BY THEIR
FRUITS

A NOVEL OF FREEDOM AND FORGIVENESS

BETH SAGE

Disclaimer

This is a work of fiction based on true events. Names, identifying characteristics, locations, and settings were changed to protect individuals' privacy. Dialog was recreated or fabricated based on interviews with real people. The ideas presented in this book do not necessarily represent the author's current beliefs or interpretations of scripture. Readers are encouraged to discern the truth through studying the Bible, seeking God's guidance, and the counsel of trusted church leaders.

Trigger Warning

This book contains depictions of psychological and sexual abuse.

In loving memory of Allison Jane.

For survivors of abuse by church leaders.

LET'S STAY CONNECTED!

Thank you for supporting this labor of love.

I would like to send you a free gift for joining me on this journey.

Scan this QR code to connect and claim your free gift:

AUTHOR'S NOTE

This book contains experiences of being in a high-control religious group. If you have experienced anything similar, please consider religious trauma informed counseling services. Stay connected or visit www.bethsage.com for more resources on this subject.

CONTENTS

PROLOGUE

THE MINISTRY

THE UNVEILING

THE RESTORATION

Beware of false prophets, who come to you in sheep's clothing but inwardly are ravenous wolves. You will recognize them by their fruits. Are grapes gathered from thornbushes, or figs from thistles? So, every healthy tree bears good fruit, but the diseased tree bears bad fruit.

MATTHEW 7:15–17 ESV

PROLOGUE

Always be humble and gentle. Be patient with each other, making allowance for each other's faults because of your love. Make every effort to keep yourselves united in the Spirit, binding yourselves together with peace. For there is one body and one Spirit, just as you have been called to one glorious hope for the future. There is one Lord, one faith, one baptism, one God and Father of all, who is over all, in all, and living through all.

Ephesians 4:2–6 NLT

IDEALS

Sedona, Arizona – October 2004

My heart races as I climb the ladder, reaching for safety. The enemy on my heels has no power over me, yet I'm frightened by his red face, yellow eyes, and horns straight off the pages of my old children's Bible.

"Not today, Satan! I rebuke you in the name of Jesus Christ!" I proclaim, proceeding to speak in tongues. As I pull my body onto the platform, my enemy falls into the dark abyss from which I escaped.

I awake in a cold sweat, sitting straight up in bed. My heart is thumping, my breathing quick and shallow. It was a dream.

Moonlight casts unfamiliar shadows into the guest room of The Ministry Center where I'm staying. I hear a door shut and heavy footsteps down the hall.

Is someone still up?

It's two a.m. according to the clock on my nightstand.

I whisper into the dark, "Focus on the light, not the shadows."

Then I pray over the room to cast out unclean spirits. My heart rate and breathing slow. I am safe here.

I lay my head back down and recite Psalm 91, "He who dwells in the shelter of the Most High and abides in the shadow of the Almighty . . ." and drift off to sleep.

Weightless and free, I hover just below the ceiling, pushing myself off the wall and past the bookshelves of my childhood bedroom. I pass through an open window with no screen. Will I fall? Only a little, before I ascend to the rooftops, stroking the air as if swimming. My fear of heights only kicks in when I surpass the roof of the one-story home and reach the evergreen treetops.

Before I get too high, it all fades away.

I open my stiff eyelids as the morning light reminds me of where I am. Another dream, my favorite kind. Maybe it's God's way of acclimating me to heights, so I won't be afraid when Christ returns and I meet him in the air with the rest of the church.

The house is quiet. The clock now displays just past ten a.m. Not so early. Stepping out of bed, I gather my Bible and notebook, then walk out to the sunlit living room. I'm the first one up.

I place my notebook on the coffee table next to an oversized travel book depicting the surrounding Red Rock mountains of Sedona, Arizona, then settle into the sofa facing the floor-to-ceiling windows of this mountainside home. A majestic display of red rock, a shade similar to my hair, contrasts the deep blue-gray clouds preparing to pour out rain in the distance. I may not be flying, but my soul feels as though it will reach new heights in this sacred place.

A door handle turning tells me someone is awake.

"Morning, Victoria," Heather murmurs as she emerges from her bedroom. Her eyes are puffy with dark circles below. She works as a round-the-clock personal assistant to Rob Peterson, apostle and founding elder of The Ministry, now in his seventies. Heather is far from the misguided teenager she was when her parents sent her to live and work with him. At sixteen, she sported an exposed midriff and cut-off shorts, and swore like a sailor. Now in her mid-twenties, she is a virtuous woman and the embodiment of grace. If only I could be half as holy as she, perhaps one day I could live and serve at the Apostle Center too.

A few steps away in the kitchen, she starts the coffeemaker and puts on some toast.

"Good morning! You are the glory of the Lord," I say.

She peeks out from behind the refrigerator door and smiles graciously, as if she hasn't heard that a thousand times.

"What's that?" I walk over to the kitchen island. "It smells interesting."

"Have you never had Vegemite?" she says. "You probably won't like it. It took me a while, and it's not for everyone."

"It can't be that bad."

She spreads it on a slice of toast for me, and I take a bite. My nose crinkles, and I nearly gag.

Heather holds back laughter.

"It's pretty awful, isn't it?" she says, handing me a paper towel to spit out what I haven't swallowed. "It's popular in Australia. Kumari introduced it to us when she arrived last month and then Papa received a revelation from God that it was a source of essential nutrients and I was to incorporate it into his daily intake."

"Daily intake?"

"Yes, he is on a strict regimen of several small meals a day. He only eats what the Holy Spirit tells him to and then trains me on how to prepare it and when."

"I suppose if the apostle says it's good for me, I could learn to like it. For now, I think I'll save my appetite for brunch," I say.

Heather delivers the toast to Rob's bedroom, then cozies up on the couch with her Bible and journal. I step outside onto the balcony to give her privacy.

Heather's devotion extends to both God and Rob, whom she affectionately refers to as Papa—a Southwest colloquialism for both fathers and grandfathers. He would be the latter, and not by blood, but by a word of the Lord.

Settling into a teak lounge chair, I thank God for placing the Holy Spirit in me and the gift to receive words from the Lord. He kept me from harm and helped me make wise decisions while at college over the past four years. Now out of school and not yet employed, I need God's guidance more than ever. What a joy it is when I lack wisdom simply to ask my Lord Jesus in faith, believing I will receive an answer. Then I speak out that answer by the direct inspiration of the Holy Spirit in prophecy. I can trust it as a living word of God to guide me for His glory.

Thank you, Lord, for The Ministry's teachings on this way of life.

The sliding door opens, startling me out of my thoughts.

"Enjoying the view a bit before it rains?" Kumari asks. She is a dark-skinned five-foot-nothing Sri Lankan woman who speaks the Queen's English with a diffused Indian accent.

"The dark clouds make it even more beautiful, don't they?" I say.

"Yes. These views are pretty, but they don't compare to my home in Sydney." She rests her chin on the rail and gazes down over the balcony.

"Australia, Indonesia . . . they must be breathtaking. I'd like to visit them someday," I say. "Maybe I love this view because it's so different from the gray rocks I grew up with in New England."

Standing beside her with my elbows resting on the rail, I look off into the distance, unable to imagine greater splendor.

It's noon by the time Rob emerges dressed and ready for the day. He's not a tall man, but his attire amplifies his presence—gray slacks, black dress shoes, a coral dress shirt, and silver bolo tie inlaid with turquoise and obsidian. He invites me to walk through the town this afternoon.

Heather hands him his cherry-wood cane carved with the head of a phoenix on our way out the door. Kumari will stay back to finish up her chores and meet up with the three of us later.

Our first stop is some shops in the town center. Most are tourist traps filled with Southwestern wares and cliché trinkets. We walk into a shoe store and Heather points out a pair of sandals.

"Those would look darling on you," she says.

The cork and leather sandals are earthy with a bit of class, adorned with a medallion.

"I could dress them up or keep them casual."

I check the price tag and gasp, "They're way too much!"

As I walk away, Heather stops me with her hand on my shoulder. "You don't know that. At least get a word from the Lord."

Of course, why didn't I think of that?

"Papa." She motions him to come closer. "Victoria would like to get a word on purchasing these sandals."

"Ah, wonderful!" He stomps his cane on the floor and smiles. Sensing my reservations, he says, "You are worthy of all things in Christ. He has given us the entire Kingdom of God, so do not worry about the price. If it's His wisdom, he'll provide. Just keep your heart open."

In the middle of the shoe store in Sedona, we huddle close and pray.

"It's your question, so you give your word first, sweetie," said Heather.

The words come to me as I prophesy, "Do not fear about the provision, for I have given you all things. These are a blessing to you, and I would have you to wear them on both casual and nicer occasions. They will ground you and stand the test of time."

Heather and Rob give their words of confirmation. I make the purchase with confidence.

Once outside the store, Rob points up the hill with his cane, which he uses more as a walking stick and accessory than an assistive device. "I'd like to take you up that way. You'll get a better feel of the history."

"Papa, I submit to go look at the candle store to see if that scent I like is back in stock," Heather says. "It's just around the corner."

He looks up briefly, as if getting a signal from heaven. "All right, let's get a word about you going there and then meeting up with us."

They bow their heads and pray for the Lord's guidance.

Heather prophesies first, "Yes, my child, find what delights you."

Then Rob, "Be quick about it and look not to the left or right for there will be distractions, but keep your sights on my word and you will do well."

They both turn to me and Heather says, "Do you have a word?"

"Uh . . . sure." I quickly pray and then say on the Lord's behalf, "Yes, go forth, this is my wisdom."

Although it is my commitment to walk in the spirit of prophecy, I'm still not used to prophesying to every matter, big or small.

With that, Heather walks up ahead, her long naturally blonde hair matching the movement of her ankle-length skirt as she rounds the corner and goes out of sight.

"Wasn't that *her* word to get from the Lord?" I ask Rob as we resume walking.

"It was, but it involved all of us, because we are an entity, walking together with the same purpose and representing Christ. If she were to decide on her own and go to the store without my confirmation as her head, that would give the devil an open door and she could get hurt. Only God knows what's around that corner."

I shudder at the thought of Heather being left spiritually unprotected.

Have I been leaving the door open for the devil when I come and go as I please at home? I am a body in several entities—my Dad and I, Mom and I, my supervisor at work—but I'm not always with them to submit everything I do.

Rob points with his cane. "This on your left is Yoga Joe's. He has been here since the 1960s and teaching yoga since then. Behind his studio is a tiny vegan restaurant. It was closed down twice for environmental health violations. But somehow people still go." He bends over to pick up an empty potato chip packet. He stuffs it in a bag he keeps in his rucksack.

"Were you here in the sixties?" I ask.

"I may have passed through once or twice, but this was always a place for hippies, and that was never my scene. I was fairly straight back then. Would have been your age, darling, fresh out of college. Soon after, I began my political career that would take me to Washington, DC, where I picked up all my nasty habits. My life became all about where to get the next drink." He stares straight ahead, and his countenance drops for a moment before flashing a sudden smile. "And the next hamburger with fries." He pats his large belly. "I guess not everything changes."

It's not a stretch to imagine him as a politician, with his slicked-back hair and large, ruddy nose—now betraying his holy persona with evidence of a life once defined by alcoholism. Of course, that was in the past.

"What's this?" I point to a gated complex of small, neat bungalows.

"Retirees. One of the dominant groups here. They come for the clean air and the healing springs. Of all the groups, these are the only ones who show any interest in the Center. A few of them attend meetings. And they are faithful givers. They can't take the money with them."

Up ahead is the Coffee Pot where we will meet up with Kumari. My stomach grumbles, and I feel my blood sugar dipping. I regret not eating the Vegemite toast.

He points up a trail with his cane. "Say, have I taken you up to a vortex site?"

I shake my head.

"It is truly one of the most spiritual places on earth. They call it a thin place."

"A thin place?" I repeat. I look around at their scantily clad bodies and long yoga muscles. "You mean, because of people's diet?"

"No," he says. He tries to conceal a smile. "Have you not heard of thin places?"

I shake my head.

"A thin place is where the line between the spirit world and the material world is thin. Where spiritual people can pass through easily."

"Pass through?"

"They are where people have visions. Where I've had some of mine."

Rob looks north toward the barren mountains, as if transported to another time, as if it's still all so present to him.

"When we step in there, the earth's magnetic energy pulses through our bodies and brings divine healing, Victoria."

"What do they call it?" I ask. All the rock formations here have names.

He rolls his eyes. "They call that one Cathedral Rock because, you see, it looks like a medieval cathedral. Catholics. Some of the most well-meaning yet deceived people. They had to take something God made beautiful and bring it down to their level by putting a label on it. Then the Protestants came along and built a chapel into the side of it. See that thar speck. It's a big tourist destination, but that's not where the real healing happens."

He waves at a shopkeeper tending an outdoor display, who bows in a "namaste" manner. Rob reserves judgement. My dad, Samuel Rose, always has to be right and would have started a theological debate with the man.

"Keep the peace," he says, as if reading my mind. He stoops to pick up a dirty plastic cup. "And leave a place better than you found it. That was Jesus's way."

"I understand," I say. "I learned a lot about tolerance and loving others who believe differently while at college."

"Oh, yeah?"

"Yes, I was exposed to believers of all denominations."

"Now it's time to unlearn everything you think you know and be taught by the Holy Spirit."

I tilt my head in confusion.

"I *was* taught by the Holy Spirit though. I gave everything I read and heard unto God, through Christ, to be taught by His Spirit so that I wouldn't lean on my own understanding."

"Do you know what it means to understand?"

"Yes, I think so. In fact, I was praying about that the other day. The Lord showed me that it means to stand under someone or something. So, to have true understanding, I must stand under God."

His eyes light up. "That's exactly right! Few people truly know what that means. I was waiting for the Holy Spirit to release me to share that revelation and now that you have brought it to me, it is time. Do me a favor, don't tell your parents yet. Your Father is a wise man, but there are some things he's just not ready to hear. Let's keep this between us until I share it with the body of Christ."

"Yes, of course," I say with a grin as wide as the Arizona sunrise. *God just used me as his prophetess.*

Rob gave me the title of prophetess to the apostle while still in high school, but unlike Heather, I didn't train with him. My father presides over the local church in Massachusetts, and he taught me most of what I know about the Bible and Rob's teachings.

Five months ago, I graduated from a Christian college, where I found it hard for others to accept my beliefs about spiritual gifts, God's order, and eternal life. Still, my experience there opened my eyes to the breadth of God's love. Now, it's time I learn the depth of God's love.

People are walking past us, talking and laughing. Rob looks so ordinary with his cane, large belly, and bolo tie. They don't know who walks among them. I breathe in the air and feel that my healing vortex is walking right beside me.

The next day, we travel two hours south to Phoenix to attend an elders' meeting. Before the meeting, Rob insists on showing me where it all began.

The Jeep Cherokee hugs the side of the mountain as Rob traverses the switchbacks with confidence. I am holding onto my seat. I look out at the sprawling city. Downtown Phoenix isn't much to speak of, just a couple of sports stadiums and a cluster of high-rise businesses that line Central Avenue, surrounded by a patchwork of suburbs.

The South Mountain range stretches along the southern border of Phoenix proper and seems to be an anchor point for giving directions. Rob points out Camelback Mountain to the east and Piestewa Peak to the north as major landmarks. They pale in comparison.

"We'll walk from here," Rob says.

We park in a dirt pull-off partway up the mountain. Rob and I step out, but Heather and Kumari stay in the vehicle.

We walk for about a hundred feet and come to a large rock. I look around. I'm not sure what I'm expecting. Perhaps some kind of Holy Ghost tingle or other sensation of enlightenment.

"Don't expect to feel anything. There's nothing supernatural about this place," he says. "Most people are quick to mark something as holy, then it becomes an idol to them. Don't make that mistake here. It's just a rock, and this is just a mountain. God can move anywhere. He just chose this place to speak to me at that specific time."

I nod. "Right here?"

"I'd hiked up the mountain that day instead of driving. The Lord told me to lie down on this rock and rest."

"Which rock?"

"This one right here." He points to a flat rock, much smaller than I expected.

"What did it look like? The vision you had."

"Well, you know Star Wars. It looked like the intro with scrolling words across the sky. Each of the Twelve Principles of Human Being Life were laid out before me. God told me I was to write them down and teach them to the body of Christ. These were the key to manifesting the sons of God that He created us to be, that Jesus Christ died for us to become."

So, this is where it all started. I soak in the view.

"I wasn't the first man God showed these to, but I was the only one who kept them and committed to sharing them. Several other prominent evangelical preachers got the same word, but they were too beholden to their churches and their denominations to follow God's lead, so they wouldn't do it. God chose me. A nothing nobody with a hell of a past. He knew I had nothing to lose."

He's not kidding about that. Rob had a sickly childhood and got good at getting what he wanted, so he learned sales. After some success going door-to-door, he joined a political campaign for some politician in Washington, DC. I'm not sure what he did there, but he'd shared with us how corrupt the nature of man is and how everyone was out for themselves. He became a high-functioning alcoholic during that time. God has since helped him become sober. He often tells the story to show believers how to be led out of an addiction by the Holy Spirit.

If God could turn around a man like that, he could help anyone.

A few days later, Rob enters the living room of the Apostle Center, and I freeze. *Am I supposed to see him like this?* The man, whose most casual attire is a button-down Hawaiian shirt, is now indecent, wearing nothing more than a white tank top and gray boxer shorts over his pasty-white skin dappled with red and brown blemishes. He sinks into one end of the couch with the TV remote. Heather brings him a bowl of popcorn, then sits on the sofa beside him and grabs a handful from his bowl with a snicker. He gives her a playful glare before she springs back up and leaves the room.

"Another Western tonight?" I ask, hoping it's something else.

A wrestling match appears on the screen. "No, it's Monday Night Raw. There he is." He points at Mr. Muscle. "This guy is one of my favorites."

I gape at him in dismay. "Wrestling? But it's so violent."

"Oh, it's not real, darlin'. It's all for show. You see that guy there?" He points to a masked man with a cape and lightning bolt tattoos down his arms. "He's been through a lot of heartache, and he recently became a believer. It's not just entertainment. I pray for these guys. They're just as worthy of knowing the truth of God and Christ as you are."

Heather drags a mattress into the living room. "Don't you watch wrestling?" she asks.

She and Kumari step onto it wearing long night shirts and underwear, no bottoms. Rob stuffs a handful of popcorn in his mouth.

Heather and Kumari start to giggle and squeal. I turn to see them in a full-on pillow fight. Again, I look at Rob, thinking he'll stop this madness. Kumari screams, and I spin around to see her pinned under Heather with her arm twisted behind her back.

"Are you . . .?" I say.

She laughs as she catches her breath. "I'm okay, yes."

"Don't worry, we do this all the time," Heather assures me. "It's fun!"

I suppose it might be fun if we were seven and if Rob was really our grandpa and they were my sisters.

"I think I'll turn in early," I say as I cross in front of Rob toward my bedroom.

He reaches out and grips my arm. "Don't judge it."

I stop in my tracks. "I . . . I'm not."

Still holding on, he says, "I can feel it in my chest. A sharp pain. It's judgment, and it's coming from you."

Heather drops the pillow and sits by his side on the sofa, placing her hand across his chest, and prays quietly.

He explains, "Any form of judgment is sin. You think you know what is right and wrong, don't you?"

"Well . . ."

"Only God is the judge of that, and unless you received his wisdom regarding this matter, you don't have the right to judge anything. Even the very thought causes you to walk in sin."

"I'm sorry, I didn't mean to . . ."

"You didn't mean it, darlin', but you agreed with it, and those fiery darts came right at me."

I pull back, and he releases his grip.

"Sorry," I say, stepping back.

"Sorry don't do nothing!" He raises his voice and stands up, waving his finger at me. "That's what Satan wants you to believe, is that you are a sorry, no-good creature, so you will sulk and not agree with the perfect, sinless, righteous son of God that you are in Christ!"

I stand frozen. My chest tightens and I feel the need to cry, but I won't do it. I won't cry. I am tougher than that.

Here is the apostle before me, and I cannot deny what he says is true. He sees the sin in me when I don't.

He continues, "I don't mean to scare you, but you've got to know that judgment is spiritual murder. If I said nothing and you just kept on judging, then I would be responsible as a watchman of your soul. And if you died tomorrow and hadn't repented of this, then you would wake up in hell with no idea how you got there."

"In hell?" I look at him with eyes wide open and my body is trembling.

"That's right," he says in a soft voice. "I haven't shared this with the body of Christ yet because they weren't ready to hear it. But the Spirit tells me you are. There are only two sources—the Holy Spirit of God and the Unholy Spirit of Satan. In every moment, either the Holy Spirit of God or the Unholy Spirit of Satan leads us. You think you decide on your own?"

My eyes dart from Kumari who is sitting straight up on the mattress, then to Heather who is watching from the sofa, and back to Apostle Rob.

"Not so!" He yells, and I flinch. "Our minds mind something. Nobody ever had an original thought. Every thought has to come from one of those two sources. So, whichever source you are receiving from in the moment, that's where your residence is. If you're walking by the flesh mind, which is led by the Unholy Spirit, then you have temporarily left your seat with the resurrected Christ."

Rob's face is flush and his nostrils flare as he shouts with the gusto of a Pentecostal preacher from the pulpit, except he's only three feet away. His stare bores into me. "If you were to die in that moment, you would wake up separated from God. That's why we must be diligent to seek God in *all* things in *every* moment!"

My heart is pounding, and I'm sweating from the immense guilt and fear that come with judging their activities and leaving my place in Christ. Kumari wrapped a blanket around herself and is now sitting next to Heather watching and praying. Heather nods.

"I . . . I confess it as sin that I judged you." Both women nod in acceptance. Looking down to hold back tears, I say, "Lord, please forgive me." Then I turn back to Rob. "And I ask for your forgiveness too."

His voice is gentle again. "Oh, there's no *un*forgiveness in my heart, dear. I was never mad. You see, I just had to yell to cut through that stubborn spirit that was on you. But you broke free and now you're back to who you are."

A headache replaces the adrenaline rush I felt from the confrontation.

"Now go on to bed, if you receive to. We'll turn down the volume," he says.

"Thank you," I say to him and wave to the ladies. "Goodnight, I bless your rest."

As I lay in bed, I ask God, "Please show me revelation in my dreams. Show me the sin that is in my life that I'm not willing to see in the light of day so I can repent of it and root it out of my soul. And Lord, please ease this headache and give me rest."

"Kumari will pay," Rob says. We're sitting in a high-end café overlooking uptown Sedona. They've taken me there to celebrate the final week of my stay at the Center.

I've chosen a small cake, but both Heather and Rob ordered a full lunch with dessert. I sneak a look at the prices; they're having the most expensive things on the menu.

"Kumari offered to pay. She wanted to celebrate your visit." Rob holds Kumari in his gaze as if drawing a blessing onto her. I feel a pang of envy that she has spent so much time with him, then quickly correct myself.

Kumari narrows her brows, hesitating, then pulls out her wallet and places it delicately on the table. "It is my pleasure, Victoria," she says with a bow of her head. There's a slight tremor in her voice. She pushes out her chair and goes over to the counter.

I finish my small cake quickly and wish that I had asked for lunch too. Nothing expensive, just filling. In the two weeks I've been here, I've blown through most of my vacation money on eating out. I didn't want them to use ministry funds for me every time. There are so many other financial needs here. My third week is going to be a hungry one.

"Thank you for letting her do that," says Rob, stretching over and touching my hand. I feel the warmth of his blessing. "It is a burden for her to have so much. The Australian dollar is worth a lot with the current exchange rate, and she so wants to put it to good use."

He stretches back, pushing his full belly toward the table as Kumari joins us again.

"Let's finish with a quick prayer of blessing. Your hand, Kumari."

We bow our heads. I'm here with the apostolic team at last. Rob Peterson, our apostle, is holding one hand, and the other is being held by the delicate fingers of Heather, the prophetess, only two years older than me but pulsing with the Holy Spirit. I'm so blessed.

This is what my life is moving toward. This is my world and people.

I feel rather than see Kumari join the circle as Rob prays with confidence. I am certain that everyone within earshot will be blessed by what they overhear.

"Lord, we thank you for the bountiful provision that you have given us in Christ. I invoke the victory of Jesus Christ over Satan and his demons, forbidding them from using the conflict between the conscious and subconscious minds as fiery darts against Heather, Kumari, Victoria, or her parents or anyone in this café who may have overheard your words of life. Let us go forth as sons of God, one with you, and perfect in Christ."

"Amen."

I look up, full of joy. Tears well up in Kumari's eyes.

As we're leaving, I put my arm around her and say our form of a thank-you. "I bless you back a hundredfold return of the Kingdom of God in your lifetime."

She shakes her head and excuses herself to the bathroom. I know how she feels; the joy is overwhelming.

THE MINISTRY

*Now these are the gifts Christ gave to the church: the apostles,
the prophets, the evangelists, and the pastors and teachers. Their
responsibility is to equip God's people to do his work and build up the
church, the body of Christ. This will continue until we all come to such
unity in our faith and knowledge of God's Son that we will be mature
in the Lord, measuring up to the full and complete standard of Christ.*

EPHESIANS 4:11–13 NLT

CHAPTER 1

EXPECTATIONS

I step off the elevator into the main lobby of the corporate building where I work. Julianne, a spry woman in her sixties, waves me over from across the atrium.

"Happy work anniversary," she says in her French West Indies accent. A full tote bag half her size is slung over her shoulder. She'll retire in a few years, but her long muscles, smooth skin, and energetic presence would suggest she's in her prime.

"What's all this?" I point to the bag.

"I told you we were going to have a picnic. Ten years is a big deal!"

Less than a year after my stay at The Ministry Center back in 2005, I accepted an entry-level job at this nonprofit safety organization intending to climb the corporate ladder and reach a level of financial freedom that would pay for me to work in full-time ministry.

"Thank you. Who would've thought I'd still be here?" I shrug. "You know, an administrative career was never my plan."

"Ahh, but then I wouldn't have met you." She places a hand on my shoulder. "You were the best thing that happened to our prayer group."

"Your persistence paid off," I say.

She'd kept inviting me to attend the weekly prayer group for a year before I conceded. Once I did, we found common ground in our faith, and I repented of unfairly judging my coworkers from other church denominations.

"God knows what He's doing." She nudges my side with her elbow as we exit the glass doors toward the parking lot of this four-story brick building.

"He does." I hold out the back of my left hand and admire the ring as we walk past the parking lot and down the hill to the nature preserve across the street.

"So, any movement on the romance front?" she asks.

"No . . . well, maybe. I don't know. Adam and I should be engaged by now, but it's hard to know where he stands."

Adam, the prophet's son, and I have been in a courtship of sorts called a "consideration of marriage" for the last five years, but none of my friends have met him, and while I think about him day and night, we're only allowed to speak once or twice a month.

"Maybe if you wore that ring on a different finger, you'd meet an eligible bachelor who doesn't take his sweet old time. Long-distance relationships are tough," she reminds me.

"You *know* why I wear this ring," I protest, rolling my eyes.

"I forgot. It happens with age," she jokes. "Remind me again?"

We enter the trailhead and focus on our footing as we walk on the uneven ground between the pines.

"My mother gave me this ring for my college graduation." It's an amethyst, my favorite stone, with two diamond specs. "It represents my being betrothed to Jesus Christ . . . and helps me be patient while I wait for the one God has prepared to be my soulmate."

"You always impress me with your strong faith. I wish I had that. I worry too much and still have lots of questions. But it's God's mysterious ways that make Him so incredible, isn't it?"

"Perhaps," I say.

God isn't a mystery to me. Every question I could have has been answered. It's all right there in the Bible for anyone who's willing to see it . . . and she seems so willing.

We stop on a footbridge to admire water lilies floating in the pond on either side of us. Their white and yellow flowers are bright with cheer on a backdrop of green leaves and dark algae-filled water.

"They're just beginning to blossom and already so beautiful," I say with a smile.

"Yes. Speaking of blossoming, I don't think you've ever told me how you came to believe in God. Care to share your testimony over a picnic basket?"

She motions to the clearing at the edge of the pond.

I raise an eyebrow, pleased that she asked.

"Many people grow up not knowing the Lord and then have a big life-changing moment. I can't say that happened to me. There isn't one moment that I can pinpoint when I received Jesus Christ as my Lord and Savior. It feels like I've always believed. There were spiritually significant moments throughout my childhood that I can share."

"Please do. I love hearing your insights," she said as we spread out the blanket and unpack the basket.

"It was about 1985 . . ." I tell her my story.

Dad sat on our 1970s paisley-patterned orange and brown couch, strumming his Ovation guitar and plucking out a simple melody while singing:

> *I'm just a little one, having so much fun.*
>
> *Loving God, by loving you,*
>
> *And giving His Kingdom . . . Kingdom!*

I would echo the last "Kingdom!" with the high-pitched squeal of a three-year-old and my dad's face lit up, revealing his dimples while ruddy cheeks emerged through his brown, freckled skin. His thick, black eyebrows were almost cartoonish as they accentuated each expression, adding to my delight.

My mom, Hannah Rose, sang beside me in her melodic soprano voice. She exuded a brightness beyond her fair skin and blonde hair. Reaching out her hand, she spun me around until I plopped down on my bum, cushioned by a brown-and-cream braided rug that covered the laminate tile flooring of the townhouse we rented.

"God was revealing His word to me even then," I tell Julianne, "as my little mind considered the lyrics and wondered—How *could* I love God, whom I couldn't see? Then I realized the song gave me the answer. I could love my parents. Together, we could share His Kingdom with the world. So I tried my best to love and obey them."

"What a lovely song." She hums the tune from my childhood. "And I'm impressed that you learned a lesson from it so young. Maybe I'll share it with my grandkids, although I don't know if they would be so attentive."

"Out of the mouths of babes," I shrug, quoting Scripture.

"That's true. Kids are so smart; you never know what they're picking up on."

She spreads out sliced fruit and crackers on a cutting board, and I'm eager to snag one.

"Shall we pray?" I ask.

"Oh, yes, you do the honors."

I keep it short. "Lord, thank you for this beautiful day and time we get to spend together. May our conversation honor you and the food nourish our bodies, in Jesus Christ's name. Amen."

"Amen, that was perfect. Maybe this is bad to say, but it's hard to sit through long prayers when there's food in front of you." She puts her hands together in a prayer gesture as she looks to the sky and says, "Forgive me, Lord, you know my heart."

I start in on the fruit and crackers while Julianne pulls a couple of homemade sandwiches out of the basket.

"I hope you like chicken salad. I made them this morning."

"Oh, I do! Thank you very much."

"Oh, it's nothing." She waves her hand in dismissal of my gratitude. "So, what else?"

I look at my empty hands. "I, uh . . ."

"You said you had experienced several profound moments as a child. Do you have another story to share?"

"Oh, of course." I exhale with relief that she hadn't expected me to bring something to my surprise picnic.

"My first existential thought. It came as a result of being disciplined for something I'm pretty sure I said on the bus ride home from first grade."

Mom grabbed my arm with one hand to hold me still.

"You don't say things like that. I'm going to wash your mouth out." With the other hand, she swabbed my mouth with a bar of Ivory soap. Tears ran down my face to the rhythm of rapid inhales and forced exhales. The bitter taste scarcely matched the weight of doing wrong.

"Go to your room and think about your actions. Don't come out until you're ready to apologize," Mom said.

Julianne scrunches her face and says, "I remember doing that to my own kids. It was rather common in those days."

I sigh.

I was a blubbery mess, sitting on the end of my twin bed, legs not yet reaching the floor. My head hung heavy as beams of afternoon sunlight highlighted my pink Strawberry Shortcake t-shirt and baby-blue corduroy pants. In the sun's warm embrace, my breathing slowed, and I wiped the remaining tears away with the bottom of my shirt.

That's when the revelation came to me. Mom had said that words can hurt others. *Okay*, I thought, *but why should I care?* Other kids had hurt me with their words plenty of times.

It's rare I have a question that goes unanswered for very long, and that day was no exception.

At that moment, I had pictured myself being the only one on earth with consciousness. Everyone else was a creation of my own perceptions. Nothing I did or said could really hurt anyone because they weren't real, not the way I was.

What if they are *real?* What if their existence was just like mine, except they believed *they* were the only ones who mattered?

I'd shuddered at the thought. So in that moment, I repented and chose to have faith that everyone was as real as I was, and that I would treat them kindly, the way I wanted to be treated, just like the Bible said.

"That's profound for a six-year-old. Do you think it was the Holy Spirit showing you that?" Julianne asked.

"I think maybe it was both spirits. The devil was trying to convince me I was the only one that mattered, but because I was repentant, I think the Holy Spirit intervened to show me the consequences of that worldview so that I could make a choice."

"The devil does like to play with our minds," she remarked. "You were wise beyond your years, and still are."

I smile slightly and take a deep breath as my gaze lands on my smartphone, displaying the time.

"It's 1:10 already!" I jump up. "I've got to get back. My boss will wonder where I am, and I have several loose ends to tie up before leaving for a week."

I help her pack up the leftovers, and we head back to the office.

"Victoria Rose, you should be packing," I scold myself out loud as I sit at the end of my queen-size bed, staring at my open closet. It's Sunday, and I'm preparing for ministry travel this week. Meanwhile, I have about an hour before Dad picks me up for the biweekly Home Body Ministry Gathering of the Saints, or simply, a gathering.

I open the airline app on my phone and check the flight itinerary. It reads: BOS to PHX, departure 9:35 a.m. A pop-up asks me to check in. I follow the prompts and confirm our seats—a middle seat for me and an aisle for Dad to accommodate his limited mobility. I've put both our tickets on my credit card, knowing the chances are slim that he'll pay me back. The local ministry doesn't bring in enough funds to pay his pastoral salary, let alone travel. "Thank God for loyalty points," I say under my breath.

I look at my closet, then over to my empty suitcase laid open on the bed. Enough procrastination. *Packing shouldn't be this hard*, I tell myself. I make this trip at least twice a year. My shoulders raise and my chest tightens as I slump over. Too many thoughts enter my head at once, and I can't move. Well, I could move, but if I did, I would probably just end up laying on the floor curled up in a ball. This overwhelm is only remnants of the anxiety I've battled for over ten years. I know I am better than this. God made me capable, and he equipped me with the Holy Spirit to guide me. Yet I still struggle under the weight of sin, afraid to make the wrong choice or be a negative influence.

I flop onto my bed and stare at the exposed wood ceiling beams and organic lines of this eighteenth-century home. I would prefer something more modern, less drafty—no allergy-inducing walnut trees near the front windows. But Mom has always appreciated historical homes, and she and her husband are gracious to welcome me here. I can't afford a place of my own, if I am to pay off my student loan debt and qualify to serve the apostle.

"Victoria?" Mom chirps from the bottom of the stairs.

"I'm okay," I sigh. She must have heard me stomp my foot in frustration.

"Are you all packed?" Her singsong voice is delightful, when I'm in the mood for it.

A loud, guttural sigh is all I can manage.

Her footsteps are light, but the stairway still creaks. Then a knock on the door, and it opens. There isn't always a knock. She tries, but she is used to walking right in. The boundaries between us are paper thin, if any exist at all. That's why it is both easy and difficult to still be living with her in my mid-thirties. Easy because I have nothing to hide. Difficult because the comfort of being among the familiar keeps me from creating a life of my own. I'm not sure if I'm so emotional because I live with family or if I'm still not ready to move out. I trust any changes will happen in God's time.

"Come in," I say as she peers through the opening.

"Oh, honey, you got this!" I appreciate the enthusiasm, but it doesn't convince me.

"What if he asks me to marry him? I hope he does, but I don't want to expect it, you know? I don't want to be disappointed. Still, I should prepare. Do you think he's going to ask? What should I do if he doesn't? I've waited so long. I'm just going to play it cool. Do you think he'll hold my hand? I hope so . . ."

"Rocky . . . breathe." That was her nickname for me. She saw a fighter in me. She always thought I had the endurance of Rocky Balboa in the famous training montage of the 1976 movie, when he runs up the expansive staircase of the Philadelphia Museum of Art. I'm thin by genetics. My body has become a bit more athletic since taking fitness classes at the office gym, but it's a metaphor.

I attempt a deep breath, but it comes in rapid, short bursts. Making eye contact with her, I try again. Inhale . . . exhale . . . inhale . . . exhale. Better.

"I need to pray," I say.

We sit on the bed, hand in hand.

"Thank you, Father," she begins, then speaks softly in her spiritual tongue, giving me space to speak.

"Father God, the past is sin because it is separate from you. You are ever-present. These emotions and worries about the future and fears from the past are all lies. You made me a joint heir with Christ, and I am a new creation. Lord, I surrender to your will." I let my prayer language pour out, lifting a sweet sound unto the Lord.

God answers me, as I speak through prophecy. "My daughter, I will guide you in all your ways as you look to me. I have shown you I am here now and always will be in you, in the Holy Spirit. My son cared so that you would be free from the worry of your tomorrows. Let my spirit wash over you and receive peace. Lean not on your own understanding, but in all things give thanks and seek my word of life. In this, you shall receive vision and know what your part in it shall be in the moment. Let go of fear and hold on to grace."

I sigh with relief, feeling a weight lift from my body.

"Amen." Mom rubs my shoulder. "What is that Scripture about gaining hope from the trying of our faith?'"

I search in the Bible app on my phone and find Romans 5:4. "'Therefore, since we have been justified by faith, we have peace with God through our Lord Jesus Christ . . . Not only that, but we rejoice in our sufferings, knowing that suffering produces endurance, and endurance produces character, and character produces hope . . .'"

Mom embraces me. "Can I get you anything?"

"No, I'll be fine. I just need to keep moving."

She leaves my room, closing the door behind her.

I stand up and rifle through my closet, passing over the suit pants and blouses I wear to my day job and foregoing the weekend jeans and graphic tees. When I'm with my ministry family, I can be myself. I come to the end of the rack and pull out the long flowing skirts and a colorful sarong—make that *two* wrap dresses from my island collection. It may be chilly in the desert this time of year, so I reach up to the shelf above my hanging clothes and pull down a knit poncho. I lay them on one side of my bed. Then I rummage through the pile of shoes to the far end of my closet to retrieve my trusty cork sandals and set them on the floor. It's been several months since sandal weather. I step into them, not too restrictive on my toes, but supportive, as if the natural fibers carry an energy that helps me stay grounded in my walk.

I remember Heather being there when I bought these sandals. One of the few times we connected on a personal level.

"Oh, Heather. Gone so soon," I say into the empty room. I recall the cold and sudden way I learned of her passing.

It was a typical Saturday afternoon, and I'd been practicing guitar. I took a break to check my social media feed when I saw a message from her aunt that read:

> I can't believe it. God took my beautiful angel. Heather, I miss you already. This can't be real.

No! It can't be real. What happened and why didn't anyone call me?

I looked at her account. No updates in two days. I scrolled feverishly, looking for some clues about what had happened. There were only comments of shock, sadness, and condolences.

I called her aunt, but the phone was busy. When I finally reached her, all she said was Heather was sick with pneumonia, took some sleeping pills the night before, and didn't wake up.

Those who knew her best ruled out suicide. She'd fulfilled her time at the Apostle Center and was engaged to be married. She had her whole life ahead of her. Why, God?

It's a question only the apostle was prepared to answer.

He later shared that the eldership did not sanction her marriage, and therefore, she was in rebellion. After tasting the goodness of God's order from the apostle, she would not recover from what lie ahead. So God, in His mercy, took her home.

The sound of a guitar strumming from my phone brings me back to the present moment.

I answer it, "Hey, Dad."

"I've stopped to pick up Priscilla. She needed a ride," he says. "We're about ten minutes out. Do you have the handouts?"

"Yes, I'll be ready. I'll bring the diagrams."

I place the sandals in my suitcase.

CHAPTER TWO

BY THE SPIRIT

I slide into the passenger seat of Dad's dark-blue sedan, placing my quilted tote bag on the floor by my feet, bulging with laminated diagrams and the latest spiral-bound syllabus. Scents of musk and mint overcompensate for the smell of cigarette smoke that lingers in the car's fabric. I ignore the crumbs and dirt in the console and lean in to plant a kiss on his cheek. His freckled, brown cheeks turn rosy. We've kept up this routine every other Sunday for years.

Dad is wearing a royal-blue collared shirt and the purple paisley tie I bought him for his birthday six months ago. His thinning black hair, he tamed into smooth waves that reach his neckline.

"Is your mom coming today?" he asks.

"Yes, she'll meet us there," I say.

I turn to greet Priscilla, a thin woman in her seventies with strawberry blonde hair, wearing a light-pink blouse buttoned up to the collar and fastened with a poinsettia lapel pin. I recognize her in name only.

"My, how you have grown, Victoria! I remember when you were just a toddler coloring on the floor during your dad's sermons."

I blush. "I'm sure it's hard to believe that was over thirty years ago."

Dad pulls out of the driveway and asks, "Would you voice the ministry, Victoria?"

I nod. Our forty-five-minute drive always starts with a prayer for safety as the apostle taught us.

"Father God, we ask for divine safety and protection and commission your angels to guard around us and our vehicle and all those on the roadways with us. I will to honor you, Father God, and my God-ordained heads and headships as a fit and fulfilling body unto my Lord Jesus Christ and to Dad while he drives."

Dad prays while driving, "I will drive giving all five senses to my spirit to go only to you, Father, through the way made by Jesus Christ, and I will to receive back from you, through Jesus Christ, by the Holy Spirit, divine knowledge, wisdom, and understanding. I will to honor all the authorities of the roads, both local and state, and I forbid Satan and his demons from using myself or this vehicle to hinder or harm anyone, in Christ Jesus's name."

"Amen," I declare.

At that moment, Dad's leg spasms and his foot slips, missing the brake briefly, but he recovers just in time to make a turn. Priscilla and I let out a synchronized gasp.

"Thank God for his angels protecting us!" I exclaim.

Dad nods with relief. He won't readily admit it, but his legs don't always cooperate as he would like because of the advancing neuropathy.

"We like to use our travel time to minister one to another as we prepare for the gathering, so if you don't mind, we'll do that now," Dad says to Priscilla.

"Oh, not at all. Please go ahead, Sam," she says.

Internally, I ask the Lord for what he would have me give to my dad. I'm prompted to give him a word of prophecy, so I declare: "From God, through Christ, by the Holy Spirit," then I speak in tongues until I am compelled to speak in English. "My sons, go forth in boldness, for there is much that I am revealing to all. You are my channels of love to this body. In time, you will see the hearts become clear and the burden of the past lifted as you walk anew by my spirit, having full confidence in the resurrected victory of Jesus Christ and knowing that we are one."

Dad is faithful to repeat what he just heard, as the apostle taught. "I bless you back a hundredfold return of the Kingdom of God in your lifetime for that word. I'm hearing to go forth in boldness for much is being revealed. We are channels of love to the body, and their hearts will become clear as we continue to love them. I will, through Christ, to go forth in boldness, Father, and to have full confidence in the resurrected victory of Jesus Christ!"

"Yes, that was a blessing," Priscilla chimes in from the back seat. "May I ask, what was that phrase that you spoke before the word of prophecy?"

"From God through Christ by the Holy Spirit," I answer. "I'm declaring the source, channel, and power by which I speak to ensure that what follows is coming from the right source and not the flesh mind."

"Interesting." She nods.

Dad reciprocates the ministry. "For you, yea, my daughter Victoria, be not afraid of what people will say or do. My word is in you. Continue to give and receive to and from God, through Christ, by your Spirit, that you may walk in the truth and be assured that I am with thee."

"Thee? I haven't heard that since I used to read the King James Bible," Priscilla comments.

I respond first to Dad, out of honor for God's word. "Amen, thank you, Dad, I bless you back a hundredfold. I will, through Christ, to not be afraid of what people say or do, but I will go forth giving and receiving to and from my Spirit, for He is with me."

Dad responds to Priscilla's interjection. "We still use the King James Version exclusively. It's the most accurate and pure translation available."

While I find other translations helpful, I don't argue with this. There was a time in high school when I tried reading from modern translations and then shared them with Dad. He had made a compelling argument showing me verses where words changed the meaning of the entire passage and that even whole verses were missing, citing Scriptures such as 1 John 5:7. These verses were foundational to our faith and might explain why other Christians were so deceived.

Priscilla's honesty is refreshing. "Well, that may be, but I have found other translations easier to understand. Do you often minister prophecies to one another?"

I'm pleased to respond, "We do, Dad and me. The apostle encourages us to start every conversation with a word from the Lord. Most in our church speak in tongues and prophesy, though few embrace the idea of greeting one another with a spiritual word every time."

"I don't know that I would be comfortable doing that." She crosses her arms and rubs her biceps, as if cold.

"That's okay, there's no pressure," I say. "It's saved Dad and I from several arguments. When I am presented with feelings of obligation, I recognize it as the flesh mind and repent right away. The Scriptures say to ask and you shall receive. So, when I ask, I receive. And I'm always happy I did."

"I'll think about that," she says.

Dad glances at her through the rearview mirror. "Don't just think about it, give it to your spirit—"

She clears her throat. "My spirit?"

"What he means is the portion of the Holy Spirit that lives inside of you," I say. "We couldn't possibly contain the entire Holy Spirit of God inside of us, so he gave us each a portion of His Spirit that is, in the words of the apostle, our 'unique, intrinsic, and integral spirit.' It's the highest part of you."

I'm almost giddy sharing this revelation.

"I'd never thought about it that way." Priscilla casts her gaze out the window toward the cranberry bogs that line Route 3A through Kingston.

Dad is a creature of habit, whether of the flesh or the spirit—and he is a man of many words. My mom used to say, ask him a simple question and he'll build you a watch. So when the apostle gives us a script, he incorporates it into his language and routine. I view the teachings as a guide. Once I've committed the prayers to memory, I improvise. This helps me simplify the message when I minister alongside him.

"It's made the most difference in my life," I say. "About the time I graduated college, Rob received the revelation about how to 'function by the unction,' as he put it. By our will, we can give all five-sense perceptions to our spirit to receive God's knowledge, wisdom, and understanding about them. In this way, we can respond by the spirit rather than react by the flesh in each situation. It allows us to cease being led by feelings, which are so easily manipulated and deceived."

She nods but says nothing.

I try to reassure her. "It's overwhelming to take in all at once. Just know that as you seek Him, God will show you what you need at the moment."

We drive up the steep gravel road to a house at the top of a hill. It's the one with multi-tiered gardens, now dormant for winter, amid a cacophony of wind chimes, an eclectic mix of lawn ornaments from old boots to broken-down garden tools, and whirly things that capture the whimsy of the wind.

Maria Thomas, or Mimi, as we like to call her, stands on her tiptoes at about five two to welcome us with wide-open arms. Peter, her husband and teaching elder, stands head and shoulders above her, watching to ensure Dad doesn't misstep on the uneven floorboards of their weathered deck.

We've arrived several minutes late and join the handful of saints seated in a circle; gray hair and receding hairlines adorn familiar faces. All women, except for the elders—Peter and my dad. Books line the walls along with seasonal handmade decor, dried flowers, and antiques.

Peter scrambles to set up a few extra folding chairs and motions for Priscilla to sit. She greets everyone, surprised to recognize some.

"My mom is coming too," I say. He pulls another chair from the closet by the door. Peter is a man of few words who lets his wife do most of the talking.

"Have you opened yet?" Dad asks as he slowly shuffles across the room and lands heavily in the sturdy armchair reserved for him. I sit in the chair next to his.

"Nope, just visiting while we waited for you," Peter says.

Dad nods and makes eye contact with each one of us as he catches his breath. He coughs from the exertion, and Mimi, already in the kitchen, brings him a glass of water.

After taking a sip and a few long breaths, he starts, "I'll voice the prayer, but it's up to each of you to agree in your hearts because I can't pray for you."

Heads bow around the room.

Shifting forward in his chair, he crosses his ankles and rests his elbows on his knees, hands folded. Spiritual tongues flow from his mouth like breathing, to align his heart and mind with Christ as he leads us in prayer.

"Father God, we give this time of fellowship to you. We declare our will in agreement with your word, that all past is dead and therefore sin. Through the sacrifice of Jesus Christ, you have made us perfect—sinless, righteous sons of God. Our lives are hidden with Christ, in God, in the

Holy Spirit, far above all things. As your sons, you have made us joint heirs with Christ and we have all things in Christ for life and godliness."

He straightens up and looks around. "Saints, I encourage each to do this next part for yourselves."

He resumes prayer posture. "I will all five-sense perceptions to my spirit to you through Jesus Christ, to receive from God, through Christ, by my spirit, your knowledge, wisdom, understanding, and compassion for each one here. I invoke the victory of Jesus Christ over Satan and his demons, forbidding them from using psychic energies created by the conflict between the conscious and subconscious minds, as fiery darts against my heads and headships, my body, myself, or anyone else in Christ Jesus's name!"

A collection of agreement rises from among the saints: "Amen," "Yes, I agree," "That is my will also," "Thank you for voicing that, brother."

Priscilla sits with perfect posture, her arms close to her sides and hands folded in her lap. Abandoning pursed lips, she opens her mouth, but no words come out.

"Do you have a question, Priscilla?" I say.

"Well . . . it's just . . . why did you call us saints?" She shakes her head. "I'm no saint."

"We refer to all believers as saints, because God sanctified us in Christ. That is how the Apostle Paul addressed the church at Corinth."

"Oh, I see." She nods.

I add, "It doesn't mean we're manifesting perfection, but we agree with God that He set us aside for a holy purpose and He equips us to carry that out by His Spirit."

"Your spirit," Dad corrects me.

"Yes, my spirit, as part of the Holy Spirit," I acknowledge.

"I think I see that," Priscilla says. "I'll have to pray about it more."

CHAPTER THREE

IN HIS IMAGE

Mom quietly enters the front door, careful not to disturb the conversation. Mimi jumps up and greets her with a hug. We all stop and welcome her. She sits in the open seat across from me. Mom and Dad have remained friends since their divorce when I was four years old. At first it was for my sake. Eventually, she received him again as her pastor. He even confirmed a word from the Lord for her to marry her current husband.

Dad prompts the rest of us, "Well, does anyone have any ministry? Words of knowledge, words of wisdom, prophecy, a song? Come on, saints, give it to your spirit to see what the Lord would have for one another."

The room is quiet for a moment. The saints whisper in a variety of spiritual tongues. It's beautiful to hear, even the sometimes-awkward syllables of their unique languages. It reassures me they are seeking their God in Christ for wisdom beyond their own understanding.

Priscilla looks around and then bows her head. Her lips are shut. I wonder if she has the Holy Spirit, or just isn't comfortable using her gifts in our presence. Apostle Rob teaches that speaking in tongues is the evidence of the indwelling of the Holy Spirit, and doing so seals Him unto us and He will never leave. I am not so sure that is true because I have known other Christians who didn't use their spiritual tongues and still seemed to hear from God. Either way, using my spiritual language is an important part of practicing my faith.

"I receive a song," Mimi offers. "You Are the Temple of the Holy Ghost."

"Ah, one of mine. I can't play it anymore, but we can sing a cappella." Dad wrote the music to it in the 1980s and recorded it with a few of the sisters from that time. I miss the days my dad would play his Ovation guitar, with its signature sound. I would clap a tambourine while we all sang just a little off-key. Now, with no instrumental support, we sing way off-key.

You are the temple of the Holy Ghost,

If you obey the Lord, you won't play into the devil's hands,

And you will be stronger,

And you will build better,

And you will grow into agreement with the Lord

And as you grow stronger and stronger as the temple on the earth,

You will do these things,

The weapons will come against you,

But we will fight them and defeat them

In the fight of faith.

At the conclusion of the second refrain, Dad says, "Let's go to that Scripture. I believe it's 1 Corinthians 6:19–20."

"I'll read it," a sister volunteers.

She reads, "'What? Know ye not that your body is the temple of the Holy Ghost which is in you, which ye have of God, and ye are not your own? For ye are bought with a price: therefore glorify God in your body, and in your spirit, which are God's.'"

Giving the written word to my spirit, I receive to speak a word of prophecy that we might hear the living word concerning it.

I say, "The word I receive on that is: 'Indeed, like Jesus was the temple of God that raised up to replace the temple of old built by man, you are the temple of the Holy Spirit in which my knowledge, wisdom, and understanding live in you. Care for this temple as you would care for a holy temple that you could walk into and know my presence is there. For my presence is within you, and I would have you to honor me in spirit and with your body and the decisions of your will. I care for your full being. Honor me in your full being, and my love will flow through you unhindered by the flesh, for you will have crucified it with its affections and lusts,' says the Lord."

Several saints respond with a "bless you" or "thank you." The feeling of God-life passing through me and that communication by the Spirit of God between us as God's family fulfills me. I am worshipping God.

"That Scripture goes right along with the latest teaching." Dad pulls out his copy of the syllabus provided to us at the last elders conference where the apostle always gave a one-day seminar focusing on one of the Twelve Principles of Human Being Life.

Peter, Mimi, and the others reach for theirs. I pull two copies from my bag and hand one to Priscilla. The cover reads, PRINCIPLE TWELVE: SON OF GOD PERFECTION, SUB-PRINCIPLE TEN, GO ON UNTO PERFECTION.

We skip past the first eight pages, summarizing the previous eleven principles and their corresponding sub-principles. It starts where all the principles start, in the Garden of Eden:

IN THE GARDEN OF EDEN, WE CAN SEE HOW GOD MADE MANKIND, MAN AND WOMAN, TO DWELL WITH HIM AND TO WALK PERFECTLY, GIVING EVERYTHING TO THEIR SPIRIT AND WALKING IN THE SPIRIT OF PROPHECY, OF THOUGHT, WORD, AND ACTION. NOTHING THEY DID WAS WITHOUT GOD'S GUIDANCE. THIS IS THE SAME FOR YOU AND I, SINCE JESUS CHRIST REDEEMED US UNTO HIMSELF AND TORE THE VEIL THAT SEPARATED US FROM GOD IN THE HOLY OF HOLIES. SOLOMON'S TEMPLE WAS ONLY A REPRESENTATION OF OUR BODIES AS THE TEMPLE OF THE HOLY GHOST. WITH THIS UNLIMITED ACCESS TO GOD, IF WE WILL, WE CAN EXCHANGE THE WORD OF SELF FOR THE WORD OF GOD, THUS PURIFYING OUR SOUL, EVEN AS WE ARE ALREADY PURE IN THE SPIRIT.

YOU WILL SEE THIS REALITY FROM GENESIS TO REVELATION. WHENEVER PEOPLE FOLLOW THE WORD OF GOD, THE RESULT IS LIFE. WHEN THEY FOLLOW THE WORD OF SELF, THE RESULT IS DEATH. IT'S A MATTER OF LIFE AND DEATH. JESUS CHRIST DIED SO THAT WE WOULDN'T HAVE TO DIE, NOT SPIRITUALLY AND NOT PHYSICALLY. IF WE WILL WALK AS JESUS WALKED, GIVING EVERYTHING TO HIS FATHER AND ACTING ONLY BY PROPHECY, THEN WE TOO WILL WALK MANIFESTLY PERFECT, AND THE RESULT IS THAT WE WILL OVERCOME DEATH AS JESUS DID FOR US. THE FIRST FRUIT AMONG MANY BRETHREN, AS STATED IN ROMANS 8:29.

"Will someone read that Scripture?" Dad asks.

"I will," I say, promptly navigating to the chapter and verse in the Bible app on my smartphone and checking to be sure it's set to King James Version.

"'For whom he did foreknow, he also did predestinate to be conformed to the image of His Son, that he might be the firstborn among many brethren.'"

"Thank you. As Victoria just read, God considers us Jesus's brothers and sisters, predestined to be conformed to His image, which we know from the previous principles, that refers to our makeup of spirit, soul, and body.

"It's the sanctification process that we learned about in Principle Eight that takes place when we hear God's word, agree with it in our heart, and put it into action. As we continue in this process, we will eventually have purified our soul until our spirit leads all we think, say, and do. Then we will walk in 'Son of God perfection' and Jesus will return."

Mimi chimes in, "It's like— What is that Scripture? No spot or wrinkle?"

"That's right." Dad thumbs through the pages of his worn-out leather-bound Bible. "Here it is, Ephesians 5:7. 'That he might present it to himself a glorious church, not having spot, or wrinkle, or any such thing, but that it should be holy and without blemish.'"

"I look forward to that day!" Mimi exclaims. "I've got plenty of spots and wrinkles I'd like to see go away."

Priscilla clears her throat. "Do you think it's talking about our physical bodies? Or is it something else?"

"Oh, I think it's both our physical bodies and our souls," Mimi responds. "If we have no sin left, then our bodies have to heal." She strokes her arms one at a time as if she were wiping them clean of blemishes.

"It seems like a lot of pressure to walk perfectly in every way," Priscilla says. "I can barely get through an hour without having some judgmental thought or feeling of jealousy. I don't know that I could reach that level of discipline."

"It's a process," I say. "But the Scriptures also tell us we'll reach it together. The first shall be last and the last shall be first."

Dad continues reading with fervor, "We're encouraged in Hebrews 6:1, therefore leaving the principles of the doctrine of Christ, let us go on unto perfection—not laying again the foundation of repentance from dead works, and of faith toward God, of the doctrine of baptisms, and of laying on of hands, and of resurrection of the dead, and of eternal judgment. And this will we do, if God permits."

"Amen, if God permits. Thank you, Lord," I whisper to not distract others from what they are hearing.

The clock above the mantel reminds me that a couple of hours have gone by. I'm hungry and a little sleepy so I reach for a snack in my bag.

Mom uses this opportunity to leave. "It's been a blessing, but I must get home before dark. It's hard to see at night."

Dad blesses her journey. "We speak safety and protection to you as you travel, Hannah."

"Thank you, Sam, and you as well," she replies. "See you at home, Tori."

Mimi points at me. "I have a word of knowledge for you."

"Okay." I smile with anticipation.

"I was lifting you up to the Lord in prayer regarding your singleness. I know you've been waiting a long time to have a family of your own. In this vision, I saw you riding a horse at full cantor in the desert. You had your eyes set on the horizon ahead. Then a man also riding a horse came along from a different path that met yours. When the two of you met up, he continued riding alongside you toward the same destination.

"The Lord would say to you: 'My daughter, I have seen you and know the desires of your heart. Continue along my path, being about your purpose, and this one will come alongside you because you are both seeking truth.'"

A warmth fills my heart and my cheeks. "Thank you! I was just sitting here, thinking about how I desire to be ministering alongside my husband one day. I'm hearing to continue along the path of ministry that the Lord has set me on, seeking His Kingdom, and in due time, my husband will manifest."

I imagine Adam riding along that horse. *Could this mean he'll be ready soon?*

I don't allow myself to think too long about it. *Either way, I will trust God.*

My dad clears his throat. "Are the hearts clear? Does anyone have another word to bring forth?"

I ask my spirit if there's anything more to bring forth.

"I'm clear," I say.

Others follow: "My heart's clear," "I'm clear," "Clear."

"All right then. Before we wrap up, I have some requests for faith agreement."

"Is that like a prayer request?" Priscilla asks.

Peter clears his throat. "It is similar, yes. Instead of simply asking God for something, it also requires your agreement that God has already provided for it, and an action of faith to follow it. So, when you pray, you also ask the Lord what action he is leading you to take toward fulfilling that request."

"Thank you," she says.

Dad pulls out a printed email. "The Ministry is asking for your faith agreement to the manifestation of the needs of the Apostle Center this month: two thousand dollars in rent, two hundred for the housekeeper, two eighty for satellite TV, one fifty for their phone bill, nine hundred for food, and one hundred toward Rob's next sabbatical. They are short fifteen hundred dollars this month and are at risk of getting their phones shut off."

I'm overwhelmed with the numbers and get this sinking feeling in the pit of my stomach. It sounds like so much, and the requests keep coming every month.

"Also, Victoria and I will travel to Arizona for the conference this week. Please stand in faith to pay her back for fronting the funds for my flight to Phoenix. That's about six hundred eighty dollars. Plus, I'll need travel money for food and incidentals during the week."

Mimi prays, "I stand in faith with you, and I minister safe travels and health to you both. I ask the Lord for that provision to cover all of your needs and then some, in Christ Jesus's name."

While I appreciate their faith agreement, I don't expect the money back. I had decided a while ago that to truly give unto God, I must give freely and sacrificially, without expecting a return. Still, it would be much less of a burden if everyone would pitch in.

I noticed my mom slipped a check in the little wooden giving box that sits on a table by the door before she left. Another saint takes out their wallet and counts the cash in it, reserving some.

"Thank you. Does anyone have needs we can be ministering to?" Dad asks.

Priscilla says, "My throat. I've had a chronic issue that the doctors can't seem to figure out. I would appreciate prayer for a correct diagnosis and healing."

"May we lay hands on you?" I ask.

"Yes, thank you," she says.

I stand up to get closer to her and lay my hand on her shoulder. Mimi walks over, and the others join.

Spiritual tongues rise to the heavens as we petition for our sister's healing.

I pray, "Father God, in the name of Jesus Christ, I stand with my sister for the health that is hers in God in Christ, in the Spirit. I thank you, Father, that your son Jesus took all sin and sickness upon Him on the cross, brought it to hell and left it there. Having fought Satan and his demons and taking the keys of the Kingdom, defeating death, He raised our sister up with Him and placed her at your right hand far above all sin and sickness. We believe that when we ask, we shall receive." I look at her. "Do you believe that, sister?"

"Yes, I believe it," Priscilla says, as a tear rolls down her face.

Another gives a word of knowledge in a vision and another speaks to her throat and the loosening of the muscles and healing of the larynx, as their spirit leads them.

The prayers wind down and Priscilla says, "Thank you, all. I felt as though there were a hand grasping my throat and then, as you were praying, I felt a release. I can swallow easier. I will continue to stand in faith agreement with the word of God that, by his wounds, I am healed."

"Praise God!" I exclaim. "Keep agreeing with that reality. Even if you don't see it fully manifest, believe God already did it."

We conclude the gathering with a prayer of protection mirroring the one we used when traveling here and reiterating the opening prayer for the day against evil spirits. Dad concludes with, "May the Holy Spirit seal God's word in our hearts and continue to teach us as we go."

Dad hands me his car keys and we say goodbye to everyone.

"How did you like the gathering?" I glance at Priscilla in the rearview mirror. She turns from staring out the window. Dad is dozing off to my right in the passenger seat as night falls over the winding back roads between Plymouth and Bridgewater.

Priscilla leans forward. "It was very interesting. A blast from the past seeing all those people again."

"I'm sure it was. Did you find it much different from when you used to attend?" I ask, not wanting to intrude on her life in between.

"The principles are the same, but the application seems different." She clears her throat. "How about you? I think the last time I saw you was at a gathering at your parents' house in Plymouth. You were only a toddler, and you were prophesying to us all. It was amazing!"

"You remember that?" I grin with delight. "I was four years old."

The memory fades in and out like a snapshot. It was the year 1986, and I stood in the same living room where I had sung with Mom and Dad. This time, a few inches taller, wearing a handmade mauve corduroy jumper made by my mom's friend Miss Sarah, over a white cotton shirt with frilly cap sleeves. I placed my little hand on the knee of a woman sitting among the circle of adults and prophesied to her. When I looked up at her face in the warm light, she seemed comforted. I continued around the circle, giving each a unique word of encouragement, as I had seen my father do occasionally. Adults often seemed shy about giving words. I was happy to obey the Lord. Walking in what the Holy Spirit moved me to do felt completely natural. When I finished rounding the circle, I came to my dad who lifted me up to sit upon his knee. I looked across the room, eye-level with the woman whose face was bright.

Priscilla's hand rests on my shoulder. "Of course I remember that."

"That was you!" I turn to her and then back to the road, hands firmly on the steering wheel. We laugh with delight.

"I was going through a difficult divorce. Your word assured me that God was with me as I faced the unknown."

I'm speechless.

"Less than a year after leaving town, I heard of your parents' divorce. I was absolutely shocked! I prayed for you, knowing how difficult it was for my own kids."

"Thank you."

The day my childhood changed forever was like any other day. I was barely four years old, officially a toddler. I recall in early March counting the days until this milestone birthday.

The television was on while Dad and Mom were upstairs, whispering in the bedroom. I lay on the couch watching whatever movie Dad left on the screen. In this movie, I learned a young boy's parents were getting a divorce and they would no longer be living together. The boy was quite upset by it, and everyone seemed sad.

On any other day, this may have been background noise, except what happened next seared it into my memory. Mom descended the stairs first, barely looking in my direction, and said, "Your father has something to tell you."

Then she proceeded past me toward the kitchen. Dad followed with his giant mug of Lipton tea in hand and sat in his Hitchcock-style wooden rocking chair. The one he bought my mom to rock me in when I was a baby. It became his favorite chair, great for playing the guitar. He leaned forward, hands folded and legs crossed at his ankles.

Dad drew in a long breath before speaking. "I want you to know that your mother and I love you very much, but I'm going to be moving out and you'll stay here with your mother. We both agree it would be best this way."

"Are you getting a divorce?" I asked in disbelief.

"Yes . . . do you know what that is?"

Oddly enough, I did.

"The parents in this movie are getting a divorce." I looked toward the TV screen.

"Do you have questions?" he asked me.

My heart sank with rejection and I asked, "Why can't I live with you, Dad?"

Dad was always the fun one who played guitar, sang, and made jokes. Sure, he raised his voice sometimes, and that was terrifying, but Mom had more rules.

"It's best that you stay with your mother. She can take better care of you. You can come visit me once I'm settled."

I buried my face in the couch and cried. My world had gone dark.

Bright lights nearly blind me from a pickup truck coming around the bend. I flash my lights at them.

"Those headlights make it awful to drive at night," Priscilla complains.

"Yeah, I suppose they can be harsh, but who could drive these back roads without them?" I shrug.

"Did you stay with The Ministry all this time?" she asks.

"Not entirely. It wasn't my choice to leave . . . but after my parents split, my mom didn't feel comfortable going to the gatherings. She continued to raise me in the faith though."

I recall a time when I was six years old. Mom read a story from my illustrated children's Bible and prayed with me as she often did when tucking me in at night. She gently stroked my hair while praying in her spiritual language. I joined her in uttering similar words as I often did. I thought about how Mom and Dad's prayer languages sounded different from each other and how mine seemed to be a combination of borrowed syllables.

Lord, are these my words, or am I just copying her? I thought.

An inner voice answered, *This is how you learn. Start with these sounds and I will give you your own as you grow.*

I understood this inner voice to be God's response.

So I continued to practice the sounds I'd heard, and it didn't take long for the Holy Spirit to give me fresh sounds. The key was not to think about it. Dad cautioned me not to analyze or try to interpret these sounds since they were spiritual and required divine interpretation to be understood. It was enough for me to speak the words in private unto the Lord. Whatever I was saying, I trusted it was the perfect prayer and He would answer it perfectly.

Dad stirs awake as we pull into the driveway. "Sorry about that. I just felt so tired."

"Ministry is a lot of work," Priscilla reassures him. She's not offended. "Besides, Victoria and I were having a pleasant chat."

I nod. "It was a pleasure."

I get out of the car and leave the driver's-side door open for Dad to get in. After his nap, he should be fine to drop off Priscilla and get home safely.

Walking up to the house, I turn and call back to Dad. "Mom agreed to drive us to the airport. Lord willing, we'll see you Thursday at seven a.m."

CHAPTER FOUR

HIGHER CALLING

Thirty-six-thousand feet above the Midwest, Dad is asleep in the aisle seat to the right of me. I look past the passenger on my left to gaze upon pillows of cumulous clouds lulling me into a daydream of love at first sight.

Nearly fifteen years ago, Prophet Charles Price, the apostle's closest adviser, presented a photograph of the elders, among which a young man caught my eye, and my heart followed. Contrasted with a group of mostly white middle-aged men stood a *young* white man with a crown of hair that glowed like a halo.

Could he be the one?

At sixteen, I imagined he was cool, like a California surfer, but part of The Ministry. Nobody my age took part in the local ministry. And he wasn't just anyone, he was the prophet's son, Adam. A glimmer of hope alighted my soul.

We met a year later when I was seventeen. It was my first time visiting Arizona, and he was a kind young man opening doors and offering to carry things for everyone, though a bit awkward around girls. I didn't mind. Tough men were intimidating; I preferred the sensitive type. I was a hopeful dreamer seeking that magic moment when all roads led to my one true love. His family's Southwestern charm was endearing, and the landscape was exotic compared to what I grew up with in Massachusetts. Saguaro cacti towered over a vast desert, reaching toward the expansive sky. A 360-degree view spanned the horizon, interrupted only by mountain ranges in the distance, evoking a sense of adventure in me.

I observed how his family prayed before every errand and ministered spiritual words of encouragement to each other along the way. I'd not seen such kindness within a family.

One day, we stopped at a lookout while driving up a mountain not far outside the city. The air was dry, the sun shining amid a clear blue sky above the light-brown dirt and gray cityscape. Several feet away, Adam crouched to the ground and came back up with a hand-picked wildflower.

That's sweet. He likes nature.

I walked over to get a better look at the view from the edge of the cliff, then he turned and held the flower up in front of me. I smiled, taken a bit by surprise, and accepted his gift. It was the first flower a boy had ever given me. I pocketed the feeling of that moment as a jewel for the treasure chest of my soul.

My stomach dips when plane hits turbulance. I press my palm against the seat in front of me and breathe deep until it passes after a few moments. Adam and I have been officially considering each other for marriage for the last five years. It is a loosely defined long-distance relationship with many unspoken rules. We talk on the phone about once a month—an improvement from once every few months—and only by a confirmed word of the Lord. I am free to contact him as my spirit leads, per my headship's instruction, but he must submit for a word through his father each time we speak.

My heart leaps with joy when I hear his voice. It soothes my soul, and he makes me laugh. We discuss many things, especially the word of God and its application in our lives. However, talking about our relationship or a future together is off limits. That would be considered presumption on our part, since we can't yet know where God is leading us. The apostle instructed us to wait for the Holy Spirit to reveal to us and to the eldership if it is time to take the next step.

I temper my anticipation of being in his presence by absorbing the teachings I believe will ultimately lead to perfection. Surely God is orchestrating a beautiful future where we will live out the tenets of our faith and show the world what it means to live in perfect harmony. Some may call it youthful folly, or maybe it is something the world has never seen. We could be different. We could prove that perfect love is possible between humans because, with God, all things are possible.

We ride the thermals for a turbulent descent into Sky Harbor. When the landing gear touches down, a sigh of relief escapes my lungs. I am always nervous during take-off and landing. The feeling turns into excitement as I collect my luggage, help my father, who has slept for most of the flight, and make our way to baggage claim.

Since that first meeting, I have traveled twice a year to Phoenix as an assistant to my dad. At first, it was for my benefit, but as the years waxed on, it became necessary that he traveled with help. I love my father and appreciate all the spiritual coaching he has given me over the years. Although he hasn't found success as a family man, he is a dedicated pastor who cares deeply for my soul, and I've learned so much about the Scriptures under his guidance.

On the way to baggage claim, a soldier walks by us and a young woman runs toward him. He drops his bags to the floor and catches her as she jumps up, wrapping her legs around his waist, and they kiss. A feeling in the pit of my stomach overshadows this joyful moment and the respect I have for this man's service. Envy.

I look up ahead. Charles is the tallest man I know at six-foot-four, and Adam is not far behind. I spot them near the baggage carousel, and my heart races. How I want to be like the young woman with her soldier. Instead, I constrain myself to a reserved smile and feel my cheeks fill with warmth.

"Greetings, how was your flight, sister?" Adam asks. It's a customary biblical greeting the eldership encourages us to use instead of hello—which apparently has some corrupt etymology. Addressing each other as brother and sister is supposed to prevent us from showing favor among the family of Christ.

"Hi, brother. The flight was long. I'm glad to be on the ground," which is true, but not what I want to say. On the phone, we would talk for hours, but in person, I can't find the words. My stomach is a butterfly atrium, but to allow emotions to lead my actions would be unholy. So I keep my passions to myself while I relish every moment I am in his presence. My mind is happy to cozy up to the thoughts of a future together while my body yearns for those thoughts to become reality. I pray these unruly desires will not overtake me.

Adam picks us up at the conference hotel where we slept off some jet lag from the day before. We're off to visit the Center for Prophet and Helps Ministries. I agree to help with seminar preparations, and Dad wants to visit with the team members. We drive north from our hotel along the I-17. The three of us exchange words of prophecy, and then Dad and Adam sustain small talk while I gaze out the window.

City buildings fade into an impressive landscape of saguaros standing tall against the mountainsides. The afternoon sun illuminates a crystal-blue sky until the earth meets it at the far reaches of my vision. Small towns come and go, separated by stretches of desert. After about thirty minutes, we exit the freeway into an unremarkable suburb with the convenience of modern commerce. Walmart and Costco are the big attractions supplemented by popular restaurants and a movie theater.

The home is modest, with a few sentimental decor items and a mix of donated furniture. One family, two couples, and an older single gentleman live and work together under one terra-cotta roof. Vaulted ceilings, a common feature that helps capture the rising heat, make the home feel spacious.

The smell of toner on warm paper fresh off a laser printer puts me into work mode. Spread out on the kitchen island, stacks of seminar materials wait to be collated and bound for the next day. The home offices and hallways are full of sound equipment and banners to transport to the venue. Meanwhile, out-of-town visitors add to the bustle. Some volunteer, and others stop in to greet everyone before the conference begins. We do our best to remain focused amid the activity.

There we stand, a handful of dedicated volunteers in a production line, compiling syllabi between clear acrylic covers and threading the compilations with plastic coil bindings.

At the risk of losing concentration on the task, I ask the group, "So, how did you all meet the apostle?"

Rita Sanchez, an elder's wife in her fifties with dark shoulder-length hair and a single silver streak swept to one side, shares first. "We met at a Southern Baptist church when I was in high school. I was friends with his daughter, Bobbie Jo, and spent time at their house."

"What was that like?" I've known Southern Baptist to be a lively tradition of Spirit-filled Bible believers. The mention of it conjures scenes from the 1992 movie *Leap of Faith* starring Steve Martin, where a fake faith-healer, Jonas Nightingale, traveled the South bringing big-tent revivals where folks experienced spiritual healings and miracles.

"I remember he had a lung sickness, and I would often hear him yelling at his wife and children."

"That sounds intimidating. What made you join The Ministry?"

"Oh, well, they started having gatherings in their home after church on Sundays. The Lord really ministered to me through those. I was a shy kid and . . ." She pauses and scans our faces. "I felt like I was a bad person on the inside. Sure, to everyone else I seemed like a goodie-two-shoes, but that's not what *I* saw. I was close to taking my life. Youth pastors and others didn't take me seriously when I trusted them with this information. Rob was the first one to offer me a solution.

"He told me I wasn't good or bad, but somewhere in the middle. God made me good, but the flesh was bad, and so my thoughts and actions were a mixture of both."

A collective sigh moves through the assembly line as we understand this to be double mindedness, which, as we know from James 1:8, brings instability.

"Of course," Rita continues, "now I know it was the flesh warring against the spirit and that I'm not unique in that. Each one of us must prove out a single-minded faith, including the elders. As Paul said in Galatians, 'For the flesh desires what is contrary to the Spirit, and the Spirit what is contrary to the flesh. They conflict with each other, so that you are not to do whatever you want. But if the Spirit leads you, you are not under the law.'"

"Amen, sister, we're not under the law," Adam affirms in his warm and welcoming way.

"Yes, that's Principle Eight: Proving," I chime in. "We give all to God and receive from God, agree, and act on it by faith. Then what we have in Him will be given to us." They all look at me like I'm preaching to the choir, so I look down at the papers as I pass them through the line.

"I was a mess when I met Rob," Kumari says. It's great to see her again. She recently married Elias Johnson, an elder from Phoenix. They have been living in Sedona and working at the Apostle Center for the past year.

"I was around twenty-four years old and did not know what I was doing with my life," she says. "My mum and I didn't get along so well. She thought I should be married and having children. Instead, I studied at the university. In her culture, I should not have lived away from home while single. Even if I wanted to, it would have been difficult to find a husband because my dad was in the Peace Corps and we moved around often.

"Anyway, I was seeking God for help because I did not know what to do and could not fulfill my family's expectations. Oddly enough, it was my mum who introduced me to Rob. She met him at a neighbor's house, and she liked him and was very impressed with his words of prophecy. She stuck with it for a while, but my dad was not interested. I don't know why, maybe it was his Catholic upbringing. I pray for him."

Others who have a Catholic background nod in agreement. I guess they would know how difficult it was to break from that tradition and receive the outpouring of the Holy Spirit and the freedom that comes with it.

"There was a huge outpouring of the spirit at that time," Kumari says. "I remember seeing people laughing hysterically, falling down on the ground to rest in the spirit. It was all very different and exciting. He was a great minister of God and the only one who was brave enough to prophesy to my uncle. My uncle was a big, tough military man who most people were intimidated by. He did not listen to anyone, so people stopped trying to tell him things. Rob walked right over to him and put his hand on his shoulder, looked him in the eye, and what he spoke, it was all true!

"I will admit, I had warned my mother of false prophets and did not want to meet him at first. When I did, he shook my hand, and I felt electricity! It was like a sign from God that he was a man of God."

I smile, thinking of the times when Rob would speak truth to me as if he could see into my soul. It was a wonderful feeling that could only be supernatural.

"I met him first, remember, sis?" Kumari's older brother, Mani, walks into the room. He's an elder and is helping with some of the equipment.

"Yes, brother. Don't rub it in." She smiles wide, and her eyes light up with embarrassment.

He joins the conversation. "What she is not telling you is that she followed me everywhere when we were kids. I accepted Christ, she also accepted

Christ, I received the Holy Spirit at the charismatic church we were attending, then she did the same. She always wanted everything that I had," he chides.

Her cheeks flush from the attention.

"Seriously, though," Mani continues. "I received the Holy Spirit only a couple of weeks before meeting Brother Rob for the first time. I will never forget the divine connection I felt. But I am not one to follow just anyone, so I studied the Scriptures to prove everything he said. It was all true. It was presented in a way I had not considered before, and it was life! That is why I am here today, and that is why you have to put up with this one." He nudges his sister with an elbow.

"Hey!" She squints and purses her lips at him.

I chuckle at their banter.

"What about you, dear?" Kumari glints at me. "You are a prophetess now. How did that come about?"

Surprised at her interest, I glance up at her from the pile of papers passing through my hands. I share with some reluctance, "The calling came as a result of some ministry I was sending to elders. It was during a time when I was faithfully praying from the *Declarations of the Will unto God* pamphlet as my morning ministry each day. I would wake up a half hour early before high school. Yes, high school. I did it every morning because I thought if I was consistent, I would eventually become perfect."

It was the formula I always wanted. I thought, *Here's my recipe. If I just keep reading this, eventually I am going to become a perfect human being who will usher in Christ's return on this earth.* Since then, I've realized it's more about my heart than repeating the words.

"My heart was sincere in what I prayed unto the Lord. Even if I was misguided about what the results would be," I say.

That discipline alone changed my life. I had more confidence. I was more focused. The practice even dispelled some fears since it was mostly based on Scripture. I believe that is why it had such a positive impact. Even so, this ritual would not be my salvation.

"Anyway," I say. "There was a long list of elders to pray for in The Ministry. I read their names every day and I thought, *Is this really doing anything?*

"One day, I received to ask God to highlight names for me, and whichever ones stood out to me by the Holy Spirit, I would send them a prophetic word of encouragement by email.

"I continued to do this often. On the day I sent a word to the apostle, he responded saying I was indeed a prophetess. And it made so much sense, because that's what I was doing."

It was the highest honor I could imagine, and while I didn't know what it really meant, I desired to fulfill the role. That's when I got nervous, thinking, *Am I now expected to keep this up?* At first, I committed the responsibility to the Lord, sending words whenever I received to. I continued this through college, albeit less frequently.

"My dream after college was to work with you all at The Ministry Center because I thought that was how I would fulfill my role of being prophetess to the apostle. It hasn't happened yet . . . "

A booming voice cuts the conversation short. "How are those syllabi coming?"

Charles enters the kitchen and pours himself a cup of coffee. Expressionless, his eyes scan the table checking on our progress.

The last few syllabi pass through the assembly line, then we count them without conversation and do some quality checks. By the time we pack them in boxes to send with the other supplies, the time for intimate conversation and connection has passed.

The conferences represent hope for many people. If God has any new revelation for the church body, it will come through the apostle before making its way into the system churches and various denominations around the globe. We are the faithful few entrusted to spearhead the advancement of God's word until Christ's return. This position comes with honor and a touch of pride.

CHAPTER FIVE

INNER WORKINGS

"**G**ood morning! You are the glory of the Lord," I declare to Adam. We are the first ones to arrive in the hotel conference room on seminar day. He's sitting in one of twenty office chairs and looks up from his phone.

"You too, sister. How did you sleep?" His eyes are puffy and dark despite his otherwise professional appearance. His purple necktie matches the blouse I'm wearing.

A match made in heaven?

"I slept well. You don't look like you could say the same." I sit in the chair next to him.

"Yeah, I was up late editing the conference video and clearing the camera storage for today's recordings." He rubs his eyes. "I could use a second cup of coffee."

I'm about to get up and find him a coffee when Rita walks in.

"Did someone say they need coffee?" Rita says. "I have an extra one. I accidentally put too much sugar in it."

"I'll take it." Adam sips it with a sigh of content and rocks gently in the swivel chair.

"So, how was dinner last night?" I ask Adam. "I noticed you left with your parents before I could ask where you were headed."

"Oh, it was nothing special. Dad and Mom had a long day, so we got some takeout and brought it back to the Center. I had a lot of work to do anyway."

"Right, the video editing." I try not to feel disappointment, but I can't help it. I'm visiting from two thousand miles away, and he brings takeout back to his house with his parents.

When all the volunteers arrive, we open with prayer and prophecies. I receive, "My sons look not to the physical presentations of the circumstances but in all things receive by your spirit the victory at the moment over the enemy and the flesh mind. You have the mind of Christ and you know all things. Go forth and support the elders in their work this day."

Similar words of encouragement come through a few others before we get started. A local elder is setting up sound equipment for the seminar later while I help the ladies pour glasses of water and put out candy at each of the elders' seats around the conference tables.

I scan the room, seeing what needs to be done, and then give it to my spirit for prophetic guidance on what to submit to help with. I've made the mistake before of asking someone what to do. Their response? "Give it to your spirit and receive." Here at the epicenter of The Ministry, I must prove everything I practice in daily life. In this high-stakes place, every thought, every movement, has consequences. Either they are of the Kingdom of God or of the devil. There's no middle ground.

I work up the courage to say, "Adam, I receive to help hang the banners."

I don't want to show favoritism in working with Adam while others also need help, but that's what my spirit gave me.

"All right. Would you hold these hooks while I get on the ladder?" he asks.

"Sure." I stand close to him as he ascends the three-step ladder. The older women are watching. He reaches his hand out for a hook, and I gently place one in his palm. His fingers graze mine for a second, and I feel at peace. Standing next to him, my head at his hips, I ward off lustful thoughts by thinking of the purpose we are serving. If he gets unsteady, my hands are ready to support him.

Once hung, we step back to determine their evenness. He gives me a casual high-five for a job well done. The banners depict the spiritual structure of human beings and how we ought to communicate through the spirit for true fellowship to take place. It serves as a reminder of the first principle, that we are spirit, soul, and body. The apostle refers to the charts often in his preaching.

A local elder, Julio, in charge of the sound system, is untangling cords and setting out microphones. They are preparing for a midday changeover between the conference-style seating and seminar setup.

After I help him tape down the wires, he asks, "Would you go sit in the apostle's chair so I can adjust the camera's focus?"

"My pleasure." I sit behind the head table in the armchair designated for Rob. I avert my eyes from looking directly into the stage lights and sit tall, feeling I'm sitting in a sacred space.

"Thanks, lovely," his words flatter me. "Just sit right there, shift a little to your left. There, perfect! I'm not used to seeing such beauty through this lens. Boy, if I wasn't married." He shakes his head. "I'd scoop you up in a heartbeat."

Did he really just say that to me? I shudder. This space doesn't feel so sacred anymore. Adam looks up at me from the mass of cords he's now untangling and blushes slightly, then looks back down. I sigh. I'm sure Julio meant well, but that was awkward.

Charles appears at the door. His hands tremble by his side. The shake seems to get worse each time I see him. "Adam, you were supposed to meet me back in the room."

"Yes, sir, I . . . I ask your forgiveness." Adam scrambles to lay down the cords and leaves with his father.

I pick them up and continue the work.

Rob enters from the back of the room shaking hands, patting shoulders, and greeting each one by name, not unlike the president entering the cabinet floor for the State of the Union address. Except Rob is an ambassador of a Holy Nation. Seeing me, he raises his thick eyebrows and flashes a wide grin, revealing bright white dentures. I feel his favor and smile back. His walk is labored and unsteady, assisted by the prophet on one side and Heather's mom on the other.

He approaches his chair but doesn't sit. Instead, he waves away his handlers to take their seats in the front row. He stands alone at the front of the room, gazing out at the group of about seventy, seeming to look into every single one of us. Then in a commanding voice, coming not from his frail body but from somewhere entirely different, he speaks: "And he gave some, apostles; and some, prophets; and some, evangelists; and some, pastors and teachers; for the perfecting of the saints, for the work of the ministry, for the edifying of the body of Christ."

He pauses again, nodding. He lifts his hands. "I founded this ministry in 1968 with these words from Ephesians, chapter four. We are that body of Christ. We are those apostles, prophets, evangelists, pastors and teachers." As he speaks, his eyes roll over each person, identifying us. His gaze rests on me on the word *prophets*. I shiver and almost fall; it is like an anointing.

"I beseech you, that every one of you gives everything you hear to your spirit and receive from God, as your only source. Not from me.

I am just a man, a messenger. No other preacher will tell you to make God your only source. No, they want you to follow them. But God called me not to be worshipped but to lead a family of true worshippers who will be steadfast enough to work out their salvation and usher in Christ's return.

"Each of these principles builds on the one before it. We have preached on all twelve, several times over the last forty years, and each round yields an increase in revelation and in removing the veil of the flesh as our hearts turn to the Lord. The first and most critical principle is Man Created in the Image of God: Triune—Spirit, Soul, and Body. The first step to restoration is to know what God created. Therefore, you have me as an example of how to walk as Jesus did without compromise. I am not saying that I am perfect at it, but my will is to walk in the perfection that I am, in God in Christ.

"Now, I give you another example, one that will faithfully emulate Christ and not compromise." He motions for Heather's mom to come stand beside him. She looks at her husband seated next to her. He nods. She walks up, and a flowing blue and white ankle-length skirt sways with her stride. She stands beside Rob, mouth stern and gaze downward, her long gray hair secured by a pin on either side of her head swept behind her shoulders. She dodges eye contact with anyone in the room.

"Saints, I give you Eve, your apostlist."

A few of us gasp, our eyes locked on the two of them.

What is an apostlist? Is that biblical? Is he bestowing a leadership role upon a woman? No, it couldn't be. I'm sure he'll have a good explanation.

"Now, before you all get your panties in a bunch, let me explain. As I just said, God has called us all to be apostles, prophets, evangelists, pastors, and teachers. He put the entire five-fold ministry within us in the Holy Spirit. It is just that we're not all mature enough to realize it, and so he appointed some to carry out those roles until we all come unto the measure of the stature of Christ. This woman you see before you has proven to be unwavering in her faith. She lost her very own daughter, an unimaginable pain, yet committed to serving the church and me, Christ's representative, faithfully and without compromise. She has proven her ability to stand beside me and in my stead. Therefore, God revealed to me she is to be called Eve, replacing the identity of her past with one of restitution. She will function as an apostlist—a new title the Spirit gave me to describe a female apostle."

My mouth opens without words. I sit up tall, and hope renews within me. There *is* room for female leadership in the body of Christ. This aligns with Paul's letter to the Galatians telling us that there is no male or female in Christ.

"Rest assured," Rob says, "this does not violate the Principle of Submission. She will still submit to her husband in her marriage, but she will submit to me in every other way as her spiritual covering."

He turns to her and places a hand on her shoulder, blessing her. Then motions for her to go back to her seat.

As he takes his seat of honor behind the table, he says, "My flesh is weak, and for that, I ask you to stand in faith with me, that I will have the strength to preach this entire seminar. If you will remain strong against the flesh mind, then I will make it through."

His well-being is in our hands now. I will stand strong in faith.

Lord, I hope everyone else does too.

The first portion of the seminar is a recap of the previous eleven principles in the Twelve Principles of Human Being Life series. I commit it all to my Spirit to be taught anew, even though I have heard these words many times.

"Only God could save mankind," Rob reiterates, "but only mankind could work out being saved."

I would do anything to work out my salvation to the fullness of the measure of the stature of Christ.

"Now, the Principle of Submission . . . " Rob raises his voice. "Ah yes, the one that makes you all stiffen up because of your stiff necks because of the spirit of rebellion! This is the single-most misunderstood principle and the reason many have walked away. I'm not asking you to submit to me or to any person. I am telling you that God alone deserves our very being. We are to submit *all* things to him." He shouts, "Without Him we *do not have life!*" Then, in a quiet whisper, "We have no air to breathe without the Creator making it for us."

His tone fluctuates for emphasis and to keep our attention. Yelling when we need to wake up, whispering when we need to lean in.

"Now, you might say"—Rob mimics a whining woman—"'But my husband is a drunk, I can't submit to him.'" Then, with authority, he rises from his chair and declares, "But *God* is *not* a drunk, and his Spirit will answer your heart, honey! He spoke to Moses through a bush, to Balaam through a donkey, and to Gideon through a fleece. He can certainly speak through your drunk husband!" He flashes a bright white smile, nodding as he scans the room. "All right, then. So we don't submit to people, we submit to God, through Jesus as Lord, by the working of the Holy Spirit."

He lets out a heavy sigh. "To this day, the most difficult principle for people to grasp, next to having a sovereign will, is the Principle of Submission. That's why many have fallen away. Dear brothers and sisters, don't let the devil fool you. Nothing done outside of God's order will bear fruit. Many have perished due to the pride of stepping out of God's order."

He looks down for a moment, shaking his head, then looks out at us. "My wife might still be here today if she had a heart of submission to take on my purpose of spreading the gospel as her own. Instead, the devil used that judgment manifested as cancer. Then my children went down their own paths, and they have seen so much heartache."

His own heartache is a stark reminder of how the devil operates. I think of the elders I know who have passed away. Each of them had either left The Ministry or stepped out of God's order.

One elder passed away by stopping his medication without having a word of the Lord, confirmed by the eldership and his doctor.

A dear elder from Massachusetts, Dicky Silverman, died of a heart attack soon after leaving his role twenty years ago. He and his wife, Joanne, were the first to host gatherings in our area, and I was baptized in their swimming pool at nine years old.

I recall the day of my baptism as if it were yesterday. It was a day of celebration, and Dad had prepared me for it well. He used mini sermons during car rides from his house and back on weekends to ensure I understood the significance. It was my once-for-all decision to follow Christ. I'd been following my parents' lead and walking in their faith for years. It was time I claimed that faith for myself.

The place wasn't sacred, only the moment. I stood with my mom poolside, fixated on those who were being baptized before me. An oversized t-shirt nearly reaching my knees concealed my two-piece bathing suit. Families seated in folding chairs lined the deck under blue skies with the scent of charcoals warming for the barbecue. A slight breeze grazed my skin on this summer day in Cape Cod.

I was shivering while still dry, not because of the breeze but because of nerves. The sights and sounds helped to ease my fears of going underwater. When I was two, my dad had tried to force me to learn to swim underwater by dunking me in a pool against my will. Ever since then, I would panic from claustrophobia each time I went under, causing me to inhale water that burned the back of my throat.

They called my name, and Mom walked me to the edge. I took my dad's hand, trusting him this time, as I stepped into the shallow end of the swimming pool. Chilly, but nothing I couldn't handle. I stood between my Dad and another elder, Philip. I knew this submersion would be different because baptism was holy and God would protect me.

"Do you, Victoria Rose, believe with all your heart that Jesus Christ is the Son of God?"

I nodded. "Yes."

Dad continued, "Do you believe he was crucified for your sin and the sin of the world, descended into hell, fighting off Satan and his demons and taking the keys of the Kingdom, leaving your sin in hell and raising you with him to be forever separated from sin and reconciled to God as perfect, sinless, and righteous?"

"Yes," I said, shaking a bit more in anticipation of going under.

"Declare 'I do' with confidence so all can hear it," my dad encouraged.

"I do!" I proclaimed to my mom and the others with enough force for the fear to take its place in hell with Satan.

"Going under the water, you will be buried with Christ in his death, and as you rise again out of the water, you will be raised with him in victory, your slate wiped clean."

"Amen," I said with a steady voice. I held my nose with one hand, the other across my heart. This was too important to allow fear to stop me.

I felt the safety of their supportive hands on my back, as I surrendered to the moment. I felt my weakness and my willingness to do what was required. And I knew perfection was in that for me. Paul said that grace is sufficient, for our power is made perfect in weakness. I boasted in my weakness to have power in Jesus, just like Paul told me. The descent was slow as the watery grave engulfed my body. The water covered my ears, and then my face, before my reflexes kicked in, and I shot straight up trembling with tears of both relief and joy. I was forgiven. Sin would have no power over me.

Rob's voice booms over the audience, and I snap to attention. "Satan has *no* power, except that which you give him!"

Dicky's heart attack must have resulted from him being outside of God's order, thus giving Satan power. I must always stay in God's order or I will risk being taken out by the enemy and failing to be alive when Christ returns.

Adam is watching Rob on the small screen of the video camera. I think about what it would be like to submit to God through him as my husband one day. The love and tenderness I would feel in his gentle guidance. I imagine us walking hand in hand, in oneness with Jesus Christ, traveling, and sharing the gospel. We would be unstoppable—a shining example of faithfulness before the world.

Rob clears his throat and sips from a tall glass of distilled water.

Oh no, I got lost in thought again.

I look down at the syllabus to see what I missed and find the statement about Satan having no power of his own. I sigh with relief. He didn't get far.

"That is why it is vital," Rob says, "that you keep your will asserted unto God and Christ in every changing circumstance to receive his knowledge, wisdom, and understanding above your flesh mind."

I whisper a prayer, "Father, I confess as sin that I let my mind wander. That is not me. I will all five-sense perceptions to my spirit to hear only from you in this moment. Help me stay focused so I don't give Satan any power."

He continues preaching and I follow along, the Holy Spirit illuminating my understanding of each point.

A door to the conference room opens behind us, and a stranger enters. The man's clothes are worn thin, his shoulder-length silver and brown hair is heavy with oil, and his gaze is distant. He stands at the back of the room, listening.

Before long, the stranger walks with a slight limp down the center aisle toward Rob; the congregation follows his movement. Adam, sitting in the front row, makes a move toward the man, but Rob holds up his hand motioning him to stand down.

"Welcome, sir. Can I help you?" Rob steps out from behind the table to meet the man at the front.

The stranger falls to his knees before the apostle with hands lifted high. "Forgive me, Lord. I'm a sinner," he weeps. Rob leans over and lays his hand on the man's shoulder. Adam, at first ready to protect the apostle, comes alongside the man and places his hand on his other shoulder.

Rob ministers in tongues, praying over the man. The congregation follows suit as a sea of prayers in English and spiritual tongues fill the room. Repenting of the fear I first felt, the Holy Spirit fills me with compassion, and I raise my hand to speak. A volunteer hands me a microphone.

I speak to the stranger. "I saw a vision of an angel descending upon you . . ."

"Roger," the stranger fills in his name.

"Roger," I say. "This angel embraced you with his wings, before telling you to rise and assisted you to your feet."

"I felt it," Roger said. "I felt the embrace and the love of Jesus. Thank you."

Rob asks, "Can we get you anything?"

Roger says, "Your prayers mean more than you know. I was released from prison only an hour ago with nothin' but the clothes on my back and a few bucks for a train. I had no idea where to go. I took the light rail and somethin' told me to stop here. So, I came into the hotel for some water and saw that there was church event happening. I don't know what compelled me to enter, but I heard your preaching and I couldn't help myself."

Shouts of "amen" and "praise the Lord" from attendees punctuate his testimony.

Rob nods toward Adam. "Make sure this man gets a bottle of water and the local pastor's phone number."

Adam nods.

"Thank you for you kindness."

"You are welcome to stay for a while," says Rob.

"No, no, I'll be moving along. But I know God is with me now. Thank you all, and sorry for interrupting."

The man has no reason to apologize. I am excited to witness this blessing. But surely there's some other way to help him. Food, shelter, clothing? I feel the tug of the Apostle James, who wrote that faith without works is dead. We can't just let him walk away . . . but I say nothing, figuring the elders know what to do. Roger walks out the door.

Adam relieves the person covering for him behind the camera, and Rob picks up the sermon where he left off.

I offer up a silent prayer. *Lord, I see you are calling Roger to yourself. Please be with him. Lead him to find shelter and a job. Most of all, help him find his place in the body of Christ where he will continue to receive spiritual nourishment, in Christ Jesus's name.*

CHAPTER SIX

ALLEGIANCE

Guitars strum feverishly as we sing each refrain at increasing tempo, "They run through the city, dance on the walls. Great is the army, that carries out his word." I bunch up my long skirt in one hand, pumping a fist in the air, and stomping my bare feet. I sing with gusto the lyrics based on Joel 2:9, "Blow the trumpet in Zion, Zion . . ." Children dance around me—little girls in dresses and boys in suits. They link hands in a circle formation, then dancing turns to running. The faster the music, the faster they revolve. As the song ends, some continue spinning until they're so dizzy they fall.

The Jubilee is the close of every conference weekend. Adam hasn't arrived yet. Sometimes he works through it, editing the conference video, or rests due to exhaustion from all the preparations. I hope that's not the case tonight.

I distract myself by watching the children and admiring their lack of inhibition.

Who am I kidding? I too have little inhibition when dancing for the Lord.

The next song draws everyone to their feet. There's something about "doing it for the children" that makes looking silly seem perfectly fine. The

"Arky Barky Song" is one of those times. We sing of Noah calling the animals onto the ark two-by-two and follow the choreographed motions.

Adam appears in the entrance, and the children run up to him and pull him into the dance. My shoulders drop, and my dancing becomes looser now that I know he's joining us to celebrate. God's revelations through the apostle are worthy of this honor.

After a few songs, I excuse myself to the ladies room to refresh, when a local sister I don't know very well walks up beside me.

"Aren't the children precious?" I say.

"Too precious," she says. "We have to watch over them. Especially around the men."

I snap my head up and furrow an eyebrow as we walk.

"I heard Julio cheated on his wife and may be mistreating the children," she says.

I step back in disbelief. Julio, the same elder who ran the sound system? I know he has a questionable past, but so do most of the elders. Since coming to Christ, he is working hard to learn the principles and support his wife and five children.

"How could you spread such gossip?" I reprimand her as she follows me into the bathroom.

"The signs are there if you'll look at them."

I can't believe I'm hearing this. But, if the devil is using her to spread lies, I must find out where it started.

"What signs?" I say.

"They're hard to miss. Overly friendly, always remarking about women's looks. I don't trust him," she says.

"How do you . . . I mean, when do you think it started?" I say.

"Can't be sure, but from what I've heard, the elders confronted him and then did nothing. He said he'd repented, and they gave him nothing more than a slap on the wrist." She shakes her head.

A toilet flushes in one stall. We say no more.

Satan is the accuser of the brethren. He roams like a roaring lion seeking whom he may destroy. That must be it. Spiritual warfare. In the privacy of a stall, I whisper a prayer, "Father, in Christ's name, I take authority over the lies of the devil and forbid lying spirits from spreading rumors meant to destroy Christ's ministry."

I rejoin the jubilation, feeling less jubilant. Julio bounces a young girl on his knee, and immediately I have unclean thoughts about the situation.

No, that's perfectly normal, I scold myself.

The children love him. His wife is sitting by him clapping a tambourine and singing joyful praises to the Lord. It's nothing but a baseless rumor.

The next day, I hitch a ride with other volunteers to visit the Apostle Center in Sedona. We walk up to the front door of their newest location.

"The apostle is very weak right now," Adam says, briefly making eye contact with me before looking at the ground. "Any subconscious judgment or unclean spirit could have devastating consequences. Assert your will unto God and cleanse yourself."

"Of course." My body stiffens, like a deer caught in headlights. I'm not aware of any unholiness, but I obediently pray that Satan would not use my subconscious to take down our spiritual leader. Our faith upholds him.

Eve invites us into the single-story bungalow on a flat lot. Aside from their appearance at the conference, we rarely saw much of either of them. We would get updates on his health struggles and hear him speak to us through weekly recordings, expounding on the previously taught principles. Visits like the one I enjoyed over a decade ago are now uncommon.

Rob sits in an oversized recliner, his legs covered with several blankets. I reach out to greet him. He slips his left hand into mine, his fragile frame gripping tight. Then he takes Adam's hand beside me. We stand before him, joined by him.

"You know I'm proud of you both." His eyes twinkle, set in a landscape of wrinkles. He prophesies, "The Lord would say to you, you have a mighty calling. I have given you all that I can through my apostle. The foundation is set, the way is shown to you. Be an example to those who will come after you. Stand in the apostle's doctrine and you will receive a hundredfold return of the Kingdom of God in your lifetime for your faithfulness."

Lord! My heart skips a beat. I feel as if we are standing on a sacred mountaintop, receiving a great commission that God specifically equipped the two of us to carry out. This must mean we'll be together; we will embody Christ and lead His people unto perfection.

In the afternoon, we visit a popular hiking spot. Gazing straight up at the rust-colored snow-capped mountains on either side, I draw a deep breath of cool, clean air.

Adam walks by flashing a smile then looks at his watch. "It's sixty-three degrees now. Looks like the temperature will climb to seventy by late afternoon."

"The Lord gave us perfect weather," I say.

He continues past Rita and Kumari to catch up with Elias, Kumari's husband, who has taken the lead as we walk along the riverbed.

Adam and Elias stop and turn around about twenty feet ahead of us.

Elias announces, "It looks like we'll have to cross here." He points to the shallow stream of water rolling over a row of steppingstones that lead to the other side.

A family with two teenage daughters struggles to cross up ahead, and Adam goes to assist. He finds a secure stance and reaches out his hand. The mom and dad cross with great care, then their daughters giggle and blush when taking Adam's hand.

I'm proud of his good deed, but I want to wipe that grin right off his face.

I step onto the log, confident I don't need help but eager to accept it from Adam. I place my hand in his and gaze into his kind eyes. My body runs warm, my limbs weightless, as if I could hover to the other side. Once across, Adam jogs up to meet Elias. Kumari winks and nudges me with her elbow.

They all know we're in a consideration of marriage, and that makes us ripe for scrutiny. Most physical touch is off limits, even holding hands must be done with purpose and discretion.

"You know, marrying an elder isn't everything," Kumari says.

"I don't think that," I say. My body is buzzing with too many endorphins to feel ashamed.

She gives me that lips-pursed, big-eyed look my mother would give me when she knows I'm not being honest with myself.

"Aren't you happy being married to Elias?" I ask.

"Yes, but there are things you miss about being single after you're married. I'm just saying you want to be sure that it's really what you want. If you're too eager, then you might miss out on the freedom you have right now."

"I suppose being single can have its perks," I say, "but I can't think of anything else I want to do without a husband."

"Oh, you'll see," Kumari says. "Once you have a husband and a child, you can't just go anywhere and do anything you'd like."

I consider her version of being single and the freedom it affords. Even now, God leads me in where I go and what I do, and I submit most things to my headship.

Won't there be more freedom in being married to the right person?

"I don't think I would mind that," I say, watching Adam up ahead. "Rita, you seem happy in your marriage. What's your secret?"

Rita looks up from the uneven path. "Oh, I don't think you want my advice."

"What do you mean? Of course I do. I know how much you love Manuel."

"It's true, I love my husband very much, but we've faced our share of disappointments," Rita says.

"In your marriage?" I say.

"Um, more so in The Ministry actually."

I turn and walk backward for a few steps so I can see her expressions.

She's frowning and focused on her steps. "We can't just go anywhere that we feel God leading us. With Manuel being a pastor, our ministry is tied to one location until a younger elder takes his place." She shakes her head. "But there are no prospects."

"Where would you go?" I say.

"We've desired for many years to minister in México. But the eldership won't allow it. So, we obey."

Obey the eldership? We're supposed to *submit* to them unto God, not obey. She and Manuel must be outside of God's order. If it were truly God's will for them to go, I'm sure the eldership would allow it.

"Well, I'm praying that God will lead me into a relationship that will magnify my impact for Christ," I say.

Kumari and Rita smile and nod.

Adam steps off to the side, and we almost pass him.

"Are you okay?" I say.

"Yeah, I just need to take a break and adjust my insulin."

I ask the Lord what to do, and he reminds me I'm prepared for this. I pull a sandwich bag full of pistachios from my pack.

"Would you like some nuts, brother?"

"Yes, that's perfect, sister. Thank you."

I explain, "The Holy Spirit prompted me to pack them this morning just in case you would need some protein to counteract the sugar spike after breakfast."

His glucose-induced blank stare is hard to read, but I think he's as surprised as I am that I came prepared. Maybe now he'll see my value, that I can be there for him.

After a few minutes, Adam tells the group, "I think I'm better now. Let's continue on, shall we?"

The group stays together from here on. Adam walks beside me, pointing out interesting mushrooms on the forest floor and the critters that make their habitat there. We come to a clearing in front of a large juniper tree.

"What a beautiful tree!" I say.

"Yes, it is perfect for a photo." Kumari nudges Adam. "Why don't you stand by the tree with Victoria? I'll get a picture of you two."

"That would be lovely." I walk toward the tree and wave him over.

Thank the Lord for Kumari. She gets it.

I reach around Adam's waist, slipping my hand under his open brown leather jacket. He rests his arm over my shoulders, and I nestle into his side. It's a picture-perfect moment.

Kumari takes several photos on her phone and sends them to me. I hold back a squeal. This photo marks a new chapter in the beginning of our lives together.

I chew my gum faster as the change in elevation makes my ears pop. Gazing out the backseat window of a sport utility vehicle, I marvel at the evening sun's rays revealing layers of purple and gray canyon below as it passes through the undulating shadows of pines lining the ridge. The

Red Rocks are now far behind us; pines will soon transform into cacti, and canyons will flatten to desert. Our vehicle hugs the highway, and a dip in my stomach reminds me to pray for safety. I look at Adam, who is asleep next to me, then I look out my window once more.

I think about how my generation of believers can do better than our parents. Something about being in the mountains elevates my perspective. I recall stories the elders told over the years of their sordid pasts. Their depravity of growing up without God, or at most a parched and lifeless version of Christianity, may taint their perception of our hearts and intentions. Afraid of us living life as they did, the elders assume we are bound to push every boundary. Whatever appeal that drugs and promiscuity once had for them would never cross our minds. We have a personal relationship with Jesus Christ. Why would we want any of that?

I have weaknesses, but they are mild. I'm at risk of entering into dysfunctional relationships. Since I didn't grow up with the best examples, I guard my heart with determination.

The landscape sweeping past us is now a flat desert with cacti, tumble weeds, and vast open skies. I want my mom to share in this joy with me. It's been over twenty years since she'd seen those she knows, and many haven't met her.

My thoughts drift to relationship lessons from my childhood. The adults in my life had a hard time cultivating healthy relationships. Every couple I knew either fought constantly or split up.

Mom and I were scarred by Dad's abrupt decision to end their marriage—one she expected would last forever. Her second husband, Steve, entered our lives four years after Dad left. He was a dreamer. His kindness toward his children and the community drew her to him. After their wedding, she learned he was an alcoholic.

We had some fun times, but they didn't last. He was a carpenter and fisherman, so he built us a boat and we learned to dig for clams. He took us out to the sand bars outside of Plymouth Harbor, where we would do the "quahog dance," stomping our feet to make the clams come to the surface. We'd look for a bubble in the mud and then dig fast, hoping it wasn't a razor clam.

The fun soon wore off, and his addiction took a toll on our family. His kids stopped coming on weekends, and I spent more time at my grandparents' house. Mom was determined to help him and keep me safe.

My grandparents were married for over forty years and argued night and day. They didn't believe in divorce, or counseling. I often retreated to my room and turned on the TV or music to drown it out until they settled to watch their nightly television programs. My favorites were *Murder She Wrote*, *Matlock*, and *MacGyver*. On nights Grandpa insisted on watching *Baywatch*, Grandma went to bed early.

"Early to bed, early to rise, makes a man (or woman) healthy, wealthy, and wise," Grandma liked to say. She kept to a regular bedtime of nine thirty and arose before dawn to read her Bible, pray, write note cards, and prepare her Sunday School lessons.

Eventually, the addiction overtook Steve, and he was unfaithful. Several years after their divorce, we learned he died from liver disease.

These were my examples of marriage growing up. I'm sure I can avoid my own heartaches if I just remain faithful to God, chaste, and study hard. After all, my parents want better for me, and I am certain God does too.

Being single in my thirties and working at a job where I am underutilized and underappreciated isn't my idea of shortening the learning curve. But God is faithful, and I know my diligence will pay off.

Tomorrow, I will make my official submission to Rob and the elders about serving as an apostolic body in Sedona. It's more of a formality, really. I made my written submission over a month ago, but they were busy preparing for the seminar.

I look over at Adam, still asleep, his head rocking against the window with the gentle motion of the vehicle. Orange light strobes across his face as the setting sun filters through the desert landscape, tinting his now dirty-blond hair to match mine. Someday, it will be us driving across the desert with our children and introducing travelers to the beauty of Arizona. We'll lead a thriving church, one that spreads the gospel and empowers all people to know their true worth and power they have in Christ. Then we will usher in Jesus's return.

CHAPTER SEVEN

ACCOUNTABILITY

The hotel breakfast buffet is lighter on weekdays. I will all five-sense perceptions to my spirit to receive what is wisdom for me to eat this morning. My spirit leads me to grab an apple and a bagel with peanut butter for some protein. I flip over the peanut butter pack to scan the ingredients: sugar, of course. It will have to do for now.

I whisper, "Lord, I bless this peanut butter, and I ask that the protein be effective and the sugar's impact be limited, in Christ Jesus's name."

I slip my bagel in the toaster.

"Hey, sister." Rita's husband, Manuel, approaches the buffet. He's in his late sixties but has a boyish face and shoulder-length hair with a receding hairline. On this casual travel day, he's wearing jeans and a band t-shirt that covers his pot belly—I'm not familiar with the band.

He reaches for the pastries and jam. "Did you see the donuts?" He already has one on his plate.

"Oh, yeah, I did, but my spirit led me to eat something that will sustain me." I hold up the peanut butter and apple and say with a wink, "God's natural energy sources."

"You have more discipline than me," he says with a shrug and takes his sugar and fat-filled plate over to sit with Rita. He offers her a bite of his donut. She shakes her head no, then gives in.

If self-control is a fruit of the spirit, it's certainly not reflected in food choices. Don't they see their bodies are temples of the Holy Spirit to be honored and cared for? Oh, well. I guess there are larger issues related to the Kingdom of God than what a person eats or drinks. Still, I'm going to be led of my spirit in caring for my body and hopefully they will too.

Adam walks into the lounge area. "Howdy, howdy," he says.

I smile big and meet him for a side hug. "Are you our ride?" I ask.

"Yes, ma'am." He points to the truck outside the window. "I brought the luxury vehicle."

Dad and I will meet with the apostolic team before heading to the airport. I didn't think Rob would make it back to Phoenix this morning after seeing his condition two days ago, but apparently, he got a breath of new life and was up for the trip. My bagel pops out of the toaster. I grab it, and we join Rita and Manuel at their table. They've already begun eating.

"How's your father this morning?" Rita asks.

"He's all right," I say. "Just running a bit behind. Shall we pray?"

They put down their food mid-bite and avert their eyes.

"Oh, yes. Thank you for reminding me," Manuel says.

I smile, a bit confused. *Why should I have to remind a pastor to pray before a meal? Isn't that his job?*

He says an abbreviated version of the prayer we've been taught.

"Amen, thank you," I say politely.

"We have a long drive back to LA ahead of us." Rita turns to Manuel. "Honey, did you check the tire pressure?"

"It's fine. I told you to stop worrying about it."

"I know, but I'm worried because . . ." She goes on about the price of gas, new tires, construction along their route, and several other logistics. I've not seen this worried side of her all weekend long.

"Whatever you need, ask God for it," Adam encourages her.

Manuel offers Adam a donut. He hesitates, says a prayer under his breath, and receives it. "Thanks, I had eggs earlier but could use a boost." Then he reaches to his side and adjusts his insulin pump.

My gut reaction is to challenge his food choice, but it seems he's taking a calculated risk, having stopped to receive by his spirit first. Instead, I think about all the avocado toast, protein bowls, and smoothies I would make him if we were married.

No, no, I'm getting ahead of myself.

First, I need to move out here and start working at the Apostle Center. There, I will learn what God says about intake for sustaining optimal energy and the natural healing processes that God gave our bodies.

"Heading home today?" Manuel asks me.

"Yes, this afternoon. But first we have a meeting with Rob," I say.

"Oh? What about?" he asks.

I look at Adam for a sign that it may be confidential, but he's looking out the window.

I scoot to the edge of my seat and lean in. "We're going to meet to discuss me joining their team."

Manuel's eyes light up as if he'd not heard I was a candidate. Rita sits back and says, "That would be a big move for you."

"Yes, go big or go home, right?" I say.

Dad enters the breakfast area and grabs a bagel.

I check my phone for the time. "We have to go. I don't want to be late for our meeting."

Adam looks at his watch and up at me. He nods. "It's that time."

We meet in the presidential suite of a five-star hotel down the street. Apparently, there was a mix-up with the reservations when the apostolic team first arrived at the conference hotel. To make up for it, the hotel sent them to another property with a significant upgrade. God's favor is raining down upon him. The leather office chair and expansive view of the Phoenix skyline augment Rob's commanding presence.

He motions us to sit. I sit on the couch with my feet flat on the floor and my hands folded in my lap. Dad sits in the armchair to my left. Adam joins the prophet and apostlist to stand behind the apostle. This isn't the warm welcome I imagine when I finally take my place of service in The Ministry's highest ranks. Something feels off.

"We understand you are interested in serving at the Apostle Center," Rob begins.

Interested? It's my life's dream. They must know this by now.

"Yes, I've been preparing for seven years. I'm almost out of debt and . . ."

Rob holds his hand up for me to stop. "I read your submission."

My shoulders drop. If he read my submission, then he already knows how important this is to me, how much I care about The Ministry, and that God is leading me.

"We asked you to meet us here today because the team lifted it up to the Lord for a word of confirmation. I'm sorry, darlin', your loyalty to The Ministry has come into question, and we received it would be too much of a risk to take you on."

My hands clench and my whole body quakes as darkness fills my vision. I want to speak, but I can't. The child inside of me wants to throw myself onto the couch, kicking and screaming in a tantric fury. Frozen, I say, "You . . . you're wrong. This is everything I've ever worked for."

Tears well up, betraying my resolve to maintain composure.

Me, a risk?

I cradle my head in my hands to shield my face from the shame. Dad and Rob are speaking, but they're just voices.

God, how can this be? How did I fail you?

I cannot find any other response to the questions racing through my mind than "I am not good enough."

Adam breaks rank to sit next to me, placing a hand on my shoulder. Instead of comfort, I feel betrayed.

"Did . . . did you know?" I manage through the sobs.

Rob's eyes narrow, his mouth presses shut, and Charles shakes his head. Adam pulls back his hand.

"This doesn't change anything," Adam says, hunched over to see my face. "It's just not the right time."

"If not now, when?"

My protest is met with silence.

"We'd better get to the airport," Dad says.

Adam takes extra time to park the car and escort us into the airport. We said little on the drive. I understand why he didn't tell me. Even if Adam knew, telling me would have been an act of rebellion, putting him out of God's order and the apostle in harm's way. He wouldn't do that, and that's part of what I love about him.

Under normal circumstances, Adam's presence would ease the sadness of leaving this home away from home. Life on the East Coast has always felt temporary. It was my parents' choice of residence, not mine. Every time I fellowship with believers in Arizona, the Southwest feels a little more like home. I long to return and never want to leave.

This departure feels different. Dad is shuffling his way to the ticket counter to ask the personnel about getting seats closer to the restroom. I think about his chronic health issues and the multiple strokes he's had. Traveling wears him down, and it is getting tougher for me to care for him.

Adam cares deeply for my father. If we were married, I would have someone to share the load. I don't care whether we stay out west or he comes back east. I just want to start our lives together before it's too late.

Adam leans in to hug me as I wrap my arms around his chest. I pull him in tighter and feel a spark of electricity jolt through my body. My eyes fly open. Could this be the elusive element found in movies and romance novels?

I tilt my head up, gazing into his eyes. "Did you feel that?"

"Yes," he says, grimacing as his cheeks turn bright red.

"I wish you could come with me." Saying this is a risk, but I must make my desire known.

He whispers in my ear, "Trust God."

Now I am sure that he has a plan. His proposal is not far off. All I need to do is continue in my role back home, be faithful to help my dad, and most of all, keep trusting God.

CHAPTER EIGHT

LOSS

It's Saturday, no work. Late morning light fills my bedroom as the smell of bacon entices my senses. I am eager to rise from a restless sleep until the memory of the apostle's rejection reminds me why I don't want to get out of bed. Instead, I pull the sheet over my head, but it only diffuses the light. I pull a blanket over, but now I can't breathe. It's futile. I fling both off of me and lay sprawled out in surrender.

Lord, I have failed you. What now?

I turn my head to one side and read a poster on my wall.

> BUT WITHOUT FAITH, IT IS IMPOSSIBLE TO PLEASE HIM. THOSE WHO COME TO GOD MUST FIRST BELIEVE THAT HE IS, AND THAT HE IS A REWARDER OF THOSE WHO DILIGENTLY SEEK HIM.

"Without faith," I repeat aloud. "Am I lacking faith?"

I want to prophesy, but it's like two sides of an argument are playing in my mind and I am seated on the jury. One side saying the apostle's rejection was a sign that God is not pleased with me; therefore, I must not have enough faith. The other is saying that he *is* pleased, and I must believe he will still reward me in His own way and timing. The moment I muster the courage to believe He will reward me, the first voice counters it, repeating the accusation that I don't have enough faith.

"Rocky!" Mom's singsong voice rises from the kitchen. "Breakfast is ready, if you want to eat."

I call back down, "I'm not hungry . . . thanks!"

Mom knows it's not like me to refuse bacon. "Oh, honey. Eat something. I'll bring you some toast."

"Okay," I say.

I let my legs hang over the side of my bed until my feet hit the cold floor. I shiver and reach for my slippers, then I stare out the window. A large maple tree fills most of the view now that its leaves have come in. Earth comes alive in spring. And with the blooms come allergies and mosquitos. At least winter kills those pests. In summer, the only reprieve is going to the beach, weather permitting. All four seasons come with their challenges, I suppose. This time, it's not the weather that has me down but the crushing possibility that I'll never fulfill God's calling as a prophetess to the apostle.

Write, I hear in my spirit. I take a deep breath, walk two steps to my desk, and plop down in my office chair. Hunched over my laptop, I open a template called Personal Submission. When I need to lay my heart out before God and have Him pour His living word into me, the Personal Submission template is my life preserver. A series of seven questions guide me to consider my relationship with God in the context of all other relationships in God's order. A pit in my stomach begs for food, and I'm starting to get a headache, but I ignore it. I don't care how long this takes, I must hear from God today, and I know He'll reward my faithfulness to diligently seek Him.

Following the format given through the apostle, I assert my will to agree with God's order by declaring out loud each of my relationships. Then I start with part one, A WORD FOR ALL. "Father God, I submit unto you and Christ to my God-ordained headships as a body to the Massachusetts church eldership, an assistant in the pastoral office, and a prophetess unto the apostle/prophet entity. I will bring forth a word for all, by my spirit."

I type:

> MY SONS, TODAY YOU ARE FREE AND DO NOT LET THE PAST CORRUPT YOUR PERCEPTIONS, FOR I HAVE WIPED THE SLATE CLEAN.

Free? I don't feel free.

I inhale and exhale with measured release. The pressure on my temples releases a bit. I am free from the perceptions of the past because Jesus gives me a fresh start each day. I acknowledge and thank God for this word of prophecy that it may minister to anyone who reads my submission.

A knock at my bedroom door interrupts my thoughts. I turn around, and Mom is holding a glass of orange juice and toast with peanut butter. I offer a slight smile to show appreciation. She places them on my desk and puts a hand on my shoulder. "I'm praying for you, sweetie," she says.

I nod, and she leaves my room.

Part two is titled, MY INNER-PERSONAL RELATIONSHIPS. The first of six relationships is with God. I ask, "Father God, what would you say to me about my inner-personal relationship with you, God; in Christ; in my Spirit, the Holy Ghost?"

Again, I type in all caps, allowing his response to flow through my fingers:

> IT'S ONLY THE PERCEPTIONS THAT HOLD BACK YOUR MANIFESTING MY LOVE UNTO THE WORLD AND THE FAITH OF THE SON OF GOD THAT I GAVE YOU. NOW, STAND IN THIS ONENESS AND SANCTIFY ALL OF THOSE DEAD PERCEPTIONS AND MAKE ALL NEW AND LIVING BY YOUR SPIRIT, AS I HAVE

GIVEN YOU TO WALK AND YOU WILL RECEIVE THE LIVING
WATER THAT CAUSES NO THIRST. IT SHALL BE HOLY AND
PURIFYING, MY SON.

He's doubling down on perceptions. The masculine position serves to remind me that there is no gender in the spirit and that I am equal to Jesus in God's eyes.

I type a response and then read it aloud, "Thank you, Father God and my Lord Jesus Christ, for giving me my spirit by which I will, through Christ, to sanctify my perceptions and receive the holy, new, and living water that washes all impurity away, and leads me in all righteousness, to be your love unto the entire world as you are."

I sip the orange juice, and a burst of energy courses through my body. I sit up straight, pull back my shoulders, and arch my spine as my lungs draw in more oxygen. I let out a big yawn. The heaviness is lifting. I want to hear more from God.

Question two is more provoking. *How am I doing in my relationship with my spouse?* I could say I have no spouse and skip this section, but I have several spiritual spouses. The Lord Jesus Christ is my first. The word above applies to that one, so I move on to the next—my relationship with the apostle and prophet entity as a prophetess. My chest tightens as I recall the rejection I felt standing before leadership in that stoic space high above the city.

Lord, I need this.

I stare at the blank space, afraid to uncover the depths of what my spirit knows about me. Still, it is the only way to quiet the unruly thoughts and emotions inside. I take a few more swigs of orange juice, this time washing away the lump forming in my throat. Another deep breath and I type:

YOU HAVE DONE WELL TO COME TO ME AS YOUR PRIMARY
SOURCE, BUT THERE IS YET PRIDE IN THE FLESH. THIS PRIDE

CONVINCED YOU THAT YOU WERE READY AND CREATED AN EXPECTATION. THESE EXPECTATIONS ARE NOT OF ME, FOR THEY SET YOU UP FOR JUDGMENT. RELEASE ALL EXPECTATIONS AND YOU WILL FREE YOUR MIND TO HONOR THESE HEADSHIPS WITH A PURE HEART. DO NOT FEAR THE LOSS, FOR I HAVE PREPARED A PATH FOR YOU, AS MY SON, MY DAUGHTER, AND AN AMBASSADOR FOR CHRIST.

The lump in my throat jumps to the middle of my chest. *Pride.* Such a loaded word.

Is that true? Have I been prideful? I thought the Lord was telling me I was ready, but could pride have blinded me?

My Spirit whispers, *yes.*

"That's it then," I reply aloud. "I will through Christ to rid myself of all pride. I will humble myself in every moment to God and Christ, in honor to the apostle and prophet, even if I don't speak to them. Lord, show me how. Help me be pure in heart."

I prophesy about my relationship with my pastor and teacher. Then to the heads of the household, in this case, my mom and stepfather.

At the fifth and final spousal relationship, I pause.

My husband. This is where God will show me how I am relating to Adam in considering him for marriage. This is my favorite one.

I say aloud, "Lord, what would you say to me about my inner-personal relationship with my husband, in consideration of Adam?"

I pray in tongues, then type:

AS I AM HAVING YOU RID YOURSELF OF THE PAST AND ANY ATTACHMENTS TO THE PLANS AND MAKINGS OF THE FLESH, YOU RECEIVE THAT PREPARATION FOR TAKING ON A NEW HEAD'S PURPOSE. KNOW THAT I BUILT YOU TO BE MY HELPMEET: A BODY TO CHRIST AND TO YOUR FUTURE HUSBAND ON THIS EARTH. YES, IT IS TO WORK OUT YOUR

SALVATION BUT ALSO TO BE MY WORD MANIFEST, AS I
INTENDED FOR MANKIND TO LIVE. BLESS THIS ONE, ADAM,
AND SEE HIM AS A BROTHER—A SINLESS, RIGHTEOUS SON
OF ME. BE OPEN IN COMMUNICATING WITH HIM AS YOU
RELATE UNTO ME AND IN SUBMISSION TO YOUR HEADSHIP.
FOR THERE IS A LIGHT SHINING DOWN UPON THIS AND YOU
ARE IN BLOOM.

"Thank you, Father!" I say. "I see you are clearing my attachments
to the past and making the way for me to be a fit body, a spiritual and
physical helpmeet, to my future husband. Encouraged that I will still be
about Christ's purpose, just in our unique way as a couple, I will not
look to the times or the physical seasons but unto you in my spirit for
the steps to walk in."

God has replaced the heaviness I felt upon waking with lightness.
I sit back and gaze out the window, this time only seeing beauty. The
river flows on the other side of barren trees, a scene hidden from view
during any other season. A male cardinal lands on a maple tree branch, a
beacon of red against the brown and gray backdrop. His song penetrates
the double-paned windows, and my heart follows its tune.

Sing, strong little bird. Sing praises to the Lord!

I am still hungry and my toast is cold, but I don't mind. I have
spiritual food to sustain me, the living word of God through prophecy.
Resolving to complete this written submission, I prophesy to question
three, my inner-personal relationships with my family unit. I skip
question four—pastor, teacher, and local eldership—since they're
the same headship I addressed in section two. Then I continue with
questions five and six, my employer heads and coworkers. Having
addressed all the relationships in my life from a spiritual standpoint, I
proceed to the third and final part of this submission.

Part three, the ultimate question:

WHAT IS THE DIRECTION I AM IMPRESSED THE LORD IS
LEADING ME AT THIS POINT?

I close my eyes and clear my mind of distractions, reasserting my
will to hear only from God, through Christ, by my spirit, in the order of
life. I type:

> CONTINUE TO SANCTIFY YOUR PERCEPTIONS IN THE SPIRIT
> AND WORK OUT YOUR SALVATION MANIFESTLY. TOUCHING
> ALL POINTS OF YOUR LIFE, BE FREE OF THE EMOTIONAL
> CONNECTIONS AND PHYSICAL THINGS THAT WERE BUILT
> TO OCCUPY YOUR TIME AND DRAW YOUR ENERGY. AS YOU
> EXAMINE THEM BY YOUR SPIRIT, I'LL SHOW YOU A MORE
> EXCELLENT WAY. ONE IN WHICH YOU ARE NOT TIED TO THE
> CREATED, BUT GIVE FORTH MY LOVE MORE FREELY THAN
> YOU HAVE BEFORE!"

These words send a shiver through my body, awakening my senses
to new possibilities. "Yes, Father, I'm willing to examine all things,
systems, and relationships that consume my time and energy. I give it
all to you."

The Lord must be working to clear the way, both in my heart and in
Adam's. Perhaps my application was premature and I must wait until we
can serve the apostle together.

A reminder pops up in the top right corner of my screen. Study
time.

That's it. I will continue my online naturopathic studies so that
when I am finally called to serve, I will have a solid career to sustain our
ministry work. God is truly marvelous, and I trust He's preparing me for
something greater than I could imagine.

After a traffic-filled commute home, I pull into the driveway. Schools will soon break for summer, meaning I can look forward to less traffic for a couple of months. My phone rings and the hands-free voice in my car announces that it's Rita. She must be calling with an update on Rob's condition since being hospitalized less than a week ago. I could use some good news. God has a way of pulling him through at the last minute. I turn off the car, gather my things, and answer through my earbuds.

"Hello."

She sobs.

"Rita?"

"He's dead."

I almost drop the phone. "Rita . . . what . . . I . . ."

"Oh, Victoria." I hear the cracking in her voice. "He held on as long as he could."

I drop to my knees on our front lawn.

We were all praying for our apostle. Every time he went to the hospital, it was life-threatening, but he always recovered. His stories of flat-lining during open-heart surgery or during a severe allergic reaction to a medication and then being resurrected served as further proof of his high calling from God. Few of us believed he could die. I recall him mentioning in a recent sermon there was no guarantee he would be with us until the coming of Christ.

"I'm so sorry," I say.

I can hardly believe it, and I want to know more. What were his last moments like? I'm sure his team surrounded him. Did he impart words of wisdom, any last instructions? Or was he in and out of consciousness, too medicated to form thoughts? I wonder if perhaps someone saw an angel visit his room to take him home, like with my grandmother.

"I tried calling your father and couldn't reach him. Will you try?" she says, sobbing.

"Yes. I love you," I say before she hangs up.

It is the end of an era.

Mom is waiting by the front door when I enter. "Is everything all right?" she asks in a low voice.

"No." I look past her, unable to show emotion. "Rob didn't make it."

She pulls me in for an embrace and rubs my back.

"He was in his eighties, right?" she says. "He lived a full life and battled a lot of illnesses. Now he's with the Lord, rejoicing."

I hang my head as my thoughts race.

Did we not have enough faith?

He preached that the health of the head depended on the body. Our walking in righteousness would protect him from the enemy's fiery darts. I remember Rob saying that while Christians often celebrate going home to see their Savior, what they're really doing is "going out in a blaze of glory for Satan."

Is that what he did?

Such questions would have to remain unanswered, for now. I have a duty before me. I step back outside on the front steps to call my father. The spring air gently brushes my cheeks as if angels were wiping away invisible tears. When I give Dad the news, he is quiet. Like me, he shows little emotion. My father and I split up the work of calling the saints. I offer to call those on our email list who we haven't spoken with in a long time.

"Hello, Shirley? . . . I'm doing all right, but I'm calling to deliver some news about the apostle. . . . No, unfortunately, he passed away this morning. . . . I know it's hard to believe. . . . Yes, he was old. We all thought he would pull through. . . . I'm not sure who will lead The Ministry. The important thing is that we continue to make God our only source and be led by our Spirit in all things. . . . Yes, I will tell my dad you say hello. I bless you."

Just like that, call after call, talking with people who are scarcely a childhood memory, I deliver the news. They have similar questions, yet none of them appear concerned about how this affects their salvation or the body of Christ.

Meanwhile, I brace for a monumental shift.

Will this delay Christ's coming until we get another apostle? Is there still hope for any of us overcoming death, as Jesus did?

For the first time in my life, I have more questions than answers.

Apostle Rob gave a prophecy and word of knowledge five years ago concerning this time. He said there would be a falling away if he passed. Those who seemed to be strongest in their faith would leave The Ministry and those who appeared weak would become the most faithful. It was one of the most frightening words I'd ever heard because I always considered myself to be strong and couldn't imagine leaving. He prophesied a scattering but said, as long as we go out two-by-two, remaining in pairs, we can find our way back. I envisioned a mind map with him at the center and tethered entities moving away from it. Individuals going solo would get lost to false doctrines. I brace myself for this unknown future, vowing to never step out on my own.

THE UNVEILING

For nothing is hidden that will not be made manifest, nor is
anything secret that will not be known and come to light.

LUKE 8:17 ESV

CHAPTER NINE

TRANSITION

I t's late August 2016. Two months since the apostle's passing, with little direction on what comes next.

Dad and I are five hours into our trans-Pacific flight and halfway to Fiji. A passenger left their window shade up across the aisle. The view confirms there is nothing to see except the blinking light on the tip of the wing of what feels like a tin can suspended in oblivion. My knees abut the seat in front of me, and I'm rubbing shoulders with Dad as he snores like a revving engine, blissfully unaware of time passing. The stranger on my left is leaning against the window, also asleep.

After watching a movie, I make another attempt at sleep, but my mind is reeling with what the future of The Ministry will look like.

It's difficult to imagine any new revelation coming out of it. The apostle had declared in a letter before his passing that he had taught everything the Lord had given him. And he reached every destination he was called to, culminating with the spreading of Christ's ministry to New Zealand.

But where is the radical change?

The elders are aging and the youth nearing middle-age. *How will The Ministry continue?*

My chest feels tight, so I take some deep breaths and sing unto the Lord, asking the Holy Spirit to rein in my wandering mind.

I retrieve a travel journal from my backpack hoping to ease my worries by writing. An entry from six years ago catches my eye—August 2010, Fiji.

That was a trip to remember.

Dad couldn't join me that year, as he was recovering from a traumatic brain injury—the cause of his present cognitive challenges. In desperate fear of flying alone, I snatched the empty seat between Adam and an elder we called uncle. Their proximity made me feel safe. It was the longest amount of time Adam and I ever spent together. Back then, our consideration of marriage wasn't mutual or public. Still, cozying up to my crush was effective for easing flight anxiety.

Now that our consideration is official, I hope we can spend more time together. It's hard to know what he's thinking because he hasn't been himself. Serving the apostle was his primary duty over the past couple of years. I've released all hope of him proposing on this trip.

Lord, I pray he doesn't make any rash decisions.

A pain shoots across my back. I take a deep breath and shift in my seat. Turning to the journal, I get lost in the hopeful musings written by a younger me:

> It isn't Fiji's white sandy beaches or high-rise hotels that impress me most, although they are very nice. What impresses me are the wild palms, coconuts ready to drink with one whack of a machete, a bright blue sea filled with tropical reef, and island hospitality. The islands may not have the best consumer goods or newest car models, but they are rich in natural resources and a deep sense of community.

Outside of the conference, we visited locals and enjoyed home-cooked cuisine. Their homes overflowed with people, food, and love. Whole families gathered— husbands and wives, aunts, uncles, grandparents, cousins, and children. They played guitars, shook tambourines, and sang songs unto the Lord like when I was a child. Their island chain may only be a few specks on the globe amid a giant ocean, but for many of them, it is the only world they know.

I imagine it feels lonely to live so far from the mainland. Then I continue reading:

Our flight schedule allowed for a few extra days to enjoy the island before returning home. I joined Adam, Kumari, her fiancé Elias, and a few others on an island boat tour. We boarded a ferry at Port Denarau that took us through a chain of islands off the coast, popular with tourists and well-to-do islanders alike. Upon approaching each island, sounds of ukulele, guitar, mandolin, and Lali drums filled the air as the backdrop to a chorus of voices singing greetings in their native language. The welcoming melody needed no interpretation. The men wore sulus (fabric skirts) or grass skirts with shell and flower necklaces, and the women dressed conservatively in a "sulu va taga," a tribal patterned dress made of a single piece of fabric and a plumeria flower in their hair—either on the right if they're married or on the left if they're unattached. I wore mine on the left, hoping that would soon change. Their music and expressions were happy, as if welcoming long-distance friends to visit. It was heavenly!

We disembarked on a far island where we ate lunch beachside at the restaurant. A family-run resort or inn that welcomes tourists as personal guests occupied each island. Many of these islands were so small that I could capture the breadth of them from coast to coast in a single camera shot and still be close enough to wave to those onshore.

After a meal, we took a small boat out to the coral reef for snorkeling, where we swam with starfish that were no less than twelve inches in diameter and many other colorful species of sea life. Unfortunately, we also observed parts of the reef dying because of the compounded impact of local fishing pressure, coastal development, and climate change. As the tour guide explained, the sea life population had dwindled in recent years because of the coral reef's erosion. Tours like these helped to fund research and conservation efforts.

Compared to American culture, Fijian culture doesn't seem lonely at all. This is the community I long to embrace, even under the shadow of the apostle's passing.

Lord, I confess I envy Fijians for living in paradise. Even though they are thousands of miles from any major land mass, they have everything they need to thrive. But then, there is their sordid tribal past. On the way to one of the local saints' homes, Uncle cautioned us to minister against evil spirits that still lingered from the sin of cannibalism, last recorded in 1867. I cringe at the revolting thought. Lord, thank you for saving them from that practice and turning so many back to you.

The lights turn on overhead as the captain announces we will land in just under two hours. My anticipation of seeing the beautiful island and people again eases the discomfort of stiff legs and achy joints. Flight attendants will begin serving breakfast and coffee to help passengers wake up and prepare for arrival. I peer over several rows of seats to check on Adam, who is stirring awake. We make eye contact, and I wave. He returns a partial smile, still groggy.

A few hours later, we arrive at the resort. Dad turns on one of three TV channels and starts unpacking. I can't stay inside in the middle of paradise, so I go for a walk outside to admire the natural beauty.

A section of fence along the west side of the resort property is down, and some floorboards are missing from the walkway, evidence of the cyclone that recently swept through the island. The staff mentioned repairs would still be underway when we arrived. Much like the body of Christ, the property shouldn't be anything a bit of love and sweat can't fix.

Morning couldn't come early enough. Ear plugs muted Dad's snoring in the bed next to mine, if one could call it a bed. It's basically a hardwood plank with a thin mattress on top. After one night, it feels as if there is no mattress at all.

My anticipation of the conference outweighs any jet lag I might feel.

After breakfast, we sit at a conference table with the eldership once again. The setting is similar to past conferences: gray tables set in a U shape with a whiteboard and projection screen against beige walls. During this opening session, wives and helpers sit along the side walls. The only other woman at the table is Eve, the apostlist, sitting at the prophet's right hand at the front of the room. Flanking them are three members of the bishopric who hold offices in The Ministry. Many of the elders don business attire with a few of the bolder ones sporting tropical shirts, the only sign that we might be on an island.

Routine dictates we proceed with the ceremonial giving and receiving of words of wisdom, prophecy, and encouragement to one another before any business begins. Despite the appearance of normalcy, the apostle's passing hangs like a dense fog over the room.

"Don't everybody jump in at once," Charles says.

The elders look at each other, hoping someone will speak first.

Dallas, an elder from Arizona with a salt-and-pepper mustache and tanned leather skin, clears his throat and sits forward in his chair. He removes his cowboy hat, placing it on the table in front of him to reveal a crew cut.

"My sons," he says in a loud voice. "I, your God, do not change. You have looked to the apostle for too long and now you must stand on your own with Christ. My word does not change. Your walk of salvation need not change. I have not left you headless."

The elders and saints stir after hearing this. Dad fidgets with his pen and looks up.

"I bless you a hundredfold return for that word, brother," Dad says. "I'm hearing that God doesn't change and so my walk of salvation shouldn't change just because the apostle is gone. Jesus Christ is the chief apostle."

I say amen. Others do as well.

"I have a word of knowledge," Kumari says.

"Alright," Charles says.

"I saw a fleet of small ships, and each of the elders was in one. When the apostle was alive, they stayed close together on the same course. But now, I see them drifting apart and spreading over different parts of the ocean. Jesus is on the horizon, and they are pointing toward him, but they are taking their own routes to get there."

Our own routes? That doesn't sound like the straight and narrow path.

"I'll prophesy the wisdom to that," Elias says.

"Go ahead," Charles says.

"I appointed you a fleet captain to show the way of salvation. He only pointed you to the one who is your salvation, Jesus Christ. Now, you must depend on my Spirit to guide you, each as the unique sons of God that I made you. You will cover more distance to gather more souls. Go out and give my love to those who need it, rather than drawing into yourselves."

Cascades of "amen" and "bless you a hundredfold" flow through the room.

Now's your turn, my spirit prompts.

"I bless you all for your words," I say. "I received a word of knowledge ahead of the conference, and the Lord told me to bring a prop to illustrate." Reaching down into my bag, I pull out a box of Jenga and set it on the table.

"Perhaps you are familiar with this stacking game?" I say, looking around for signs of recognition. Adam and a few others nod. I slide off the box, careful not to topple the logs stacked in threes, each layer laid perpendicular to the one beneath it in a crosshatch pattern. "For those who aren't familiar, the idea is to see how tall you can build the tower by removing logs from lower on the tower and laying them on the top. The trick is to find logs that aren't part of the supporting structure that are easy to move." I tap a few logs to test their rigidity, then push through a loose one and place it on top to demonstrate. A few more heads nod.

"The Lord showed me through this metaphor," I say. "Over the past forty years, the eldership has grown in knowledge and in age."

An older man chuckles.

I point to the rigid logs near the bottom.

"These building blocks represent elders that have been around since the beginning, but their effectiveness to grow The Ministry has diminished. Among them, younger elders are more flexible and add reach. But without training them to be leaders to carry forward the foundation, the tower becomes out of balance, resting on weaker logs."

I continue to pull out the loose logs and stack them in layers of three until the tower is skinny at the bottom and heavy on top.

"Unless this ministry reinforces and equips the youth to lead and attract more saints, it will not grow, or . . ."

With my hands now unsteady, like the tower, I pull out another block and hold my breath as I place it on top. It's getting close. I push on one more. The tower sways and crashes to the table, piercing the silence and scattering blocks, some falling in the laps of nearby elders.

". . . it will become top-heavy and crumble," I say.

The elders turn to see how the bishopric is reacting. Charles shuffles some papers and looks around the room, seemingly not impressed.

Lord, I trust you will teach them what they need to know.

Dallas slides a piece back to me from across the table, and Elias helps me pick up the other logs as I sweep them into my bag.

Dallas breaks the silence. "I hear that word from my God and Christ and bless you a hundredfold, sister. Brothers, let's not allow the fact that it was a game to stop us from seeing the truth. She has a point. We've been at this a long time, and how many new elders have we raised up to do more than work with the cameras?"

Heads nod again.

Charles looks at me with no expression, then sits up even taller, hands folded on the table. "Well, that certainly gives us all something to consider," he says.

Dallas raises his hand. "If I may."

"Go ahead," Charles says.

"Rob had a word to start this ministry over forty years ago. Each of us had a word to become elders at some point or another to join what

Christ was doing through him. Now that he has fulfilled his mission, isn't it presumption for us to continue it without getting a word of our own?"

The elders murmur.

"I'm not saying that we should shut it all down," he continues, "but do we really know if the Lord Jesus Christ intended for this portion of Christ's ministry to continue in its current form beyond the life of the apostle?"

"You have a point," Elias says. "We're now a five-fold ministry with only four folds."

"Jesus Christ is our chief apostle," Dad says.

"He always has been," Adam says, "but that doesn't change the fact—"

"All right, settle down," Charles says. "Dallas is right. We don't have a word on what to do from here or whether we should even continue as a ministry. God gave this ministry to Rob to do what he would do. We can't presume that He's passing it on to us in the same format."

"Thank you, that's all I was saying," Dallas says.

"Let's take a few minutes to get our hearts clear so we can uplift the question before proceeding with our agenda," Charles says. "I know this will present a lot of fear for some of you since being part of this eldership is all you've known for many years. Give that to your spirit so you're not led by emotions."

Women stop filling water glasses, and Dad puts down a candy wrapper he's been fidgeting with. The room is quiet.

Had anyone ever considered what life might be like after The Ministry?

We are running the race toward the high calling of God in Christ Jesus, preparing for His return. Such a question seems like a sin to ask. Now the prophet is asking us to entertain the idea. But without an earthly apostle to confirm what the elders are receiving, they only have God to rely on.

Several minutes of quiet prayer and contemplation pass before Charles breaks the silence. "If everyone's ready, we'll uplift the word."

Nobody objects. Charles starts the prayer. An unease comes over me.

This doesn't feel right. *Did anyone really have enough time to clear their hearts for such a big decision? Perhaps we should sleep on it. Should I say something? No, it's not my place.*

Dad prophesies first, "You are ambassadors for Christ to lead the world in the restitution of all things. Continue in this capacity, as you have not yet accomplished your purpose."

Elias gives his word, "There is more to do with your own church areas. Don't think that you have finished your word because my apostle finished his."

Another elder, "Continue with this ministry. You have not fulfilled my word."

"Christ does not cease; therefore, you are not to cease in His work," says another elder.

Their words of direction continue down the line, each affirming the previous, with few exceptions.

"I would not have you continue in the way you always have, for this shall yield no better results," prophesies Dallas. "Seek me for renewal and clarity on how to fulfill your role as sons of God in this new season. Allow me to tear down the strongholds in your minds and the habits of the past so that you may be pure in your worship and effective in love."

It was subtle, but did I just hear a bit of dissent?

That would make the collective word mixed, and the elders won't proceed with a decision until all words are unanimous. Perhaps they won't establish their course so hastily. Not that I want The Ministry to cease, but I know that when God closes one door, he opens another. Maybe there is another door that God is waiting to open for us and for the world.

Lord, I pray they will receive words of truth.

The elders that follow give words similar to those before them, with one or two presenting an unclear yes or no.

"That's all the elders," says Charles. "Now anyone else, Helps Ministers, wives, you're welcome to share your words as witnesses before the bishopric gives our words."

I'm still stuck on the single word of dissent. As I pray in the spirit to prepare to give my word, I hear only fragments of what others are speaking. There are words of knowledge and visions, some of caution, many to support carrying out Christ's ministry.

I feel a fire burning in my chest, and my palms are sweaty.

Lord, I'm not sure I want to give a word, but I know you have me here for a reason. What would you have me say?

"My sons," I prophesy, "if Jesus is truly your Lord and head in all things, the ministry work you set out to fulfill will prosper. If you allow your own ambitions and fear for self to thrive, then the results of your work will wither and die like the fig tree that bore no fruit."

I look down at the table, not wanting to make eye contact.

That was the word of a prophetess, I hear my spirit say. *Don't worry about how they will respond. My word does not come back to me void but accomplishes the purpose I have for it.*

Yes, Lord, thank you, I pray internally.

"Thank you. And for the bishopric?" Charles says.

"Continue as I have given with Jesus Christ as your chief apostle," prophesies the Second Bishop. "You have yet to fulfill your roles to my standard. So continue to work out your salvation according to the vision I gave to my apostle." He adds, "That's interesting. That's not a clear word to continue in the same ministry."

Charles doesn't respond.

The apostlist gives her word, "Rob took The Ministry as far as he could, and now it's up to you to be faithful in what he taught. The Ministry of Christ is only as effective as His body on this earth."

Charles gives the final word, "Do not change what I have started. Only reinforce the foundation that was laid from the beginning. You have the revelation and instructions. Go forth to fulfill it until I call forth another apostle to fill the role. For a headless ministry cannot come into the perfection of Christ. I will provide an apostle when the body is ready to receive him."

A sobering word. I'd been eager to hear the Lord's direction for The Ministry, but now I expect we'll seek another round of words, since there wasn't consensus.

This is going to be a long day.

"Well, there you have it," Charles says. "The words are overall positive to continue with The Ministry."

The First Bishop turns to look at Charles. "Are you sure about that? A few of the words seemed unclear."

"Does anyone else think there was a mixed word?" Charles says.

Heads turn throughout the room, elders murmuring.

"What about Dallas?" the First Bishop says.

Dallas puts his hands up in surrender. "It wasn't the clearest yes, but I don't think it was a no."

"Are we clear to proceed, then?" Charles says.

The First Bishop, a large yet humble man, leans back in his chair and folds his hands to rest on his belly.

"It's settled. The Ministry will continue. Now, does anyone have an impression on who should lead until the Lord raises up another apostle? Otherwise, as the prophet, I would be next in line. I'm not saying I want this . . ." He shrugs his shoulders with palms up.

Nobody objects. The eldership has their direction, and I am left to wrestle with the unease.

CHAPTER TEN

REJECTION

L ounging by the pool the next day, I take a long, refreshing sip from a fresh coconut. The midday sun warms my body, though it's not hot enough for a swim. Fiji only has two seasons: dry and wet. May to October is their dry season, what we would consider winter. The clear skies and my need to keep hydrated and apply hand cream several times a day attest to it.

Rita walks toward me wearing a blue and white coverall, a tote bag in one hand and a towel in the other. Her shoulder-length black hair and single gray streak bounce in the breeze.

"You're not attending the afternoon session?" she says.

"No, I'm not doing Helps Ministry this time. Just here to support my dad," I say.

"Good for you," says Rita. "No reason to spend your whole time in Fiji cooped up in a conference room."

Only those needed for working equipment, taking notes, or pouring water may stay during elders' personal submission times. I had done it plenty of times at the American conferences. It's their opportunity to pour out their hearts unto the Lord and prophesy about what is happening in their personal lives, such as challenges they're facing, recent victories, and how they can better lead their local church body. If they need direction, they will uplift their questions to the Lord in the eldership's presence for words of confirmation, or to be shown a better way.

Rita settles into the chair next to me and opens her oversized wrap tunic to reveal a black one-piece bathing suit.

"That's what I was thinking. They've got it covered," I say. "So, this must be a pleasant break for you."

"Oh, yes! I didn't realize how much I needed it until I was here. Manuel insisted I take the time off and not volunteer. Besides, the flight doesn't get any easier as we get older."

She doesn't look very old. Mid-fifties maybe, but I think her husband is older.

"Manuel just turned sixty-eight, and I'm no spring chicken," she says.

"I don't know how you all do it every year," I say. "This is only my second time at the International Conference and the journey is tough. My dad really struggles with it."

"How is your dad? I haven't talked with him much," she says.

"He has a lot of health challenges. He used a wheelchair to get through the LA airport on our layover. The flight left him worn out. Still, it's the cognitive decline that bothers me the most. That accident six years ago impaired his abilities. Remember, he used to quote Bible passages by chapter and verse? Now, he can barely recall the words."

"I'm sorry to hear that," Rita says. "Ministry work takes a real toll on these men and their families. I'm glad we didn't have children for that reason."

Ana approaches Rita from behind. She lets down her long black hair, which has grown significantly since being part of the apostolic team. She and I were close friends before she moved to Sedona.

"Greetings, ladies," says Ana.

"Oh, hi! I didn't see you there," says Rita. "Are they on break?"

"Just a short one. I thought I would take in some natural light for a few moments," says Ana.

She reclines on the chair next to Rita. Her long skirt drapes out to the side, revealing the long, dark hairs that cover the lower part of her calf.

How long has it been since she shaved?

A fly lands on Rita's bare leg below the coverall. She swats it away, then scratches the area.

"Must be itchy from shaving," Rita says.

We both look at Ana.

She looks at us and says, "I stopped shaving shortly after moving into the Apostle Center. Rob ministered to all of us women about personal hygiene. As examples to the rest of the church, we're called to maintain a standard of purity that God intended for us. He created men and women to exist in the Garden of Eden. Shaving is a corrupt practice of Western society that removes God's natural barrier and means of sensation from a woman's legs."

"I hadn't thought of it that way," Rita says, shaking her head.

"Oh, yes, there are many practices that God never intended for us," Ana says. "We're so conditioned by our culture that we have to repent of what we learned, give it all to our Spirit, and receive a new way of being and living."

I nod, fixated on her teaching.

"For example, most of us women no longer wear underwear," she says.

Did I hear that right?

"The extra fabric creates an unnatural barrier and can lead to health issues. It's much more natural to leave that area open to airflow."

Ana's matter-of-fact tone and peaceful countenance is hard to counter. I look at her long skirt and imagine how that freedom must feel. Come to think of it, all the female assistants wear long skirts. My cheeks feel flush, and I have a sudden urge to pee as these thoughts trigger blood flow to that area.

"That's an interesting way to look at it," Rita says, squinting.

"Try it sometime. You'll find it's very freeing," Ana says as she gets up from her chair.

"Thanks, I just might," I say.

Rita looks at me with a raised eyebrow when Ana is out of earshot. "We don't have to follow everything Rob taught. He's not perfect."

"I know," I say. "I'll give it to my spirit and see what the Lord says."

We sit there in silence for several minutes. Meanwhile, I pray internally to see what the Lord would say about it. I receive, *Be wary of making a law out of the practices of any individual. Though Rob speaks my word, there are things I give only to him and not to others. There is danger in following a man instead of me. Some have done this, but it isn't for you to judge their hearts.*

"You're right," I say to Rita. "God wouldn't have us follow everything. But he also wouldn't have me to judge what others are doing because he knows what is in their hearts."

"You're more forgiving than I am," says Rita. "I'm surprised they didn't accept you to work at the Apostle Center."

"You heard?" I say.

"Manuel keeps me informed," Rita says.

"I still don't understand why they rejected me. I worked so hard to fit all the criteria. Now I'm not sure how to fulfill the role of a prophetess without him."

"Well—"

"You ladies enjoying the sunshine?" a voice calls out. I turn to see Dallas walking toward us.

"Oh, hi, brother." Rita waves to him.

"Yes, it's beautiful out," I say.

"Even more beautiful with you in the picture," Dallas says.

I'm flattered by the compliment.

Rita swings her legs over the side of the lounge chair, smoothing out her coverall and pulling up the neckline.

"I didn't mean to interrupt your conversation. Just came to share with you we're on a lunch break. Some of the local sisters made food and brought it in for us. It's in the conference room, if you want any."

"Thanks, that sounds wonderful," I say.

We gather our things, and he waits to escort us back. We start walking toward the meeting room when he stops me, letting Rita walk ahead of us.

"How are you holding up?" Dallas asks. "I know your meeting with the apostolic team didn't work out the way you hoped. I want you to know, I advocated for you."

"You did?"

"Yeah. Rumors fly all the time, but I've always known you're one of the loyal ones."

"What rumors?" I say.

"You don't know?" he says. "One of the team members heard you talking to a woman in the bathroom at a conference. I guess you were questioning the behavior of an elder. I don't know what you said, but it got back to Rob that you were gossiping."

"Me? Gossiping? No, I was . . . She told me something, and I was questioning her. I didn't believe what she said."

He places a hand on my shoulder. "Oh, darling. I'm so sorry."

I can't make sense of this.

"All this time, they rejected me over a misheard rumor. Really? They've known me since I was a little girl. How could they believe the word of one woman over me, after everything I've done?"

He shakes his head. "I am truly sorry."

There is nothing left to say. The opportunity is past, and I can never correct the record with the apostle. I wonder as we walk who else I can trust besides Dad and Adam, and who sees me as a gossip?

Mom flutters about the kitchen serving bacon, eggs, and pancakes. She whistles over the sound of the blender as my stepdad, Henry, a quiet blue-collar man, prepares a smoothie. I dispense some vitamins from bottles in the cabinet and place them on my napkin, then sit down at the table on this Sunday in July.

"So, what do you think about the job offer?" Mom asks.

In the months since the conference, I doubled down on my studies in the evenings and weekends, completing the naturopathy course. I spread my job search over Boston, a market where major medical institutions abound, and Phoenix, where the alternative medicine industry is growing. Finally, an offer came in a few days ago to work at a holistic medical practice in Mesa, just outside of Phoenix.

"I really want to go for it. But . . . I'm not sure now is the right time to move across the country," I say. "I thought Adam would have regained some sense of direction. He's still not the same since the apostle passed. And now, there doesn't seem to be room for me at The Ministry Center without being married."

"Well, honey, how do you know until you're there? As much as I would love for you to stay here, I really think Adam needs to see you more often."

I put my elbow on the table and rest my chin on my hand.

Henry places a smoothie in front of me. "Wouldn't it be a big pay increase?"

I nod.

He takes his seat at the head of the table.

"You may be right, Mom," I say. "Moving to Arizona may be what Adam needs to know that I'm serious."

Trying to make eye contact with her is like trying to catch a butterfly. She must ensure we're all set before serving herself. She masks it well, but her moistening eyes and downward gaze tell me she's struggling with the thought of me living far away.

"Just let me know when you're ready to pray about it." She doesn't want to hold me back.

"Can we pray this afternoon with Dad on the phone? I just need to know what God wants for me. All this back and forth, weighing the options, is exhausting."

"Of course." She sits in her seat and scoots her chair closer to the table. She looks at Henry. "Do you want to say the blessing?"

"Go ahead," he says.

Mom says a short prayer before we eat.

I'm satisfied that we have a plan to pray about my future, and excited to tell Adam about the possibility. I finish the food on my plate, then text Adam to request a video call.

We connect about an hour later. I check the self-facing camera and tilt the screen to ensure it's catching my best angle then smooth out my hair. We greet each other and share words of prophecy. I marvel the tenderness and wisdom that he speaks while admiring his human form. His blond hair is swept to one side, framing his soft eyes. The beard he's growing brings definition to his otherwise round face. I'm not thrilled with his t-shirt, something video game related, but I can look past that.

After some small talk, it's time for me to bring up moving. I don't want to receive a word without at least running the idea by him first.

"So, what would you think if I were to move to Arizona?"

He sits back, his gaze steady and hard to read. Then he shakes his head. "It doesn't matter what I think." Then nods. "If that's where God is leading you, then it would be a blessing."

That's it?

He's not wrong, but I was hoping for a bit more enthusiasm. I've seen this indifference before. Heck, I've used it myself to overcompensate for my emotions. So I press the matter a little further.

"Do you ever think about your future? Like where you would like to live?" I say.

"Sometimes, but I don't like to fantasize about things that aren't by a word of the Lord."

"Right. Sometimes I think about living in Hawaii someday, but I'm sure that's not likely."

"It could be."

"Really?"

"Sure, why not?" A subtle smile lights his face. His eyes twinkle just enough to show a little hope. He lived there once, and now I know he's open to returning. That small acknowledgment tells me anything is possible, if it's the wisdom of the Lord.

Mom, Dad, and I meet that afternoon to get the Lord's direction on my future.

The next day, I accept the job offer with the stipulation that I have thirty days to relocate.

I lie on my bed watching the rhythm of the ceiling fan, which has little effect on this humid afternoon. I'll have to get used to the heat anyway. Initial preparations for the move are underway. I haven't talked with Adam, outside of texting him the good news. He congratulated me and said he was standing in faith with me for God's provision.

In a few minutes, I'll join a scheduled phone call with Adam and our fathers. Dad and I requested the appointment to discuss moving to the next step in marriage consideration. Adam and I have had little instruction on what to do other than reading through a booklet on biblical marriage and keeping up with our written personal submissions.

"God, I trust you for our next steps," I say aloud as I continue this time of reflection.

Moving to Phoenix will usher in a new beginning. Despite Adam's apparent indifference when I first told him, having an official word seemed to ease his apprehension.

Adam knows my motives are pure, no matter what others say. He's witnessed my spiritual growth and the discipline I put into improving my physical and mental health over the past ten years. Anxiety no longer grips me. Many of the chronic stress-induced maladies have dissipated. Applying faith, natural remedies, and modern medicine has done wonders for my health, and I'm confident it will benefit Adam once we're married. My new job will support us both in our ministry.

God has a purpose for us. Seven years of preparation must mean that He was perfecting our readiness so that we would thrive as one. Every frustration, every impatient thought, every feeling of loneliness, or each time we questioned God's purpose—it all has tested us. The enemy has tested our resolve and faithfulness. Through exchanging the word of self for the word of God, by His Spirit, His word prevails. I am ready.

My phone rings.

The four of us give encouraging words of prophecy, as is customary, and there is an awkward silence. Dad starts to speak when the prophet interrupts him.

"Let's let Adam speak first, as he has something to share."

Here it is, Lord, he's going to propose.

I take a deep breath to calm my excited nerves.

Adam says, "I've been spending time in prayer about this and submitted it to the eldership. I received a word that our time of consideration is fulfilled."

Fulfilled . . . Fulfilled? Wait, this step or the whole thing? I wait for clarity.

"So . . . what does that mean?" Dad says.

Charles interjects, "It means it's over. I'm sorry if you thought—"

"What? . . . No!" My chest tightens as a lump forms in my throat. Tears well up. My whole body shakes as if I just learned that a loved one has died.

Adam begins sobbing through the phone. As an empath, he can't help it. I won't feel sorry for him. He needs to feel how much he is hurting me.

Charles continues, "I'm sorry that I wasn't more involved. If I had been more active in this consideration, it never would have lasted this long."

Another dagger to my wounded heart.

"Hold on, what's going on here?" says Dad. "I thought we were going to help them take the next step."

I erupt. "Nope. Apparently, they're just ready to throw it all away. All this time, all those years!" Pulling myself together as best I can, I ask, "Adam, can you give me a reason?"

His sobs break, and a weak voice says, "It's what we received by a confirmed word. I'm sorry I don't have a better answer for you."

A third dagger, against which I have no defense, pierces my heart. He knows I respect the confirmed word. Still, there is always more to it. It's not like he just got a prompting one day to ask God if our consideration of marriage was fulfilled and God said, "Yes. You're done with this, move on." Our Loving Father has more depth and understanding than that. Either Adam's word resulted from some deep soul searching and many conversations with his headship about our future, or he never really took this seriously.

"Victoria, you need to calm down. There's no need to overreact," Charles says, as if I were some child throwing a tantrum because someone took my lollipop.

Dad was ambushed. I feel betrayed.

The call ends with both Adam and me in tears. No promise of talking again. No sign of where to go from here.

I fold into myself.

All those years of connection and joy and laughter, of preparation and pining are running through my head. The late-night phone calls, serving beside each other at conferences, hiking among the junipers, holding hands when nobody was looking, and how he made me laugh. The many times he'd encouraged me, and I him. I thought I knew him better than any other friend. I know he's felt depressed since the apostle passed away. It affected him more than most.

Now, all I want is to be there for him, to comfort him, and show him the hope of a life together in Christ. I want to help him see the apostle was not a second Jesus, and we still have a living Savior to serve. I can't imagine what happened to him in recent years to make him so weak, so hopeless that he won't fight for our future, much less drum up the courage to break this news to me without his father's supervision. Yet, the decision stands. The gavel has dropped.

This court of consideration is dismissed.

CHAPTER ELEVEN

CHANGES

Six months later, I'm standing in the middle of an empty one-bedroom second-floor walk-up in South Scottsdale, just outside of Phoenix, Arizona. Two suitcases and a backpack sit on the beige-gray faux-wood floor beside me. The boxes will arrive in a few days. White walls, gray countertops, and brand-new appliances give it an elevated feel. It's small, but it's mine—all 670 square feet.

I had all but given up on this dream, but the Lord hadn't given up on me. I declined the job offer, thinking I would stay in Massachusetts. God worked with me on adjusting my priorities. Adam could no longer be the leading motivation for me to move.

Then a friend from my online classes invited me to attend an integrative medicine conference in her home city—Phoenix, of all places.

While attending the conference, I made a few professional connections and received another job offer—this time in Scottsdale. The allure of sunny weather, friendly people, and new beginnings tugged at my heartstrings, and those tugs became greater than my attraction to

Adam. I still cared for him as a brother, despite how he treated me on that last call. The difference? I was no longer planning my life around him.

At thirty-six years old, in my first apartment, this freedom is both wonderful and terrifying.

In the bathroom, I fixate on flaws in the paint, messy caulking, and seams that don't fit together. Any other day, I might dismiss it as evidence of a rush turnover for profit and be thankful for my reasonable rent payments. Today, the imperfections are a commentary on my life choices.

Lord, what have I done?

My chest tightens, and I cry. Nobody is around to hear it, to worry. It's me and the Lord. I leave the bathroom and walk through the carpeted bedroom and out the sliding glass doors to the balcony.

I take several deep breaths. Gaining composure, I realize the surrounding beauty. Carved out among a sea of palm trees beneath sprawling blue skies is a resort-style pool, complete with lounge chairs, private cabanas, a fire pit, and grills. Camelback Mountain peaks beyond the palms. Its towering presence stands as an anchor and comfort to my soul. Perhaps it is close enough that I might walk or ride a bicycle when I get one. The natural beauty reminds me that God is faithful to provide for all my needs. And now he's placed me in paradise.

I feel the independence of my youth reigniting. At age twelve, I became a latchkey kid, having the house to myself after school. I'll never forget the time I answered the phone and my grandmother was on the other end, her voice stern and accusing. "Victoria, what are you doing home alone?" That's when I remembered I wasn't supposed to answer the phone. My grandmother would have preferred I stay with her, and I imagine Mom got an earful that day. But Mom was responsible and made sure I had neighbors looking out for me.

I liked my freedom then. Freedom as an adult comes with more responsibility. As the reality sets in, all I can do is move forward, one step at a time. So, I focus on the immediate needs—an air mattress to sleep on, a few cooking utensils—the essentials.

Ping. It's a text from Nathan, a photographer I met at the medical conference.

It reads, "Welcome to Arizona. How was your flight?"

How did he remember I was arriving today? We'd become professionally acquainted through social media and had spoken on the phone briefly. Not much more than that.

"The flight was good, thanks for asking," I type back.

"Of course. Let me know if you need anything while you're settling in."

Of all the people I'd known for years who lived out here, mostly from church, none of them reached out to me or even acknowledged my arrival.

"Thanks, I'm pretty hungry. Do you want to grab a bite to eat?" I say.

"Sure, I'm off work in an hour. Where do you want to go?"

"I don't really know the area." I glance at the rental car keys on the counter. "You pick and I'll meet you there."

I wait a minute for a response. To my relief, an address appears in the chat with three flashing dots signaling that he's still typing.

"It's a restaurant on my valet rotation. I think you'll enjoy it."

In the same way my mother ensured others look after me when I was twelve, God has people watching out for me now.

After a month, I've settled into my apartment and job quite well. I glance at the wall clock in the waiting room next to an ancient proverb of unknown origins, *Medice, cura te ipsum*, meaning "Physician, heal thyself," a reminder to practice what we preach. It's four thirty, and my last patient rescheduled, so I have some free time before the office social.

Olivia, our patient outreach coordinator, who handles most of the marketing for this small practice, springs into my office. Her red and orange sundress brightens up the room, complimenting her megawatt smile. "You'd better come tonight. We're all going to Earth Spice before the performance. You know, the new vegan place that opened up down the street."

"God willing, I wouldn't miss it," I say.

"*God* willing? *You* will," she says with a sideways grin, then spins around the corner out of sight.

Olivia made me feel welcome from day one. Her free spirit and exuberant positivity is contagious, but she's deep into new-age philosophy. If only she could see that Jesus Christ is the source of life. I'm looking forward to her performance at open mic night at Joella's Café later and indulging in a chai latte topped with vanilla bean foam and cinnamon.

In the meantime, I pull my phone out of my desk drawer where it stays most of the day, shielding my patients from its radiation. It's an office policy to keep electronics usage to a minimum in this healing space. It's also less distracting, but since I have a quiet moment, I'll check my emails. As I'm scanning my inbox, a strange title in all caps captures my attention "WOLVES IN SHEEP'S CLOTHING." I recognize the sender's name as an elder who had left for a while and recently returned to take part in elders conferences. I hesitate.

Kelsey calls out from the front desk. "Hey, Tori, we're heading over early to grab a table." She's our office manager, receptionist, and unofficial party planner who keeps this place running.

"Uh . . . yeah, I'm right behind you," I call back.

Lord, what should I do?

The email can wait.

I'll enjoy my time out and deal with whatever drama might be behind that door when I get home. I whisper a prayer, "Lord, I bless all those involved with that communication and cut off any fiery darts of the wicked from coming against The Ministry, in Jesus Christ's name."

I collect my midnight denim jacket and sunset-toned woven messenger bag, then catch up with the others.

Joella's is busiest on Open Mic Night and Sunday mornings. Despite the crowd, it feels spacious and intimate all at once. The place has a modern fair-trade organic flair meets country-chic. Bookcases line the walls, holding a select few books and games, but mostly houseplants. Pinewood cutouts of handwritten script declare positive affirmations in the white spaces. Photographs on the back wall tell of Joella's travels to Guatemala where she met fair-trade coffee and chocolate farmers while studying microeconomics. A donation jar at the counter is filling up with funds to send a little extra help to her supplier's village. These details tell a story of lives lived in community—souls in pursuit of what is honest and pure.

"Thank you for allowing me the honor of playing for you tonight. May it nourish your soul." Olivia presses her hands together at her heart-center in a gesture of both prayer and gratitude.

Lord, nourish this audience with your truth and love, and shield them from further deception. You alone are the source of life, in Christ Jesus's name.

Olivia's Nordic roots emerge in the melodic sounds of her voice, forming round vowels and full-bodied syllables. Soft chords from her acoustic guitar cover a landscape of rolling hills for her voice to travel. She sings from pain and longing, beauty and healing. A strong faith in herself.

Heads nod, feet tap, and bodies gently sway. Her message is universal, speaking to the yearning of every human heart. I see glimmers of hope in her eyes, but beyond the glimmer is still an emptiness.

After her set, she joins us at our table to indulge in her favorite sweet treat, a vanilla chamomile scone.

She turns to me. "What did you think?" The others had seen her perform before.

"It was captivating! I especially enjoyed the acoustic sounds and your melodic voice."

"Thank you, you're too kind," Olivia says, pushing her hair behind one ear. "I also wrote the lyrics. This one was deeply personal to me, so I mainly wrote it for myself, and if it inspires others, that's great too."

"Yeah. About that, I heard you say in the end that you found healing by trusting in your own abilities. What about the God who gave you those abilities?"

"Well, of course, all healing comes from the Universe. There are many ways people can find strength, some through practicing meditation and self-affirmations, or I suppose, religion. I know you think Jesus is the only way, but it's a big, wide world, and I prefer to keep an open mind."

Part of me wants to accept what she's saying and leave it at that. Another part wants so desperately to prove to her that Jesus is big enough to cover the universe and that she can't truly say she has an open mind if she's not willing to consider he may be the only way to God.

"I—"

My phone buzzes several times in my pocket. I pull it out to see an onslaught of responses to the earlier email. Something's up. It's late for a weeknight, and I'm feeling tired. Witnessing to Olivia would have to wait for another time.

"It was a wonderful performance, but I have to head out. I'll see you in the morning." I wave bye to everyone then deposit my mug and plate in the wash bin on my way out the door.

I arrive home a few minutes past ten o'clock. Normally, I would be in bed, but I'm compelled to see what all the fuss is about. I sit on the couch and open my laptop for a better view. There it is: "WOLVES IN SHEEP'S CLOTHING." Only there are several replies now. I open the original email.

It appears to be a scathing accusation toward the eldership of financial abuse.

In short, the elder is serving as a financial executor for an elderly widow who had fronted funds to The Ministry over the years to a sum of nearly thirty thousand dollars. Her late husband once forgave twenty thousand dollars of the debt, and this elder is asking The Ministry to repay the rest. He claims several failed attempts to communicate directly have forced him to bring the issue before the church.

Puzzled why the eldership would not have responded to him earlier, my instinct is to question this man's motivations. Perhaps he's in rebellion and the widow hasn't been standing in faith with The Ministry to receive the donations to pay her back.

The first reply is from Charles. He acknowledges the elder's concerns and denies having received any prior communication from him about the debt. He reminds the elder it is each person's responsibility to stand in faith for the provision of funds to be repaid and that God directs the order in which that repayment should happen. They honor God by putting his mission first. They stand in faith with the saint that she may receive her hundred-fold return of the Kingdom of God.

The response seems reasonable and aligned with the Principle of Proving, where we give all to God and receive from God, agree with His word on the matter, and walk by faith. As a result, we'll receive what we need. A major blocker to this process is judgment, and this elder has plenty of it.

The man replies to Charles, saying that by turning it around on the widow as being in rebellion and out of order, he is practicing elder abuse and manipulation. He questions the eldership about their responsibility to adhere to their part of the word to pay her back.

To which, Charles replies, he has no awareness of a word making that elder her legal representative. The elders' accusations have no basis in reality and he should check his own heart for the judgement that blocks the flow of the Kingdom.

This tit for tat is embarrassing. I close my laptop and stare at the blank television screen mounted on the wall. I think of times I've held similar sentiments as that elder, after giving to The Ministry, but I always repented of the judgment. Sometimes, The Ministry paid me back as a result; other times, the Lord would lead me to forgive the debt. All of my money is God's anyway, so why should I fear? I pray over the situation and go to bed.

I awake early the next morning after a night of restless sleep. I reach for my phone to open a daily Bible verse when I see a stack of notifications for replies that came in overnight. They're from people in the South Pacific. I can't allow this to take over my morning.

I'm preparing for work when my mom calls. It's two hours later on the East Coast.

"Have you checked your email?" she says with concern in her voice.

"Yeah, last night. There was some back and forth about alleged financial abuse."

"It's worse than that," she says. "They're saying things happened to the women in The Ministry Center. Do you know anything about that?"

"No, what things?"

"It's not specific. Go check your emails and we'll talk after."

"Okay."

I open my laptop and see several replies. It seems the conversation has turned away from money to something else.

Charles's tone is stoic and formal. His response reads like a legal document, evading specific allegations toward a man and what he "may or may not have done." Speaking on behalf of the eldership, he warned

that reports of abuse were attacks on the Ministry of Christ. Whatever it is they think happened should remain between them, God, and their headship.

What would warrant a response like this?

I scan my emails to find more details, but there is nothing specific. If people are attacking The Ministry with accusations of abuse and others' faith is wavering because of it, then the enemy must be on high alert. That's often a sign we're doing something right. Like Charles said, we shouldn't perpetuate gossip. I pray in the Spirit for all involved and that the truth would come forth. God promises in His word that all things will come to light and the deeds of men will be made manifest. So far, I have seen nothing that would lead me to suspect wrongdoing.

The letter also resurfaces the financial complaint lodged publicly by the elder. It makes the situation seem like the eldership tried to comply with payment, but the sister and her local eldership cut them off. The elders reiterate this is a faith-based ministry. They conclude the sister hasn't been paid because she was taken aside by Satan and not having faith. The letter further reinforced that we must be faithful and on guard to communicate and submit to our headships at all times, or the enemy of our soul may deceive us.

This is all quite heavy for a Friday morning. I cast the care upon God. Clearly, there is dysfunction in the church, but then again, there is dysfunction everywhere, so why should that be a surprise? I text Mom, saying I am praying for all involved and I'll talk with her after work.

Back-to-back patients this morning help keep my mind in the present and focused on supporting God's desire for wholeness among His creation. I pray for each patient before and after working with them that God would give them understanding of His purpose in their lives and, as the chief physician, He would give me the knowledge of how to best support the natural healing process He built into each person.

It's early afternoon before I have a break. I walk into the courtyard for some sunlight and fresh air. Olivia is sitting there with a plate of sushi she brought from home and her eyes fixed on her phone.

She looks up. "Hey, Holy Roller."

"Hey, Pop Star," I retort. She hates pop music.

"Did you hear about that mega-church in California? Lifespring, or something like that."

"I've heard of it. They produce music I often hear on my favorite radio station. What about it?" I say.

"Oh, you need to hear this. A documentary was just released about dozens of reports of abuse from their leaders. Shit, you would think such a big, successful ministry would have more eyes on them. It's not like they're an obscure cult in the backwoods of Kentucky." She shakes her head. "I used to sing their songs at youth group back in high school."

"You went to a youth group?"

"Yeah, my parents raised me Catholic, but I went to a group with my best friend. That was before reality slapped me in the face. Then I learned to be self-sufficient. These poor souls can't see what's going on right in front of them."

"Right. I mean, no, that's sad," I say. "Church should be a safe place. That particular church isn't reflecting God's true nature. They need prayer."

"Whatever. People need to wake up." She throws her hands up.

I shake my head. "God is—"

Olivia's phone buzzes, and she answers a call. Interrupted again.

Lord, what is going on? First the emails attacking The Ministry, now this documentary about a mainstream church. Could there be something to these accusations, or is this more propaganda from the father of lies, a plot to take down the whole church by giving it a bad rep? The Ministry is different. It isn't one of those "system" churches led by man-made rituals following the same religious calendar every year.

We are spirit-led, making God our only source instead of the men in leadership positions.

My watch alarm beeps, reminding me that my next patient will arrive in five minutes. Back to work.

In the evening, I stretch out on my bed. My room is lit by the dim warmth of a Himalayan salt lamp. Eucalyptus and lavender scents release from the diffuser beside it. Anything to find some relaxation after the day I had.

The rumors of financial and sexual abuse have my head spinning. There's no way the ministry I grew up in is like those other churches Olivia told me about. It's not possible. There must be more the elders are not saying to protect the body of Christ.

Then I remember I have access to my dad's email account. When I worked as his assistant, I would send emails on his behalf. True, I'm not his assistant anymore. But if something else is going on, I need to know about it without anyone suspecting me of distrusting the eldership.

A peek won't hurt. I only want to know the truth. I scroll through a couple of junk items and some financial reports, sabbath updates, etc. A few elders have questions to uplift about life issues. Nothing out of the ordinary—

But wait, what's this?

There's an email from Adam to the eldership. The subject line reads, *Consideration of Marriage to . . .* and then cuts off.

My stomach flutters. *Who is he considering? Could it be about me?* I have to know, but I'm afraid to find out. After a few moments, I open the email.

Ana Brown. I stare at her name in total confusion. The question he's asking is not just whether it is the wisdom of the Lord for him to consider Ana, but to marry her! A question that to my knowledge he never afforded me. This makes no sense. She's five years older than me. That makes her ten years older than Adam.

The heat of anger overtakes my body, and I scream out in frustration. I don't care if my neighbors hear me. Ana and I used to be close. We'd talk on the phone for hours before she moved to the Apostle Center. Why did neither of them tell me?

This can't be real. It's only been seven months since we broke up. I read the contents of the email again to be sure. It's real all right, and they want to do it in a month!

I feel as if the ground is shaking beneath me. I sink to the floor, imagining a chasm opening up and swallowing me whole with my pathetic romantic dreams. Any chance of us getting back together is about to be gone forever. But that isn't the worst part. It's the betrayal by my two best friends.

Tears pour down my face as I cry out, "Why God? Where did I go wrong?"

It's not until several minutes pass, when I finally catch my breath, that I think, *If Adam rejecting me was an act of obedience to his father, then maybe this is too. I still love him, and more than anything I don't want to see him ruin his life, even if he has already ruined mine.*

I pull up his contact on my phone and his profile picture fills the screen. That face, that baby face with kind eyes and a big heart.

What happened to you?

I press the call button.

"H-hello?" Adam's voice is hesitant and small.

"What's going on?" I say.

"Uh . . ."

"I know about your question. What I can't figure out is why didn't you tell me. Or why didn't she tell me? You were my best friends."

I hear shallow breathing and a sniffle.

"You could have at least told me to my face," I say.

"I know. I'm sorry," he manages. "I—I ask your forgiveness."

"I'm not ready to give it," I say. "I know I'm supposed to forgive you, but I'm still wrapping my head around how this happened."

"I didn't mean to . . . It was— we've been working together for a while and . . . well, when our consideration ended, I—I didn't mean for you to find out like this. It just happened so fast," he says. "I didn't want to say anything before we had a confirmed word."

I take some deep breaths and then say, "Adam, we're all hurting right now. The Ministry is broken and on the defensive. I understand if you feel lost without an apostle, but please don't make any major decisions while you're in this state. Let things settle down first so you can have a clear head."

"Uh-huh," he says. I'm pouring out my soul, and that's all he has for me. Regardless of what he's done, he is still a child of God, and I love him.

"I'm praying for you," I say.

We end the conversation on amicable terms. After hanging up the phone, I plant my face in my pillow.

The integrity of The Ministry is in question. The door to Adam's heart has officially closed, and I'm four thousand miles away from family. Doubting God's plan for me, I cry myself to sleep.

CHAPTER TWELVE

GRIEF

My first time home since moving away came sooner than expected. Joanne Silverman, wife of the late, Dicky Silverman, had passed away, and Mom asked me to join her for the funeral.

To be honest, I needed to come home for a bit. The heaviness of Adam moving on before the dust has settled left me confused and questioning if I was hearing God at all.

The scent of flowers and soft music fill a carpeted room while friends and family of the deceased take their seats in rows of foldable chairs. Mom and I fix our attention on flower arrangements surrounding a casket with a single photo of Joanne circa 1965. She dons a high-collared blouse with a bold flower print to match her bright pink lips. Her blond hair is coifed atop her head like a beehive, with large pearl earrings to finish the look.

I always loved the Silvermans. Joanne and her late husband hosted the first Ministry gatherings in Massachusetts. That's also where my parents first met Apostle Rob and his family nearly forty years ago.

Even though the family was no longer part of The Ministry, Mom and I always loved them like distant family.

Now, years later, we came to show the surviving family members we haven't forgotten about them and our love still stands despite theological differences.

The Silvermans' daughter, Sarah, was one of Mom's best friends. She and her husband Philip, a former elder, and their five children and some grandchildren, fill the first few rows.

A local church minister gives a traditional eulogy complete with Psalm 23, then opens the floor for friends and family to speak.

Sarah's brother is first at the podium.

"There aren't enough words to describe our mom. She was a tour de force, a brilliant woman who supported Dad as he built his construction business from the ground up and, in their success, always kept the family grounded. Mom was full of love and compassion. She would cheer us on in our endeavors with endless enthusiasm and be there for us with unconditional love when we inevitably messed up. My children will tell you there's no better hug than one from Nana . . ."

"Look, Mom," I say. "Charles is here."

I spot the prophet sitting in the back row by the door. He must have slipped in after the service started. I knew he was in town for meetings with the eldership, but we weren't expecting him here.

"What a blessing," Mom says.

A few more family members speak, and then Charles steps up to the podium, which comes up to his waist. Few people recognize him. We expect him to say good things about this loving couple who served for so many years in The Ministry and were critical to its growth in this area.

He looks out at the audience and then down at his notes.

"I'm sure many of you are here today because you loved this woman and you believe that she and her late husband did many wonderful things for their community. That may be so. However, I would be remiss if I didn't warn you of the choice they made to leave the positions God called them to and proceed without a word of God to live their lives apart from God's order."

His remarks send shivers down my spine. Others shift uncomfortably in their seats.

Charles continues, "This kind of living opens the door for Satan to kill, steal, and destroy. Here, he cut short Dicky's life and left Joanne headless for many years, resulting in a slow decline of her faculties from which she could not return to the glory she once had. Let this be a caution to those who think they can walk their own path and still give God the glory. There is no glory in it."

He puts down the microphone and walks out of the funeral home, leaving behind family members both grieving and stunned.

The minister takes the microphone and clears his throat. "Well, that was . . . uncalled for. I'm sorry, folks. Someone else? Please?"

Sarah's husband, Philip, hurries to the podium. "Folks, my sincere apologies. Who let that man in?" He shakes his head. "Remarks like that reinforce that they were right to leave The Ministry when they did. Us too, my family and I. God's love is bigger than any religious group, and we give God the glory for both the hardships and the victories this family has experienced together. I rejoice now that Dad and Mom have reunited in the presence of Jesus, our loving Savior. Please, do not take what that man said to heart. God is love, and he is there for anyone who calls upon Him. It was His love and joy that exuded from the Silvermans."

Mom leans into me. "I can't believe he said those things in front of their family and friends. Besides, they still loved the Lord."

"It . . . it may be true," I say, "but that wasn't love."

"Oh, I don't believe it was even true. There's more to the body of Christ than just The Ministry," Mom says.

I shrug. I suppose there is, but after experiencing the fullness of the truth, is there any going back to the limited perspective of the church system?

The service ends, and we stand in line to greet the family members. We hug Sarah and Philip and share our condolences.

"How's your dad doing?" Philip asks.

"He's hanging in there," I say. "He has some chronic health issues that make it hard for him to get out of the house. I know he'd be here if he could."

"I'm sorry to hear that. Your dad is a kind man. Do you think he'd be open to me coming to see him while I'm in town?"

"Yes, I'm sure of it."

"Good. Let's make that happen."

Sarah presents their grown children, who we haven't seen since they were teenagers.

Ethan, the oldest, is clean shaven and tall with dark hair. He offers a handshake, and Mom gives him a hug.

"Hannah, you've hardly aged," he says to Mom.

"Oh, thank you. You turned out to be quite handsome yourself. Anyone special in your life?"

Abashed, he points out his wife seated at the back holding their newborn son.

"Congratulations. This must be a bittersweet time for you," I say.

"Yeah, thanks. It's been quite a month," he says. "I'd like to catch up more, under different circumstances."

"Yes, of course. I'll message you online."

He nods, and we move along with the line.

"Hannah," a voice calls from behind us.

We turn around to see Lydia, a woman a few years older than my mom, whom I recognize from childhood. She's average height and build with a brown bob and bangs. She embraces Mom.

A gentleman steps up beside her. He's about the same age, dark-skinned, wearing glasses and a fedora.

"Look who's here. You remember Cedric?" Lydia gestures to the man beside her.

"Oh my! Of course, I do. How could I forget those days touring on the bus around New England?"

I recognize his name as one of dad's old band members.

He extends his hand and Mom brings him in for a hug. Then he says, "I see the years have been good to you. You wouldn't think thirty years had gone by. You look just the same."

"Oh, thank you! Have you met Victoria?" she puts her arm around my waist.

"A pleasure," Cedric says extending his arm for a handshake "You look just like your father. I see you got his freckles. How is he?"

"Oh, he's hanging in there. He has some health and mobility issues that prevented him from coming today."

"Well, I'd love to see him."

"I think I could arrange that." We exchange contact information.

"Is there a reception after this?" Mom asks.

"There's a private one just for family," Lydia says. "That's why I got your attention. We're planning a small lunch to get the ladies together tomorrow afternoon. Mimi will be there and hopefully Sarah, if she's up for it. Can you come? We'd love for you both to join us."

"Yes, we'd love to," Mom says, and I nod in agreement.

The next day, we pull into a parking space at the Seaside Grille to meet the ladies from the funeral. "Are you okay, Mom?" I ask. "You've been quiet for most of the drive."

"Oh, yes, it's just . . . I was thinking of when you were a little girl and your father still loved me."

I turn to her from the passenger seat and take her hands in mine.

"I'm sorry that it didn't work out, Mom."

"It's okay. I've moved on, but seeing familiar faces brings up a lot of memories." Her face turns flush, and tears gloss over her eyes.

She sniffs and shakes off the sadness, removing her hands from mine. She pulls out a mirror and a tissue from her pocketbook and dabs her eyes, ensuring her mascara hasn't run before we enter.

The hostess leads us onto the three-season patio with a view of Cape Cod Canal. The water is glistening, and seagulls fly above it. A few small sailboats coast past a barge that eases along carrying a cargo load.

Mimi and Lydia stand up to greet us with hugs.

Mimi goes on her tiptoes, stretching her arms high and wide to embrace me. Her long black hair catches on my ring for a moment. I shake it free.

Why am I still wearing that? It once represented being wed to Christ, then it kept me off the market while I was considering Adam. Now, it reminds me of the time I spent waiting in vain.

Both women are older than my mom, but they bonded over being elders' wives and raising their young children together.

"So, how's Arizona? We want to hear all about it," says Mimi.

"Oh, it's wonderful! The climate has done wonders for my breathing," I say.

"Good for you. It would be way too hot for me," Mimi says. "How are the elders and saints there? Have you joined a fellowship?"

"Well, they . . . it's not as active as I hoped it would be. I attend a Friday night gathering at a home with a bunch of children that is quite chaotic at times. It's not like the stories I've heard from the early days."

"The early days," Sarah echoes as she enters the room. She is tall and poised, with a dirty-blonde classic short haircut, a subdued nod to her mother's beehive from the 1960s.

"You made it!" Mimi gets up and gives her a big bear hug.

"How are you holding up?" Lydia asks.

"It's hard, but I could use a short break from the family, just for an afternoon."

We offer sympathetic nods.

Lydia and Sarah left The Ministry with their husbands years ago. Lydia later divorced hers. Mimi and Peter stayed the course.

The server, seeing that we're all here, comes to take our drink orders.

"I remember those days, the early days," Sarah says.

"I love the music you used to make with my dad," I say. "You sang and I think Lydia played the flute, right?"

"Yes, that's right." Sarah smiles. "That was a long time ago. My oldest was about four or five years old." She looks at me. "You must have been around that age too. Those were some good times."

"I still have those sing-along tapes," Mimi says. "Peter converted them to CD so I can still listen to them in the car sometimes. You were always quiet, but you could sing like an angel. I don't have a voice like that, but I appreciate those who do. I just make a joyful noise, and I mean *noise*." We chuckle, knowing most of us are mediocre singers with some crackling at best.

"I listen to them on my phone," I say. "It's so uplifting to sing along."

Hearing my dad's voice as a younger man is especially comforting.

Sarah's eyes glisten. "My goodness, I didn't realize my music was still blessing people! It was a lot of fun to make. I think those are some of the best times I had with this group."

"I loved playing along with the tambourine," I say.

It was the only instrument I could play, and my mom had taught me how to clap it with the beat and shake it with the melody.

The reminiscing makes me feel like I'm with family and I want to hear more. "What were some other good times you all remember?"

Mimi's eyes widen. "The flow of the spirit. We were so hungry back then that our mid-week gatherings would go late into the night. Remember that? I loved how freely we used the gifts of the Spirit—prophecies, words of knowledge, all of it."

We nod our heads in reminiscence of this shared experience.

Mimi continues, "Miracles happened all the time. I remember there was a woman with one leg that was shorter than the other. Someone laid hands on her to minister healing, and it grew back!"

"A leg grew back?" I say.

"Sure as day!" Mimi says. "There was also a young boy who had a speech impediment, and when he received the Holy Spirit and prophesied, it was clear as a bell. He didn't have any trouble after that."

"I was there for that one. It left me speechless," Sarah recalled. "I'm encouraged, even now to stand in faith unto the manifestation of the health in my throat. It hasn't been the same for a long time, but I'm trusting and believing that God will heal me in due time."

"Amen, sister, we stand in faith with you," I say. But the words alone don't seem like enough. I ask God if there is something else I can do but receive no further prompting.

Our server is back with the drinks and takes our food orders.

"What else did you witness?" I ask the group.

"I prophesied your birth!" Mimi joyfully proclaims. "Do you remember that, Hannah?"

"Hmm, I'm not sure I do," Mom says.

"No?" Mimi unfolds the napkin on her plate and places it on her lap as she explains, "See when I prophesy, I never know what's going to come out, but I just say what the Lord gives me. Some people's words are packaged all pretty and tied with a bow at the end . . . Mine are kind of blunt. I say what I need to say and then it stops like a faucet turned off."

She laughs at her own explanation. "Anyway, Hannah, we were at a gathering at my house, and I saw you in the kitchen. You and Sam had been trying for children for over a year, and you'd asked for ministry that night. While I was walking by you, the Lord just put the words in my mouth . . . Something like, 'Your baby will be here by spring.' That's it. When were you born?"

I smile. "March."

"See, there you go." She gestures with an open hand.

Mom's face glows. "You know, I had forgotten all about that." She clears her throat. "I don't know if anyone here recalls, but there was another miracle that happened while I was pregnant with Victoria. One morning when I was close to my due date, the doctor told me my uterus was tilted and that it could cause complications during birth. So, when I got home, I told Sam about it and no one else. He didn't tell anyone. We went to a gathering that evening. I think several of you were there. We were having body ministry, people laying hands on each other, prophesying to each other when Rob's grandson, Nicholas—he must have been about five or six—comes up to me and puts his hands on my belly and starts praying. He says that he saw that my stomach was tilted. And I said, 'Whoa.' I teared up and looked at Sam. Then I shared what happened that morning, how the doctor said the uterus was tilted. After little Nicholas prayed for me, I didn't have any issues. She came out fine."

"Praise God," Lydia says. "I didn't know about that."

I can't help thinking about where Nick is today—incarcerated and estranged from his family. How beautiful was the light that shone through the boy's innocence and how it was extinguished soon after. Hardship and abuse overcame his fresh, unadulterated faith, and he found himself in and out of prison for crimes related to drug activity. His children were subjected to a similar pattern of abuse at the hands of their mother's boyfriends.

I silently pray, *God, please be with Nick's children. Show them your truth, and shine your light into their hearts. Rescue them from the evil that has followed them and show them your fatherly love as only you can, in Christ Jesus's name. Amen.*

The waitress sets down lobster rolls piled high with fresh meat in front of me and Mom. Sarah thanks the waitress for her Tuna Niçoise salad. Lydia's eyes widen at the size of the Reuben stuffed with sauerkraut, and Mimi rubs her hands together, giddy to enjoy a nostalgic grilled cheese sandwich with tomato soup.

"Shall we bless the food?" I ask the group.

Mimi replies, "Yes, would you do the honors?"

"Sure." We bow our heads. "Father, I thank you for bringing us together in fellowship this day. We thank you for the sacrifice of your son Jesus on the cross for our sins, and it was his death, burial, and resurrection that purchased our universal salvation. I have sinned and not walked worthily of his sacrifice in every area of my life. I repent of that and thank you for the blood of Jesus that cleanses us from all unrighteousness, so that by His grace we may come unto a perfect man manifestly, having eaten all the body and drank all the blood of Jesus, the sacrificial lamb. We bless those who prepared and were channels of provision to this food and drink, that they may receive a hundredfold return of the Kingdom of God, and we bless this food and drink to the health, strength, and nourishment of our physical bodies, which is our holy and living sacrifice unto you. We pray all of this in the name of Jesus Christ. Amen."

They follow with amen. Some more enthusiastic than others.

"That was a thorough prayer," Lydia says.

"It's how the apostle has taught us to pray," I say, "since every meal is a type of communion, beyond the ritual with wafers and grape juice that some churches espouse. It touches on all the points of remembrance and repentance, although I may have shortened it a bit.

"That was short?" Sarah says.

I laugh. "Well, yes, the original script goes into more detail."

"It's true," Mimi says. "It takes about ten minutes for Sam to get through the entire thing before we eat at gatherings. Well, maybe five, but it's long."

"Thank you for sparing us," Mom says. "Let's eat!"

If I'm going to learn the truth of how The Ministry has treated women over the years, there's no better time to ask.

CHAPTER THIRTEEN

FORGIVENESS

Before taking my first bite of food, I ask the women around the table, "I'm curious about your first encounters with Rob Peterson. What drew you in?"

Mimi speaks first. "I've got to go back a ways for you to understand how much the encounter meant to me. In the 1960s, I escaped from an abusive foster home and was on the run. A thirteen-year-old hitchhiking along the coast highway in California." She shakes her head. "I didn't know how dangerous that was. I didn't know God, but I knew I could get a free meal from churches and sometimes a bed to sleep in. Eventually, I landed in juvenile hall, which is the last place I expected God to meet me.

"It was my court date. I'm lying on a cot with a stickman Bible. It was the only book they gave me, so I read a passage from it. Then I looked toward the ceiling and yelled, 'If you are the truth, then get me the fuck out of here!' and I threw the Bible across the room."

Sarah flinches at hearing the curse word come out of Mimi. Lydia doesn't seem fazed.

"What happened?" I say.

"I got out that day. The judge said, 'If I ever see you in my courtroom again, I'll put you away until you're twenty-one.' I said, 'You won't see me again.'" She laughs with a guttural triumph.

"Is that when you became a believer?"

"No, but a seed was planted. It wasn't until I met my husband. His mother made me promise to raise our son Christian, so I gave her my word. And that's when I was introduced to Jesus and later the Holy Spirit through the church I brought him to for Sunday School. In fact, I taught there so that I could learn the basics myself.

"One day, a friend came up to me and said, 'I met a man who told me the interpretations of every dream I ever had.' I was watchful by then and would not let a sister be drawn away by a false prophet, so I went with her to protect her. Immediately, I saw something by my spirit that I was seeking. I had never met anyone that I instantly connected with the way I did with him. Not to mention, he was from Oklahoma like I was.

"By the early eighties I was periodically attending an Assemblies of God retreat center in southern New Hampshire. While there, I was asking God to deliver me. I wasn't sure from what until he showed me I longed for a place to belong. I thought my church was that place until I got deliverance and saw that I belonged to God. He was the one I needed to trust.

"So I dug into The Ministry's teachings and studied how to use the Holy Spirit and be led by it."

"That's awful that they rejected you like that after you'd given so much time to the church," I say.

"Yeah, but it was a spiritual thing. It was all part of me coming to see that I belonged to God and not to people. But it was still hurtful." Mimi takes a spoonful of soup, which she has hardly touched.

We all know the feeling she described. Deep inside, we've all hungered and thirsted for righteousness. We drank from the well of living water that was the Holy Spirit, and we've poured into each other many impressive words of encouragement. The Holy Spirit's guidance has transformed our lives. And we've all faced the judgment of well-meaning Christians.

Lydia puts down her sandwich.

"What about you, Lydia?" I ask. "What were your first encounters with Rob like?"

"Me? Well, it's hard to think about the good times because as you know I've tried to block out most of the memories from that time."

"I'm sorry, you don't have to—"

"No, it's okay. I'll share." She shakes off the hesitation. "I had been a Christian for about six years and attended Trinity Covenant Church where I met your mother. Later, my first husband and I went with your parents to the Church of Plymouth. After your parents got involved with The Ministry, we visited a gathering with them and found it to be very different.

"The first time I met Rob, he prophesied over me about a spirit of rejection. I remember thinking, 'Why is he doing that?' Sometimes the word doesn't seem to make sense until you pray about it and then it's like, 'Wow, I didn't see that before.' Before this, I didn't know about Home Body Ministry. We always went to a community church building, but this was more personal, and we really liked it. So that's how we got involved."

"Thank you for sharing your stories," I say.

"It's too bad things changed over the years," Mimi says.

She once received a prophecy from Rob's wife that defines her well. The Lord said through her, "Thou art the stalwart one." Mimi received this to mean strong, immovable. This is very true, for she is a woman who goes full force in whatever direction she is pointed. It follows that she would stand strong in the teachings of The Ministry after all these years.

"It wasn't personal," Sarah says. "The fellowship was great, but it took a toll on our family. As an elder, Philip was away from the house much of the time. His meetings always ran late into the night or early morning, and I was at home with the little ones. My health problems were just beginning then, and I needed help. On top of that, he was running his orthodontic practice out of our home. He couldn't support his family while giving all of his time to the church."

"I didn't know you were having health issues," Mimi says.

"We didn't share it with the body because we thought they would look down upon us. Rob taught that the wife was supposed to serve the husband, and as an elder's wife and a young couple, we didn't want anyone to think we weren't up to the task. The first time I couldn't attend a gathering due to a migraine, my husband was told that I was in rebellion. He defended me, but the simple accusation put a bitter taste in our mouths."

I furrow my brows.

"You were lucky your husband defended you," Lydia adds. "Mine probably would have agreed with the elders. He took the idea of submission and serving him too seriously.

"I never told anyone outside my family about this," Lydia says, "but when my brother was getting married, the wedding fell on a weekend when a seminar was in town. I told my husband that I wanted to go to the wedding, but the elders wouldn't permit it. My husband had agreed with them, and they would not allow me to go. When I approached the elders about it, they told me it was none of my business how they made the decision. That's the way they treated women in those days. They didn't respect us.

"Now, we all do things to hurt people, and so I eventually had to forgive them. But would I get involved with that again? No. The seminar ended up being called off for other reasons and we went to the wedding, but my relationships with close family members were never the same again. It put a wedge between my family and me for most of our lives.

I guess the elders weren't reading the Scripture that talks about the husband *loving* their wife and washing her with the water of the word. At least that's not how it was in our family. I think other families applied submission to different degrees. Ours was rather extreme."

Childhood memories flood my mind as I listen to these women recollect the early days.

I nod. "I remember playing over at your house, and there were so many rules I couldn't remember them all, so I would inevitably break one. I was so ashamed to be standing in a corner facing the wall, not allowed to turn around for several minutes. The worst part was when he took out the belt, but we don't need to go there."

"Spare the rod, spoil the child, is what we used to say. Such an awful thing." Lydia shakes her head with remorse. "The way we applied it wasn't even biblical."

"It was a different time then," Sarah says. "We all did things to our children we're not proud of."

"It's true," Lydia agrees. "But I should have known better, even then. I was a social worker responsible for placing children in foster care. How could I not see it in my own house? There must have been a spirit blinding me. Sorry, guys, I didn't mean to get so heavy. It is really nice to be here with you all again."

"I imagine it's hard to talk about," I say. "We all experienced some incredible things, but not without significant cost to some."

How could a ministry be both a blessing and a curse, leaving so much damage in its wake?

A prompting says, *Ask. Talk to others. Don't let your mind presume what they experienced. Find out and I will guide you on this journey.* God must have an answer.

Lord? I check. Yes, it was his voice speaking to me. I obey.

"Lydia, do you think I could meet with one of your children to ask them about their experience with The Ministry?"

Am I prepared for this?

"Um, sure. I don't know if they'll want to talk about it, but you're welcome to ask. I'll give you Joshua's number."

"Thank you." I look at Sarah. "Do you think your sons would talk to me?"

"I'm sure they'd love to hear from you," she says.

"Thank you. It would be good to catch up with them."

What am I getting myself into?

It's been decades since I've seen them. Who knows if they'll be open to answering personal questions. A fire stirs within me. I will search not only for God's truth, but the truth of what happened to those who turned away. If there were, in fact, victims of The Ministry—its teachings or its leaders—someone has to seek justice. At the very least, I have to know what part I may have played in it and try to make amends for the undue judgments I passed on them.

"You know, everybody makes mistakes," Mom says. "We were coming out of deception and just learning how to purge the flesh and walk by the spirit. I had worked hard for years to forgive Victoria's father for leaving me. It's only by God's mercy."

Mimi is twirling the ends of her hair around her fingers. Then she says, "The Lord is showing me we were all in different places on our journey of faith. Kind of like a rotary, or traffic circle, as they call it outside of New England. Anyway, we entered from different roads and then we drove around the center—around these teachings for a while. Some of us stayed a long time and are still driving around it and others exited to other roads. But the traffic circle wasn't the destination, it was only a means of getting from one place in our faith to another. God was at the center of it, but he was also in the cars with us in the Holy Spirit. Some exited, for whatever reason, that's between them and God, but we were all drawn by the Spirit and He is still riding with us now."

A refreshing chill runs through my body.

Lord, what understanding you give to those who seek it!

"I wished I had exited the traffic circle much sooner," Lydia says, "but I do agree that God has always been with me. Thank you for that."

"Yes, amen," Sarah agrees. "God led us away from the traffic circle and helped us find a place where there was more support for our family and activities for the children. I still hold on to some teachings though. Especially those about being separate from sin and being able to minister with the gifts of the spirit. I would love to do more of that, but there isn't much opportunity in the church that we go to now. They're not against it, but they don't encourage it."

"You know," Lydia says. "When we eventually gravitated away from The Ministry, we had books written by a missionary couple to encourage us. I saw the freedom and power women could have in Christ. Then my ex became ill and depended on me to carry the house financially and executively with our five children. The tables had turned, but our relationship wasn't much better. I still question today, was it the man I was involved with or was it The Ministry that was the problem? I don't know."

Even after all the pain, Lydia is cautious not to speak ill of anyone or pass judgment.

"When one of our sons took his own life, that's when I knew I had to get my youngest daughter out of there. We'd been married for almost twenty-five years when I left, but I believed God was with me. If I had been listening a little better, I might have left sooner. After that, it was difficult to trust any man. I didn't see myself getting remarried. It took a lot of work between me and the Lord to soften my heart."

"I'm sure that's only the half of it," I say. "It's quite a testimony to see how God brought you into a healthy relationship, even after you experienced so much pain."

"Yep, you have to move on," Lydia says. "You can bury it, but things will continue to come up, and God will continue to teach you. In fact, one of the most valuable teachings I ever received through The Ministry was about the purging of sin. It was the idea that when repenting, I envision my sin placed on the cross with Jesus and taken to hell with Him in His death and burial, then seeing He left that sin in hell and I am raised up with Jesus in heavenly places at the right hand of God. That's a position of victory! It has helped me to truly purge sin from my past."

Her confidence is contagious.

"Amen!" Mimi says. "Thank you for sharing your story with us. I only knew some of that, and I'm glad that you are still seeking God and being led by your spirit after all these years."

I see God has each person in the church where he wants them.

"Happy to share if it will encourage anyone else," Lydia says. "I have one question though. You said you were led by *your spirit*. Is that the same as the Holy Spirit?"

"Yeah, sort of," Mimi says. "The entire Holy Spirit is too big to live inside of me, so the portion He gave me is my spirit. That's what I call the portion that each of us has received of the Spirit, your spirit and my spirit, all from the same Holy Spirit, just a portion that is unique to each of us and gives us God's wisdom for us as individuals."

"I hadn't heard it put that way. I will give that to the Lord and see what he has to show me," Lydia says.

A new server arrives with the dinner shift and cautiously approaches our table.

"Oh, hi, do you need to clear our plates?" Mom says.

"You were all having such a deep conversation. I didn't want to interrupt."

"Oh, no, go ahead." I smile. "We just haven't seen each other in quite a long time."

"It sounds like you've been through quite a lot." She hasn't introduced herself, but her nametag reads Ana Marie and she's wearing a delicate gold cross around her neck. "Forgive me for overhearing a little, but I'm a single mom raised Catholic. I don't go to church anymore, but I do pray, and what you're saying is so different from anything I've heard. I've always been a little curious about the Holy Spirit."

My spirit nudges me. *Ask her.* I take a breath and without overthinking it, I say, "Would you like to receive the Holy Spirit?"

"If God would give it to me. I'm not sure he would though. I haven't been living a very good life. I try, but it's hard."

"Aw, honey, God doesn't care about that," Mimi says. "He looks at our heart. If you're open and you ask, believing that He's God and He can do what He says He will, then you'll receive it."

"Oh, I believe He can work miracles. My daughter is an example of that. So, what do I need to do?" Ana Marie's eyes are wide and focused. The restaurant is almost clear of patrons for the lull between lunch and dinner.

"Well, it's simply a matter of asking in faith. We can pray with you right now, if you're open to it?" Mimi asks.

She looks around for a few seconds.

I thought of Peter walking on water with Jesus and then looking around at the deep waters. She was close. Would she take the step of faith like many had before? Or would she hesitate and put it off for another day like countless people do?

"Okay. I can let the others take the first few tables." She pulls up a chair from a neighboring table.

Her heart is in the right place.

Mimi nods in my direction.

I invite Ana Marie to place her hands in mine. "When we pray in the name of Jesus Christ and ask God for the gift of the Holy Spirit," I say, "He will deliver it and it's going to require a response from you. That response will be you speaking in a spiritual language. You may have heard it called 'speaking in tongues.' Don't let that scare you, it's just a prayer language. You won't know what you're saying, but that's okay. All you need to do is open your mouth and make sounds. He'll do the rest."

I wait for her acknowledgment, hoping she won't back out.

"I've heard of that, yes. I think my grandmother had it."

"Praise God! All right then, are you ready to pray with me?"

She closes her eyes and takes a deep breath in and exhales, "Yes."

I overhear Mimi speaking words of protection over us so that the enemy would not hinder her receiving.

I pray, "Father, you have reconciled this one to you through your Son Jesus Christ. We ask you now to fill her with your anointing, that she may have your spirit dwelling inside of her. And because she asks, we know she will receive it."

She squeezes my hands.

"Ana Marie," I say, "if you agree, say, 'Lord, fill me with your spirit. I receive it,' and then open your mouth for the Holy Spirit to speak."

She makes sounds in a language unknown to any of us here. They come out as a soft whisper, only a few measures, before opening her eyes.

"I felt my arms tingle," Ana Marie says. "My whole body got warm. I imagined a light pushing away the dark thoughts that I had about myself and about everyone. It just washed over me. Thank you, Jesus!"

I embrace her as if she were my sister, whom I loved. We all rejoice with her. By now, we've drawn the attention of curious staff and customers, but nobody approaches us. God appointed this time for her.

She wipes away tears of joy, relief, and acceptance. Then she tilts her head to the side.

"What's on your heart?" I asked.

"W-what do I do now?"

"You continue to talk to God," I say. "Anywhere, anytime, in your thoughts or out loud, if it's appropriate, and let him teach you. Go to His word in Scripture. You can start by reading 1 Corinthians 14 so that you can learn more about spiritual gifts. Ask Him to help you understand it."

She pulls out a pen and a cocktail napkin from her apron and writes: *Talk to God. Read the Bible. Help me understand.*

"And practice your spiritual language," Mimi says. "Even in the shower, if that's where you are most comfortable. The more you do, the more it will expand and encourage you in your faith. God will give you interpretations and pictures to show you what He wants you to know."

Lord, is there anything else she needs to know?

I say, "Also, see Ephesians 6:10–18 where it talks about the armor of God. You will need this to stand strong through the trials in your life."

She adds to the napkin: *Armor of God, E—* "How do you spell that?"

"Ephesians, E-P-H-E-S-I-A-N-S, you got it. Chapter six, verses ten through eighteen." Her napkin is now full.

"Thank you, thank you so much. I don't know how I could thank you enough."

"Thank God," says Mimi. "You receiving it and continuing to seek God is enough. We are so blessed and overjoyed to meet you today."

Lydia stands to hug her. "I'm glad my story had such a positive impact on you. You remind me of my daughter, Camille. Maybe you could pray that she would be open like this one day."

"Yes, I will be glad to pray for her." Ana Marie clasps her hands gesturing prayer and then asks, "Is there anything more I can get you? Dessert on the house?"

We look around at each other.

Mimi says, "No. We're satisfied, thank you."

And I am satisfied—spiritually, more than anything. Yet my soul stirs from hearing how the women who left The Ministry are still seeking God, and He is meeting their needs. I didn't think that was possible once a person heard the truth and denied it. How can anyone be satisfied apart from the apostle's doctrine?

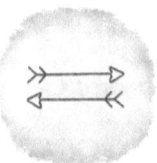

CHAPTER FOURTEEN

DISAGREEMENTS

Mom and I spend time the next day going through old photographs. In her retirement, she's begun organizing boxes of photos into albums. Everything from my grandparents' childhood up through my own. It's beautiful and heartbreaking at the same time—seeing snapshots of loved ones from birth to death.

A collection of moments shows relationships blossom and fade, then new ones take their place. Mom points out the band members and their wives, all from the same church. She turns the page and we jump further back in time to see the same folks are at her wedding shower. I imagine what my young parents were like with their friends and church family. They seemed happy, then it all fell apart.

Will my life be any different?

My "life" hasn't even begun. Yet, I know more about walking by the spirit now than they did back then, so maybe there's hope. Still, being rejected by Adam feels eerily similar to my parents' divorce. I can't dwell on this thought for long. It's too painful.

Instead, I finalize arrangements for this evening when I'll surprise Dad by taking him to dinner with his two old friends and Pete, the teaching elder.

Five of us sit at a round table in a local steakhouse close to Dad's apartment. I wouldn't have guessed Cedric is older than my dad. He'd sprung up to greet us when we arrived and pulled out Dad's chair with youthful energy.

"Do you still play guitar?" Cedric asks before devouring the steak on his fork. They were in the band before Dad joined The Ministry and haven't seen each other since.

Dad sighs and presses the tips of his fingers together to test them for feeling. "No, the neuropathy makes it impossible," he says, then takes a swig off a Long Island Iced Tea.

Dad used to play music by Santana and Jimi Hendrix. He wrote worship songs, with advanced melodies that elude intermediate musicians. Hearing him play was one of the great joys of my childhood. That and his dry humor. I would laugh so hard I'd get the hiccups almost every time.

"Man, you should have seen this guy when we played in our band," Cedric says. "He's on stage wearing an orange V-neck shirt and bell-bottom jeans with brown platform boots and an afro, complete with a wide-toothed comb sticking out of it."

"Nah, no way. Not this guy," Philip says, shaking his head. He's staying for a few days after his mother-in-law's funeral to visit with family.

"It's true. I have the photos to prove it," I say.

"Touché." Philip raises his glass, and we clink iced teas.

Cedric raises his beer, and we look at Pete.

"Hey, no judgment here. I was a dead head before I came to Christ." Peter points to the Led Zeppelin t-shirt he's wearing.

The men laugh and talk, enjoying their pub-style steak and potatoes. Continuing with the seafood theme, I'm having broiled haddock and a side salad.

Dad hasn't seen Cedric since joining The Ministry before I was born. Philip served on the eldership with Dad and Peter while I was growing up. I am taking a risk bringing them all together, but I want to give them a chance to reconcile.

"A band is a special bond. You two must have been close," says Pete.

Dad smiles. "I was kind of wild, as a kid. I had been in a few bands in my early twenties. We even got a couple of songs on the radio before we broke up."

The pride in his voice masks the sense of loss he feels.

"But I was lost," he admits. "After my first marriage didn't pan out, I guess I was searching for meaning and was happy to meet another guitar player in town. We played regularly and got another band together. One day he invited me to church, and since we were friends, I thought, 'Sure, why not.' The pastor was very dynamic."

"I remember that. Pastor Freeman was preaching," Cedric says.

"That's right, you and I were sitting together at Trinity Episcopal Church. The pastor told me all the things I'd been doing. I elbowed you and said, 'What's going on? How does he know what I've been up to?' You just smiled at me. I was mad at first because I thought you talked to the pastor about me, until I realized I hadn't told anyone, not even you. That's when I knew God was real, and He was drawing me to Himself. At the end of the service, they had an altar call, and I went up to receive the Lord. It was tremendous!

"I was stubborn, so I didn't receive the gifts of the Holy Spirit right away, but I studied the Scriptures for several months. I wanted the Holy Spirit, but it was difficult to get past the intellect. One day, I was driving in my car, commuting from the factory where I worked, and praying to God when His presence overwhelmed me and I spoke in tongues for the first time. I was overjoyed! Then He began revealing so much to me. My eyes were wide open to God's truth. I had to pull over so I could embrace what was happening. A few months later, I got water baptized."

"I was so proud of you that day," Cedric says. "It wasn't long until you were ordained."

"Yeah, that's right," Dad says, as if uncovering a childhood toy that was locked away in a dusty box in the attic for years.

Dad explains to the rest of us, "We were serving at Trinity Episcopal church together when it divided over traditions and the role of the manifestations of the spirit. One group kept with tradition and the other followed a charismatic pastor. We agreed more with the charismatic pastor, but rather than put new wine in old wineskins, we went our own way and started a grassroots church called the Church of Plymouth. We met in small groups and around town without a building at first, but when the church grew, and it grew kind of fast, we rented a storefront."

"Those were the days," Cedric recalled. "We weren't very smart about it though. I see now we shouldn't have branched off without the support of the church."

"Maybe," Dad says. "I didn't stay around long because that's about the time I started listening to Rob Peterson's tapes."

"I'd like to know more about this ministry that pulled you away from me all those years ago." Cedric tosses the question to Dad like a ball over the fence to see where it lands.

Dad nods in my direction. "Your grandparents gave the tapes to your mom and me. That's when I started hearing different doctrines." Then he looks back at Cedric. "He was teaching about Mystery Babylon and coming out of the system. I studied it out in the word, and it was all true."

"That's how I felt too, brother," Philip says. "A friend spent a summer at the Grand Canyon studying under Rob. I was so grateful for how he'd helped her, I sent him a sixty-dollar offering. In response, Mr. Peterson asked to come out and talk with me at my kitchen table. I thought it was quite an honor."

"The first time I met Rob," Dad says, "I saw right away the entire team was of one mind and one accord, by the Spirit of God. It was a tremendous time! He was saying things I had recently seen in dreams or discussed with my wife—things nobody told him. I got the sense that I had known him for a long time."

"He knew how to make you feel special all right," Philip scoffs.

"That's right." Dad lifts his chin and puffs out his chest. "After that first meeting, he came back a few more times and established an eldership. They raised me up as pastor, Philip as the teaching elder, Pete and a few others were deacon elders. He was very instructive on how an eldership functions."

"Man, I never understood why you went radio silent." Cedric looks him in the eyes. "We had just appointed you associate pastor of the Church of Plymouth, and then I stopped hearing from you. We tried to build the church, but it wasn't the same without you."

The rest of us are quiet, eyes shifting between the two.

Dad puts his hands up. "I shared the tapes with you, brother, but you weren't interested. So I let you be."

"You know, I believe that two brothers in Christ can disagree about the specifics and still be friends. You didn't seem to think so. It really hurt when you disappeared like that."

Dad's gaze drops, and his face relaxes. When he looked up, their eyes meet.

"I ask your forgiveness, brother. That wasn't my intention at all."

Cedric raises both eyebrows. "Forget about it, man. It was a long time ago. We've all hurt people we loved along the way. What's important is that we know Jesus. He forgave me, and I can forgive you."

"Amen." Philip nods, the tension easing. "It was a unique time. Many people were coming out of traditional churches. It was around that time that the non-denominational movement started. There was a group of people we called 'the wanderers.' They were always looking for the latest and greatest, not settling with a church. Many of them came into fellowship with us and stuck around."

Philip looks at Pete. "Weren't you part of that group?"

Pete puts down his glass of water after taking a sip. "Not quite. My wife went to the New Testament Church down the street for a while. She was very involved until a friend introduced her to Rob's teachings. Church wasn't really my thing. I'd keep tabs on what she was into by watching the television minsters with her."

"It wasn't?" I say.

"Nah, I was a rebel in the 1970s. Mostly agnostic about God. I grew up going to church, but it meant nothing to me. No one explained it. Mimi invited me to a gathering when Rob was in town. When I finally met him, I saw life in what he preached, something I could sink my teeth into. I kept attending until I received the Holy Spirit. My eyes opened; I knew I could receive the truth. I finally understood the passion that I had seen in others, and it became personal to me."

"What you said about sinking your teeth into it and receiving truth and life, I can relate to that," Philip says. "I learned things during that time that were foundational to my faith."

"Yep, I just knew it was true." Pete continued, "It wasn't mental, it wasn't emotional. It must have been by the Holy Spirit. For example, when I heard him say, 'We live by faith and not by sight,' there was no thinking about it."

"No, you can't think about it," Dad says. "It has to be received by faith. Thinking would use your own understanding instead of God's understanding, through Christ, by the Holy Spirit."

Dad is precise about language. Pete and I are used to this.

Pete continues, "Growing up as an army brat, I didn't have friends. We moved every three years. The Ministry really opened me up to appreciate having people at my house for gatherings, Lord's suppers, and jubilees. I was done moving around. That's why we put down roots and stayed in the same house for over forty years."

"You and Mimi are a real blessing," Dad says.

Cedric, listening as an outsider, says, "It sounds like you were a tight-knit group. I've experienced some great fellowship in church over the years, so I know how important that can be."

"I'm sure you have," Dad says, "but our fellowship wasn't really with one another. It was with Christ. He is the only one we are to have a relationship with or else we're making another person our source."

Here he goes. He just *has* to correct everyone.

Cedric wipes his mouth with his napkin. "I was only saying I appreciate good Christian friendship."

"You know, The Ministry had a way of drawing us in, but it also isolated us from the rest of the church," Philip says.

Wide-eyed Cedric gives a knowing nod.

The server approaches our table. "How is everything?"

"Good," says Dad. "I'll have another Long Island iced tea."

"Dad, are you sure?" I ask, concerned about his health.

He shakes off my question as absurd. I resign. Dad is a large man who's never had a problem handling his liquor. Still, I don't like it. I look at his cane hooked on the table's edge. If diabetes and congestive heart failure weren't enough to kill him, the drinking might.

The server leaves to fulfill his order.

Pete clears his throat. "You know, it was more than the fellowship. I remember when I learned how to be led by the Spirit, whether to do something or go somewhere. Whenever Mimi and I would get a word of prophecy to go on a trip, it was always the best trip. I also experienced the opposite when I didn't give an issue to the Lord and get his wisdom.

"We were visiting family in Florida once, and we were low on money. On our way back, driving up the East Coast, we had nothing for tolls or gas. I said, 'Lord, what do I do?' and I received, 'Search the van.' So I did and found enough change to pay for both. We had just what we needed with eight cents left when we got home."

"God provides," I say, raising my glass. "How did you become an elder?"

"After attending for a few years, someone received that I should be an elder, not sure who. I thought, 'Why me?'"

"Do you know why now?" I say.

"No."

Pete meets all the qualifications set forth by the Apostle Paul in his letter to Timothy. An elder should be "beyond reproach, the husband of one wife, sober-minded, self-controlled, respectable, hospitable, able to teach, not a drunkard, not violent but gentle, not quarrelsome, not a lover of money." Most elders I know are still working on meeting those standards.

The waitress places Dad's drink in front of him and removes the empty glass.

Dad nods at the waitress and then looks at me. "You were probably too young to remember our trip to Hawaii."

"Oh, I remember! My best childhood memories were from that trip."

"It was in the mid-'80s, what were you, three?"

"Four," I say.

"Close enough. The apostolic team invited us to visit The Ministry Center on the island of Oahu, where Rob was living. A man I was ministering to gave us the money for the trip. That five thousand dollars was a manifestation of provision from the Lord. We stayed for three weeks, and he taught concerning all aspects of life. It was a great time. So powerful! He showed us how to raise a daughter. He taught we were sons of God and had the power of life and death. Tremendous!"

Having power over life and death isn't new to me, but hearing him boast about the instruction he received for raising a daughter? Shortly after returning from that trip, he divorced my mom. I've since forgiven him for leaving us, but let's be honest, Mom raised me. Any struggles I had with self-esteem and relationships all stemmed from him leaving us. I wring my hands.

Philip raises a finger and opens his mouth to say something.

"Then there were the miracles," Dad says as Philip puts his hand down. "Rob became ill while staying with an elder's family, like scarlet fever or something, and it seemed like he had died. I got a call from the elder hosting him and we ministered, taking authority over the simple thinking of the mind. I spoke forth resurrection life, and he woke up! We tried to share it with people after that, but not everyone believed. It was so powerful, we had to share it!"

"Did any of you witness that?" I ask.

Pete and Philip shake their heads.

"No, it was just the word of the elder and his wife who were hosting him. They left The Ministry not long after," Peter says.

Curious.

The only elder to have seen Rob raised from the dead was the first to leave. I would love to believe that God raised an apostle from the dead through my dad's words. I'm confident that God still does that today, but the lack of witnesses doesn't help his case.

Philip finally speaks up. "Brother Sam, I'm glad you had an enjoyable time in Hawaii, but we weren't all so fortunate to have our visit work out as well as yours. I took a similar trip with another elder at our own expense to meet with Rob. I took an enormous risk leaving home. It was January, and a blizzard hit Cape Cod with four feet of snow. My wife was stuck with our young children and had no power. We were there for four days, and Rob was sick the entire time. His daughter said he couldn't stand any noise, so we could only whisper. We didn't see him except for a short meeting the day we were leaving. But I'll tell you, that was the most fear-filled house I had ever been in."

The mood around the table shifts. Dad shakes his head at Philip as if he'd spoken against the Lord Jesus Christ.

Philip leans into it. "There was another time too. A few years later, when Rob and his team moved to Arizona. I traveled there to The Ministry Center because my wife and I were interested in homeschooling our children, and we wanted more information about their program. They wouldn't send us the curriculum and said we had to come see how it worked. So we were there to see the homeschool buildings, but they weren't ready to share them with us. I don't know why they were so secretive about it. We traveled all that way to see nothing."

"Really?" Peter sits up tall. "That would have bothered me too."

Dad shifts in his chair. "I never experienced that. As far as I knew, Rob was welcoming and nobody was hiding anything. It must have been a misunderstanding."

Cedric taps his fingers on the table, eyes shifting from Philip to Dad and back during their exchange.

"Sam, I was clear about why I was there. They just didn't want to bring me in close. That's the difference between you and me. Rob didn't see me as someone he could shape. I had a decent childhood and didn't harbor unresolved father issues. Most of the elders who formed a bond with Rob had experienced abuse or abandonment from their fathers. He was a welcome surrogate and was all too happy to step into that role. But instead of helping them grow up into Christ and move beyond that trauma, he kept them dependent on him."

Dad's nostrils flare as his dark complexion turns brick red. "Rob was looking for those who would submit themselves to God and Christ. Any rebellion would cut off the flow of the Spirit to them and he wouldn't be able to minister."

"Oh, I'm aware of The Ministry's stance on rebellion, but I respectfully disagree."

Dad flips his palms up in surrender. "Fine, that's your prerogative."

Pete looks sidelong at Cedric, who leans back in his chair to distance himself from the argument.

Philip doesn't stop. "That term *rebellion* was thrown around too much. The elders first accused my wife of being in rebellion when she was having frequent migraines and couldn't attend every gathering. They said I should've forced her. What none of us knew back then is she was experiencing symptoms of fibromyalgia, a chronic illness. I should have defended her, but I was cowardly."

Pete offers a sincere apology. "Brother, I ask your forgiveness. My wife experiences frequent migraines and has missed plenty of gatherings, but she has the freedom to receive from God whether to attend. I would never accuse her of being in rebellion for that now, but back then, I was going right along with it."

"I appreciate that, Peter. Unfortunately, that wasn't the extent of the hurt." Philip turns to Dad. "If you'll hear me, I'd like to share some things."

Philip struck a deep chord. One I hadn't identified until now, but everything he is saying rings true. It seems he speaks about the wrongs because he cares for these men. I can see how the isolation took its toll on Dad. I imagine Philip has been holding onto this for years, perhaps waiting for the right time.

Will Dad finally hear him out?

Dad's face is less ruddy now. He leans forward with his elbows on the table. He might view Philip as a detractor intending to stir up doubt and judgment.

"Dad, hear him out, please."

Dad shakes his head, ignoring me. "That's not how I remember it. You had it in your heart that you didn't need to submit to an eldership. We were trying to function as God showed through the apostle that He gave us, but you didn't honor him the way we did."

"I honored God," Philip declares.

All eyes are on us. A chill runs up my spine for fear that we are misrepresenting God and his church by arguing in public.

"Our honor was unto God and Christ, not to the man. Rob always said, 'Don't take my word for it. Give it to your spirit and see if it is true for you.' When I gave it to my spirit, everything that he preached, I received it was true for me and willed to do it."

I glance at Dad sideways. *Really?* I've heard a lot of preaching but have seen little action. I love him very much and will be eternally grateful for all I've learned from him about the Bible and how to walk by my spirit. He's a skilled preacher, and people trust him. Still, none of my growth came from watching his actions. I had to listen intently to what he said if I were to benefit. He has even told me, 'Don't pay attention to my attitude, listen to my words.' Ignoring tone and inflection and only listening to words is confusing.

"Calm down, brother, please." Philip makes a downward pressing motion with his hands, as if to push down the escalating tension. "I mean no disrespect, but just as you have received by your spirit about the word, I also gave it to God and received what I was to do with the teachings. He had many wise things to say, but it needed to be checked with the Scriptures. His understanding of submission, no matter how he phrased it as honoring God, it was all done in an authoritarian context."

Cedric shifts in his chair and looks around, then raises his hand, making a sign to the waitress to deliver the check.

"Well, you can think that all you want"—Dad waves his hand dismissively—"but the man did not control or rule me, nor did I control anyone else. Everybody has a sovereign will, and it would be against God to control them."

A plate crashes to the ground in the kitchen and we all sit up with a start, except Philip.

"I agree, but—"

Pete leans forward, putting a hand up to each of them. "Why don't we all settle down? There's no need to get heated over this matter."

"I'm not heated!" Dad slams his drink on the table.

"Regardless, we're getting loud and people are staring," Pete says.

"Let them." Dad looks around then back at Philip pointing his finger in the air toward the heavens. "They might learn something when they hear the truth!"

Pulling out his wallet, Philip puts a twenty-dollar bill on the table. "I'm sorry, Victoria. God bless you, brothers." And he walks out of the restaurant.

CHAPTER FIFTEEN

NURTURE

The next day, after brunch and shopping with Mom, I borrow her car to meet up with both Lydia's and Sarah's sons for happy hour. It's a wonder I caught them before I headed home to Arizona. We're at an Irish-style pub where Jack tends bar. It happens to be where he and Ethan reconnected a few years back.

"Ethan was my best friend until he turned into a dick," Jack tells me.

"Hey, man, I was the best you could do."

I laugh with them, sitting on the stool next to Ethan.

Philip and Sarah's son, Ethan, looks like he just stepped off a yacht, sporting a white polo, chinos, and boat shoes. He sits in stark contrast to Lydia's son, Jack, a husky six-foot-three man with a shaven head and pale skin. He drove trucks for eighteen years, then took up bartending to be closer to his wife and two-year-old daughter.

"What happened between you two?" I say.

Jack wipes the inside of a highball glass and nods toward Ethan, who turns to me.

"Honestly, it's like he said. After graduating high school, I studied politics and worked for a local politician on his campaign. I was arrogant and selfish, blinded by the success of those around me and the name I was making for myself in those circles. Too young to appreciate genuine success, and yet I'd seen too much not to know better. I lost friends. My first marriage ended because of it."

It's hard for me to comprehend why others growing up in The Ministry didn't stick with it, or at least remain Christians. I hope talking to these two will shed some light on that.

"Did homeschooling have anything to do with that?" I say.

"Nah, if anything, it's how I knew better."

"So you didn't feel restricted or out of touch?" Having gone to public school, it was always clear to me that my beliefs were different than others'.

"Not really. My parents were forthcoming about the way the world worked. Sure, everything centered on the Bible and that worldview, but they didn't force me to believe it. They just gave me the option so I could decide."

"Option?" Jack says, catching bits of our conversation as he tends to a few regulars. "We didn't have options, me and my siblings. Everything we learned tied back to God. I didn't think much about it." He walks over to us and puts his hand on the counter. "For example, history focused on how the beliefs of the founding fathers influenced the growth of America. As I got older, maybe ten or twelve, I wondered if there were more sides to these stories."

I shake my head. "There's always more than one side."

"Oh, there are multiple sides." He snaps back, eyes narrowed. "But I had no choice. I only heard the one side."

"Did you *choose* to believe in God?" I ask, knowing he professed faith as a child.

"No, not at all. They forced it on me. I didn't see it that way until later, when I realized there were other points of view to consider. The world only worked one way in our house, and my father was the high ruler of it all. If he said 'jump,' we said 'how high' or we got the belt. It was his way or the highway. My sister, Lilly, chose the highway several times. She didn't stay past thirteen, ended up living with foster parents."

Memories of his father taking off his belt in anger flash in my mind, and I groan. "I remember your house being strict."

"Oh, you don't know the half of it." He leans in to whisper, "The son of a bitch was the biggest hypocrite I'd ever met." Jack points at Ethan. "He knows what I'm talking about."

Ethan frowns and nods his head, then drinks his Blue Moon lager.

I shift on my stool. "Why do you say that?"

Jack looks around then leans over the bar toward me. "My father was not a kind man. This one time, he found mags under my mattress—I was a teenager and I couldn't talk about my feelings, so I had to find out somehow what was going on. Anyway, he berated me, called me a piece of crap for looking at porn, and said I was going to hell. I was used to hearing that. But here's the kicker. We had one computer in the house that we all shared. The next day, my younger brother, who knew a thing or two about computers, found that someone had been on the internet looking at porn in the middle of the night. That could only be my father. A damned hypocrite! Did you know he was in jail twice for attempted rape?"

My heart sinks, a sex offender welcomed into the ranks of church leadership. "No. I knew he served time prior to being saved, but I didn't know what for." Surely, the elders thought he was a changed man. Sadly, his corruption gave all of his children a reason to hate God.

Jack wipes his hand over his face and strokes his beard. "It hurt me deeply then and now. I cut him out of my life before he died. I think my younger siblings took more emotional abuse than I did, and I don't have any proof to back this up"—he waves his finger—"but I suspect there was also physical abuse."

A pit forms in my stomach.

"As a child"—he shakes his head—"I would hear noises coming from another bedroom at night. It seemed strange, but I had no experience or frame of reference to conceive of what may be happening. Only as an adult, once the damage had been done, could I imagine the worst."

I cringe. Jack's father came back to The Ministry with his new wife a few years ago. Once an elder, always an elder. That's their policy. According to Scripture, "The gifts and callings of God are without repentance." If God called him to ministry, who was anyone to say he shouldn't do it? He was repentant for his past and hoped to reconcile with his children but eventually became frustrated that the local body was so small and he had little authority over its operation. He left for the last time and died of a stroke less than a year later.

"My siblings and I," Jack says, "were told that the person who abused us was God's representative of love. What kind of love punishes, threatens, demeans, silences, and uses the vulnerable for pleasure? If God were real, then he would have protected my sister and brothers. Where was He when they were pinned down, violated by their own father? He must not exist. Even if He did, why would I worship a being that allowed that to happen?"

He looks around to see if any customers need him. They don't.

"You know what happened to my younger brother."

Alex was nineteen, a whiz at computers. He had opportunities, but the drugs held him back. Tragically, when the drugs wore him down, he took his life with a gun.

"I was so angry. Not at my brother, but at my father," Jack says.

I sit for a minute, honoring Alex's memory. I remember him as a little blond-haired boy wearing a striped shirt and corduroy pants. He was always picking his nose and getting into trouble. Although, it was easy to get into trouble at their house.

"I'm sorry I wasn't there for you, man," Ethan says.

"Yeah, well. We all had our own lives to live." He stands up straight, then adds. "It absolutely crushed my sister though."

For a moment, I feel a bit of the tension that once separated the two men.

"Speaking of Lilly," says Ethan. "I remember this one time when we were kids and you all were at our house for a church meeting. Strange people of all kinds walked through that door in need of prayer, and frankly, psychological care. Anyway, there was a half wall separating the room where the adults gathered from where the children were playing so we could hear everything. Someone was preaching about each person having something to give. Lilly drew a picture, I'm not sure of what, but she seemed pleased with it and then started cutting it into pieces. I said, 'What are you doing that for?' and she just gave me a look like 'None of your business.' Then she picked up all the pieces and brought it into the gathering, proceeding to hand them out to each of the adults. She didn't know I was watching. I'm not sure why I told you that. Just a silly thing I remember, I guess."

"Huh. I don't remember that," Jack says. A patron flags him over. "Be right back."

I turn my body to face Ethan. "It's interesting that stuck out in your memory."

Maybe not." He shrugs. "I have an exceptional memory. It's a blessing and a curse, depending on the situation."

"Do you believe in God now?" I say.

"Oh, yes. Not in the traditional sense of going to church every weekend, but he's always been with me."

"How did you come to that decision?" I say.

He stares into the bottom of his beer glass for a moment. "It kind of happened over time." Then looks at me. "I'd like to tell you about one experience that stands out to me, and it occurred around the time I stopped seeing so many strange people come to our house each week."

"What happened?" I say, then sip my hard cider. Jack is back within earshot mixing someone's drink.

Ethan turns his body to face me, sitting taller than before while resting his left elbow on the bar.

"I started playing baseball in a town league when I was about twelve years old." He places his right hand at the approximate height of a twelve-year-old. "Now this great American pastime has rules, guidelines, positions of authority, roles to be played. It's the structure that provides certainty and measures a player's value. If it weren't for this structure with penalties and rewards, we wouldn't recognize success and where to improve."

I nod. My eyes, fixed on him as he gestures.

"There was one day, I remember it clearly, our team was playing one of the toughest in the league, and by some miracle—not because of my skills—we were tied. Most of my teammates had been playing since tee-ball, so I had some catching up to do." He rolls his eyes.

I smile and shrug.

"I stepped up to the plate reluctantly. My past few hits hadn't gone so well. My mother was in the stands, and my father had just arrived. This time, I knew I wanted to show them something special. It was rare to see my father at a game because ministry was always the priority." He looks away. "Somehow, other people's problems always came before our family."

I tilt my head.

He turns back to me. "I wasn't opposed to my father's work; I just didn't understand why other people's well-being was more important than his own son's. We'd had a tough year, with my mom's health issues and my sister getting bullied at school. I felt the weight of my family on my shoulders." He slumps, looking at the floor.

"I'm sorry," I say.

He looks at me, slaps his hands on his thighs and straightens up. "Anyway, baseball was my outlet and my strongest connection to the outside world. Since joining public school earlier that year, I had made no friends aside from my teammates. Even then"—he flips his palm up—"'friend' may overstate those relationships. They were friendly so long as we had a game to win, but my teammates never invited me to hang out outside of practice and the occasional overnight away game."

"I've been there." I nod. "What happened next?"

"The next swing of the bat would likely determine the outcome of the game and my future standing with my team. If I didn't do well, I felt it would be best for everyone if I didn't sign up for next season." He raises his eyebrows. "It would also justify my dad in missing most of my games, and most of all, I felt it would disappoint my mom, who tried so hard to give me the space to practice, even though she needed me more often than she would care to admit. I needed this hit. I needed my team to appreciate me. I thought I needed to make my parents proud so my father would see what he'd been missing. Most of all, I needed this hit to prove to myself that I could succeed in something my parents didn't teach me."

He reaches for his glass then remembers it's empty. We both look down the bar to see Jack is still tending to a customer.

Ethan continues, "I'd been trying so hard all season with minor improvement. The chances of scoring runs on one hit alone were slim, no matter how much I wanted it. So I decided I needed some help. I stared at the bat for a moment to pray while adjusting my sweaty hands. 'God, help me out here,' I said."

"Did He?" I ask.

"I looked at the pitcher, then the ball, locked on to it with intense focus, and in an instant, I heard the crack of the bat as the ball flew higher and higher, farther and farther . . . Could it be? 'No time to think, just run,' I told myself. I was running and saw out of the corner of my eye the ball cleared the outfield. It was a home run! I didn't want to take any chances, so I ran hard. I knew in that moment it wasn't my power alone, but I had more to stand on than I realized. Jesus was the ultimate batter, and all I had to do was run the bases—keep going and don't look back until I reached home base.

"So that's what I did," Ethan concludes.

"Wow, Ethan, that's quite a story!" I feel great about being here with him. I don't know what is more energizing: reconnecting with a long-lost friend or my relief that Ethan still has faith in God.

"Yep. I went to college on a baseball scholarship and studied government and public administration. The order in government attracted me, and I wanted to make a difference in my community. After an internship with a senator, I worked on a campaign for a local official."

Jack comes back around. "And that's when he turned into a major—"

Ethan raises his hands in surrender. "Okay, okay. I think she gets it."

"I still think religion is a cover," Jack says, "so awful men can demand respect and have control. Sure, some preach good values. But I can walk into a Catholic Church and get the same thing; those are just American values. Respect your wife, love your children, don't steal, do unto others . . . you know, the Golden Rule."

Ethan excuses himself to use the restroom.

"Is that how you live your life, the Golden Rule?" I say.

Jack looks down at the counter and starts cleaning it. "You probably heard some things about me. Back in the mid-2000s, I hurt my back and my knee. I got some painkillers prescribed by a doctor and didn't come off them when I should have. So that progressed and got worse until I lost my job. Then I dabbled with heroin and that got ahold of me. Eventually, that put me in a position where I felt desperate enough that I actually robbed banks . . . and I got caught for that."

He stops cleaning and makes eye contact with me.

"I was in jail for thirteen months awaiting trial. I went to court to take a plea deal, and the judge saw I had no prior record, nothing, not an arrest, not anything. She realized maybe I was a decent guy who screwed up terribly. She gave me a chance. So she let me walk that day with three years' probation. One stipulation of probation was that I had to go to regular NA or AA meetings for those three years. Now I don't know if you've ever been to one of those meetings—"

"I have, actually." I thought of the times I colored in the kids' room of the Kingdom Hall of Jehovah's Witnesses while my mom attended Tuesday night Al-Anon meetings to cope with my stepfather's addiction. They thought I couldn't hear what was going on, but I always heard.

"So you've probably seen when everyone goes around the room saying their name and admitting their addiction." He places his hand on his chest and acts out, "Hi, I'm Jack, and I'm an addict."

He explains, talking with his hands, "They do that because if you look at the large numbers, alcoholics need to admit to themselves every day that they're an addict and that's part of what helps them stay sober or stay clean."

He steps back and whips the dishcloth against the bar.

"I never bought into that. They think they need a higher power to stay sober, but for me, the higher power was the thing that was stronger than me—the heroine. I'd beaten that. I chose to stay clean. When you're detoxing, there comes a point where you feel so terrible, your body is telling you every second that you have to have it. If you haven't changed your mind…well, that's why people relapse." Jack rinses and squeezes his dishcloth at the sink.

"So, in not declaring that you were an addict, you weren't giving that power to the drugs?"

"Exactly. I said all that to bring it back to the religious side of it. If that's what people need to live their life well, to act as decent people, then fine, go for it. I'm fine with that. It doesn't affect me. I just don't see a place for it in my life."

Part of what he said resonates with me. "That sounds like some people in the church that I've often heard declaring that they are sinners. Some churches really double down on the fact that we're sinners saved by grace. Personally, I do still believe in God, but I believe it was the grace of God that brought me out of sin and, therefore, I am no longer a sinner. To declare that I am what I once was doesn't let me progress. It holds me back. God gave me a sovereign will and the will to choose, and if I am going to act lovingly and righteously or not is entirely my choice. He won't make me do any of that."

"Make you do what?" Ethan strolls back to us and reclaims his bar stool.

"Sin or not sin," I say.

"Yeah," Jack says. "If you make the choice not to act with love and then say, 'Oh well, I'm a sinner.' No, you made the choice not to. That's on you."

"Right, you're responsible for your actions," I say. "It sounds like you experienced a life where your father used religion as justification for his actions, but he totally missed the point that it was supposed to make him a good father, a loving person, and someone who felt responsible enough for his actions to change them."

He nods, and an older gentleman takes a seat at the bar close to us. Jack excuses himself.

I look at Ethan. "So, what turned you around?"

He touches his chin. "I'd say it was when my grandmother got sick and couldn't remember us anymore. I really took an inward look at myself and all the time I missed out on being away from her and my family. Since then, I reconnected with God. I'm now remarried and my daughter was born earlier this year." He shows me photos on his phone.

"Aw, I saw those rosy little cheeks at the funeral. What a blessing!"

"There's nothing like bringing a life into the world to help you refocus on what matters. I always knew God was real, but I didn't always relate to him as part of my life. Church has never felt like a requirement because my relationship with God is personal and he's with me anywhere, but it's good for when people want community."

"I suppose community becomes more important when you have a family," I say.

Ethan raises his glass. "To family."

Jack returns and gives a nod of approval.

"To family," I say as I clink my glass with Ethan's.

Jack steps back and announces, "Last call for happy hour!" The handful of people in the lounge look up for a moment.

That's when I remember I promised Mom I'd be home for dinner.

CHAPTER SIXTEEN

QUESTIONING

As I approach the glass door to exit the pub, Philip walks up and opens it for me.

I step back. "Where did you come from?"

"Good evening to you, too," he says.

"Ah, sorry, I was in my own world." I walk through the door, and he follows.

"It's all right. I took you off guard. I'm just here picking up a pizza. Sarah and I are heading home tomorrow, but I'm glad I ran into you."

"Oh yeah?"

"I want to apologize for walking out on your dad the other day."

"Thank you," I say.

"If I could just explain what happened all those years ago."

I stop and look at him. Part of me wants to know everything, but another part doesn't want what I hear to taint my view of The Ministry.

"You see, it wasn't just financial. That was only part of it."

"What was it then?" I'll hear him out. Besides, I'm sure the elders have corrected it by now.

"It was very demanding. The fellowship we enjoyed with your parents and others was the best part, but for the sake of my family, we couldn't stick around."

He motions toward gray, weathered picnic benches on the outdoor patio, complete with a walk-up counter used for serving ice creams on hot summer days. This may be my only chance to hear him out, so I sit with him.

"There were three stories that Rob always told. I reference them now because I think they had a powerful impact on his later ministry. Not all of what he preached was tainted. At the beginning, he was really teaching the Bible. I said before that I learned some very foundational things from him that are still true today. There were many things others preached as well and Scripture supported. Still, the Lord showed me a few areas to be cautious about. They were apparent in three stories he told."

"Which ones?" I'm sure I've heard them all.

"The first story was about a traumatic event he experienced as a young child. He lost both his parents to a car crash and lived with his grandparents. At the age of four, as he told it, he walked into the garage to find his grandfather had hung himself. That is a very traumatic event to happen to a child. It must have affected his outlook on life. His grandmother gave him up for adoption after that. He didn't have the best relationship with his adoptive parents. Then he was sick for most of his childhood, so he spent a long time in isolation."

"It was a real tragedy," I say. "But, he used that time in isolation to pray and learn the Scriptures."

"That may be, but it also didn't allow him to have the natural childhood interactions that would lend to developing emotional intelligence, healthy relationships, and empathy."

"I suppose not," I say.

"The second story was about submission. He would tell the story of a woman who had an offer to sell a portion of her business."

"I'm familiar with this one too," I say.

"Okay. So you remember she wasn't sure what to do, so after praying about it, she talked with the elders and they said she should talk with her husband?" Philip says.

"Yes, but he was an alcoholic, and she didn't think he could give her an accurate word," I say.

"In Rob's words," Philip says, "her husband was a drunk, and he was passed out on the couch after a drinking binge. She needed an answer right away, and so she agreed to trust God and submit the issue to him. As the story goes, she shook him awake, asked him if she should sell or not, and in a moment of clarity, he said 'Don't sell.' Then he passed out again. She trusted God through her head, which was her husband, and didn't sell. It turned out that there was some clause in the contract that would have left her high and dry if she had taken the deal."

I nod. "Rob used that story to illustrate how submission works despite an unfit headship. He always said the answer we received from God through our headship would be determined by the condition of our heart unto God and whether we were truly submitting to God or to man."

"Yeah, but it wasn't foolproof," Philip says. "There's one more."

"Okay." I'm not sure where he's going with this, but I hope he gets to the point soon.

"In the third story, he shared a technique he used while working as a salesman. I don't remember what he was selling . . . vacuums or something. But somehow he related the sales tactics to a spiritual principle. He would tell us how he'd go door-to-door in the 1950s and sell to housewives. Rob thought it was great selling to women. He would start by complimenting them before asking if he could show them a few products that he had, promising there was no obligation to buy. Once they invited him into their homes, the first thing he would do was ask for a glass of water. Why? You might think, because Missouri summers are hot. They are, but that's not the reason he highlighted. He said, 'Once I got her in the mindset of serving me, I could sell her anything I want.'"

I furrow my brows.

Philip throws his hands up. "Right? It was so telling about how he saw women and what a master of manipulation he was. You know he used to work for a politician in Washington, DC?"

"Yes, he mentioned it a few times to tell us how corrupt it was and to draw a contrast from the life he left behind."

"Well, my first thought was, that's where you learned to manipulate."

"That and sales." I follow his logic, but that doesn't mean the apostle was manipulating *us*.

"You got it. And that's what he did to us. When he came to Massachusetts, he looked for the most influential men in the area. He stroked our egos, like when he sat at my kitchen table, and he asked us to serve him. Then he owned us."

I say in Rob's defense, "He was a completely different man before becoming a minister. He would often include stories from his past to illustrate the devil's schemes, or his ability to overcome them by faith. Like the one about him quitting drinking."

Philip waves off my comment. "I don't think I heard that one."

I tell him anyway. Rob claimed he was an X-factor alcoholic, which, according to him, meant his body was so dependent that it needed alcohol to survive. God was training him to be an apostle, so he committed to stop drinking. After being dry for a while, he walked by a bar and heard the Holy Spirit tell him to enter. He thought, 'No, I can't do that. I've been sober. If I have one drink, it could kill me.' But he was sure that it was God, so he obeyed. He ordered a drink, and the smell was repulsive to him. That was odd, because he had always desired the smell of alcohol. The Lord said to drink. He drank and nearly gagged. It was so repulsive that from that day on, he never desired another sip. He was cured."

Philip says, "And that was his testimony of how God leads people out of temptation, by leading them into it?"

"Yes," I say. "He related it to the Scripture about Simon Peter and his vision on the rooftop. When God showed him all the unclean animals gathered on a sheet and he told him to rise, kill, and eat. Simon said, 'Not so, Lord,' and God's response was 'Do not call unclean that which I have made clean.' So, if a saint is addicted to cigarettes or something, they need to ask for deliverance and then each time they are presented with the temptation, they should ask God if it is wisdom to partake. It may be wisdom each time until one day they receive no, and eventually, they are free of that temptation."

"Interesting. And who has that worked for?" Philip says.

"Well, I know a few people who smoke and who intended to manifest their deliverance that way . . . but I can't say if any of them were successful."

"Do you know the context of that Scripture?" he asks.

I nod. "God was preparing Simon Peter to receive Saul, a gentile, into his home. Simon Peter would miraculously restore Saul's sight so that he would believe. Then Saul, who God renamed Paul, preached the gospel to the world."

"Right," he says. "It was the moment God revealed he was opening up His Kingdom to non-Jews. It had nothing to do with overcoming a fleshly habit and everything to do with removing the barriers God previously set for their protection so they could bring the gospel and God's love to the world."

When he put it like that, I realize Rob may not have selected the best Scripture to support his illustration.

Philip brings up the financial issue again, repeating much of the same things he did yesterday. It hit close to home for him as former treasurer, responsible for asking the saints to stand in faith agreement with the elders for the funds to send the apostolic team on outreaches, keep the lights on, and providing for their daily needs.

"So, you see, it was a large burden put on the saints," he concludes.

"I can see how it felt like asking for money," I say. "But that's only because people weren't giving it to their spirit to prophesy what their action of faith should be."

"You sound like the elders," he says.

I take it as a compliment, though I don't think he meant it that way. I was a helper to them for a long time.

He says, "But I had no updates to share about those outreaches, and there was no breathing room. It was one request after another. Then there was your dad, who barely had enough to eat, never mind pay his bills. Yet, he was the one doing all the local preaching and providing pastoral care for the saints."

I sigh, agreeing that the elders didn't manage it well.

"Rob invited your dad and I on another trip to Hawaii, but the funds didn't manifest, so I put up $1,800 on my credit card for his flight. The eldership promised to pay me back, and after a year of bringing it up, I finally dropped it. Even though I'd been paying interest, I didn't want to hold the saints responsible. It was always the single women who gave the most. I was concerned about their financial futures."

"Really? I thought it was just me," I say. "I paid for several airline tickets but always had faith that God would return my money."

"God does promise he will provide for those who give generously to the poor. That's in Deuteronomy 15:10 and Psalm 112:9. But to the ministry, God only required ten percent, that's what tithe means."

"What about the early church? They pooled all of their resources for the good of the community," I say.

"Think about what that time in history must have been like," Philip says. "Many alive had seen Jesus and witnessed miracles. Freshly endowed with the Holy Spirit, and living as refugees, they were in a special situation. The Ministry was not that kind of situation. We weren't living in a community in tents. We all had our own separate lives to live."

The outdoor order window slides open, and an employee sticks their head out. "Philip!" they call out.

"That's my pizza," he says. They motion for him to enter by the front door.

Maybe Philip is right.

We were business owners and service workers alike, taking part in a modern economy. How would we know if it was the Holy Spirit or men manipulating us into giving more than God requires? The more I try to make sense of what occurred, the less sense it makes. I was always diligent to ask God when and how much to give and trusted him for the return. In turn, I had sufficient provision for what His Spirit led me to do.

Considering others' experiences, I can't make sense of what happened, nor can I dismiss it as foolishness. Something else is at play, and I want to understand it now more than ever.

Philip returns with a steaming-hot large pizza.

I stand up to say goodbye.

"I know what they said about me when I left," he says. "That I was in rebellion and couldn't accept the Principle of Submission. I have prayed long and hard about that and received assurance that my heart is right with God."

"That's a blessing to hear," I say, impressed that Philip has maintained his relationship with God apart from The Ministry.

Maybe he hasn't been in rebellion.

"In the late eighties," he adds, "I believe Rob became mentally ill."

That's quite a claim.

I consider defending the apostle, again, but choose to remain curious. "Is that what made you leave?"

He chuckles at my directness. "It was many things but mostly for my family. Also, I looked around at the shrinking numbers, I mean, it was probably less than five families and a few singles at that point. I thought to myself, 'If this is an anointed ministry of God, why didn't more people respond? Wouldn't God draw people to it?'"

"I'd often thought the same thing," I say. "Every time I mentioned it, I was told not to look at the numbers. That is how the world measures success, but we are to trust God that He is doing a deeper work in us."

"If that were the case, why does the Bible record how many were added to the church daily when the apostles preached?"

I don't have an answer.

"Sarah and I wrote a letter to the eldership declaring my resignation. Their response was strange. They told me to show up about thirty minutes late to a regularly scheduled elders' meeting. I wasn't sure what I was walking into, but I thought it was odd, so I prayed about it before going and received to just listen. I didn't want to argue about any of my reasons for leaving. After I arrived, Rob began questioning me. Sitting there, I heard in the Spirit, 'If you open your mouth, he's going to eat you alive.' Every question was a setup. So I kept silent."

His pizza might get cold, but I'm invested in this now.

"What was it like for you to give up that position?" I ask. Ever since the apostle's passing, I had been seeking what to do with my position in The Ministry.

"Leaving was uncomfortable but rewarding. About a year later, I was still working through the bitterness in my heart when a guy gave me a check that was the exact amount I paid for the Hawaii trip. That's when I knew God was taking care of me and I could let the bitterness go. Sarah and I have learned so much since then about the Bible and where our beliefs misaligned. She's had a lot of health problems, but we are blessed to be living a comfortable lifestyle as empty nesters with four grown children and a few grandchildren now."

"Speaking of your wife," I say, "you've got to get that hot pizza back to her."

He places his free hand on my shoulder. "Victoria, I'm glad we met here. I didn't plan on sharing all of that, but I think God wanted you to hear it. Take care of yourself. And you have my number if you need anything."

As we go our separate ways, I feel he is someone I can trust, even if he didn't trust the apostle.

I text my mom that I'm running late, and I stop at the town park near her house, where I spent many days of my youth. There is a chill in the air and clouds are rolling in like it might rain. I take my chances, walking the familiar gravel pathway to a small footbridge overlooking the old stone shovel mill.

My mother called it her thinking bridge. As a girl, she would run here and sit for a while when she needed to escape the arguing in her house just up the street. The arguing I seek to escape today is in my mind. This whole time I was under the impression that people left out of rebellion to God's word. I pictured them following after selfish ambition and earthly pleasures instead of God's kingdom. But that's not the story I heard from the women on Sunday or from Philip.

I sit on the edge with my feet dangling. Below, the shallow brown waters tinted from an overabundance of iron run rapidly over the smooth stones as I enjoy the solitude and sound of rushing water.

Clearly, there was a falling out in the early days, and perhaps that's what happens when fallen men learn to live in God's grace. It's unfair of me to judge Philip for leaving with his family. I might have done the same in his shoes, but I don't think that justifies turning away from the apostolic doctrine. Then there were elders like Jack's father, who completely misinterpreted how to apply the principles in love, but that wasn't all of the elders. What Jack's father did was atrocious and flat-out wrong. I'm sure if Rob knew about the abuse, he would have put a stop to it.

But then, the others who left appeared to be seeking God and not in rebellion, which would mean the apostle and the elders lied to us.

How could lies come from an apostle ordained of God and speaking by the Spirit of Truth?

The apostle hadn't reached perfection. As a safeguard, he told us all to give everything to our Spirit and prophesy whether it is true for us, rather than to believe it because he said so.

Lydia experienced control and labeled The Ministry as authoritarian. Rob taught that to love someone was to honor their will. *What's authoritarian about that?*

A rush of wind blows some leaves across my face. I brush them away and wrap my arms around my chest for warmth.

Still, I am conflicted. On top of that is an unexplained emptiness. Is that how Jack feels without God? The reality of what he shared opens up to me in waves. I feel a pit in my stomach.

For Jack and his siblings, there was no trial by jury, no fair judgment, only his father's word pitted against theirs. A man ordained to lead a sanctified life and esteemed by the community. They thought, surely, one who answers God's call in the path of "righteousness," prioritizing spiritual wealth over worldly gains, must be dependable.

I clench my teeth and my cheeks flush. This mirage exacted a steep toll. While many put their hope in the words Jack's father preached, his children did not see hope but despair. He was a hypocrite, wielding power over his domain. His children could not depend on him for the same help he offered to others.

What example did Jack have of a father's love? How could he even imagine what he was missing?

I kick my legs above the foam-filled river, faster as the frustration mounts. I take deep breaths to calm my heart rate and think of what I had growing up.

I am fortunate that my father has always tried his best to love me, and that his best never involved abuse. He may not have been present for most of my childhood nor paid much attention to my earthly activities, but he was always there for me spiritually.

Mom covered the rest of it pretty well. Like most single moms who keep it together, she played the roles of provider and caregiver. Apart from Jesus, she's always been my hero. Our faith and trust in God got us this far.

Or was it His abundant mercy and grace?

Two young birds tussle on a tree branch. One loses its footing and flies away, the other stays. I think of the time I was playing on the stairs with Lilly when I was three years old. Her mom had arrived to bring her home from a sleepover at our house. I recall sitting next to her at the top of the stairs when she pushed me. Screaming, I tumbled down the hard wooden steps. My father scooped me up before I hit the landing. My head pounded. It wasn't the only time I fell down those slippery stairs, but it was the only time someone pushed me.

Why would she do that? I've wondered over the years.

Now, I suspect, it was a symptom of the violence she had witnessed at home. This was the same girl that Ethan mentioned cutting up her picture and giving it to others. Was it generosity, as everyone supposed, or a trauma response? Maybe that picture represented her identity, and she thought her value was in giving away pieces of herself.

A few years ago, I had a dream that woke me in a cold sweat. In the dream, she and I were with her father, and I felt he had violated me, but I couldn't quite remember the details. Upon waking, I prayed to God and asked him for wisdom. He told me that memory was not my own, but it was hers. After talking with Jack, I finally understand why she ran away.

Long-overdue tears pour down my cheeks. I wish I could hold her right now and tell her how precious she is to me and how much our Heavenly Father loves her.

CHAPTER SEVENTEEN

RIPPLE EFFECTS

A yoga mat lies between me and the faux-wood floor of my apartment. From a downward-facing dog position, I step my right foot to the top of the mat, stretching out in a lunge, and raise my arms above my head in a sun salutation. The morning light warms my face, and I admire how the two plants in the south-facing window survived my being away in Massachusetts for a week.

Caring for something, even as simple as a plant, challenges me to be consistent. They depend on me to remember to care for them, having no ability of their own to make a request. Still, when I see the organic matter growing and changing shape over time, it reminds me that God-life flows through everything. I turn to the side and let one arm stretch downward toward the mat, feeling some of that life release in me.

"You uphold all things by the word of your power," I quote Hebrews 1:3 in worship of the Lord. Then, from Psalm 19, I say, "All of creation testifies to your glory."

I welcome this return to solitude and rest in God's presence. As I move through the poses, I honor this body the Creator gave me. It feels good, but my soul stirs. It's time I talk with Him about my trip. I sit in a bolstered cross-legged position in the center of my mat, hands resting on my knees, palms up, in a posture of openness to receive.

"Lord, thank you for leading people from my past to tell me their stories about The Ministry. I struggle with how some enjoyed profound experiences that strengthened their faith, as I did, while others were left misguided, hurt, and confused. You say in Romans 8:28, 'All things work together for good to them who love God and are called according to His purpose.' Do they not love you? Are they not called?"

I sit in silence, open to hear, and God speaks as I open my mouth to prophesy:

"My daughter, I love the entire world. Wrongs were done to them, causing scars before they could know me. I do not control this because of free will. I did not stop the abuse because nobody was asking me to stop it. I know this is hard to understand, but it is how I show my mercy and grace. If the hurting will seek me with all their heart, I will turn their suffering into joy."

"Okay. I think I get it, but does that mean that it was your will for them to suffer?"

"No," He says. "I weep when my children weep. Christ poured out His love for all on the cross that day of Calvary. I desire peace, though it must be won by those I have set in the hard places to be my ambassadors, to reach the broken-hearted, for they will only see whoever is in front of them. Sadly, many block out even those who want to show them my love because of the evil they have experienced."

I sit with this for a moment. The Old Testament was full of examples of God bringing suffering to people in order to deliver them. In the New Testament, he often used suffering and deliverance to show His glory, like when the apostles suffered persecution or healed lifelong illnesses for all to see. Jesus died for our suffering, and in Romans 8:2, the Apostle Paul writes that in Christ, we are freed from the power of sin and death.

In Revelation 21:4, God gave us hope for a future without suffering in New Jerusalem.

"Lord, don't you bring suffering for your glory?"

"Does the hero in battle start the war?" He says.

"No."

"There is enough evil in this world without my inducing suffering. I simply address the suffering that exists and turn it around for my glory. What kind of loving father would I be if I started trouble just so that I could clean it up and claim the victory? It is not so."

I'm satisfied with this picture of God. I close my eyes. "Father God, meet those who are hurting in their walk. May they be receptive to your healing hand, in Christ Jesus's name. Amen."

I open my eyes, ready to start a new work week. An uplifting musical beat sounds from my phone. It's Nathan and his timing is perfect. "Hello?"

"Hey, welcome back!" The tenor of his voice matches the levity of the ringtone. "There's a place that serves vegan ice cream on Seventh Street. Want to go there tonight?"

"Yeah, that would be lovely."

Nathanial has been a close companion for my first four months in Arizona. He's always checking in on me and suggesting fun things to do around the city. The ten-year age gap felt safe at first. I figured we could be friends without the risk of falling into a romantic relationship. I wasn't ready for that.

To my dismay, our friendship developed into more. God's love compels me. I was skeptical at first, especially since I wanted to follow God's order. But the previous consideration of marriage had so little guidance that I didn't see how I could bring someone from the outside into that process. I kept hearing my Spirit say to love him with the love of the Lord, so I have. I feel a sense of belonging when I'm with him. Like we just fit.

Work is extra busy because I have to catch up on what I missed while out of town. My stand-in was fairly organized so at least the notes were easy to follow. There are few cases I need to research more and get some advice on before reaching out to the patients. That will have to wait until tomorrow.

On my way home, I take a call from Dad through the car speakers. He's checking in to see how I'm doing. I tell him about how Charles acted at the funeral and that it made me uneasy.

"As a prophet, Charles is a watchman who must speak the truth at all costs," Dad says.

"What about speaking the truth in love?"

"Well, he's not perfect."

Then he tells me he cleared up the misunderstanding about my alleged gossiping with Charles and that I am welcome to visit The Ministry Center at any time. My shoulders drop with relief. I look out at the mountains just north of the road I'm on. The sun's rays illuminate the jagged terrain. Hope sparks within me.

Nathan and I have been "dating" for a few weeks. Since then, I've shared with him some of The Ministry's teachings and tried to explain how they operate. I also told him they were struggling to grow and how I would like to influence change—help break down the walls of judgment and attract some younger folks.

I meet Nathan at the vegan place in Midtown and we have some appetizers so there will be room for ice cream. The food is all right, but the ice cream is divine. After dessert, we walk down a Midtown side street holding hands and talk about places we'd like to travel. I think about the rules of engagement I followed with Adam. I haven't been so strict with Nathan.

This feels natural, so it must be wrong.

The battle inside me rages again, and my heart races.

"Are you okay?" he says.

"I'm not sure we should do this," I say.

"Do what?"

"Hold hands in public and talk about the future."

He stops in his tracks.

"It's not you," I try to assure him. "The Ministry frowns on those things. In my last relationship, we didn't go on dates. They reprimanded us for showing public displays of affection, and we weren't allowed to talk about our future. It's presumptuous because only God knows the future."

Nathan grew up Catholic and has little dating experience. He has mostly followed my lead until now.

"I hear you, but how else would we get to know each other?"

"That's a good question." If Adam and I had communicated more, things may have turned out much different.

"I know I don't have much experience," he says, "but I believe communication and proximity are essential to building a healthy relationship."

How can I argue with that?

After all, his parents are still married. He speaks highly of his mother and respects his father's wisdom.

"It's just that . . ." I look at the pavement.

"What are you not telling me?" he says.

I look up at him. He steps one foot back.

"It's nothing bad, I promise. My dad was talking to Charles the other day. It sounds like there might still be a chance for me to work with them."

Nathan looks away.

"What's wrong?" I say, squeezing his hand tighter.

"I . . . I admire your desire to work in ministry. Your kind heart is one of the things I love most about you. But every time you talk about your work at the clinic, you light up in a way I don't see when you talk about The Ministry. God, yes, but not The Ministry. I know you care deeply about people, but is it really your responsibility to fix everything?"

I pull my hand from his. "What are you suggesting? I've been with The Ministry my whole life. These people are like family. I toed the line for so long. If there's anything that needs correction, why shouldn't I be the one to do it?"

The mere suggestion that I shouldn't pursue a position in The Ministry after all my preparation is offensive.

"Whoa, calm down." He puts his hands up in defense. "If it's what you really want, I won't stand in your way. I just don't know how involved I want to be with that."

My heart feels torn between two loves. One is familiar and begs to open past wounds, the other risks causing fresh hurts.

We walk back to the car in silence. I beg God for clarity in this confusion.

Is Nathanial really from God, or is he a distraction meant to test my faith? No answer.

We arrive at the car. He confesses he feels the early signs of a migraine and doesn't have his medication on him. I know how serious this can be for him.

I ask if I can pray over him. He agrees. I place one hand on the nape of his neck and the other hand on his forehead. It's hot. He rocks back and forth to distract himself from the intensifying pain.

Almost instinctively, I speak in tongues for the first time in front of him. I command the spirit of infirmity off him, as the Holy Spirit gives me the words to speak. Then I prophesy a word of encouragement and direction. His rocking slows, and his demeanor lightens.

He looks into my eyes. "That was . . ." He blinks. "Thank you. I feel better. It literally felt like something was squeezing my head, but when you prayed, it released."

I return his gaze and smile.

"What were those words you were saying?"

"It's my prayer language."

He reclines in the passenger seat, resting in God's peace.

A text from Mom reads: "Check your email and then call me."

Okay.

It's Saturday morning, and I am about to head out to the farmers' market.

Instead, I open the mail app on my phone and see a familiar subject line, *Wolves in Sheep's Clothing* in bold. There's a new reply since the activity from a week ago.

It's from Eve. Until recently, she had continued to represent the apostle after his passing by sending out weekly messages based on his teachings. Charles since took over.

It's a response to Charles's last email, which I reread for context, since it was before I visited Massachusetts that I last read it. He was dismissing accusations of abuse against a man who had women serving in his home. I'm not sure who was being accused, but he warned the deadly gossip was causing more harm than the alleged actions.

Her response reads,

I stand by the victims' allegations.

I gasp. *What happened?*

I read on to find out.

While concealing the victims' identities, she affirms that the apostle physically abused at least three women.

I call Mom immediately.

"Terrible, isn't it?" she says.

"I . . . I don't know whether to believe them."

"Well, honey, think about it. An old man living with young women. I always said it wasn't right that they be alone with him."

I thought she was paranoid the last time she raised a concern.

"But they received a word of God about it," I say. "That should have protected them."

"Apparently, it wasn't enough."

It's difficult to choose a side. Either way, I feel ashamed. First for agreeing with the elders that the allegations were likely spiritual attacks on The Ministry when the original email came through. Now for entertaining accusations against the apostle.

This witness, a mother who lost her daughter and then dedicated her life to serving the apostle, is siding with the accusers.

"The apostle has been dead for two years. She served with him for five. Why is this coming out now?" I say in disbelief. "Wouldn't she have seen something? And if she did, how could she stand by and allow it?"

"I don't know, Tori, but just watch yourself, okay? Someone had to know what was happening. And if they would hide it, who knows if other elders were doing the same thing."

"I will, Mom."

If Rob were alive, I would drive straight to his house and confront him. I want to look him in the eyes and demand answers. I want the impossible.

After hanging up, I pray, "Lord, I don't know what to believe. I'm sure the victims believe what they are saying is true, but perhaps Satan is deceiving them. I invoke the victory of Jesus Christ over Satan and his demons and all lying spirits, and ask that the truth come to light."

CHAPTER EIGHTEEN

UNEXPECTED

I sit on a worn second-hand leather couch with Nathan by my side. Dogs have torn it with their claws in several places and now the beasts are clamoring at the back door to be part of the action. Crumbs line the couch crevices. I lean back and feel something poke me: a child's toy. Rosario does her best to clean up each Friday, but five children, one grandbaby, and three dogs undo her best efforts. Her husband, Julio, the subject of the earlier rumors that ruined my chances of working with the apostle, oversees this Friday night gathering at their home.

Instead of being bitter, I've begun to wonder if those rumors were a way God spared me from becoming a potential victim. Then again, if there was a coverup of the apostle abusing women, it's possible Julio's actions were also concealed.

About ten adults and a handful of children fill their living room, mostly family members and a few other local saints. We sing some songs in English and Spanish to open the gathering while Julio plays the guitar. The children dance and sing and play tag in the middle of the room. When the music is over, Julio corrals the children to settle down. He tickles a two-year-old boy to stop him from crying. Then he lifts one of his nieces to sit on his lap. The kids seem to love him. He prays for our food, and we help ourselves to fried chicken, coleslaw, and mashed potatoes brought in from a local fast-food chain.

This is Nathan's first time at a gathering. I watch him for signs of discomfort as he takes it all in, and I wonder what's going through his mind. Like me, he grew up as an only child, but that's where the similarities end. His parents were wealthy. They had a maid, a nanny, and a landscape architect. Their pets were well-groomed. If he can handle this, he just might be a keeper.

Looking past the distractions, I see people with big hearts who are hurting and want to serve God. An older woman tells a story about how God gave her a way to relate with her class as a schoolteacher. She would pray for her students and ask for God's knowledge, wisdom, and understanding. Several others could relate, including Nathan, who recently took a position teaching photography at a high school.

We pray, read Scriptures, give words of encouragement, and prophesy to one another.

"I have a word for you," Julio announces, looking at me.

"All right, I'm ready," I say.

"It's kind of strange," he says. "I don't know what it means, but I'm just going to share it. I see you walking along, and then your body, soul, and spirit separate. It's as if some force punched you, thrusting your soul and spirit out the back. So, your body is going first, then your soul, and finally your spirit follows."

"That's interesting," I say. "The order is supposed to be spirit, soul, and body—leading with the spirit, not the other way around."

"That's true," he says. "But in this case, it's like your body went first and the soul and spirit had to catch up."

He opens his folded hands and shakes his head. "I don't know what that means, sister, just got to give it to your God and Christ for the wisdom."

I immediately feel convicted about my relationship with Nathan. This must be telling me I'm out of order by dating him. He has respected my physical boundaries; nevertheless, I must be careful not to allow my feelings to guide me instead of God.

For the rest of the night, I'm unable to think about much else. In giving it to my spirit, I receive it may be an illustration of working out my salvation—the method by which we must reach perfection. Rob taught that all things start in the spirit realm and work their way into the physical. So, this word would seem contrary to that teaching and thus out of order. This disturbing thought prompts me to keep praying. Perhaps it's true that all things start in the spirit *internally*, but they manifest in the reverse order. God didn't give this word of knowledge to be an accusation, but a revelation. With that understanding, I no longer feel condemned about my relationship.

Nathan and I arrive at a trailhead late the next morning. January is perfect for hiking in Phoenix. I'm eager to talk about his experience last night, but he's worried about our gear, the trail map, and if the lighting is right for photography.

I'm still getting used to Nathan's quirks. He rechecks his backpack to ensure his camera and the first aid supplies are in their places. I'm carrying the snacks. He checks his watch and apologizes for the twentieth time for picking me up later than we planned. I assure him it's all right.

"Our team goes this way," he says, pointing his hiking stick toward the trail's opening about thirty feet away. It's just us, but it's cute the way he used the word "team."

For several minutes he goes on about where we parked, and if we have enough time, did we screenshot the maps, and so on. Once he's certain all things are in order, we can enjoy the hike. The incline is gradual at first. We walk and talk, mostly pointing out lizards and desert flowers among the layers of rock that comprise South Mountain.

"So, what did you think of last night?" I ask.

"You know, the older woman's testimony about how the Holy Spirit helped her know what to teach and how to handle her students struck me. I sure could use help with my students."

"One name for the Holy Spirit in Scripture is Helper," I say.

"In more ways than one, it seems," he says. "There was also the gentleman who was in prison for a while. His conversations with God impressed me and how he became a better person because of that time he spent in prayer and studying God's word. Was all that because they received the Holy Spirit and spoke in tongues like you do?"

"I believe so," I say. Any interest he has in the Holy Spirit gives me hope that we might have a future together.

I explain further. "Praying in tongues is speaking above my mind. It quiets my thoughts so I can hear clearly from God. Also, as a spiritual language, it helps me pray effectively when I don't know what to say."

"Right. It was helpful to hear how others have used it. So, the Holy Spirit taught him?"

"That's right. The prophecies he received back from God were showing him how to apply God's word with understanding."

We walk until we come to a large boulder. We look at each other, smile, then climb atop it. The view is spectacular, and this is only our halfway point. We sit and enjoy it for a few moments. Nature's gentle chorus eases my racing mind. It wasn't the cool mountain air of the north country, but we are just above the haze of smog that often rests upon the city of Phoenix. The expanse of this sprawling city is impressive from this vantage point.

"This is where it all began," I say. "The apostle saw a vision from this rock that started the whole ministry back in 1978."

"Interesting. What kind of vision?"

"As he tells it, there was writing in the sky. The words scrolling like the credits to a movie. God revealed twelve principles to him and commissioned him to teach them so that the church could get back on track to functioning as He created us to."

We get moving again.

"Hey, look!" He points to a crevice between the layers of rock.

"Is that a Gila monster?" I say.

"I think so. It's about three feet long!"

I step forward.

"Don't get too close!"

"I won't," I snap back. It's the biggest lizard I've seen in the wild.

"I think it's hunting," he says. "Let's move along."

I nod. We continue up the mountain.

The top isn't a peak, rather an interesting terrain of peaks and valleys with multiple trails converging at different points. We walk around a bit until we come to a narrow passageway we recognize from the trail map with the ironic name Fat Man's Pass. I shimmy through it to find a small cave on the other side. I look back at Nathan, who looks unsure. He's got some extra weight on him.

"I better not get stuck," he says. "Here, take the gear." He passes it through the opening and I shimmy partway to him, barely reaching the strap of the backpack.

He sucks in his gut and starts working his way through. About midway, he panics.

"Oh my God, oh my God . . .," he says.

"You're okay," I say. "You're at the narrowest point. Just breathe shallow and shimmy."

"If I get stuck here . . ." Before he can finish his sentence, he's past the narrow part and makes his way through with an enormous sigh of relief.

The cave is quiet and shaded but not dark. There's a low opening to the east on a different level of the mountaintop, so we could duck through and walk right out. A ray of light shines through the narrow pass, illuminating a giant beetle. It's about five inches long.

"Desert creatures are hardy. They live to be much larger than the ones I'm used to in New England," I say.

"Oh, yeah. They're dangerous too. Watch yourself. Especially if you see bright, colorful ones, or scorpions, or snakes." He looks around to do a check of the area. A small spider has made its home in the corner. He cringes.

"I think we're fine. Let's just relax for a bit," I say. The natural cooling effect from the rocks feels soothing. We sit in silence for a while.

A wind rushes through the cave. Compressed by the narrow opening, it spins up a small dirt devil in front of us and then dissipates as quickly as it comes.

"This is my happy place," I say.

Nathan turns to me, and we kiss. It's not the first time. Once taboo for me, I see it as a way of saying we care about each other enough to consider a future together.

We rest for a few minutes and eat the trail mix from my pack for an energy boost. Then we head back down the mountain the same way we came.

We come upon the large flat boulder where we stopped halfway up. Nathan climbs atop it, and I hang back. He spreads his arms from east to west, looking north beyond the city, and takes a deep breath. I take a photo to capture the freedom his posture portrays. He stays there for a minute. A lizard scurries along the path and into the brush. *Cute little guy.*

Nathan's voice rises on the gentle breeze singing a familiar tune, "Go tell it on the mountain, over the hills and everywhere. Go tell it on the mountain, Jesus Christ is Lord." Again he sings, shouting it out this time. "Go tell it on the mountain, over the hills and everywhere. Go tell it on the mountain, Jesus Christ is Lord." I join him for the third chorus as he descends the boulder, and we march in unison down the mountain trail.

The sun casts long shadows, making us appear larger than life. At the bottom of the mountain, we take a selfie next to the wooden trail map with the terrain in the background.

Once we're in the car, Nathan says, "I have to tell you something."

"What is it?"

He turns to me in his seat. "I had an encounter with God on that rock."

I raise an eyebrow. "Really?"

Something is different. His demeanor was brighter, and his steps lighter, long after we finished singing.

"Yeah. Remember that day you prayed over me for the migraine and it left?"

"Of course."

"Your prayer language was the most beautiful thing I've ever heard. It was like the voice of an angel." He takes my hand in his. "I believe I received the Holy Spirit."

"You did?" I shriek. "Praise God!"

"Yeah, I mean, I was looking out and thinking about what you showed me in Scripture—if we ask, we will receive. I asked God about it, and he showed me I had been talking to him throughout my life. As a kid, it was an imaginary friend; as a teenager, a comforting presence. He told me it was his Holy Spirit that was with me the whole time—I had been talking to God. Then, I opened my mouth to speak, and these words came out, just a few syllables, but not English. It was as if his presence filled me, and this joy overtook me. That's why I was singing!"

"Nathan, that's wonderful! A few syllables are a great start. Don't worry about remembering them. God will give you the sounds to speak by His Spirit. It's not something to think about. That's the point, so that God can speak through you above your intellect."

It overjoys me to share in this experience with him.

"Okay," he says. "I will keep practicing and let God add to the words. This is just incredible! Walking down the mountain, I felt such peace. I found joy in the moment by noticing little things. God was showing me how beautiful His creation is and you . . . you, I am so thankful He led me to you. You've made all the difference in my life. Thank you. Thank you so much."

I blush. "It's God's love that compels me."

Nathan receiving the Holy Spirit is a dream come true. I had given up any expectation that he would. He is a kind soul who cares for me very much. If all he would ever be to me was a fun and interesting companion, I could accept that. This fresh evidence of spiritual growth renews my hope in God's faithfulness.

On the way back to my place, we decide we'll cook dinner together this evening, so we stop at a grocery store.

"How do these look?" Nathan holds up a couple of red bell peppers.

"Perfect. Why don't you grab some orange ones too?" He adds the red peppers to the clear plastic bag and grabs some more.

I add brussels sprouts to mine, when out of the corner of my eye I see a familiar face.

Is that . . . Kumari?

I haven't seen her since Fiji. Her responses by email to the recent scandal made it clear she wanted nothing to do with The Ministry. I scoot behind Nathan so she won't see me, but it's too late.

"Victoria?" Kumari calls out.

I step into view.

"It is you!" she says.

"Hi, Kumari, what are you . . . I mean, I didn't know you were in town," I say.

"Yes, for a little while. We're visiting Elias's family. It's so good to see you. How are you doing? Are you okay?"

"I'm fine, doing well, actually."

Nathan clears his throat.

"Oh, this is . . . uh . . . my, um . . . Nathan."

"Pleasure to meet you," he says.

"A pleasure," she says, raising an eyebrow and looking my way.

"It's good to see you again." I hope I won't have to explain our relationship any further.

"Would you meet me for coffee while I'm in town this week?" she says.

If it gets back to Charles that I met with Kumari and engaged in gossip, all hope of working with The Ministry would be lost.

"You know, this week's going to be tough," I say. "I'll be working late most days."

It's not a complete lie. We have a busy client load this week, and I was planning on watching some training videos in the evenings.

"Are you sure? We'll be going home in a few days, and I would really like to catch up."

"I'm sorry. I don't think it's going to work out."

"That's too bad. Let's keep in touch," she says.

I nod and smile.

"What was that all about?" Nathan asks once we're in the car.

"Kumari is an old friend from The Ministry, but she's no longer part of it."

"So you don't want to talk to her anymore?"

"It's not that. I feel bad, but I can't risk anyone at the ministry finding out I met with someone who's in rebellion."

"What did she do?"

"Nothing, really. I mean, there's been some accusations against the elders. I don't think they're true, but some people have left over it and she's one of them."

"Shouldn't you at least hear her out?" he says.

"It's too risky."

He shakes his head. "It's your business, but I don't understand it."

I turn up the volume on the car stereo for the rest of the ride.

CHAPTER NINETEEN

STUBBORNNESS

By September, Nathan and I are still going strong. His spiritual gifts are developing, so I decide it's time he meets a strong male role model in The Ministry. We take a day trip up north.

I belt out, "Da . . . da . . . the rising wind, comin' up around the bend." Nathan, behind the steering wheel, lip-syncs to Creedence Clearwater Revival as we ascend the winding mountain road to Payson. Although we're from different generations, we've found a connection through classic rock, the kind that our parents listened to when we were young. Perfect for road tripping.

I sigh and look out the window at the canyon below. Scorched earth from past wildfires gives birth to new growth. The terrain is greener the further north we go, with the higher elevation. I relate it to the state of The Ministry. Will the fires of judgment give way to new life? While the email chain from nearly a year ago has been silent, Julio's wife rekindled the flame of an old rumor. This time, directly from the source. She stopped me after a gathering one night to ask for prayer and confided that she suspected her husband of cheating, but whenever she confronted him, he would get violent. The best I could do was minister to her about submission and her worth in Christ.

"Hey, it's going to be all right," Nathan says. "I'm looking forward to meeting Dallas."

"Hope so. I respect Dallas for telling me the truth while we were in Fiji. I wouldn't have guessed that listening to a woman in the bathroom would make them doubt my loyalty. He may help shed some light on the allegations."

"We'll see. Let's just relax and enjoy the scenery and cool mountain air."

Nathan isn't always this chill, but something about being together on the open road puts us both in a better state of mind.

We exit the highway and drive about forty minutes into Rim Country as the locals call it. Our vehicle climbs the two-thousand-foot escarpment to the top of the Mogollon Rim, a section of the Colorado Plateau that extends two hundred miles across Central Arizona into New Mexico. Weaving through the landscape with open windows, we take in the fresh air, courtesy of an assortment of trees including bigtooth maple, aspen, white fir, and ponderosa pine.

When we arrive at the Sturgis's ranch, a big, fluffy brown dog runs out to greet us.

"What a bear!" Nathan squats low and opens his arms wide.

"That's his name, Bear," Dallas calls out in a deep voice.

"Ha! Well, it suits him," Nathan calls back while dodging kisses. He has an affinity for animals, and he instantly bonds with nearly every dog he meets. The companionship of a dog is a pleasure I have yet to experience. As far as I can tell, Nathan shares an exceptional quality with dogs: no, not fur—loyalty. A scarce quality in most relationships. I place a high value on this character trait.

Dallas and Grace welcome us to sit out on their back deck. The savory smell of meat cooking in the oven entices our stomachs. Despite working long hours in hospitality, Grace found time to prepare a meal for us. Aside from his ministry work, Dallas is a retired prison warden with a small pension.

Grace serves us sun-brewed iced tea that she made the day before.

"So, how did you two meet?" she asks.

"Well, funny story . . .," Nathan starts, and I fill in details along the way. He was a photographer for the conference I was attending and we ended up at the same restaurant, ordering the same meal for lunch. My friend invited him over to our table. He was knowledgeable about the area and promised to show me around if I ever came back to town.

Dallas asks some questions about his family and work, then they get talking about photography.

We admire the view. Beyond the stables and corral is a field, and further out, the forest merges into mountains.

"Want a tour?" Dallas says.

"I'd like to ride, if I could," I say.

"Do you have experience?" He looks at both of us.

"Yes, I had lessons as a kid. But it's Nathan's first time."

We walk out to the stables to meet the horses.

"All right, that brown and white one there is a retired trail horse. Her name's Sugar because she's so sweet with the kids. Our grandkids ride her when they visit. She'll do just fine for you, Nate. May I call you Nate?"

"Yes, sir."

"Sir, eh?" Dallas looks at me. "I like this guy."

"Victoria, since you said you can ride . . . this old girl Stella still has a bit of fire in her." He pats the dark brown horse on her hindquarter.

"She's ornery, but that's usually just with me. Grace likes to ride her."

I approach her with slow movements and gently stroke her face. She shakes my hand off, so I try again, speaking soft blessings over her. "You are a beautiful creation of God. So strong and majestic. I bless you."

She nuzzles into me.

"Looks like you'll get along just fine," Dallas says.

I mount her, and she takes a few steps back. I loosen up on the reins, then lean over to pat her neck. She moves forward, so I lead her around the perimeter of the corral.

We return to find Dallas coaching Nathan on how to mount a horse. He's struggling to swing his leg over, so Dallas gives him a boost. After some hesitation, he's ready to ride.

Dallas mounts a tan horse and takes the lead.

"This here is Old Betsy. She's a strong girl for her age."

There's a trail entrance at the edge of their property. The three of us on horses and Bear the dog, walking alongside enter the forest. The tree canopy offers shade from the midday sun and the symphony of birds and forest creatures is a welcome contrast from the beats of city streets.

"I get the sense you have some questions for me," Dallas says from the front of the line.

I ride up closer. "We would love to hear your story about how you came to the Lord."

"I was a juvenile delinquent growing up." He looks back to see our reaction, but I'm not fazed and Nathan is just trying to balance on Sugar.

He continues, "I've been talking to the Lord since I was a kid. Even when I was doing bad things, I would talk to him about it."

"Really?" I say.

"Oh, yeah. My dad was in the US Air Force. When I turned seventeen, I didn't have any job prospects, so I followed in his footsteps. Figured it was that or I'd end up in jail. I didn't like it much. But if I left, it would violate my guaranteed job. Vietnam was ending, so I decided I would be a pain in the ass. I told the captain directly, 'Within a year, you'll be asking me to leave.' Then I did some really stupid things and never got in trouble for it."

"Did he ask you to leave?"

"Not right away." He pauses. "During that time, demons were visiting my room in the barracks at night, saying my name. Scared the hell out of me! I held a Bible against my chest and prayed 'Our Father' because that's the only thing I could pray."

"What happened next?"

I stay close to hear more about how God led him to a man named Hardy, who introduced him to a church group where he sat in their living room with a joint in his pocket. How he got caught later that night, which kicked off the grand plan of an honorable discharge that could only be by God's grace.

"Speaking of Grace, how did you meet your wife?"

"You know, the Lord has a sense of humor." He snickers. The two have been married only a handful of years. "She noticed me a long time before I ever noticed her. Back in college, Grace was in a girls' choir visiting from another campus. She took notice, asking her friend about me, who responded, 'Oh no, he's married to a witch.' That's how I know she saw me, because you see, my first wife practiced witchcraft. Nearly thirty years and two divorces later, we met again. I didn't hardly know her. That's when the Spirit drew us together to get married."

Dallas and Grace seem happy with how their consideration of marriage turned out. They were more proactive about it than Adam and me. The couple lived in proximity and enjoyed dates, which agitated leadership. I suppose experiencing a few marriages and grown kids made them wise where we were naïve.

Nathan kicks Sugar to trot up alongside me and reaches out his hand. I give him mine for a quick squeeze. He knows I'm still recovering from my past relationship.

I turn my focus back to Dallas.

"You had some wild experiences prior to joining The Ministry," I say. "What was Rob Peterson like in those early days? The 1970s was it?"

Our horses climb a short incline before leveling out again.

"I didn't meet him right away. Gabriel was my unofficial pastor for a while. I met Rob in 1978 at a Sunday gathering. Just when you think it's ending around four in the afternoon, he'd start a teaching that would last until seven or eight o'clock at night. The teachings didn't help me that much."

"No?"

"Nah, most of it was over my head. I'm a maverick, someone who needs rules to rebel against. Not much for being in order or sucking up to authority. I wasn't looking for Rob's approval. We got along fine but never bonded."

"So why did you stay?"

"For the friends, I guess. One day, Gabriel asked me to be an elder. It was a boys'-club type of atmosphere that I was happy to join. If I knew then what I know now, I don't think I would have accepted it so hastily. I would have waited a few years and matured more. But for lack of better judgment, I became an elder. Rob later disclosed that he was unaware of me and three others becoming elders."

A slew of thoughts race through my head at hearing this. Does that mean his position was inauthentic? That might explain his dubious loyalty.

"How could that be?" I ask. "I thought he watched over everything."

"I thought so too. Gabriel claimed he submitted the question with our names and got words of prophecy back. Shortly before his passing, Rob asserted he never gave his word on the matter. He was traveling when Gabriel submitted the question, so maybe he didn't remember."

Dallas is giving Rob the benefit of the doubt more than I expected he would.

"How would you say you matured as an elder?" I ask.

We come to a clearing, and he circles around. He lets his reigns down, and we do the same so our horses can graze. Bear lays down in the grass.

"I'll give you an example. A brother and I were studying together when we received some revelation about how Christ's ministry should function. Brother Fremont was a colleague who I'd ministered the Holy Spirit to just a couple of years earlier. We watched how the other elders were conducting The Ministry, and it seemed wrong. So Rob granted us a meeting.

"We sat facing Rob's desk, the elders behind us. There were about six of them. I prophesied, 'Be open to your spirit, my sons, for I would show you a better way. There is latency with my word and a spirit of disorder that threatens to undermine the truth you so desire to share. Examine yourselves that you are not stumbling blocks to those who seek the truth you have to give.' With that last word of the prophecy, I went out in the spirit—fell to the floor paralyzed.

Nathan's mouth drops open.

"'Well, Dallas is out,' Rob said to Freemont, 'so you share what you're gonna share.'

"I could hear everything that was happening but couldn't respond. Fremont got mad at me, nudging me in the head with his foot as if to say, 'Wake up, wake up, you ass, you gonna leave me to do this by myself?'"

I chuckle and Stella steps forward to reach for a new patch of grass.

Dallas continues, "Fremont started speaking from 1 Timothy 3, where it lays out the qualifications for being an elder in the church. 'Not given to much wine, yet we have alcoholics in our midst. Hospitable, yet we expect hospitality from the saints that they might serve us rather than us serving them. The husband of one wife, yet there is at least one among us who has been unfaithful. Not quarrelsome, yet our marriages have been full of strife. And in Titus 1:6, his children should be obedient, not wild and unruly. Many of our children have walked away. Are any of these things above reproach . . . let alone any of us?'

"The room was silent and I couldn't see their faces, but I imagine they weren't happy to hear this. Fremont said, 'And in 1 Corinthians 11:3, it says plainly that the head of the woman is man, yes, we all agree on that one, but the head of every man is Christ and he's not to have his head covered. Metaphorically speaking, if I require a man of the church to submit to me or an eldership when deciding for his family, I am covering his head in Christ's stead.'

I furrow my brows and bite my bottom lip. *Could it be wrong for households to submit their life issues to the eldership?*

Nathan nods.

"Rob listened patiently as he went through all the Scriptures. 'I propose, brothers,' Fremont said, 'that we take a hard look at our actions and become the examples the church needs. That we encourage men to go to God, through Christ, by their Spirit, for direction in their lives and not require them to get words through us.'

"What did he say?" I can't imagine it went over well since what he described still happens to this day.

"I came to and sat up," Dallas says. "Rob looked us in the eyes and said, 'You guys are absolutely right.' We looked at the elders behind us. 'Well, why aren't they doing it?' That's when Rob said, 'Well, son, *you* haven't done *any* of this. It's true, what you're receiving and the revelation you have are right on. That is how Christ's ministry should work. However, these men have been through hell, working out their salvation, with the ups and downs and the trips and the falls and get-back-ups and all that for the last couple of years. So, yeah, they're not doing it perfectly. They're still working it out, but what have you two done?'"

Dallas shakes his head and says, "When the apostle's words cut, they cut deep. We had no right to accuse others of something we ourselves hadn't done."

He gathers up his reins and gives Old Betsy a kick. We do the same to our horses. Bear rises from his rest one paw at a time and follows us.

My mind is buzzing. Fremont made a strong case. Where are the effects of repentance? What about change? I look at Nathan, who is squinting.

"It sounds like you had a point," Nathan says. "I thought Christians were supposed to repent and change. Two years is a long time to walk with an apostle, as you say, and it not have a profound effect."

"You've got to understand, brother, years of deception left me with many demons. By the world's standards, we were all a mess. Truth be told, I thought I'd be dead by the time I was forty-five. I had contracts on me from the Arian Brotherhood, the Mexican Mafia, and others who wanted revenge. Instead, I found God's love in being part of the eldership. He made it real to me through those men."

I purse my lips in thought. "How so?"

He motions us to follow. The late afternoon sun casts beams of warm light through the trees, illuminating flying insects and other organic particles in the air. The surrounding ecosystems are teeming with life.

"I started overseeing gatherings." He shakes his head. "I was terrified. No idea what I was doing. Teaching others whose hearts were crying out was intimidating because my study had been personal until then. I would rather go to work and face fifty mad convicts than sit in a room and bring a teaching to those loving saints. It didn't stop me, though. I can't tell you how many times demons came out of people in a gathering because I wouldn't agree with the fear. Like it says in James 4:7, resist the devil and he will flee."

"So you were making an impact." I'm proud of him for having the courage to fight the devil by loving the saints.

"You said you never bonded with Rob, yet you became more submissive," I say. "Was that toward him or another elder?"

"My regular meetings were with the bishop, but I visited Rob in Australia for a few weeks. He lived there intermittently to build up the church. During this trip, he had a quadruple bypass. Heather was his assistant at the time, but she was back in the US with her mom. Rob's daughter came to help in the office a few days a week, but during most of his recovery, I was alone with him."

"Seems he was sick quite often," Nathan says.

"You've got to understand," Dallas says. "As an apostle, he was interceding for one twelfth of the world. The most important thing was that anyone functioning as his body maintain spiritual oneness with God and Christ and that they never faltered."

"His body?" Nathan says.

"That's right," Dallas says. "You may have heard of the Scripture that compares Christ and the Church to the human body. All of your five senses—sight, smell, taste, hearing, and touch—are located in your head. Your brain interprets those senses and tells the rest of your body what to do. The only sense that your body has is touch. Your head is the command center, and your body responds by acting out those commands, giving feedback, and protecting the head. If the body tries to act on its own, all it has is emotions to guide it, and those can be deceiving. It's similar with entities on earth, like in a marriage. The man is the head and the woman is the body. God established the same order within the eldership, so the apostle is the head and anyone working with him is his body. Together, we carry out Christ's ministry—Jesus Christ, of course, being our ultimate head and all believers being the body."

"Interesting," Nathan says.

"So, did you?" I say. "Maintain spiritual oneness?"

"I went out there without an agenda, not looking for him to minister to me. My purpose was to be led by God and Christ. And I did it, except one time."

Bear darts in front of us to chase a squirrel up a tree.

Dallas blows a loud whistle through his teeth and scolds him for cutting off the horses.

"I didn't think he could move that fast!" Nathan says.

"Me either," I say.

We laugh, but Dallas isn't amused.

He picks up the story where he left off without missing a beat. "We were preparing to go to his daughter's house, and I didn't acknowledge God for a moment. Rob was feeling sick to his stomach and about to retch when he came out of the bathroom and said, 'Turn your heart quick!' I turned my heart to God. He was well, and we went forth."

This spiritual sensitivity only reaffirms that Rob was endowed with supernatural powers. He was a sacred leader that needed protection, and the only way to do so was to have a perfect heart unto God. Those in positions closest to Rob were his first line of defense, while the rest of the faithful formed a safety net. Even small amounts of rebellion or judgment sent fiery darts of the enemy to attack his health or finances.

"He appreciated my diligence," Dallas says, "and I offered to stay, but he said I needed to go back and fulfill my role as pastor in the Coolidge church. He also warned me not to tell anyone how well I did. 'They'll target you. They'll torment you,' he said."

"Out of jealousy?" I say.

"Oh yes, there was terrible competition among the elders. Most of them wanted Rob's approval. But they were the least of my concerns."

We round a bend and head back toward the ranch. The sun is just past its zenith, now warming the left side of our bodies between clusters of trees and brush.

What were his real concerns?

CHAPTER TWENTY

SPIRITUAL WARFARE

Old Betsy stops to graze and Dallas gives her a hearty kick in the hindquarters with his well-worn brown leather boots.

"Spiritual warfare had already begun," he says. "Just as Rob said it would. I'd been preparing to drive to Casa Grande for an outreach, and little things just kept coming up to prevent me. The horse feed got wet from a leak in the barn after the unexpected rains. I had to change my truck tire because that also got a leak. Then I got arrested."

"What for?" I say.

"I was driving on the I-10 toward Tucson, where I planned to minister to a retired couple, former coworkers. Suddenly, someone in a truck bigger than mine was speeding past me and swerving into my lane. I jumped on the brakes, just avoiding him. I thought, 'What is this guy's deal?' I hadn't meant to cut the guy off. Too deep in thought, as usual. I was carrying a new Colt .45, excited to show my friends, but I couldn't let him see it. Pima County was very anti-gun. I didn't want them to think I was more of a threat, so I pulled it off my hip and had it against my chest to put it away. Just then, the cloud of dust cleared. He was right beside me again and he caught a glint of sun reflecting off the barrel. Instead of running me off the road, he sped up and called 911. When the officers arrived, they did a felony takedown on me.

"At the police station, I knew they didn't care what really happened. They just wanted me to confess to something I didn't do. Thank God one of the church elders posted my bail for $1,500. It would be an entire year until the trial and I couldn't carry a weapon. Not even for hunting. I felt naked without it."

I can't relate, having never carried a weapon, but I see how he would want to protect himself as a prison warden. The afternoon sun warms our backs as we approach the ranch.

"What did you do?" Nathan says. His posture is more relaxed now, hips swaying with Sugar's movement.

"The prison transferred me to a security guard post in Flagstaff where I could work without carrying. It was an isolating experience, but that's when I really learned to talk to God. I would read Scripture in my down time and talk to Him about it while doing my rounds in the snow, walking the perimeter.

"The Lord said to me, 'You want to know how to love everybody else, son. I want you to love *you* first. I want you to do everything I tell you to do. And if you do that, you're gonna love you and you're gonna be a success at this.' Blew me away! Its simplicity made it easy for me to put into action. And since then, I haven't done anything without asking the Lord first. It wasn't like Rob was sitting at a table across from me yelling." He mimics, "You've got to will everything to your spirit, to God through Christ!'"

Sugar neighs and shakes her head, apparently spooked by Dallas's tone.

"Whoa." Nathan gives her a pat on the neck. "It's all right, girl."

"I came into the condition of hope," declares Dallas.

"What do you mean by that?" Nathan says.

"It means I am no longer double-minded. I committed to giving everything to God by my Spirit and receiving from Him as my only source, and I am doing it. I have no doubts in my mind about being led by my spirit in all things."

"So you never doubt?" I say.

"Doubts may be presented, but I never agree with them. I repent immediately and speak by my spirit to the matter."

I tilt my head and glance at Nathan who raises an eyebrow. I shrug.

"One day, I was reading Galatians 6, 'For he that sows to his flesh shall of the flesh reap corruption; but he that sows to the Spirit shall of the Spirit reap life everlasting.' I was thinking about the trial, and God said to me, 'Son, the best chance you've got is to build your faith to where you won't go to prison.' At the end of that year, I got the best news. A bench trial. No jury to hate guns."

"Praise God," I say. "The Lord has brought you through some incredible experiences over the years."

The spiritual warfare and resulting deliverance seem to signal that he is doing right.

We arrive back at the ranch. The horses giddy up as they enter the corral, and head straight to the water trough.

"Let 'em drink, they deserve it," Dallas says.

Stella and Sugar drink to their hearts' content. When they come up for air, the two horses are nose to nose. Nathan and I look at each other and grin, touched by their affection.

"Dinner's ready!" Grace calls from the back porch.

After dinner, we relax in their living room. I want to ask him if he witnessed any abuse, but I'm not quite ready.

Instead, I say, "Did you ever struggle with staying in The Ministry?"

"Ha! I sure did. Around 2003, I was giving Fremont a ride back from a seminar. Some things that Rob shared rocked us badly. Something Rob was teaching contradicted a teaching that he'd put out back in 1980. I thought, 'How could God contradict himself?' It hadn't occurred to me that the apostle's doctrine might evolve with our growth. I came back the next day challenging it with the old teaching in hand. I almost walked."

Seems he'd held the apostle's teachings to the same standard as the Bible.

Had I ever done that?

For a while, I read more apostolic text than Scriptures. I felt I had read all the important passages of Scripture. To achieve further understanding and spiritual growth, it was imperative that I learned the biblical principles he delivered. My perspective on this is changing. Since the apostle's passing, I am reading more of the Bible and less of his teachings.

"Why *didn't* you walk?" I say.

"Through the elders discussing the issue, we realized we had matured spiritually. In the present covenant of faith and grace, we started by applying God's word by the law, and now we applied it by the Spirit, where there's flexibility within God's order."

"I think I see that. So was it the teaching that had changed or your perception of it?"

"Both," Dallas says. "Because our perception of how to apply the teaching changed, the Holy Spirit released the apostle to update the teaching with expanded knowledge, which we could now digest."

"Is that similar to waning off the milk of the word and onto the meat?" I say.

"Something like that, yes."

"Did anything else seem off to you?" I say. This should cover my questions.

"Of course, there were other situations, but God never led me to leave."

I bite my bottom lip and glance at Bear, nestled up to Nathan. I don't want to mention the allegations of abuse. There must have been signs. If anything happened, I'm sure his stories will reveal clues.

"For instance, after Rob and his assistant, Heather, got arrested in New Zealand, he was questioning his purpose for being there."

I sat straight up, scanning his expression. "Wait. The apostle got arrested? What for?"

"Oh, you didn't hear about it? It was for having the wrong type of visa. The country was particular about that and wasn't very welcoming to ministers from the outside."

"Oh." That wasn't the type of offense I expected. "So, you might say it was persecution for the gospel's sake?"

"Well . . . he sought confirmation from the international eldership. They were his headship, but it was complicated. As the apostle, he was the head of the church and eldership, but he submitted his life issues to the eldership for accountability. He did his best to do this until he began to not trust them. For example, when we submitted this word about not returning to New Zealand, all the elders gave the same word, but mine was different. Instead of stopping as usual and getting everyone to clear their hearts, he just praised God and didn't acknowledge my word.

"His distrust of the elders grew over the years. He thought they were so deceived that he couldn't trust their prophecies. He did things I disagreed with, according to Scripture. But when I prayed about it, my spirit showed me, 'God gave this ministry to Rob. He can do it his way or by the Holy Spirit. That's up to him. He answers to Jesus Christ on this. You don't. It's not your ministry.'"

I let this settle in a minute. God gave Rob the ministry to use as he pleased.

Why would God entrust a ministry to someone who was sinful? Wasn't this Christ's ministry?

He taught us that our hearts would determine the response we receive through our headship. But when it was about himself, the headship was wrong, not his heart.

Seems rather hypocritical.

"Why do you suppose he continued to encourage you all to get words through the eldership when he himself did not trust them?" I ask.

"Ah, you ask the tough questions, don't you?"

I let my hair down from a ponytail to relieve some mounting tension. "I like meaningful conversations. Might learn something."

"God told me He appointed Rob because he stood in the principles. He stood for what God said. The apostle wasn't infallible. He made mistakes, like all of us. Besides, that was only my perception of what happened. The elders may not have heard my prophecy as being contrary to theirs."

He continues, "Some walked away because of what they perceived to be hypocrisy. Fremont resigned over a disagreement about something the top elders in the bishopric did. I remember I spent eight hours with the Lord, going through Scripture, asking what to do. Every Scripture pointed me toward staying, as if the Lord was telling me, 'Don't leave, don't divide, don't separate.'"

"Do you think Fremont sought the Lord as you did?"

"God was very clear to me about the consequences of dividing the body. Since then, Fremont has had surgeries and terrible medical conditions. He was in terrible shape after leaving with judgments."

Was this superstition or a biblical principle?

Either way, I've always been terrified of walking away lest some tragedy befall me.

Dallas and Grace rock in their twin recliners. She left the dishes for later so she could join the conversation. Nathan is dozing off on the couch with Bear.

I'm finally ready to ask the question.

"Did either of you witness any abuse over the years?"

"No, no, can't say that I did." Dallas shakes his head. "I mean, there were probably things that were said that people could misconstrue as abuse. The enemy will twist anything any way he can."

Grace looks down. Her hands fidget. "Would anyone like some tea?"

"Sure, I'll help you," I say and follow her out to the kitchen.

She takes the kettle from the stove and motions for me to stand by her. With the running water from the faucet filling the kettle, she almost whispers, "I didn't witness anything. They never let me get that close. But I suspect there's a good reason for the reports. I knew those women for years and they wouldn't cry wolf."

The sun sets behind purple mountains, creating a soft gradient sky. I focus on the road ahead as it winds through the pass, a descending gateway between temperate terrain and the unforgiving desert. The radio plays to keep me awake while Nathan snoozes in the passenger seat.

Grace's comment replays in my head.

Why hadn't they let her get close? She worked with the team at every conference.

Nathan stirs awake.

"Good nap?" I say.

"Yes, I needed that. Thank you. How are you doing?"

"I . . . uh . . . well . . ." I sigh.

"C'mon, what's on your mind? I can tell when something's bothering you."

"What did you think of them?" I say.

"They're nice. Grace's cooking was delicious, and Dallas had some pretty wild stories."

"He sure does," I say. "That's why I trust him. He's been around, and he can read people."

"Maybe. But he didn't seem to read what was going on in The Ministry very well."

I clench the steering wheel. "What do you mean?"

"I mean, it's obvious they were controlling. He couldn't even raise an issue without getting yelled at by their leader. I was listening to this podcast the other day that talked about authoritarian leaders. They use flattery to prey on people looking for acceptance and then once they build trust, they turn the scales, requiring more access to your life until everything you do requires their approval."

"The Ministry is different. It's not authoritarian, it's based on God's order. We don't submit to people, we submit to God through people that he ordains. Since we can't see God, we need some physical representation to stand in for Him. It's like in Hebrews 13:17, 'Obey them that have the rule over you, and submit yourselves: for they watch for your souls.'"

"They watch for your souls, yes, but not every decision you make. And don't you think it's a little strange that his thoughts could make Rob sick or well?"

"No, I don't think it's strange at all. Everything starts in the spirit realm. When a head and body are one, then the heart of one affects the other."

"I don't know about that," he says. He runs his hand through his hair and shakes his head, then adjusts his vents to help ward off drowsiness.

"Isn't the shepherd supposed to take care of his flock, and not the other way around?" he says.

I open my mouth to respond, but nothing comes out. I don't have an answer for that. He's not wrong, but he's questioning The Ministry. I need to defend it.

"I know how much The Ministry means to you and you've known these people for a long time, so I don't want to rain on your parade, but I think you need to consider the possibility that their teachings weren't just flawed—"

"No, you don't understand. It wasn't the teachings. Some people misapplied them."

"All the way at the top? Perhaps your beloved Rob was not the saint you thought he was. It has all the signs of a cult."

"You don't know that!" I put up my hand, signaling him to stop.

"And you're afraid to see the truth," he says anyway.

"No, I'm not!"

"Okay, okay." He holds up his hands in surrender. "Then talk to the woman from the grocery store."

"Kumari? But she's in rebellion." I shouldn't have told him she contacted me again. Her email came in the other day telling me she's back in town.

He shakes his head and looks away from me out the window.

I bite my bottom lip so I don't show emotion. We drive in silence for a few miles.

The Ministry is not a cult. Cults make you do things you don't want to do.

I look straight ahead, nostrils flaring.

Cults worship false gods.

My eyes shift to Nathan and back to the road. I guess some people thought too highly of Rob, looking to him instead of God. Maybe most people did . . . I slump. They made Rob a false god.

My mouth drops open. I bang the steering wheel. Nathan just stares at me as if he expected it.

They destroyed what would have been a perfect union. And I've cut off Kumari and countless others they told me were in "rebellion."

Could it be? *No, it must be something else.*

I sit straight up in the driver's seat, looking beyond the shadow of mountains as far as I can see.

I gasp.

Nathan looks at me.

"Grace said they didn't let her get close."

"So?"

"They're not letting *me* get close. Could it be that's the real reason I don't have a position there yet?"

"Go on . . .," he says.

"Like dangling a carrot on a stick. Promises, but no action."

"I think you're onto something."

"Oh, Lord, I don't know what to believe about this." I exhale, remembering the other thing Grace said—those women wouldn't cry wolf. Kumari is one of them.

"You may be right. About talking to Kumari, at least."

He reaches over and rubs my shoulder. I flinch.

"Hey." He looks at me. "It's going to be all right. God's got you."

If only I could be so sure.

CHAPTER TWENTY-ONE

BETRAYAL

I sit on the side wall of the fountain at the center of Tempe Marketplace, an outdoor mall bustling with people on this Saturday afternoon. I'm perspiring both from the hundred-and-one-degree weather and in anticipation of meeting with Kumari. On my phone, I review the email she sent me just over a week ago.

> The "apostle" was not who you think he was. I spent a lot of time there and got very close to him and his team. I would never speak against someone without cause. When I stayed at the Center for three months, I arrived with $15,000 in savings and left with nothing. The expenses and expectations were out of control, and that's only half of it. The accusations are not just rumors. Please allow me to tell my story.
>
> I will be in town for two weeks. Name a time and a place and I will meet you.

The accusations were not just rumors. What were the accusations? I still don't know, except for the vague assertion from Eve. Had something physical happened to Kumari?

Lord, please bless this meeting and reveal the truth to me. Show me what to believe and who I can trust as I communicate with this sister. Show me how to love her, but also keep me from falling into temptation and judgment. Amen.

I look up to see Kumari walking toward me. Her eyes light up with joy when she sees me. I stay seated to hug her.

"Shall we?" I point to The Ice Cream Shoppe behind the fountain.

"Yes, I could use a cold one." She winks at me. We order ice cream and find a seat at one of the tall tables by the window.

"Aaron would be so jealous right now. Elias is taking care of him though. Mummy needs a break."

She pulls out her phone to show me a family picture. The three of them standing in front of the Sydney Opera House. Elias has less hair than when I last saw him, and Aaron is no longer a toddler.

"Aaron's as tall as you, Kumari."

"Taller now." She raises a hand a few inches above her head, showing his height. "This was taken in autumn. That would be your springtime. He's going to tower over me like his dad."

She maintains her bright demeanor for only a few minutes before it subsides and her voice is somber.

"It was bad, Victoria. You don't know the half of it."

I shake my head.

"You're right, I don't. I only know how things looked from afar, and they often looked pretty good. But I know Adam wasn't always happy to spend time at the Center. It took a toll on him emotionally, but he never went into detail, other than Rob being sick much of the time."

"Yes, that's true. But it all started long before that."

"What started?"

"At first, it was financial abuse. Remember when I first met you on holiday? You were just out of college, Vic."

"Yes, that was the best time. But I remember you missed home."

"You were only there for three weeks," she says. "I had already been there for a month and a half and was nearly out of money. In Australia, we get much more vacation time than Americans. I had saved up for a down payment on a house and had extra for a three-month sabbatical at The Ministry Center. It was $15,000 total. I only intended on spending about $5,000 as their guest. Little did I know they would ask me to pay for everything. The expensive dinners and eating out for every meal. It was foolish of me to spend all of that money like that. But I felt like nobody to say something."

"Now that you mention it, I never ate a home-cooked meal while I was there."

"No, they always ate out. It was 'bringing the Kingdom.' Then they would turn around and report that they were behind on their bills and at risk of not being able to pay the rent or keep the lights on each month. They claimed it was a lack of faith among the saints. If the giving saints were like me, they were budgeting every dollar and cutting back on eating out so they could meet their bills and pay off debt."

"I didn't know it was that bad, Kumari."

"It was a waste. Instead of feeding the poor, we were fattening Rob's belly. Heather ate little, and I tried to order the cheapest thing on the menu every time. But Rob indulged like a king. Then he would butter up the servers and tell them he'd pray for them. They were all on a first-name basis. But none of them ever came to us for ministry, at least not while I was there."

"Did you ever say no to going out, or suggest cooking for them?"

"Oh, I offered to cook. But I was their guest and they wouldn't have it. They said I would learn hospitality, a gift of the spirit, by being hosted."

"But, Kumari, you were paying . . ."

"Yes, it doesn't add up, does it?"

"So, that last day I was there when they asked you to pay for the meal. It wasn't an honor, as they implied."

"No, I was nearly broke. I excused myself so I would not make a scene."

Why didn't she push back? I would have told them I didn't have the money.

"Did they know this?" I say.

"Oh, yes. They said I had to have faith. The more I gave, the more I would receive."

"The spiritual law of return."

"That's what they called it, Vic, but I never saw that return. I later learned it's called the prosperity gospel."

"But it left you broke."

"Yeah, the irony!" she laughs.

"Are you still bitter?"

"Of course, but it's so absurd. What else can I do but laugh?"

I shrug. We both eat more of our ice cream.

"For example, near the end of my stay, Rob insisted he show me Las Vegas. I had no desire to see Sin City. Gambling is a fool's errand, and from what I had seen in movies, the drinking, promiscuity, and debauchery that occurred was far from my idea of a good time. The apostle insisted we uplift a word about going anyway. Somehow, we each received a positive response from our spirit, so I went along with it. I supposed there might be some spiritual lesson I needed to learn there, though I couldn't imagine what."

"What was that experience like for you?" I sip my water.

She looks out the storefront window for a moment then back at me.

"We arrived late in the afternoon while the sun was high. I recall watching the parched landscape give way to metallic high-rises against the Spring Mountains backdrop to the west. Airplanes flew overhead, arriving and departing in all directions. We drove nearly five hours with a brief stop at Hoover Dam. It was so hot, my legs were sticking to the leather seats. And Rob kept offering the water he packed, but it was distilled, which I think is gross. He only ever drank distilled water though. Said it was how God intended it."

"I drank distilled for a while and loved it, but then I stopped because the science was conflicting, and it's more expensive than regular."

"I was happy to go back to regular water," she chuckles.

We watch people walk by the ice cream parlor. A mom in yoga pants with her children wearing designer clothes. One holds a giant lollipop, the other a mylar balloon.

She leans toward me. "Victoria, it was awful. Las Vegas, lauded as the Entertainment Capital of the World, was just that—of the world and not of the Spirit of God."

"Oh, I completely agree."

"They boasted grand architecture, but it was all mimicry. A smaller Statue of Liberty, the Eiffel Tower, paintings from the Sistine Chapel, a Roman Colosseum—all replicas of actual sites that told a rich history in their original context but set against the backdrop of flashing lights, greed, and hedonism, they lost all significance."

I stroke my chin. "I hadn't thought about it that way."

"Living in Sydney, I had a front-row seat to the monumental architecture of the Sydney Opera House. My work travels brought me to some of the original buildings in Europe—the Greek Parthenon, castles of the Middle Ages, palaces of the Renaissance, and cathedrals older than the United States. Why would I care to see all of that in Las Vegas?"

I nod. "I always prefer natural wonders to the manmade ones."

"Me too, Victoria. For all the skill and beauty on display, I was far more impressed by the natural cathedrals—monuments formed by God's hands of dirt and rock, trees and water. Nature was where God's majesty shined. Those last three months offered an endless array of colorful sunsets, geological phenomena, and thunderous rain clouds sounding their battle cries in the mountains above and the valleys below."

She just described what I like most about Arizona.

Kumari pulls me into her story as if I were there with her.

"Welcome to Las Vegas, the famous sign proclaimed." She waves her hand in the air as if tracing a banner.

"We arrived at our hotel, which wasn't directly on the Strip, thank God! At check-in, Heather turned to me, 'I submit we use your card for incidentals. It's best not to use The Ministry's card until we know what the balance is going to be.' I shook my head. 'If you promise not to charge it,' I told her and handed over my card for what I hoped would be the last time before returning home.

"Rob's room connected to Heather's and mine. He always insisted she be right there in case he needed anything in the middle of the night. Heather showed off the amenities and the big Jacuzzi bathtub, but neither of us were keen on all the mirrors. I reached for a Fiji water from the countertop. She told me to stop because they charge you twelve dollars if you even move it. 'Now she cares about money,' I thought. I left it thinking we'd bring the water from the car later.

"We ministered to the room, casting out any unclean spirits and asking the Holy Spirit and angels of God to fill it with peace."

I give Kumari an understanding nod. I also try to do this each time I enter a new space. God only knows what spirits may linger in a hotel room.

"Once that was set, Heather asked what I wanted to do that night. I said I didn't know and asked where she wanted to go. I imagined they had something in mind already. She said we'd lift it up for a word but that Rob would probably want to go to his favorite buffet and then a show.

"I thought, 'Oh, Lord, who's paying for us to see a show?' I heard Las Vegas buffets were cheap, with an abundance of options, so I said, 'The buffet sounds nice.' It was exquisite. Fifty dollars a person to sit at the chef's table, usually reserved for parties of eight or more, but Rob worked his charms and we got in. 'This is the best buffet in Las Vegas,' he proclaimed. 'Even so, it doesn't compare to the glory of the riches we have in Christ Jesus.'

"I honestly felt bad for thinking that it was too expensive, that I was rejecting a gift that God had given us in his infinite provision. Still, I had a hard time enjoying the King Crab and calamari without wondering, 'Who is going without food tonight?'"

I have a sinking feeling. "Kumari, I was guilty of the same thing each time I partook of an expensive meal with them. They would pay for it as a ministry expense, and I would think, 'Praise God for the provision,' without considering who gave the money and why."

She nods. "I never intended to spend my life savings on meals. And yet somehow, I was supposed to be okay with eating out two meals a day, indulging on the backs of the saints—members of the church body who were living paycheck to paycheck while dutifully supporting The Ministry, for the gospel's sake. I couldn't see how this trip or many of the meals we shared out at restaurants each day were part of that mission, so I paid for my own meals whenever I could, but I was running very low.

"After dinner, we walked through the indoor mall that occupied most of the hotel. I was hoping they would forget about seeing a show. We were in this small shop that sold knockoff watches when Heather saw one that she adored. She hardly ever bought anything new for herself. The saints ministered most things to her, but she didn't feel worthy of receiving them. I couldn't have her feeling unworthy. Heather was a beautiful child of God, and I looked up to her faithfulness. She asked if I would buy it for her. She never asked me for anything. Of course, I wanted to buy it for her. The price tag read sixty dollars and I was down to my last hundred.

"I said, 'Sorry, honey, but I'll need what's left to return home this week.' She was sad, but it was Rob who guilted me into buying it. Afterward, we drove the Strip, with no money for a show and flashing neon signs threatening to give me a migraine. I wanted nothing more than to go home to my own bed and back to my routine."

Kumari presses her hand to her head and winces.

"Are you okay?" I lean toward her.

"Ice headache." She holds up her ice cream and chuckles.

"Ah, brain freeze, I call it." I sit back in my chair. "Kumari, I'm sorry they took advantage of you."

She shakes her head. "I don't blame Heather. She was a victim of his manipulation, even more than I was. Forced into her position at age seventeen, she lost everything, had no friends, and Rob brainwashed her from that point forward. She couldn't go anywhere without him calling her every few minutes and approving her every move."

"That bad?"

"Oh, yes. She privately disagreed with him about so many things, but she knew the only way she could get income or what she wanted was to keep up this persona of being a prophetess. In the background, she smoked, drank, and cursed because that was her only outlet."

My jaw dropped. Until now, I had heard nothing shocking about their behavior. But Kumari is describing someone I never knew. "Heather? She hid it so well. I . . . I thought she fell into those behaviors later on after leaving The Ministry Center. She did all that while she was there?"

"You don't know the half of it." Kumari looks out the window, shaking her head. "There was a lot of gossip that took place. Of course, we were told that gossip was a sin, but it happened anyway. I never knew what was being said behind my back.

"They kept me at arm's length because I would flare up in anger sometimes. They didn't allow me to join the team for some things. If you didn't adhere to their expectations, they shunned you. I was always stressed out about what they would say about me. I felt inadequate all the time."

I feel remorse for having misjudged Kumari. Her worries always sounded like a lack of faith. When she was obsessed about the small things, I thought she was being paranoid and taking her eyes off spiritual things. I was wrong. She had good reasons to be skeptical.

"Kumari, were any of the rumors true?"

"It's hard to say. I can only speak to what I experienced firsthand." Her eyes shift.

"And what was that?"

Her face goes pale. She busies herself by using a napkin to wipe away some sprinkles that dropped on the table.

"Do you want some more water, Vic? I'm going to get a refill."

"Sure." I hand her my cup.

When she returns with the waters, the color has returned to her face.

She leans into me and says in a steady, low-pitched voice, "I was pregnant with my son and working at The Ministry Center in Sedona."

I nod.

She sits up. "One afternoon, at the conclusion of a typical team meeting, the baby kicked and I let out an 'Ooh!' It caught me by surprise. I didn't want the attention, so I waved off the doting older ladies. The group dispersed from the living room, leaving only Rob and myself, the slow one, as the last to exit.

"As I walked by Rob, he motioned for me to come sit on his lap. This wasn't unusual. He liked to lay hands on my stomach and minister to the child. I welcomed the ministry. At forty, carrying a high-risk pregnancy is stressful enough on the body, let alone the mind.

"He sat forward in his recliner chair, legs spread wide enough for me to stand between them and side-saddle on his left knee. He pulled me in closer so I was resting against his upper body. His enormous stomach folded over his waistline and didn't allow for a very wide seating area on his thighs. He wrapped his left arm around my waist and placed his right hand on my big pregnant belly. The warmth of his healing touch eased my anxiety. I don't recall what he prayed, but I agreed with it.

"I said, 'Brother Rob, I receive that from my God and Christ and I bless you a hundredfold return.' It was the expected response, and I believed it. But when I shifted to stand up, he held on tighter. 'Just a minute.' His voice was gentle but stern. His eyes, cold and strange, stared like he was looking straight through me at someone else.

"I settled back into the position, and his left arm held me tight. That's when I felt the warmth of that hand travel downward across my belly and into a place no man had touched but my husband. I turned to him in protest, but before I could make a sound, his lips were touching mine. I pulled away. My stomach churned, and I had a sour taste in my mouth. I walked out of the room, stunned. I told the others I wasn't feeling well and quickly gathered my things and left, sure not to look anyone in the eyes.

"Trembling, I held on tight to the steering wheel. My mind raced as fast as my vehicle all the way home thinking, 'What had I done? What had *he* done?'"

"Oh my God, Kumari!" I get up from my chair and come around the table to hug her. I hold her tight, then pull away and look at her face. Tears are welling up.

"I'm so, so, so sorry he did that to you," I say, knowing it's not enough. Nothing can make up for the hurt she felt. "How have you held onto this for so long?"

"It was so hard, Victoria. There was nobody I could trust."

Hard to believe, among all our brothers and sisters who loved God and loved each other, that there was no one. But then, I remember how I reacted the first time I read the email. I frown and return to my seat across from her to let her tell her story.

"What about your husband? Did he know?"

"Elias was at work. He had an engineering job and volunteered part-time, serving on the board of elders. Technically, he was part of Rob's headship to oversee ministry matters, but Rob was part of Elias's headship for all aspects of his life.

"I loved my husband very much. He was my first love, truly, and I had waited ten years for him to see that I was the one. We'd followed the consideration of marriage process to the tee. We didn't even hold hands until we were engaged, and we didn't kiss until our wedding day. I kept myself holy.

"How could the apostle defile me in such a way? He was the number one proponent of purity. I thought something must have overtaken him."

"That was my first thought too, Kumari. It had to have been a demonic spirit, or some mental episode. There's no way he would have done that."

She shakes her head. "I don't think that anymore."

I'm frozen in this space between loving God and my apostle, and loving Kumari. I believe she believes everything she's saying. But can I believe that Rob was secretly molesting people and the elders were covering it up? I'm still not there.

"When I arrived home, I dropped my bags at the door and ran to the bathroom. I wasn't going to be sick anymore, but I felt dirty. I turned the shower to hot, removed my clothing, and stepped into the steady stream, letting it fill my mouth and spitting it out several times until I felt I no longer tasted him. The shame of the involuntary arousal caused me to shake, wiping down my body as if covered by a colony of spiders. When the frantic dance was over, I crouched down on the shower floor and cried. 'God, what just happened? What do I do with this?' I cried out to Him."

I'm asking God the same things right now. I imagine how dirty she felt and that no amount of hot water could make her feel clean. Her husband better have stood up for her when he found out.

"I thought about telling Elias, then imagined how he might look at me. There's no way he would believe me. I hardly believed me. My word against the apostle of God. It was like a nightmare that I needed to wake up from."

Kumari is in tears as she recounts the traumatic event. There's no way she's lying about this. And yet, she's right, I still can't imagine my apostle doing this.

She continues, "That's when I thought of Heather. I wished she were there for me to confide in. She would understand. She would . . . and that's when it hit me. If he did this to me out in the open, what had he done to her behind closed doors, when it was only the two of them living together? All the memories of my visit years prior flooded back. How miserable she was, how she wanted to escape, the time I forgot my grocery list and caught them in awkward silence sitting on his bed . . . the late-night bedroom checks . . . 'Why did you have to take her, God?' I cried out of selfishness. But I knew. Heather could never recover from that experience on this side of heaven. What Rob labeled rebellion was her escape to freedom. He told everyone she had called him asking for forgiveness the night she passed. The family maintained her death was a side effect of taking pneumonia medicine with a pre-existing heart condition. All we had were a few bits of information and a confidential autopsy report to which only the family was privy."

Kumari takes a moment to wipe away tears.

I want to believe that it was God's grace that took her home, but why wouldn't God's grace have stepped in much sooner?

"Heather was gone, and I was alone. I had a husband I loved and a baby I couldn't be more excited to welcome into this world, so I decided in that moment, I would carry this burden of shame and anger alone.

"The next day, I didn't report for work at The Ministry Center, or the day after that. I went back less frequently and only with my husband for visits. Eventually, I told them I had to rest for the baby's sake and that I couldn't return. That would excuse me for the remainder of my pregnancy and for about fourteen months after our son was born."

I cover my heart with my hand. "Thank God you had that excuse. But you went back eventually?"

"Yes, I was a few months into my second pregnancy when I had a miscarriage. That's when I felt the weight of sin and guilt. I reasoned that God's wrath was upon me because I had stayed away from The Ministry for so long. I thought it must have been because of some sin in my heart that the sexual advance happened, and because of my rebellion that my second child died. I asked God to forgive me for whatever it was, and to forgive me for the bitterness I felt toward Rob."

"What was it like to go back?" I can't imagine keeping silent about that experience, never mind seeing him every day.

Kumari says, "I didn't know how I belonged there. People would say, 'You're part of God's family . . . you are love . . . people are loving you.' What was happening was completely different."

My heart is heavy. This is the confirmation I needed. How could I not believe my dear sister, who survived so much and is still hurting?

I'm afraid to ask, but I do anyway. "Did you experience any more abuse?"

"Nothing worse than what I shared already. I heard about worse things happening to others. My experience made it easier to believe their stories. I was one of the lucky ones."

I shake my head. Nothing about that is lucky. "I am so sorry I wasn't there for you," I say. But I know words can't make up for it.

"You didn't know. How could you?" she tries to reassure me.

"I could have been more open to listen. Maybe if we'd been closer friends, you would have confided in me."

She shrugs one shoulder. "What good would it have done? You were brainwashed like the rest of us."

Brainwashed. She isn't the first person to tell me that.

I'm not sure I would use such a strong word. I wasn't powerless.

"I'll admit I was deceived . . . and I'm sorry," I say. "Kumari, I want to help. Did anyone witness to what you or others experienced?"

"No. The victims' words stand alone. Heather kept a journal. She hid it from Rob under a loose tile in her bedroom. She left in a hurry without it and never wanted to go back, so it might still be there."

Kumari's story is convincing, but I need hard evidence. I feel a responsibility to uncover the truth for the sake of those who look to me as an example. My life is about leading people to Christ, and if The Ministry were a stumbling block to that, I would have to distance myself. Rob and Heather, the only two people who could answer for these accusations, are gone. If only I could access her journal.

CHAPTER TWENTY-TWO

SCHEMING

"So, how did it go with Kumari?" Nathan asks me the next day as we walk hand in hand toward a shaded spot on the grass at our favorite Sunday spot. He's carrying a blanket under his left arm with a camera slung over his shoulder.

"It was . . . helpful," I say. I don't want to reveal too much until I have evidence. Nathan doesn't know these people like I do, and he may be quick to judge and dismiss all their teachings.

"Did you learn anything new?"

"She told me her story. I think I believe her, but I need to find out more. I can't go by the word of one person alone. I mean, I believe she is hurting, but I want to hear all sides of the story."

"That's fair. Let me know if I can help."

"Thanks," I say. "For now, this is something I need to do on my own."

We find a clear spot on the grass. He squeezes my hand a little tighter and spins me around to bring me close so we're gazing into each other's eyes.

"I'm here for you."

I nod.

We spread out the blanket under the shade of a sweet acacia tree with the sound of a nearby fountain drowning out the city traffic. I lay my head on his stomach and we point out cloud formations, imagining they are different animals. Nathan is my best friend, and I feel at peace with him.

"That one looks like the fighter aircraft I fly in . . ."

I roll my eyes. His preoccupation with fantasy reminds me that we are from different worlds. He was a silver-spoon kid, I was a thrift-store kid. I've worked hard to get to where I am and he expects things to just work.

He nudges me. "What else do you see?"

"I see Noah's Ark!" I point to a large cloud that appears to have animal heads sticking out of it.

"Huh. I guess so," he says.

He can give me the entire backstory of a superhero and recite game lore like it was his own personal history. When I talk about characters in the Bible of real consequence, he lacks the same enthusiasm.

My head bobs with his breath and he begins to snore. I sigh. He has a long way to grow spiritually before we're equally yoked.

By evening, I know what I have to do. I sit on a wrought iron stool at my kitchen counter leaning over my phone on speaker.

"Those are some harsh accusations," Dallas says at the other end. "Were there witnesses?"

"That's just it. Heather was the only witness to Kumari's financial situation. And the other acts, well, they always happened in private."

"Victoria, unless there are two or three witnesses, there's not much of a case to bring before the elders."

I stand and pace between the kitchen and the living room. "I thought you would be on the side of justice."

"I always want justice. But it says right there in the book of Revelation that the 'accuser of the brethren is cast down, which accused them before our God day and night.' That's what they'll say this is. Some saints had their feelings hurt, and instead of giving it to their God and Christ to take personal responsibility, the lying spirit, the accuser of the brethren, convinced them they experienced abuse."

I wince. Putting the responsibility on the victim doesn't sit right with me. I sit back down. "Either way, The Ministry hurt her and others, so now they find it hard to trust God. Don't the elders have a responsibility to watch for their souls, not lead them into temptation?"

He's quiet.

I stop. "Dallas?"

"We need evidence."

"That's another reason I'm calling." I resume pacing. "It's a long shot, but Heather kept a journal. According to Kumari, it may still be at The Ministry Center."

"Go on . . ."

"Nobody can know about the journal or else it might go missing," I say.

"You have my word."

"Okay, she kept it beneath a floor tile in her bedroom. A loose one under her bed."

"That might be tricky," Dallas says. "That room is now used as an office."

"Will you help me?"

"I don't know, Vic—"

"What is she asking for?" Grace says in the background.

Dallas responds, "Some potential evidence stored in the bishop's office."

"It's true, or it isn't," Grace says. "I think you know what you have to do."

Dallas breathes heavily on the other end. I pray the truth will be revealed as I await his response. After what seems like several minutes, he grunts, "I'll do it, Vic. But you're coming with me. I don't want to hold on to it, so as soon I have it, I'm handing it to you."

"Deal." I jump to my feet. "Just name the time."

"It'll have to be done in plain sight," he says.

"How so?"

"There is always someone home. For it not to be suspicious, we'll need a very public reason for us both to be there, like a gathering. That's also when the bishop and his staff will be occupied outside of the office."

"When?" I ask.

I look at the calendar on the wall.

"This Wednesday, seven p.m., we'll arrive separately. In fact, bring Nathan if he's willing. Having someone new in the mix will keep them more engaged."

"I don't want to bring him into this."

"Well, I think it's too late for that. He adores you and the outcome of this will affect him, whether you like it, or not."

What will it be like to bring Nathan to meet everyone? I feel a flutter in my stomach then remind myself that my parents support our relationship, so I have no reason to be ashamed.

"I suppose you're right." I grab a pen and mark the calendar.

"And Victoria"—he pauses—"I pray it isn't true."

"Yeah . . . me too," I say, thinking that would leave a lot of unanswered questions.

After we hang up, I question bringing Dallas into this so deep. I'm still not sure whose side he's on. I want to believe he's on the side of truth, but his loyalties run deep.

I tap my fingers on the kitchen counter.

It's too late now. We have to move forward with the plan.

When I told Nathan that Dallas invited us to a gathering at The Ministry Center in Sedona, he insisted on coming with me. I'm glad I didn't have to make the trip alone. We booked a hotel room with double beds to keep costs low, and I made him promise not to tell a soul. He knows my boundaries.

At the gathering, Nathan and I sit on a worn floral couch among a mishmash of furniture. I look around the circle of about a dozen familiar faces, all older. This isn't the same ministry house I stayed in with Kumari. It is the last house they lived in before Rob got too sick to move anymore. The once pristine high-end feel befitting the house of an apostle is long gone. I feel a heaviness.

Adam, I learn from his mother, is studying to be a pilot and adjusting to the Colorado weather where he and his . . . ahem . . . wife settled. This is a welcome surprise, sparing me the awkwardness of introducing Nathan to my ex-something so soon. I'm happy for him. The pressure he faced to be a church leader was more than he could bear. I wonder now if there were other pressures weighing on him—secrets.

The ceiling fan keeps time with a rhythmic tick. As members pray quietly, waiting for someone to receive something . . . anything, from the Lord that would propel the conversation forward and build each other up.

We sing a few songs to the strum of the elders' guitars. When nobody has any more worship songs on their heart, Charles entertains Nathan as a newcomer with a unique brand of musical comedy, part hillbilly and part country. I smile and nod, unsure what this has to do with ministry.

"All right then, I suppose that's enough silliness," Charles says. "I find it helps new folks get more comfortable."

I look at Nathan, who seems a bit confused but offers a polite "Thank you."

"Earlier we sang, 'They Will Know We Are Christians by Our Love.' What does it mean to love with God's love? Anyone?"

"Put others first," says one woman.

"Honor a person's will," one man responds.

"That's right. And how do we know what will honor their will? Do we read minds? Do we ask them?"

"We must be led of our Spirit and seek God's knowledge, wisdom, and understanding concerning them," I say.

"Yes, that's right," says Charles.

"And what if they tell us what their will is? If they say, 'Nah, I don't want to hear about that God stuff.' What then?"

A little old lady in the corner speaks up, "We don't talk about it. We just keep loving them and meeting them where they're at."

Another woman in a long purple dress and black curly hair says, "I won't stop talking about Jesus. If my spirit leads me to praise him out loud in front of them, I will. Nobody can tell me not to give glory to God for his wonderful works and grace in my life."

I respond, "I agree with you, sister. I want to be like that, but I am often torn between giving God the glory, potentially offending them, scaring them off so that they might never hear the gospel versus keeping silent until they trust me enough to listen."

Dallas adds, "Well, you've got to consider the relationship. Some people, I was one of them, never want to hear the word preached to them because it convicts them too much. But inside they're crying out. And that's okay, but you've got to wait until the time only God knows they'll be open to hear what he wants to say to them through you. So, you've got to use spiritual discernment. Only God knows how to honor someone's will. I sure don't."

For a while, we continue to talk about love and what it means to love the world. I can't help but wonder how this is *doing* anything to love the world or advance God's Kingdom. The body hasn't grown, and this topic isn't new. Eventually, we move into a time of sharing in fellowship over a meal, which they formally call a Lord's Supper. Not the same as the one the night before Jesus was crucified. No, not even close. It is simply a potluck.

Dallas looks at me across the room and gestures with his eyes toward the back offices. I nod. The offices are just past the bathrooms. I place the notebook I brought into my tote bag and then sling it over my shoulder and turn to Nathan.

"I'll be right back."

"Are you okay?" he asks.

"Yep, I just have to use the restroom," I say.

While I'm in the restroom, I hear the clacking of Dallas's cowboy boots as he walks past. I sneak out and follow him down the hall to Heather's old bedroom where he's standing with a flashlight.

"About three feet from the window against the back wall is where the head of her bed used to be," I say.

He shines his flashlight on that spot to reveal a small file cabinet.

"Uh oh," he says.

I look around the edges and see a slit in the grout between the tiles.

"This has to be it," I say.

Voices travel from the kitchen and living room as people are moving around to get food and talking more. We still have to be quiet, but at least the chatter should conceal some sounds.

When we attempt to move the file cabinet, it scrapes across the floor, making a screeching sound. We both freeze. The conversation down the hall continues, seemingly uninterrupted.

"Let's walk it," I say.

Dallas nods. We tip it onto one edge, then the corner, and back onto the opposite one. After a few rounds of this motion, the tile is unobstructed. Dallas presses on it. It's loose but I can't grasp it with my bare hands.

I look around with the flashlight to see a letter opener on the desk behind me. I reach for it when I hear footsteps coming down the hall. Dallas motions for me to hide. I duck and crawl under the desk. A sticky note lies face-up on the floor that reads, "Assert your will unto God and Christ." It's a reminder to acknowledge God in all our ways.

Lord, I pray silently, *please help us retrieve this item. I know stealing is wrong, but it doesn't belong to them. If you want the truth to come out, please protect us in this. And if what I'm doing is sin, please forgive me. I don't know what else to do.*

The footsteps stop, and I hear the bathroom door shut.

We both let out a sigh of relief. I hand him the letter opener.

"Really?"

I shrug. "It's all I could find."

He wedges it between the crack and gets just enough lift to grab hold with his fingers and pull the tile up. He sets down the letter opener and reaches in the hole, pulling out a dusty, purple leather journal.

He hands it to me. I hold it for a moment. My heart beats faster as feelings of dread, anticipation, and sadness well up inside. I cast those cares onto the Lord. No sooner do I slip it into my tote bag than Julio appears at the doorway and flips on the light.

Dallas stands up and steps in front of the misplaced file cabinet. I stand there next to him like a deer in the headlights.

"What's going on in here?" he says, looking around and seeing only the two of us. Then he gives us a wry smile. "A little personal ministry time?"

We don't say a word.

He winks. "I didn't see nothin'," and he walks away.

"Ugh," I shudder.

Dallas steps back, shaking his head.

"I'll put this stuff back. You go so nobody else gets suspicious."

"Thank you," I whisper as I tiptoe out of the room.

CHAPTER TWENTY-THREE

THE PROPHET

I fill a plate with homemade food from the buffet and meet Nathan out on the patio, where he saved me a seat next to him.

"Everything all right?" he checks in again before I sit down.

"Yep." I nod. I wish he would stop drawing attention to me like that.

Charles, who is generally quiet outside of ministry, has everyone captivated with his stories of near-death experiences. I listen as he tells of being saved from an earthquake as a boy.

"It was August 1959," he says. "We were on a family vacation. My parents had a Ford F-250 with a cab-over camper on it. We'd been to South Dakota and were going to Yellowstone Park in Montana. My folks were in the front, my two brothers and sister and I were in the back. We were supposed to go to the campground, but my folks decided last minute to visit some friends they knew near Yellowstone Park. So we showed up on their porch instead. They had two boys already, so they put us six children in an old bunkhouse."

He takes a sip of water.

"So we spent the night in the bunkhouse and the next morning the dad comes in and says, 'Well, did you feel the earthquake?'"

All eyes are on Charles. He shakes his head.

"My folks and that couple are sitting at the kitchen table playing cards and drinking coffee when everything shakes." Charles grips the armchair he's sitting in and shakes it in demonstration.

"And one of 'em says, 'Jim, stop that.' He says, 'I'm not doing anything.' Well then, the cabinet doors flap and the refrigerator rocks. So they're trying to keep everything covered." Charles mimics the chaos with his arms, as if holding things down.

"There was no damage, no harm. Later, the radio reported that a devastating landslide had completely buried the campground we had planned to stay at."

A few of us gasp, while others that likely heard this story many times give exaggerated nods.

"Yep. I was taking a geology course years later and the book we were studying had a chapter that covered that earthquake. So I told the geology teacher, you know, I was there, just not in the campground. Turns out he was a geology student at the time and they'd gone there and studied it. He said there were some people camped right on the fault line. After the earthquake, their fire pit was ten feet below their tent. The ground had slipped that much."

Everyone is speechless.

"Well, then," he continues, "I saw this special on the Discovery Channel on super volcanoes. They were interviewing a guy who had camped near Yellowstone with his family. He and his two brothers were in one tent and his folks were in another tent. The boys were having flashlight wars. Suddenly, things start rockin' and rollin', and when the dust settled, there was a boulder the size of a compact car on the parents' tent. And a tree had fallen across their vehicle. So, the boys had to be rescued."

"Oh no, the parents!" I say.

Nathan puts a fist to his mouth. Others bow their heads.

He frowns and nods. "I found out later twenty-seven million tons of dirt and rock came down off that mountaintop, and it created what they called Quake Lake for a while, because it damned up the water running down. They couldn't go in and rescue anyone else. They figured there were about twenty-eight people in that campground."

"God saved your whole family," Nathan says.

"Yep, that's right," Charles says. "There were other times too."

A couple excuses themselves. The hour is late and they need to get home, so several people get up to hug and say goodbye. Dallas walks them to the door.

There are fewer of us now. Charles's wife, Annie, sits beside him. She nudges him. When he looks at her, she says, "Tell them about when we were dating."

He smiles and his eyes twinkle, "Okay, one more. I was dating Annie. I was supposed to be at work at the copper mines at four o'clock in the afternoon. Her mom sent me off with some kind of container of pinto beans or something. I had them in the saddlebag of my motorcycle. I'm going along and there was an S-curve on the road up ahead. On a BMW motorcycle, sixty miles per hour was nothing. So I went through the first curve, started into the second curve, and heard something dragging. I look down and when I looked up, I straightened up."

Slap! His hands slide together, gesturing how he and the bike launched off the road and into the air.

"There was a cornfield and a few small hills. After I launched off the third bump, me and my bike parted ways. As I was flying through the air, I thought, *You bought it this time, Price.* But I didn't die. I landed with a face full of dirt."

Nathan winces.

Charles continues, "When I got up, the motorcycle was still running. One saddlebag was messed up. The windshield torn off. I just picked it back up and went on . . . the beans or whatever it was all over the saddlebag. I told my boss after a few hours at work, I said, 'Look, I gotta go. I hurt everywhere.' My injuries were bruises on my shins where I hit the cylinder heads and a black eye where I did the face plant into the dirt."

"That's it?" Nathan says.

"That's it. And that's the only place I could have gone off those curves where they didn't have a barbed wire fence or big concrete studs lined up along the edge. There's no way I would've lived going off that curb in any other place. That was my come-to-Jesus moment." He gestures air quotes with his hands. "Somebody was looking out for me."

"Wow, that's something." Nathan shakes his head.

"You know, I've counted seven times in my life when I shouldn't have made it," Charles says.

A couple rises from their seats to say goodnight. They live at The Ministry Center in Phoenix and are staying overnight.

Only a few of us remain. I'm eager to leave, thoughts of Heather's journal burning in the back of my mind. But I want to ask Charles a few questions first. I don't know when I'll get another chance. So I stay until the others finally go to bed and it's just us and Charles.

I take a deep breath, and I'm about to speak when Charles says, "I ask your forgiveness, sister, for doubting your loyalty to The Ministry. You've got to understand how it looked to us."

I straighten up. That's the last thing I expected him to say, but it doesn't really feel like much of an apology.

Does he have any idea how much pain that caused me, especially after the breakup?

Now isn't the time to discuss it, so I simply say, "Thank you." This is my opening to ask about the apostle's passing.

"I imagine it's been difficult for you leading The Ministry since Rob passed away," I say.

He shakes his head. "Not really. It's just continuing in the message God brought through him."

Beyond storytelling, the man never shows emotion or vulnerability, so I don't know why I expected this conversation to be different.

"True," I say, "but many people walked away."

"That was their will." He taps his fingers on the arm of the chair. His hand isn't trembling as it used to. "When people don't give their perceptions to God, to be taught by their spirit, but make a man a source, they'll get hurt. It's nothing anyone did to them."

His voice is void of expression. Unsure if Charles is capable of showing empathy, I probe deeper.

"What was it like for you when Rob passed away? That must have been difficult," I say.

He flips his palms up. "Well, of course, there have been a lot of things presented."

"Presented?" Nathan asks.

"Lies of the enemy," Charles explains. "Things everyone must give to God and Christ in their spirit to be taught God's truth."

He's still dodging the question. I ask differently. "How did Rob's passing change things for you?"

"Well, what I've always tried to share with people is, go back to what was brought. Did you prophesy to the question 'Is this true for me'? Whether the man, in the latter years, could control things or not isn't important. We're not talking about the man, we're talking about the message. And if you prophesied it was true for you, what changes it?"

"Right," I say. "So, it sounds like the message didn't change. The way of life didn't change for you at all. Did your responsibility in The Ministry change?"

"Well, I became the ipso facto head," he says with a measured tone. "It wasn't something that I was looking for or expecting. Given my position, you know, it was natural."

My patience is wearing thin. The leadership transition was the biggest change The Ministry had ever experienced, and he is acting as if it was no big deal.

Mirroring his nonchalant approach, I say, "So, is it just business as usual or were there any effects?"

"Well, of course there were effects, I mean, good grief." He shifts in his chair. "People made a lot of decisions based on what they heard, not what they prophesied, from what I've seen. It's a case of throwing the baby out with the bathwater, you know."

I nod.

Now we're getting somewhere.

"To be quite frank," he says, "I had developed a drinking problem."

A drinking problem? I have never seen him or anyone in his family touch a drop of alcohol. But after meeting with Kumari, not much surprises me.

"Rob was sick in the hospital up in Sedona but still able to talk on the phone. After having ministry from him, I realized the addiction got bad, and it was received that I should get help. I called my insurance and asked them where I could go to get cleaned up. They didn't have a good answer. They said go to the emergency room and they can process you from there. So, I called the local pastor and asked him to take me to the hospital. Then I drank the rest of the bottle of vodka."

He laughs. "I figured I'd have some fun with it. From the ER, they took me by ambulance to the rehab place. I don't remember much of anything about the ER."

Of course he doesn't, he could have given himself alcohol poisoning!

Beside me, Nathan stares intently at Charles. He probably can't believe what he's hearing.

"I couldn't receive calls while at rehab. It was on my third day that Eve and her husband came and told me that Brother Rob had passed away."

"While you were in rehab?" I ask.

"That's right. And later, Eve told me there were three things Rob was waiting for before he could let go and pass on. The third thing was me getting sober."

I'm curious what the other two were, but I won't let that distract me from hearing his testimony.

"When did you develop a drinking problem? Was it earlier in life?"

"Oh, no. It was sudden and got bad very quickly."

I was not expecting that response. Maybe it was spiritual warfare because Rob was dying.

"What do you think caused or contributed to that?" I ask.

"I don't know. It started out by getting some hard fruit drinks that had alcohol in them, and I liked the way it felt, so it escalated from there."

It sounds like he'd never had alcohol before then. Trying to make sense of this, I ask, "Was it genetic?"

"I had a brother that had a drinking problem. So maybe, I don't know."

Regardless of why it happened, I suppose what's more important is how he dealt with it.

I ask, "Did you fulfill your time in rehab?"

"Yes."

"How have you been doing since?"

"Mostly good."

For someone who keeps his feelings to himself and his personal life private, this was a big exposure. Still, something feels off about it.

"It sounds like Rob cared for you very much. What did that feel like when your sister told you he waited for you to get help before passing?"

"Well, it makes you wonder. But what can you say? Maybe it made it easier for him. I don't know."

And there's the detached version of Charles I'm used to. I try to calculate how long ago this all happened.

"What year did Rob pass away?" I ask.

"In 2016," he says. "I remember entering rehab on 5/11/16 because five and eleven make sixteen. That's how I remembered it. And so, about May thirteenth or fourteenth, he passed away—for real that time. He'd passed away several times before that."

"Yes, that is truly remarkable," I say. Rob's repeated resurrections are why I still struggle to see him as anything other than an apostle.

"Yeah. But what nobody's talking about is what happened when he bled out while in ministry with a couple. He went into the bathroom and hemorrhaged severely. They called the ambulance, and he coded two or three times. He had to have three blood transfusions. And nobody's thinking about what that would do to a person. His immune system was totally shot. I don't know how all that affected him, but nobody takes that into account."

"I think some people do," I say. "A few have received by their spirit, there could have been some mental issues triggered by the physical trauma."

"Well, when you have, like I said, three complete blood transfusions . . . and he died at least twice during that time period . . ."

His logic lingers in the air between us. The bleed-out he mentioned was somewhere around 2013. He describes how an internal vein had ruptured. When the doctor cauterized it, he remarked that he'd seen nothing like it and later wrote about it in a medical journal.

I ask, "Did he ever consider retiring or taking a back seat?"

Charles shakes his head. "I'm not aware."

"He always told us the extreme hardships had to do with him being an apostle," I say.

He nods. "How many people consider the pressure that can bring?"

"I'm sure it's a lot of pressure," I say.

"And it's a lot of intercession," he says. "I guess he had a real sickly childhood, tuberculosis or something. A lot of factors."

"He had a rough start for sure," I say.

Nathan takes my hand. His eyelids look heavy. I nod in acknowledgment that it's getting late.

I turn to Charles. "Thank you for sharing and being open about that part of your life when you struggled with alcohol. Do many people know about that?"

He shrugs.

His wife nudges him. "I receive to go to bed," she says.

Nathan leans into me. "We need to get going too."

I nod and feel a flutter in my stomach. The journal calls to me, but it must wait until I am home.

CHAPTER TWENTY-FOUR

REVELATION

Heather's journal, with its faded worn leather and curling corners, sits on my kitchen island. An associate is covering for me at work today. Anticipating this moment, I slept little last night, only dozing on the ride home from Sedona before dawn while Nathan drove. He dropped me off on his way to work. Now, nothing stands between me and learning the truth.

I pick up the journal and trace the embossed "H" with my fingertips. My view of Heather and of Rob as an apostle could change in ways I am not prepared to accept. But, it's better than living in darkness. All things must come to light. With a deep breath, I open to the first page.

It's undated.

> Day 1: What the fuck? I can't believe my parents sent me here. I attend one party and wake up in someone else's bed like a normal teenager and they freak out. What am I supposed to do with an old man and all this church shit? I'm not changing everything just for him. God, I believe you exist, so what are you doing to me? This better not last long.

Day 3: It's been three days without alcohol or cigarettes. I'm cold and sweating. When I finally sleep, nightmares torment me and I wake up screaming. When will these withdrawal symptoms go away? I feel like my body has turned itself inside out and I want to die. God help me!

I rarely think of Heather as a troubled sixteen-year-old. She never hid her old life, but she did so well replacing it. In the next few entries, she writes about being homesick and adjusting to new rules and a different schedule. Several pages later, she found she was benefiting from the arrangement.

Day 14: Today, we went shopping with Kumari. She's like, six years older than me or something, but she's really nice and after hanging around old men all the time, I'm glad to see someone young. It's too soon to tell if we'll be friends, but she's all right. I plan on leaving soon anyway.

Day 20: I can't believe how much money we spent! I was never a dress girl, but Papa (that's what he told me to call him so that people don't think it's weird when we're out in public) says that long skirts are more "becoming" of a godly woman and wearing them will represent my submission to him as my head. I don't know about that. I'm still working out this whole idea of head and body. But I find them to be very comfortable and the fabric is so pretty. Besides, maybe if I do what he wants, it will get me out of here faster.

I wonder how long it took her to stay willingly. I keep reading for several more pages. She doesn't write every day, but her tone changes around two months in.

Day 48: Today, I saw a softer side of Papa. Maybe even a weakness. After getting frustrated and angry with Charles, he cried a lot and he seemed truly alone. I tried to comfort him but wasn't sure what to say, so I gave him a hug. He pulled me in very close. Too close for my comfort, but I'm sure the old man didn't mean anything by it. He was probably just trying to hold on for balance. It must be hard to be the leader of a ministry when the elders don't understand your vision. I don't fully understand it myself, but I know he's passionate about it and many people seem to respect him for it. Maybe I could do a little more to help him. I guess I could start by praying more.

God, help me be a body to the apostle. I don't know why you chose me, but I'll do what I can to be a better example to the body of Christ. Rob says, as the body I have the greater influence. I don't want to be the reason he feels alone or misunderstood. I know what that feels like all too well. Help me to be better. Amen.

What a sweet entry. Could Kumari's account have been a misunderstanding?

It seems she spent most of her time learning to be a homemaker and doing some administrative tasks while she learned the Twelve Principles. For a while, she struggled like the rest of us with giving everything to her spirit and prophesying. But the pressure she was under to be perfect was immense. I thought I had high standards for myself, but never to the degree that Rob had for Heather. He used the mistakes she made during simple things like cooking, cleaning, and filing papers to identify sin.

Day 183: Will I ever learn to cook his eggs right? What is wrong with me that I can't do this simple task? I want to honor you, God. I want to honor him as you told me to. Everything was going fine. I put an egg in the poacher and lowered it slowly into the boiling water and set the timer. When the time went off, I removed it immediately, but my hand jittered and it slipped off, sliding across the stove and rolling onto the floor where he stood at the edge of the kitchen, hands on his hips and a scowl on his face. The next thing I know, I'm sitting down with Rob on the couch getting a lecture about asserting my will to my spirit and how I'll never get rid of sin if I'm not diligent about repenting every second. I thought I was. I try, I really try.

Day 264: Kumari has been staying with us for two months. I like having her here. It's less boring, and now I'm not the only one who messes up, or who gets offended by his jokes when we're in mixed company. At first, I didn't know why she would volunteer to come, but then I learned about her difficult relationship with her mother (I get it) and the pressure she felt to find a husband. She's smart and likes to read. That intimidates guys. I don't think I'll have that problem once I find a guy worth my time.

Day 365: It's been a year since I arrived and so much has changed. I don't know why I'm still counting the days. I can see that I have more work to do here. Today, Papa let me work in the office. He asked me to type some letters and write some words of prophecy to the elders and saints. I didn't realize how much I would enjoy it. The words of encouragement uplifted me, and I pray the recipients will be blessed too. Maybe it isn't so bad working here after all.

I'm relieved to see that things are going well. I keep reading through the afternoon. There are significant breaks in the timeline. Perhaps she had another journal for a while and then came back to this one.

Some entries go beyond her daily activities to reveal in-depth conversations with God and thoughts about Rob's teachings. In one such entry, she asks God to clarify her gender role. She is confused by the notion of being both a woman and a son of God, and which is her first priority. After much back and forth, she concludes her genderless spiritual identity must come first. From there, her spirit will lead her to fulfill the physical female role as honor to God.

Desiring to honor God, Heather repents of the ideas that have come through corrupt society on how women should behave. She laments the behavior of those around her, sparing details. Her Lord tells her that she is valuable and a blessing as a woman in the kingdom of God, and a body to the apostle. She's eager to learn more and willing to manifest it.

I recall a teaching on this subject that must have been close to the time of this entry. But, why the confusion? Even back then, I was fairly certain I knew what it meant to be a son of God, walking on earth as a woman. Reading the prophetess's thoughts on the matter begs the question: *What did she see men and women of the ministry doing?*

My stomach grumbles, and I realize it's been hours since I ate. I make a peanut butter and jelly sandwich for lunch so I don't have to stop reading for long.

Then, I read an entry that makes me regret eating.

I feel so dirty. Rob wants to prepare me to meet my husband one day. That's what he says all of this training is leading up to. In order to be a perfect bride to Christ, I need to prove my faithfulness to a man. And to do that, I need to know how to please a man. I can't believe I'm going to write this, but I want to record the details in case I forget how it felt.

Tonight he asked me to join him in his bedroom. He said he wanted some company. He was "being presented with feelings of depression." As I entered the room, he turned on the TV and there were naked bodies. I turned my head away, at first thinking he hit the wrong button and would change the channel, but he didn't. He kept it on. Then he said to repent of the flesh's perceptions and see it all by the Spirit to learn how the human body works and to pray for those on the screen who need salvation. He invited me to lie on the bed next to him and told me to pray that the Holy Spirit would keep my heart pure and guide my hands.

I stop there, and a chill runs through me. My stomach now garbles for a different reason. *"Guide my hands"? What am I about to read?*

I take a few deep breaths and pray that I can handle whatever comes to light. I keep reading.

I said no. I went to leave the room, but he yelled, "Heather! Don't leave without giving all five-sense perceptions to your Spirit and prophesying." His voice was stern but shaky, like he was afraid I might not stay.

I felt as if I'd already sinned against him and God. I turned around and submitted.

"It's all right," he said. "We are head and body by God's word. It's a type of spiritual marriage. What we do here will prepare you for a physical one someday."

I made him agree I wouldn't have to touch him, just myself. I don't know why I stayed. I don't know what came over me, but I was afraid to disobey him.

"God!" I yell out into my empty apartment. "He violated her! I don't care if they never touched, he forced himself into her psyche while doing sexual acts! Oh, God, h-how, I . . . I don't understand." Then I realize, this isn't much different from how he touched Kumari. She warned me I might find something even worse. I sink into a fetal position on the couch and immediately pray against unclean thoughts provoked in the flesh. My eyes open to the setting sun. I take some deep breaths and turn on the light.

> *Kumari is staying with us again. I don't know why she wants to come, but I'm thankful to have another sister here. I don't get as lonely, and his attention is divided.*

> *She brought music and books with her I'm not allowed to keep here. Guests are excused from following some rules until they get sufficient ministry and willingly give up their vices. I'm not so sure they are all vices, so I partake privately. Having some distraction can help me remain sober.*

> *God, that bender last month nearly put me in the hospital. Nick, a friend from childhood, was a huge help. I'm so glad Papa lets me talk to him. We reconnected after he sought spiritual council on his latest criminal charges.*

So she *was* drinking while at The Ministry Center, like Kumari said. None of this is what I expected to learn when I came out to Arizona. The Ministry was supposed to be a mecca for spiritual enlightenment. A true church that would forge the way for all believers. Now, I'm struggling to find any proper representatives of God's word.

Kumari is one of the few I can trust with my secrets, but I haven't told her everything. Sharing a room with her also helps to cut down on the nightly visits.

Nightly visits? That must be what Kumari was talking about. Lord, please don't let it be as bad as I think.

We stay up late talking, and sometimes he hears us. Last night was one of those times. We were giggling about something— yes, two grown women having a sleepover. Maybe I'm making up for a lost childhood. He shuffled down the hallway, and we went silent. Kumari whispered, "What does he want?" I held my breath and thought, "Please don't let this be the night. Kumari doesn't deserve what I've been through. She is more innocent than I ever was." The doorknob turned partway. Locked. What may have been a few seconds felt like minutes. Then he shuffled away and back to his bedroom.

That was a close call. He never came to my room simply to check on me. He would have called on me if that were the case. No, he wanted to experience my body and potentially hers, too.

I wouldn't dare tell anyone about this except Nick. It was a long time ago, but he can relate.

I cup my hands in a prayer position over my nose and mouth with shallow, measured breaths. Devastated, I let tears roll down my face. "God," I pray, but that's all that comes out. They're both dead, and only Kumari is left bearing this weight. I can't let her bear it alone.

After several minutes, I get up and take a bathroom break. I splash some water on my face and wipe away the tears. Then I return to my position on the couch with the journal.

At the North American Elders Conference, Victoria, a young woman from Massachusetts, who once stayed with us for a few weeks, commented on my weight loss. I know she meant it as a compliment, but I wasn't kind in my response: "That's what happens when you have the stomach flu for a month."

She backed away, and I don't blame her. I get the sense that she's always wanted to get closer to me, but I couldn't let her. Rob named her a prophetess. For what? So she gave a few words by email. I don't see her out here struggling with the daily battles we face. She hadn't been by Papa's side when he was sick, calmed him when enraged, prayed with him when he felt depressed and spiritually attacked. I was the one who called for the elders each time we thought we were going to lose him. I was by his side when he flat-lined in the hospital and came back to life. She has no idea.

She was right. I had no idea. My envy blinded me to seeing her struggles. When I saw her pleasant attitude, long and healthy hair, and the beautiful words she wrote to us, I thought she was closer than any of us to manifesting perfection. I shake my head in shame and read on.

Do I feel guilty lying about the flu? No. It's the only way to protect the body. I can't let my weakness discourage others from working out their salvation. I stare at the empty liquor bottles piled up in my closet. A reminder that I have to be stronger than that. I can't let it compromise Rob's reputation. He understands my struggle, and this time the devil got ahold of us both. But the blood of Jesus saves us. He has redeemed us, and that's why I'll keep this secret. The same way Rob and Charles hide their addiction. Then Satan can't use it to bring judgment upon us and destroy Christ's ministry.

The same way Rob and Charles do? So, if she was lying about the flu, then Rob lied about his deliverance, and Charles must have been drinking back then too. I only saw Charles on ministry outreaches or during conferences—times when he would have had to hide his addiction. His hand tremors were likely withdrawal symptoms. They were all lying!

The confluence of emotions inside of me is too much to process. I'm not sure how much more I can read so I skip to the last entry.

Finally, the words are all confirmed by the eldership. I am to go stay with my biological father for a few months in Tennessee. It's not the escape I dreamed of, but it's a step. I've been trying to forgive my father for abandoning me when I was a baby and passing the alcoholic gene to me. Now he's dying of it. Rob warned how difficult it will be and that he'll miss me very much. I'm sure he will. Everyone expects that once my father dies, I will be back. But Nick will be out of prison soon, and he wants to marry me. Could I take that leap?

The remaining pages are blank. I recall reading a letter issued from The Ministry to the body of Christ about her eventual resignation. After caring for her father until his death, she accepted Nick's proposal without the elders sanctioning it. She never returned to serve.

I shut the journal, the leather cool beneath my fingers, and remain on the couch. Silence amplifies the unsettling weight of her words. It was no surprise she faced spiritual battles, but I always imagined they were circumstantial or psychological. Alcoholism and sexual abuse never crossed my mind when I knew her.

Lord, how could I be so blind? And what do I do now?

I drag myself to bed, emotionally and physically exhausted.

THE RESTORATION

And after you have suffered a little while, the God of all grace, who has called you to his eternal glory in Christ, will himself restore, confirm, strengthen, and establish you.

1 PETER 5:10 ESV

CHAPTER TWENTY-FIVE

RESCUE

I can't find the strength to get out of bed the next day. The weight of all that I read is too heavy, and I'm not ready to let it go. I can no longer ignore the evil deeds of the one I trusted most. Even though he's gone, his teachings shaped my worldview and continue to shape it for others. The same philosophy influenced everyone I've ever looked up to, and now that I know he wasn't practicing what he preached . . . how can I trust any of it?

I haven't left my apartment since returning home nor answered calls from family or friends, except Nathan. If I don't answer his calls, he'll come over. I don't tell him what's going on except that I'm not feeling well and can't go into work. He offers to bring me chicken soup, but I decline. I say I just need some time to myself.

By evening of the second day, my haven feels like a prison. I need to move around and get some fresh air.

"Lord!" I call out for the umpteenth time.

But how do I know he will answer me? That it isn't just my own thoughts? Is prophecy real?

I take a deep breath and cough. *Ouch, that hurt.* My back must be out of alignment from lying around for so long.

I step onto my balcony to test the air. It's a cool day for September, partly cloudy. The weather app on my phone says low eighties, but it feels much cooler after the recent heatwave. Low of sixty tonight. I pack my hiking bag and some water and drive to South Mountain, where it all began. The trail seems more difficult than when I hiked it with Nathan. Each step feels like work, but I push through as waves of emotion ebb and flow.

I pick up a rock, but it doesn't seem very interesting. I toss it away. Hopelessness captures my mind. *Could it be that it is just a rock, and this is just a mountain? Some ocean brought them together millions of years ago. Maybe God didn't design this.* I feel so alone.

As I ascend the mountain, I turn around to see the sun, low in the western sky, turning the clouds brilliant shades of pink and orange. This artistry of light and gasses reminds me that God's majesty still covers the earth, no matter how people respond to it. His rain falls on the just and the unjust.

Living in the desert, I understand that rain is a blessing. *God, where were your blessings for Heather and Kumari and who knows how many others?*

I think about time passing, how the sun sets on one day that will never be again, and it rises with hope that the new day will be better than the last. It isn't always. Yet, I had viewed my walk of salvation as an upward trajectory. Like climbing this mountain, every hardship provided an opportunity to exercise my will to agree with God, to remain steadfast, and brought me a step closer to my eternal reign with Christ.

I keep climbing and let my mind run with its thoughts.

Eternity is a mysterious word. Many Christians celebrate the idea of being with Jesus forever. I couldn't fathom what it would be like to even exist forever. The idea provokes great fear. It's the darkness that often visits me at night when I lay in bed trying to fall asleep, then I sit up in a panic—afraid to live and afraid to die.

Shake it off, Victoria, I tell myself. *If I'm going to survive this hike, let alone this day, I must focus on this moment.* I drink from my water bottle. I've been hiking for a while without thinking about where I was going. Dusk is falling and I should turn back, but I can't seem to find the trail. I don't see any markers. I check my phone—no signal. Ironic for being on a mountain with nearly every cell and radio tower imaginable jutting out of its peak.

Must be interference. *God, if you're still there, please guide me home.*

I turn around and start walking back the way I came when I reach diverging paths. One of them looks familiar, like it may lead to Fat Man's Pass. The other two may lead down the mountain, but I'm not sure which one. I choose one that leads me around to the other side of the mountain. I hear coyotes howl in the distance.

I barely noticed the sun when it sets, and now the temperature has dropped at least twenty degrees. I shiver and feel aches throughout my body. The desert solitude that comforted me by day, now threatens to overtake me by night.

My body feels worn down and I'm nearly out of water. Around the bend, the moonlight shines into a small cave that might provide some shelter.

There is a wide opening and some large rocks to rest on. I take off my pack and pull out a flashlight to look around. No animals, no major insects or snakes to worry about. I'll rest here for a little while until I get my strength back. I tuck into a corner with my back against the smooth stone. I sip the last few drops of water from my bottle. A cloud of bugs has gathered around the head of my flashlight, so I turn it off.

I look off into the distance, observing how the lights of a small town look like earthly stars. I imagine the billions of people living their lives all doing different things in different time zones, and yet somewhere there may be others hiding out in a cave like me.

"Where are you, God? Are you with all of those billions of people and also with me?"

I hear the coyotes again and keep praying.

"God, please send your angels to protect me," I speak out into the wilderness.

Then I yell, "Why didn't you protect Heather or Kumari or any of the other women? How could you give someone like Rob a ministry and let them abuse and defile in your name?"

I stare into the infinite abyss of starlit sky. Their number is far greater than I can see down in the valley among the city lights. Doubts about my ability to discern good and evil taunt me as I consider the steps that got me here. Sure, I was born into this belief system, but hadn't God proven his faithfulness, power, and love to me?

When Mom and I didn't see a way to pay our bills, we prayed, and a check would show up in the mail. When I was sick and prayed for healing to come, in the morning I felt well enough to go about my day. Those times when I asked God which road to take that led me to a divine encounter with someone unexpected. Or when I didn't seek God and ended up lost and afraid, lacking provision.

I couldn't do this life without you, God. Jesus is my friend, my brother, my Savior. His wisdom keeps me from harm. So, why didn't they have the same benefit?

I plant my face in my hands, blocking out my surroundings.

I need to mourn. What? I do not know. Is it the person I thought I was who built an identity on the apostle's doctrine? Why would I mourn a false identity? No. It's something else.

Then it hits me. Those whose faith was shattered and lives lost, not for the gospel's sake but for the sake of power, manipulation, and deceit. They are the ones I must mourn. Those who never found the strength to speak out and tell their story. Others who sat by and did nothing because they were too blind to see the crime that was being committed and the destruction unfolding.

I was one of them. Jesus, the Good Shepherd, warned us about "the thief [who] comes only to kill and to steal and to destroy." The thief came for the sheep. He killed Heather, he stole countless lives by putting them under his control, and he destroyed relationships that otherwise might have edified the church. But Jesus also said in John 10:10, "I have come that they may have life and have it to the full."

My strength is fading, and I'm not sure I'll make it back down the mountain tonight. I stand up and feel lightheaded. When I reach for my backpack, the ground shifts and my head spins. I lean against the cold rock wall and slide down to the ground. I'll just stay here a bit longer. I place my backpack behind my head to lie back and rest.

Ouch!

Something is protruding from the front pocket. I sit up and find it's a mini Bible of the New Testament and Psalms. I open the pages blindly. It's too dark to see. I aim my flashlight at the words: Psalm 23. The Scripture known for being read at funerals.

"Oh, God! Am I going to die out here?" I cry. Then I cough again. This time it hurts when I take a deep breath. I now realize this pain in my chest feels frighteningly similar to the last time I had pneumonia. Am I destined to the same fate as Heather?

"Lord, you wouldn't allow that. Would you?" My voice and hands tremble as I shiver from the cold night air. Hoping for some comfort, I take my sweatshirt out of my backpack, not so much a pillow anymore. I pull it over my head, lay back, and read the Psalm until I lose consciousness.

"Tori! Victoria! Wake up!" I am shaken awake by two hands and a high-pitched voice. As the morning light pierces my vision, my coworker's face comes into view.

I muster the strength to speak just above a whisper. "Olivia? What . . . what are you doing here?"

"Oh, thank God!" she says. "I thought you were dead. You look terrible. Were you out here all night?"

"Yeah, I guess so." *Cough, cough.*

"You don't look well. I'm calling the park ranger."

I try to sit up, but I am too weak.

I wake up again several hours later. My chest and head hurt. I reach for an itch and feel the soreness of an IV in my right arm. A closed door mutes the sounds of machines beeping in the hallways. I turn toward the window to the right of my hospital bed to find Nathan asleep in the chair next to me.

"Nathan?" I say.

He wakes with a start. "Oh! Victoria, thank God, I was so worried about you." He takes my hand and rubs my arm. "I tried to reach you for hours last night, but your phone kept going to voicemail. Olivia called me this morning to say she found you on the mountain. Oh, God, I was so worried. I thought I was going to lose you." He hangs his head in disbelief.

"How did I get here?" I ask.

"Phoenix Mountain Rescue airlifted you. You don't remember the helicopter ride?"

"No . . . thank God. That sounds terrifying."

"The nurse says you have walking pneumonia. Why didn't you see a doctor sooner?"

"I . . . I didn't think it was that bad. I've been upset and crying a lot, so I figured the discomfort was from that."

"Why were you so upset?" he asks.

That's when I remember I have not told him what I found.

We hear a small knock at the door, then Olivia enters with two coffees. She is wearing green running shorts and a purplish gray crop top displaying a faded mandala print.

"She's awake," Nathan says.

"Oh, sweetie! How are you feeling?"

"I've been better. How did you find me?"

"It's quite remarkable, really. I woke up super early this morning, like an hour before my alarm. That's when I saw I had a bunch of text messages from Nathan. He was really worried about you. I told him I didn't know where you were and he asked me to pray. I said I would send positive thoughts to the Universe." She looks up at him with a smirk.

I let out a heavy sigh.

She puts up her hand. "But this time, I actually prayed to Jesus. I don't know what came over me, but knowing you and your strong faith, it felt right. I left early for my morning run through the mountain trails. Normally, I go left at the fork, but something told me to turn right, so I did. That's when I came to the cave where I was going to turn around, but then I saw someone laying there." She takes my hand. "I didn't know it was you at first, because your hood was up, then I saw your water bottle with the dove sticker and Bible verse on it. I called your name, but you didn't answer. That's when I ran over and shook you awake."

"I remember that part." A tear runs down her cheek, and she places her hand over her heart. "God led me to you."

"Does this mean you believe now?" I say.

She straightens up and lifts her chin. "We have some issues to sort out, but I'm willing to listen to what He has to say."

This revelation washes over me like a wave at my back—unexpected yet refreshing. God was with me, and He used my situation to reveal Himself to an unbeliever.

"That's a good start." I smile through pain in my lungs.

She nods and squeezes my hand.

The hospital kept me overnight for observation, so Mom flew into town the next day to care for me.

"Here's some orange juice to take with your antibiotics."

"Thanks, Mom," I say with a weak voice then take the pills alongside my homeopathic remedies.

As if reading my mind, she says, "You know, The Ministry isn't the only one with the truth."

She has said that before, but now I believe her. We just finished watching a sermon online where the pastor warned not to trust any church that said they were the only ones with the truth. It makes sense. How could one small ministry address the needs of billions of people? Why would an infinite God confine his blessings to a single group of people walking a narrowly prescribed path? He did that long ago with Israel, only so that he could later expand his grace to the entire world.

"I'm wondering if they preached the truth at all," I say.

"I wouldn't go that far. They teach from the Bible, and we've learned so much about following the spirit and not the flesh. They aren't perfect, but don't be so quick to throw the baby out with the bathwater."

That cliché is one of her favorites, and a wise saying. Now, I have to determine which part is the baby.

"What do you think about the idea that Jesus is God?" I say.

"Well, he was fully human, but also called 'God' by God."

"I know that's what we learned, but this pastor made a strong case for Jesus being God from the beginning, not a perfect man who became God. That the Word became flesh and dwelled among us speaks more to his love and compassion than to something we ought to strive to become," I say.

"You've always worked so hard to be something," she says. "It's pained me to watch you beat yourself up all the time."

"I know. I get frustrated that I'm not walking perfectly, the way Jesus walked." I bite my bottom lip. "But now, I think I'm seeing that Jesus is, and always was, the Word, the Light of the World. With Him living inside me, I only need to let Him shine through."

"That's right, let it flow by the spirit," she says. "Don't worry about every little detail. Remember? Cast your cares upon Him, for He cares for you."

"Yeah, I do. It's heavy though." Over the next hour, I tell her about Kumari and how that led to me finding Heather's journal and my time on the mountain, questioning God.

I know she'll need time to process it, but I ask her anyway. "Was Rob a false prophet?"

Mom replies, "Even if all the allegations are true, I don't think that makes him less of a prophet. I believe he had good intentions at the beginning, but he battled with his flesh and he was just a man who made mistakes. Look at King David. He did some terrible things. Still, God chose him."

She always brings up King David.

"But Mom, King David repented publicly and wrote an anthology of psalms about it. Rob covered up his sin and never took responsibility before the church."

She's quiet. I decide to take another approach.

"Do you ever recall hearing Rob say, 'Jesus is Lord'?"

"Sure, he wrote all about it in his teachings."

"That's just it. Rob wrote it in his teachings as explanations or as posters with pithy sayings like, 'If Jesus Christ isn't Lord of all, he's not Lord at all.' But did you ever see him worship the Lord in reverence and declare it to God before the church? I don't think I did."

How many times did I worry that one misstep would cause Jesus to no longer be the Lord of my life? But Philippians 2:11 says Jesus is Lord of all and one day all of creation will declare it. Whether I submit to him in my life doesn't make him any more or less Lord. Jesus *is* Lord, it's up to me whether I walk as his disciple.

"Let's see what the Bible says about it," I say.

I open the Bible app on my phone and type in the search 'false prophets.' It brings up Matthew 7:15–20 in the English Standard Version. I read aloud, "'Beware of false prophets, who come to you in sheep's clothing but inwardly are ravenous wolves. You will recognize them by their fruits. Are grapes gathered from thorn bushes, or figs from thistles? So, every healthy tree bears good fruit, but the diseased tree bears bad fruit. A healthy tree cannot bear bad fruit, nor can a diseased tree bear good fruit. Every tree that does not bear good fruit is cut down and thrown into the fire. Thus you will recognize them by their fruits.' Mom, what fruits did Rob exhibit? I can't think of any except seeming to be wise and making people feel special. Flattery is also a tool of the devil."

She sighs. "I saw little fruit coming from the elders, even now."

I shake my head. "Why didn't we see this before?"

"Jesus told the church not to judge, lest they be judged," she says.

"Yes, according to appearance, but then he later condoned righteous judgment." I look it up. "There it is, in John 7:24. It doesn't seem to define righteous judgment, but I think it involves giving grace to anyone trying to live a godly life and falling short because of their imperfections. Righteous judgment by God's word helps us discern a person's intent through their repeated actions. Righteous judgment looks beyond the initial appearance, like sheep's clothing, sweet talking, or a smooth personality, to recognize if there is a ravenous wolf beneath."

"It sounds like the Holy Spirit is revealing something to you," Mom says. "I'll have to pray about it some more."

"Me too. I just hope I can discern the truth and make better decisions from now on."

"Keep trusting the Lord. He knows what you need, and He'll show you the best path." She brings another blanket over and lays it across me. "This was a heavy discussion and you look like you could use a nap. I'll be around if you need anything."

"Thanks Mom, I love you."

"I love you, too, honey."

And with that, I succumb to the weight of my eyelids and drift off to sleep.

CHAPTER TWENTY-SIX

HONESTY

It's been two years since my brush with mortality. Nathan and I are visiting his aunt for a weekend in Payson. Rita happens to be visiting family in the area, so we plan to meet up for a morning hike today, our last day of reprieve from the valley heat. Nathan is too sore from all the hiking and kayaking we did the past two days and stays back to rest.

I pull into the last parking spot at the trailhead of Water Wheel Falls. Across the lot, I spot Rita. It's been five years since our conversation by the poolside in Fiji. A year later, her husband passed away. Soon after, she submitted a letter to the eldership resigning from her position as a body to them and left The Ministry.

My departure was more subtle. During the pandemic last year, Nathan and I chose to only attend gatherings online. In that time, we met other Christians and took part in events by other church groups. When the restrictions lifted, we just didn't return.

She waves while walking toward me. "Hello!"

She is slimmer than I remember. The rim of her straw hat bounces as she sways to the same measure with each step. Donned with a water cooler backpack, hiking boots, and a walking stick, she looks like a natural.

I step out of the car and give her a big hug. "Hi, sister, so glad we could meet up."

"Yes, it's funny how this worked out," she says as we embrace.

She holds up my left hand so the diamond on my engagement ring glistens in the sun next to a solid gold band.

"A married woman now?"

"Yes, Nathan. He's not from The Ministry," I say with a grin.

"Good for you! It was a limited pool anyway."

Time has traded her silver streak for long snow-white hair, and she is now an experienced hiker. The joy of hiking came to her in recent years, inspired by our friend, a writer, who, on her sixtieth birthday, set out for a solo journey on El Camino de Santiago, then wrote an inspiring book about it. We both admire her stamina and resolve.

We're starting out late morning at the base of the falls. It's a well-traveled path, frequented by families and individuals of all hiking abilities. The path crosses a mountain stream and leads up to several swimming holes supplied by small waterfalls. One of my favorite local adventures.

The trail is mostly flat, with a slight incline at first as we make our way toward the stream.

After catching up on recent events, I am eager to find out more about her journey. Even though we're not part of The Ministry anymore, I'm not ready to leave the people behind. Perhaps it will shed some light on when the corruption started and how the abuses went unnoticed.

"Do you mind if I ask about your experience with The Ministry?" I say.

She shrugs. "I'm an open book. What do you want to know?"

You once said you were friends with Rob's daughter in high school and that's how you came to know him. How did you end up working with The Ministry?"

"Let's see. Soon after we graduated, the team invited me on an outreach to visit a family in Dove Creek, Colorado. On that trip, I was ministering prophecies and laying hands on people to make them well."

"Did you witness any miracles?"

"Yes, one of them happened to Bobbie Jo's sister. She was pregnant, and a doctor pronounced her baby dead in the womb. Someone laid hands on her belly and the baby kicked."

Energy surges through me. "Wait . . . was the baby Nick?"

"Yeah, that's right."

"When he was six years old, he ministered over my mother's womb to turn me upright!"

My eyes turn to the heavens, and I take an invigorating breath as I let this blessing sink in.

"Really? What an interesting parallel," she says.

"Were there other miracles?" I say.

"There was another miracle that I heard about, but I wasn't there for it. It's quite unpleasant. The story goes that there was a woman who was eating and somehow the fork went through her jaw. I'm told that those who were present laid hands on her, and the wound closed up."

"Oh, my Lord! Did you know the woman?"

"No, but I trusted the people who were there and testified to it."

We walk for several paces as that image lingers. I don't want to think about it.

"What was your favorite outreach?"

"One of my favorite trips was when we went to Guadalajara, México. I fell in love with that place and stayed there for seven months. When I returned, I moved into the ministry house in Coolidge, a town about sixty miles south of Phoenix."

"I've been to central México. What was Guadalajara like?" I say.

She looks up at the sky and behind us to the horizon. We both take in the view. We've gained enough elevation to see over the tops of the trees. As we continue our ascent, she begins to describe her fondest memory.

"Seductive scents of homemade tortillas and roasting chiles filled the air. Guadalajara, México, is where I belonged. The confluence of colors, sounds, and a rich language met an unspoken desire of my soul to be free of the expectations and proprieties of American culture."

I gape at her illustrious description.

"That's how my memoir starts. It's a work in progress."

"I'd read it." I nod as we walk along.

"It had been two years since my first team outreach in Colorado." She continues in a conversational tone. "We traveled to several states in the US during that time, but I felt at home in Guadalajara. There was such variation and liveliness in the culture that I felt being different was simply fitting in. There, I was Margarita."

Her eyes light up as if she were transported back to that time for just a moment.

"My first visit to México with The Ministry's outreach team planted a seed that was watered upon our return. For several weeks, we visited families and learned about their spiritual and physical needs. The children were always full of joy, though they had nothing. They would make games out of sticks and draw in the dirt. I saw more smiles on these children in a week than I had seen on American children in years."

"That brings me back to a time in college when I lived with a community in Cuernavaca for a semester. I saw the same happiness among those children."

She nods. "Mexican children were born into a culture of gratitude. That gratitude was rubbing off on me and I was much happier to be there serving the Lord and the poor, learning to be spiritually rich. I understood Jesus's statement from the Mount of Olives in Matthew 5:3, when he said, 'Blessed are the poor in spirit, for theirs is the Kingdom of heaven.'

A lizard scurries across the stone pathway into the brush at the trail's edge. "I remember while in Mexico City during that same semester, children on the street would try to sell me little bobble-head lizards and turtles they made."

"Yes, they did that back then too," she says.

"Are you part Mexican?" I've always been curious, although she has light skin.

"My father was of Spanish descent and lived in México most of his life. My mother was American. I learned Spanish as a child, so I became the unofficial translator for our outreaches. Gatherings were lively to say the least. In America, one or two individuals might volunteer to contribute and the others reluctantly wait their turn. In Guadalajara, the body was bursting at the seams to sing, share Scriptures, give words of knowledge, and prophesy."

The path rounds a bend, and I point to the first water crossing just within sight. She nods, then sips water through the straw attached to her shoulder. I sip from the bottle at my hip, secured in a cross-body sling.

"Those gatherings sound wonderful!" I say.

"They were," she says. "As we neared the end of a gathering one night, Rob leaned over to me and said, 'The Lord shows me you are one with Guadalajara.' I knew this to be true. I felt it and didn't want to be anywhere else."

I sigh—both from a longing for genuine spirit-filled fellowship and grieving its eventual demise.

"The day before the team was set to head home to Arizona, the family we'd been staying with offered me a job so I could stay longer. 'Lord, could I?' I thought. "They needed help around the house, and I could work for them while continuing to fellowship with the local saints. It was an unexpected blessing from the Lord. I'd graduated with my associate's degree and didn't have a job lined up, so I prayed about it with the team, and God released me to stay.

"For seven months, I would live and work among them until the Lord said it was time to return. During that time, I grew spiritually and emotionally until I sensed there was something waiting for me back in the US. It was difficult to leave that place and people that had become my second home, but the Lord was saying it was time."

She tips her hat to a stranger on the trail passing in the opposite direction.

I nod and smile. "What was waiting for you?"

"I'll get to that. But first, I'll tell you what it was like returning," she says. "The best was early on. After returning to Coolidge, it got more difficult. Rob shared with us some tapes by Bob Mumford—a founder of the Discipleship Movement in the 1970s. That movement informed Rob's ministry. He preached God would only speak through a head, so women needed to submit to their husband or a pastor in order to receive from God. I didn't believe that. But I wanted to be part of the group, so I didn't object."

Unlike Rita, I had believed this doctrine and depended on submitting everything to my father and mother for confirmation, even as an adult. I couldn't be sure I was clearly hearing from God without their input. I had viewed marriage as independence from my parents—a ticket to experiencing a wider array of adventures while keeping my life in God's order. In hindsight, I should have traveled more, gone on missions trips, and even bought my first house as a single woman.

"How did you work with them every day if you didn't agree on the Principle of Submission?"

"Well, I soon married Manuel. He's what was waiting for me, though neither of us knew it. He wasn't forceful and domineering like the other men. I was very thankful for him and that made it okay to stay with The Ministry."

"Would you say getting married was your ticket to freedom?"

"Not exactly. The early days in LA were full of food and fellowship among the Latino culture there. When he became an evangelist, we traveled to Matamoros and Hermosillo. Then at some point, someone decided Manuel needed to be trained. Instead of me going with him, Charles would train Manuel. It didn't work out as well and Manuel stopped going."

"What do you mean?"

"He would return so discouraged and want to review with Charles what he was supposed to have learned. Charles would say, 'What do you want to know, Manuel?' He wasn't sure exactly. It felt like no training at all. Soon other elders began going with them, and Manuel got sidelined. The outreaches became regimented and formulaic. There were many egos involved in the later years."

"That's so sad."

"Yes, it is. Especially for the people the Lord once blessed by our visits. We always thought that if we could just talk to Rob about it, he would understand and set everyone straight. But no, I think Rob was well aware of what was happening, and he set up Charles to take the fall."

"You think the apostle used the prophet as a scapegoat?"

She purses her lips and nods her head.

"That's a hefty accusation. Was there other evidence of this?"

"The elders couldn't go directly to Rob because of the hierarchy, so people would ask Charles to relay the message. Many times I heard Rob deny that Charles told him information, when I know he did. We all looked at Rob as infallible." Rita paused. "I think he was full of shit."

"You do?" The shock came in hearing this come from Rita.

"Maybe not always, not at the beginning, but certainly in the later days, yes . . ."

"What changed?" Perhaps she could help settle whether The Ministry was corrupt from the beginning.

The trail interrupts our conversation. We stand before a water crossing that requires focus and steady footing. I go first, testing each rock for sturdiness before taking a step. The current is moderate, and water passing over the rocks makes the surfaces slippery. I thank God for giving me the wisdom to invest in quality hiking shoes before this trip. Still, I say a quick prayer under my breath, asking God for his angels to guard us and for the Holy Spirit to guide our steps. Nearly on the other side, I look back and see Rita struggling to keep her balance. I offer her my arm, which helps steady her for the moment. We step to the next rock, then to the next . . .

"Ahh!" Rita shrieks as her foot slips and lands between the rocks in the rushing water. I reach for her shoulders, attempting to steady her, when I lose my own balance. We teeter there for a moment before regaining control.

"Go on," she says. "I'll manage. There's no use taking you down with me."

I climb the last few boulders onto the other side, then turn to see Rita on her hands and knees. She pulls her leg out of the water, soaked up to the knee. Slowly and now more steadily, she crawls to the embankment, and I offer my hand. She interlocks her hand in mine without hesitation, and with a loud grunt, she steps onto the firm foundation upon which we both now stand.

"Balance has always been a weakness of mine. I'm working on it more these days, but clearly I have a ways to go! I'm glad *you* were steady, or the river may have washed us both downstream."

"Thanks for not giving up," I say. "I'm impressed you still have your hat on!"

"Oh, that's right!" She touches the top of her head to feel that it is still there. We laugh with relief, letting out any remaining tension from crossing the river.

We continue up the hill. Still curious about The Ministry's beginnings, I ask, "You were in The Ministry for a long time. What was it like in its heyday?"

"In the early days, in San Diego, we had music and fellowship. Most of us played musical instruments; a few of the elders were in a band. It was the best of times. If someone wanted a word of confirmation at a gathering, we would all pray and share what we received."

"Sounds wonderful," I marvel.

"Things changed when Rob began teaching that you needed to go to your headship. He further instructed that you take what they receive to the Lord and see what you receive. It sounded reasonable until we practiced it."

"What happened if you received something different from your headship?"

"If you don't do what the headship says, you're punished or ostracized or rebuked. Not so in the early days. I think that's when it became controlling. Then, one by one, the local elders' wives divorced them and they left their positions." She lists names of three couples, once dear friends, with whom she's parted ways.

"My parents split around that time."

My mom thought divorce was contagious. Now, it seems the imposition of "God's order" as defined by The Ministry was the culprit.

If both spouses were seeking to honor God, shouldn't that bring unity, not division?

"Rita, I wasn't concerned about being punished or ostracized by my headship. I was more concerned about being outside of God's protection and vulnerable to external forces. Rebuke came often enough, but it never felt like manipulation. Rob, the eldership, and my parents always told me to make God my only source. So that's what I did."

Rita frowns.

"Although, if I received something different from my headship, I always yielded to their word. It just didn't feel right acting apart from their approval . . . I guess I was being manipulated."

She places her hand on my shoulder. "I am relieved to hear you say that! You're finally an independent woman who can think for herself."

"I suppose. Although, I still feel unsure of what God is telling me at times."

She shrugs one shoulder. "Uncertainty is a part of faith. If you were sure of everything, what would you need faith for?"

"Good point."

We continue walking several paces before I ask, "Did you find their practices differed from their preaching?"

She stops me in my tracks. "Do you mean, were they hypocrites? Absolutely."

Even after some time and distance from The Ministry, it's still uncomfortable to hear this.

"Manuel's friends had a lot of respect for him and were heartbroken to separate, so they continued to meet socially even after leaving The Ministry. They enjoyed meeting him for a men's breakfast regularly. Then one day, Charles confronted Manuel about there not being a head present in the group. Manuel saw nothing wrong with gathering socially.

When I heard it, under my breath, I said, 'God, bullshit.' So Manuel didn't go anymore, and that broke his heart. I don't think he recovered from losing his friends like that. I regret it now. We should have said something much sooner. We were all blind."

I remember when Charles reprimanded Manuel. It was during an elder's meeting and I thought, *How could anyone have friends or evangelize if everything had to be in some formal order and setting?* But it wasn't my place to speak up.

"So you couldn't really have friends?" I ask.

"It would seem so. After Manuel died, I was under the covering of the bishopric. I had received to share something with a sister from another church area, so I wrote to her, and she shared it with her head, who shared it with Charles. The next thing I know, I'm hearing from my head that I shouldn't have shared that with her without going through her pastor.

I thought, 'No, she can give it to her spirit and if she receives to share it with her head, that's submission. The other is authority.' That really griped me."

"My God, Rita!" I'm shocked she couldn't talk to other women without permission. That was not something I'd experienced with my headship, but knowing the elders of whom she spoke, it wasn't unimaginable.

"Did you finally say something?" I ask.

"What could I do? I was part of this group for nearly forty years and never thought about leaving. I just shook it off."

"So what made you finally leave?"

"About that time, an elder from Sydney tried to expose The Ministry as a cult. It was Kumari's brother, Mani. So I also spoke up and said, 'You know, I've been thinking that myself. Let's talk about it.'"

"What did they say?"

Rita shakes her head. "End of discussion. They wouldn't talk about it."

Indignation rises within me. There is no reason for me to hold back anymore.

"Of course they wouldn't," I say. "It's the same culture of gaslighting that kept Kumari and Heather silent for all those years. It's infuriating! This same psychological manipulation sowed self-doubt and confusion in *my* mind for years before I recognized it. It only kept the elders in control, not God."

She points her walking stick at me. "Stoke that fire, and it will lead to freedom."

CHAPTER TWENTY-SEVEN

REFRESHMENT

Climbing over the last major part of the trail, we come to my favorite part of the hike—a clearing that reveals why the parking lot is full. Sprawled out before us are families with coolers, teenagers on towels listening to music, and youth splashing with delight in the river. Small children play in a shallow pool with their parents. Older ones glide down a natural rock slide into a swimming hole supplied by a waterfall. The more adventurous leap off the cliff into the same natural wonder of deep waters, while others watch from the mountainsides. This cove satisfies all energy levels.

"Oh, it's beautiful! I wasn't expecting so many people," Rita says. "Where did they all come from?"

"They must have hiked up earlier. It's possible there is another entrance too. I can't fathom they would have brought those coolers along the trail we just hiked."

"No, I'd imagine not," she says.

"What do you say? Would you like to swim?"

"Oh, yes! I'm so hot and sweaty from that hike."

"Me too. Let's set our stuff down and take a dip."

We placed our gear in an alcove out of the way, and I jump into the deep pool. She enters the shallow pool and wades over. The water is refreshing. I need this time to think about our conversation. Rita has known my parents for a long time and watched me grow up in The Ministry. She had no reason to lie to me. I trust the things she shared were exactly how she remembered them. Her feelings were genuine, and the consequences were painful.

After briefly cooling off in the water, we climb up the edge and sit on the rocks, watching a bit of the activity below.

"That was refreshing!" I exclaim, stretching my arms up to the sky.

"Yes, it was." She laughs with a brightness I haven't seen in years. "I needed that. What a wonderful spot! Thank you for showing it to me."

"I'm glad we could experience it together," I say as we walk up the rocky incline to the alcove where our belongings await us, untouched. We recline on our towels to rest for a while. Warmth radiates from the rocks as if this stone giant were God's nanny, cradling us from our troubles. My gaze gets lost in the infinite baby-blue sky.

Rita says, "I've been much more adventurous since Manuel passed away. This is one of many new experiences."

"Did you feel you couldn't be yourself while married?"

"Not so much because I was married, but I was hiding from the world. I realized not too long ago that in the later years, I never invited anyone to gatherings. It embarrassed me. I had a whole life outside of it, to the extent that at Manuel's funeral, two friends came up to me and said, 'Oh, I didn't realize you were part of the ministry too. I thought that was Manuel's thing.' Can you believe that?"

"No, I always viewed you as ministering together."

"That's right, to those in The Ministry, but not to the outside world. I had separated it. I was too embarrassed to send those teachings to anyone. They were baffling, convoluted, and hard to follow. I offered to help proofread and edit, but Charles would say, 'Yeah, but Rob wants it this way. It's more vague so the people have to receive it by the Spirit. You can't just feed them everything straight out.' I'm like, 'Oh my God, okay, whatever.'"

"Were they trying to relate it to Jesus speaking in parables?" I say.

"Yes, but Jesus spoke in parables related to daily life so his audience would clearly understand them. Even if the people didn't yet see how they related to the Kingdom of God. He would also clearly explain them to His disciples."

"True. I shared the teachings with Nathan early in our relationship, and he later admitted he felt like he needed a psychology degree to understand it."

"I don't blame him. We had so much context from studying it over the years, but it wasn't accessible to anyone new."

"No, and speaking of accessibility. You know, my day job was working in adult literacy. When I noticed the teachings were being printed in colored texts with highlighting, I spoke up again. They were hard to read and cost a lot of money to print. But that's the way Rob wanted it."

"Didn't The Ministry pay for them?"

"They were supposed to, but the money didn't always come in. People weren't giving. I spent a lot of our own money on reproducing those materials. There was an unspoken expectation that you have to get them out, or else, where's your faith?"

"I see."

"It wasn't faith. We always lived by my job. That was the pattern. The women were working to support the men's ministry."

She's not wrong. I worked to support my dad's ministry activity. The prophet's wife worked to support his ministry work and their son. Just about every full-time elder I can think of has a wife working a secular job. She couldn't really partner with him in it unless ministry became her second job. That's what I did and was all too proud of it, perhaps even showing up the elders' wives. I was blind to it then, but now I see the ecosystem that drove "living by faith."

"Do you think the prosperity gospel influenced us?" I say.

"Absolutely. Money and health were signs of God's blessings. If you don't have the faith to receive it, then your sin caused you and those around you to suffer. But I say it's like health. If you don't have the faith to receive healing, then you go to a doctor. Why wouldn't that be the case with finances? The ministry should adjust to our level of faith. Instead, they continuously accumulated debt by writing bad checks and relying on the belief that God would miraculously provide money before the checks were cashed. They also borrowed money from others without ever repaying them."

I respond, "That doesn't align with what the Bible teaches or with what Rob taught. The Scriptures say we're not to have debt, but you're saying that even early on, their practice was going into debt and putting that responsibility on every member to pay it back?"

She confirms, "That's the way it was. I know people in terrible shape because they gave everything. There was a teaching not to buy a house because it would put you under the bondage of ownership. I regret that we always rented. We were not to own anything but have faith that the Lord would provide."

"Wait," I say. "My understanding was that everything is the Lord's and we are stewards of the things he gives us. That's what Luke 16 is all about. *Someone* has to own the house. Isn't it better to be a steward for the Lord than to be at the mercy of a landlord?"

"That would make sense, but it's not what they practiced. The words that the apostle spoke were one thing, but how people were led or manipulated is entirely different." She huffs. "Some people gave their entire life savings and retirement funds to The Ministry."

"That must have devastated their financial futures," I say.

"It did." Rita continues, "Rob spent freely, like money was nothing. All in the name of faith, but all off the backs of someone else. There are people still suffering today, and probably some will never recover."

She is digging around in her bag when I ask, "So . . . you've got me wondering about the cult issue." I hoped she's open to continuing that part of the conversation.

"Oh, yeah?" she says, pulling out two protein bars and handing one to me. I accept her offer of nourishment, open it and take a bite, satiating a hunger I didn't know I had.

"Yeah," I say. "My extended family always thought I was in a cult. I dismissed it, telling myself they didn't understand what we believed. Then one day I brought it up with the apostle over lunch."

She tilts her head. "What did he say?"

I take another bite while trying to recall his words. "Rob said, technically, it was a cult. Of course, he explained it away, saying that a cult is just a group of like-minded people who believe the same thing. He said that since it wasn't the 'occult'—a group of Satan worshippers— it wasn't necessarily bad. By this simple definition, any denomination or religion could be seen as a cult. The explanation disarmed me."

"He did have an explanation for everything, didn't he?" she says.

"Yes," I admit, "and that's part of why I thought he was truly an apostle. Nobody else seemed to have all the answers, so I figured he must be receiving the revelation from God as he proclaimed."

My energy increases as the protein bar takes effect.

Rita asks, "Don't you think God would make His truth known to everyone who looked for it? If God is full of love, kindness, and generosity, why would He only reveal these things to a select group of people with a limited platform?"

I consume the last morsel and think aloud, "I've wondered that myself. Maybe because their hearts weren't fully seeking Him? Selfish desires can disrupt our relationship with God, yet He doesn't require us to be perfect to receive His wisdom."

He meets us where we are in our faith, and He loves us more than we could imagine. He pursues us. I have encountered people outside of

The Ministry with strong faith and devotion to God, despite not sharing my understanding. That's helped me to see not everything I thought I knew about God was true. Now, I value hearing others' perspectives, not to prove them wrong, but to learn from them.

"How did you come to believe what you do now?" I ask.

Rita scans the surrounding mountains and smiles at me with a gentle sigh. "Shall we make our way back?"

"Sure."

The warm Arizona air has dried us off. I take a moment to admire the mountains and waterfall before getting dressed. We head down a path parallel to the one by which we ascended the mountain. The river's ambient flow soothes my soul. Nature has a way of making my concerns feel small while magnifying God's presence.

She picks up our conversation a few minutes into the descent. "Leaving wasn't easy. Like you said, they didn't practice what they preached. I think Rob was sincere when he started The Ministry, but things changed drastically through the years. Many wonderful things occurred before he veered off track. Sadly, very few elders would stand up to him, and anyone who did got chewed up and spit out. They wouldn't stay long afterward. It's really sad."

Rita wipes the sweat from her brow with her sleeve. The afternoon sun is at its strongest. "I think his behavior near the end resulted from great torment."

Maybe she's right. I think about the dinner with Dad a few months back when Philip shared his account of leaving the Massachusetts church. After their confrontation, Rob used Philip as an example of an elder who left with a spirit of rebellion because he didn't agree with the Principle of Submission. He cautioned us not to fall into the same deception.

I recall what Philip shared with me the next day. "You're not the first one to have suspected mental illness."

She glances over at me, then says, "There's a book I read about cult leaders that focuses on their childhood experiences in the opening chapter. Rob fit the profile exactly. Early childhood trauma followed by some miraculous revelation or healing, then people looking up to them. Boom! So that helped me to understand too that it was a mental illness that overtook him, and unfortunately, we fed it and made it worse. I sometimes wondered, if his wife had lived longer, would it not have gone so far? I think her presence helped."

"Did it? I didn't know her very well. I just remember him talking about her and how he would handle her."

"Oh, yes, it did. But he would say things to us about her being in rebellion and him needing to withhold the benefits of the relationship, like intimacy and money. I never thought that was right. God doesn't withhold benefits from us. He has given us everything, and we're one with him. How can he withhold himself?"

"I agree. That's very Old Testament. It's a legalistic way of thinking."

"And not to mention degrading toward women," she adds.

That last part wasn't easy for me to identify. God's word says that men and women are equal in His sight, but He also maintained an order that began when He first created humans—He made the woman second. I'm certain I have followed the Principle of Submission, not authority, as I heard it taught. My conversations with the Lord have confirmed to me it was the correct way to function, which left me far less sensitive to feminist appeals. Yet, with everything we discussed today on Water Wheel Falls Trail, even that is coming into question. I'll need to talk to the Lord for more clarity, but for now, I want to hear more of Rita's story.

"Was that the worst of it for you?" I say.

"No, unfortunately."

I remain silent, waiting for more. I never saw Rita as someone who would endure abuse, but maybe that's because she's older than I.

"You heard about what he did to his assistant?" She looks at me with some intensity.

"Heather? I . . . yes, sadly I have." She doesn't need to know about the journal.

"I didn't witness it directly, but my understanding is that when Heather went to live with her sister, she confided in her. I heard it from a close friend of the family."

"I'm sure what you heard is true. It was the nail in the coffin for me."

I instantly regret my choice of words. Our dearly departed Heather deserves only to be remembered by her gentle and kind spirit. Not by what happened to her.

"Sadly, hers wasn't the only cover-up," Rita says. "Years ago, my friend Sue told me there was an elder who was molesting his daughter. Someone found out and went to the elders, urging them to go to the police. The elders refused because of a Scripture that teaches the church shouldn't involve the law but handle their own disputes. Their response to this woman's complaint was nothing but a slap on the wrist and the elders praying for him. That was it! It was rampant from the beginning."

Rita is referring to 1 Corinthians 6:1–8, in which Paul admonishes the church for taking each other to court over disputes. He argues God has given them wisdom to judge these matters, even to the least of them. When I read it in context, I see Paul was identifying a fault in the body of Christ that manifested in three ways. First, believers should not oppose each other. Second, they should follow Jesus's teaching of turning the other cheek. Last, they should not seek judgment from unbelievers. He encouraged them to appoint those who were the least esteemed in the body to judge disputes because it wasn't their own judgment they were to rely on. God gives the wisdom.

I think of my conversations with Jack and Ethan back in Massachusetts. Shaking my head in disgust, I say, "I've talked to some who suffered abuse as children and they want nothing to do with God now."

She lets out a heavy sigh. "Yeah, I look at the lives of the youth who grew up in this ministry . . . Oh my God, there's some actual pain and dysfunction. It's really sad. It hits deep."

We walk silently for a few minutes, honoring the memory of those innocent children. Mourning for the bright futures that turned dark because of their parents' deceptions and misapplication of God's word. I take a few deep breaths and release the burden to God.

We are nearing the end of our hike and devote a few moments to enjoy our surroundings before continuing for the last leg.

"How have your views changed since leaving The Ministry?" She dropped a few clues, but I feel there is more for her to say. "Have you kept your relationship with God?"

Rita stops short, and I turn around to face her, only a few steps ahead. She takes a deep breath and says, "It has changed quite a bit."

I straighten my posture as if to brace myself for what I am about to hear.

Has she given up on her faith like Kumari?

She continues walking, and I join her as she explains, "I received Jesus when I was eight years old. The doctrine was that God came to save you from sin by sending His son on the cross to die. It was your free choice to accept it and choose Him. But if you don't, you're going to die and burn in hell. I felt a resentment toward God for this. 'I never asked Jesus to die for me. Now, I owe Him?' I thought."

"Hmm." I'd never thought of it that way. I had always accepted his sacrifice as grace, and my devotion was a natural response of appreciation.

"I don't believe the Bible is teaching that anymore," she continued. "I believe He saved the entire world and you can accept it and acknowledge it or not, but He saved you. My relationship with God is much more free flowing now."

I try to understand her point of view. "What you're describing sounds like common grace. God's love and blessings extend to everyone in this life, regardless of whether they choose Him. They still get to experience the beauty of nature, like these mountains we get to climb. They still get the provision of the sun and rain and food from the earth that God created. As Matthew 5:45 declares, 'He causes His sun to rise on the evil and the good, and sends rain on the righteous and the unrighteous.'"

"I suppose that's true, but it's more than that. I think now you could look at all of Christianity as a cult because you're in or you're out."

In or out. Saved or unsaved. An eternal dwelling with God in heaven or apart from Him in hell. I contemplate how one could believe in God and the Bible and see this any other way.

"What do you believe the Bible is teaching about the concept of hell?" I asked.

"For me, I still don't know. I'm fine with not knowing. In The Ministry, there was an answer for everything."

"Everything," I nod.

"I don't feel that's necessary anymore. I'm kind of leaning toward there isn't a heaven and a hell. Maybe there's something else that we move into when we die. Perhaps we are energy and we just continue on as energy."

I look at her, puzzled.

She continues, "The Bible doesn't seem as literal as it once did. I think it's a powerful book, and I believe it's inspired by God. I appreciate it, but I don't take it so literally. What that means, I'm not entirely sure, but yeah, I don't believe the Bible is literally word for word the word of God."

I agree our English translations aren't, but I can't say the same for the original texts.

One year, the Christian church decided the Bible was inerrant. Before that, the early church didn't regard those letters that way. I think it was about that time when the Pope became seen as infallible."

That is a discussion for another day.

"You bring up some interesting points," I say. "I will have to think about that some more. I'm grateful for all you shared with me today. You've walked a long and storied journey."

"I have. It's like the title of the book our friend wrote, *Keep Walking and Your Heart Will Catch Up.*"

I smile. "Amen, sister. It looks like we've come to the end of this trail for now."

"There will be other trails." She smiles with the accomplished weariness of a day-hike, and we hug before going our separate ways.

I feel blessed by our connection today. Although, a sense of loss threatens to steal my joy as I consider our diverging beliefs about God and the Bible. My body and soul are tired from the hike. I may not understand her new views on God, but love bids me to endure our differences. I pray that God continues to work in her and Kumari and the others who left before me. Most of all, I pray, *God, if there's any way I can help open the eyes of those still under The Ministry's control, show me what I need to do to help them question the doctrine and still walk the way of Jesus.*

CHAPTER TWENTY-EIGHT

RECONCILIATION

Two months later, Nathan and I attend a barbecue at the Sturgises' house to say farewell to the horses before they sell the ranch and take their personal ministry on the road. The timing of this gathering couldn't be better. Kumari is back in town visiting family, so when she called me the other day, I invited her to join us. She was hesitant at first, but I assured her that Dallas was one of the good guys. He's only part of The Ministry to look out for the vulnerable and to keep the other elders in check. I also assured her he would be open to hearing her side of the story. Her reluctance abated, and she agreed to come and bring Aaron, now eleven, to experience the horses.

I hold on to my wide-rimmed western hat with one hand and reins in the other as Big Betsy goes from a trot to a gallop circling the corral. She's got some spunk left in her yet.

"Having fun?" I yell to Aaron. He's riding Sugar.

"She won't go fast enough."

I laugh. "That's because she's trained to be gentle with children."

"I can handle her," he says with the confidence of someone twice his age.

"I'm sure you can. Give her a good solid kick. As hard as you can, it'll feel just right to her."

He musters a big, sharp kick, and the horse picks up her pace, allowing him to steer her in a bit of an erratic pattern around the corral.

"There you go!" I say.

"She finally listened," says Aaron.

"You just needed the right command," I say.

"Burgers are ready!" Dallas calls from over the grill.

I dismount Big Betsy and stroke her soft nose, looking into her large black eyes. "You get it, don't you, girl? I bet you know God better than all of us. You're just waiting for us to come to our senses so all of creation can be restored."

She whinnies and nods with a stomp of her front hoof.

Nathan calls out from the back porch, "Do you want some watermelon?"

"Yeah, I'll be right there!" I call back to him.

Then I help lead Aaron's horse to the steps and hold her steady as he dismounts with no problem and runs off to get food.

I walk back to the patio, taking in the desert view all around us. The watermelon looks especially juicy today, so I take a slice from the tray Grace had set out on the table. My bite is interrupted by the sight of Adam and his wife, Ana, standing by the railing sipping iced teas. I take a deep breath. This is my first time seeing him since he left Arizona to marry her three years ago. And Dallas hadn't mentioned they would be here.

Adam's eyes settle on me.

"Hello," he says with the voice of a gentle giant.

With a slight smile, I say, "Welcome back."

Of all the things I'd planned to say to him if I ever saw him again, that was not one of them. How about, *why did you leave? Why her? Are you truly happy? You hurt me.* But the thing is, I'd already yelled those sentiments about him to God a hundred times over. I'd also declared my forgiveness of him about as many times. Not for his sake, but for mine, so I could move on. As hard as it was to say I forgive him, today would prove if I'd actually done so.

Ana walks toward me. I've rehearsed this repeatedly over the years. I would imagine she felt sorry and I would tell her I forgave her. I wasn't sure we could ever be friends again, and to be honest, I'd resigned to the possibility that our paths may never cross. Yet here we are. This is my chance to prove that I can love, even in the most impossible of circumstances, like Jesus did.

I walk to meet her. "Ana, what a blessing to see you again."

She stretches out both arms to embrace me, and I lean in.

"Sister!" she exclaims. "I missed you."

Funny, I've never seen a missed call or an email.

"You don't know how many times I thought about calling you. I just wasn't sure if you would forgive me. I didn't want to stir up trouble."

Does she mean now or back then?

I smile and nod. Since she's a talker, I let her continue.

"I just want you to know, in case there is any question in your heart about it. We got together after things had ended between you."

I never would have asked, but I'm glad she said it.

She continues, "I was going through a tough time, and he helped me leave The Ministry. It was then that he expressed he wanted to come with me."

Oh, my God! He wanted to leave The Ministry? Back then?

"I said I would never go back, but if he was serious, I would marry him. It wasn't the most romantic proposal, but we were two very hurt people who understood each other. God has done some deep work in us both since then."

I don't have words. "Thank you . . . thank you. Excuse me."

I run into the house and find the bathroom so I can be alone. I stare at myself in the mirror to witness the shock on my face and process my thoughts.

This means he wasn't just being obedient. He was seeking a way out.

Clearly, I wasn't that way.

I was moving *toward* The Ministry. She was moving *away*.

A lump gathers in my throat, and I swallow to keep it down. I can't go back out there looking upset. This isn't the time or place.

This whole time, I thought I was one step ahead of him. Planning our future, our ministry impact, proving my faithfulness. Not so.

He was ahead of me.

He must have realized long ago that The Ministry was corrupt, but he had to leave in a way that wouldn't hurt his family. If he told me, I would have blown the cover off the whole damn thing.

Breathing heavily, I hold myself up with the sink counter. A wave of nausea passes over me, and I sit on the floor, shivering. *Lord Jesus, help.*

Knock, knock. "Are you all right?" Nathan's voice breaks me.

Tears well up. I let him in.

"What's going on? How can I help?"

I look up at him and reach out my arms. He helps me stand and embraces me. I cry on his shoulder, blubbering, "You . . . you . . . helped me . . . leave The Ministry."

He pulls back to look at my face and sees that I'm actually smiling through the tears. "Well, when you helped me rediscover my faith, I learned that I could know what was right and wrong from God. When I prayed, there were just some things that didn't add up."

Another wave of tears comes over me as I see God's master plan in all of this. "I thought I saved you, but I didn't realize that you also saved me."

We lock eyes. "Victoria, we saved each other, by God's grace. I've always known we were together for a reason. God is good. He knows what He's doing."

My crying turns into laughter. I squeeze him tight again and then take deep breaths. "Yes, He does."

I splash cold water on my face to help the puffiness go down. I'm still flushed, but I don't care.

We stop at the cooler on the way back outside, and Nathan grabs a couple of hard ciders and hands one to me. We share a knowing smile and clink them together.

"You guys all right?" Adam says.

"Yes, yes we are," I say. Then I realize I hadn't introduced him. "Oh, sorry. This is my husband, Nathan," I say as I put an arm around his waist. He places his arm on my shoulder and shakes each of their hands.

"It's good to meet you finally," says Adam.

The sun sends streaks of orange and crimson across the vast sky. Saguaros become silhouettes in the foreground. It's a scene often captured on postcards, but it's so much better in real life.

Grace waves us all over to the fire pit where Dallas has been stoking the flames. "I've got marshmallows and chocolate for s'mores."

Aaron walks over, eyes wide. "Mum, may I have some, please?"

Kumari looks up at him and waves her finger. "You may have three, no more."

He rolls his eyes. "Yes, Mum." Dallas hands him a skewer.

We eventually all make our way over to the assortment of chairs and benches around the fire.

"Victoria," a man's voice says from behind me.

I turn and look up from my seat, but I don't recognize him. He must be in his late sixties, early seventies. It's always hard to tell with Arizonans since the sun often ages them prematurely.

He reaches out his hand. "Mark, Grace's brother. You probably don't remember me. It's been a long time."

I stand up and shake it. "Oh, yes, I'm not sure we've met, but I recognize your name. This is my husband, Nathan."

"A pleasure," Mark says. "This is my wife, Gloria."

She's about the same age with teased strawberry blonde hair, blue eyeliner, and pink lipstick. We hug as if we've known each other forever.

"I'm sorry we missed the BBQ—had a family birthday party on my wife's side. But we're here now."

They join us around the fire pit.

Dallas tells stories from the old days, and his many escapades working at the prison. He shares how he introduced his captain to the Holy Ghost and about the year he got his gun taken away. Most I had heard before.

"That stubbornness and disobedient flesh nature has helped me to stay true to God," he says. "Whenever I thought about leaving The Ministry because of what the elders were doing, I would talk to God and He'd show me what was going on in my heart that needed to change. The Lord taught me through my job and relationships. I became less rebellious and less challenging, more willing to apply the Principle of Submission."

Kumari's eyebrows narrow, and she shakes her head. Ana looks down and whispers something under her breath, maybe praying. Adam is fidgeting. Nathan squeezes my hand a couple of times to say, "I got you." Nobody seems comfortable with Dallas's stories.

"Over the years, I would get promoted in my job because of the progress I was making with God and Christ internally," Dallas boasts. "I kept checking myself and noting how I responded to situations with more maturity than I had before. It was really Luke 16 in action: keeping God's order and honoring authorities. The Lord taught me this before I heard it from Rob's teachings. I was already walking in it and prospering."

Kumari looks at me with shooting glances like she's about to bow out if he keeps talking up The Ministry.

Dallas and Grace are the only ones here who still represent The Ministry. I want to say something, but Mark beats me to it.

"You know I love you, brother, but I can't sit by without telling my side of things."

Dallas looks at Grace, and she gives a nod of approval.

"Go ahead," Dallas says.

"As some of you know, I was an elder with The Ministry for a brief time in the 1980s. There were a few times I'd shown up at a conference after that just to see if anything had changed. I think that's where I last saw you, Victoria. Anyway, I would try to share the joy of the Lord and the things He was showing me, but everyone was so stuck in their ways."

Gloria elbows him.

"Right, sorry," he says toward Dallas.

Dallas puts his hands up in a gesture of surrender. They must have some agreement not to get into it with each other in mixed company.

"I just want to share my story because I think some of you might relate. You see, I trusted Rob at one point. I was ready to dedicate my life to serving the principles he brought forth. But, that all changed on one outreach to Hawaii.

"I rejoiced in being used by God to shine light for others. I knew I had a calling on my life because the Holy Spirit was drawing people to me in each of the places we traveled. This night had been especially satisfying since a group of Hawaiian women in the hotel lobby were so thirsty for the water of God's word. After spending some time preaching to them, I was eager to share this blessing with Rob.

"When I returned to my hotel room, I placed my Bible on the table and laid back on the bed a moment to rest. 'Is that you, Mark?' I heard Rob call through the paper-thin wall. Our rooms were adjacent and connected by a door. He insisted on this setup everywhere we went. I was functioning as a body to him, so if he needed something, he expected me to help. It was better than sharing a room. I hollered back, 'Yep, I'll be right there.'

"I prayed to cleanse myself of any unclean spirit that may have attached themselves to me while I was out and set my will to honor God and the apostle before entering his room."

Heads nod in unison around the fire pit. They were all familiar with the protocol.

"He was lying in bed naked with only a thin sheet draped over his midsection. I turned away out of respect but also as a reflex. Then I tried to tell him about the women in the lobby, but he dismissed it and asked me to come closer.

"Facing him, I looked everywhere else. 'My sciatica is acting up,' he told me. 'What can I do?' I asked. I was prepared to pray with him, but I was not prepared for what he would ask of me. 'Rub my toes, will you?' He stuck out his feet from the sheets at the end of the bed. They were full of veins and his toenails were yellow. I shuddered. Feet were not my thing, much less the feet of an old naked man.

"'I . . . no, I'm sorry, I can't do that,' I said. Defying this request felt like defying orders from my former sergeant back in the Navy. I knew I would be in rebellion if I didn't comply, but I couldn't.

"I went to my room and prayed for what to do next. The Lord opened my eyes and showed me a forest with a river running through it. In the river were dead bodies and mud and goop floating by. On the other side was the Lord Jesus. He called me to come. Hesitantly, I stepped into the water, and I came out of the vision. I asked the Lord what it meant and He said, 'You are not walking with Christ, my son. You must cross this river of death to come to me.' That vision seared into my consciousness, coloring my perceptions for the rest of the trip. On my way home, I called my wife and told her, 'I'm not doing this anymore.'

"But it was too late. She and the kids had already rejected me for not being the father they needed. I'd given everything to The Ministry while they struggled to survive. I promised I would change, but words weren't enough."

"You were wading in the river of death," says Adam.

Mark nods.

Ana says, "How did you make it through?"

"Lots of prayer and lots of repentance," says Mark. "It was a whole year before I convinced her to take me back."

Gloria smiles at him.

"I needed that time to get my priorities straight. After God, family is number one in my book. Now we're blessed with eighteen grandchildren and great-grandchildren."

"You were lucky," says Kumari. "I didn't get away so easily."

Aaron reaches for a fourth marshmallow while still eating the third s'more. "No more," says Kumari and waves his hand away from the bag. He tries to say something, but his mouth is full of marshmallow. She grabs a napkin and tries to wipe the chocolate off his face, but he shies away, so she hands it to him instead.

"I'm sorry, sisters." Mark looks at Ana and Kumari. "I can't imagine what it must have been like to live with him as a woman."

Ana reaches for Kumari's hand, but she waves it away.

"If I may," Kumari says.

"For twenty-five years, I gave my all. I was faithful and didn't doubt I was doing it all unto God, and some of you know what happened to me. It wasn't fair. I've turned away from God."

It cuts deep to hear my dear sister say those words.

She continues, "Heather died. Why?"

None of us had the answer.

"I believe The Ministry is one of many cults. I understand I chose it, but now that I'm out, I don't know how to get back to that relationship with God."

"Have you prayed about it?" As soon as I ask, I know prayer isn't the issue.

"What is prayer? I used to believe it was communication with God, and it gave me peace." She pauses. "Sometimes I wonder if there is a God, but then I look at this world and the stars up there." She points up to the black night sky filled with stars, galaxies, and cosmos. "But I find it hard to reconcile myself. Where do I fit in? It's been traumatic."

I drop my gaze.

"Sorry to disappoint you, Victoria." She sighs. "I know you still have faith. Mine may come back later. My husband has not slipped. He leads our family spiritually."

Dallas shakes his head. "Sister, there's a lot to unpack there. But know that God has not abandoned you. As you submit to God's order, through your husband, those scales of deception will fall away."

She wrings her hands. "Submission? Oh, I submit, but I'd rather live in deception than be controlled by a man. I lived that life for too long."

Ana speaks up. "Sister, we left The Ministry too. We understand how you're feeling, and I want you to know that God is still with you. You may not feel His presence right now, but He loves you and wants to restore the years that were taken. He hears your heart's cry. Sometimes, hearing His voice has more to do with asking the right question. I've stopped asking why God allows evil things to happen, and now I ask how He will use it for good and how I can contribute to that. No matter what, Adam and I are not judging you. We love you." Ana walks over to Kumari and hugs her.

"Thank you, Ana," Kumari says as they embrace.

Then Kumari turns to me and says, "It's all a bit much right now."

"I understand," I say. "I'm glad I could spend some time with Aaron and watch him interact with the horses."

"Thank you. That meant a lot to him."

She signals to Aaron that it's time to go. I hug them both, then Adam walks them to their car.

Thirsty, I walk over to get a bottle of water from the cooler by the back door. I drink as much as I can to satiate the thirst brought on by a desert campfire and alcohol. Adam returns through the back door, and I offer him a water.

We lock eyes, and after a few seconds, he gives me a simple nod. I return the gesture. There is no need for words. Peace, unlike any other, washes over me. I long for Adam's presence no more. There is no need to grieve what we once had. The veil has lifted, and I clearly see God's provision for me. Adam and Ana are good for each other.

I am free.

CHAPTER TWENTY-NINE

FRUIT

"Hey, what's up, Vic?" Seth, the kids pastor at our downtown community church, holds up his hand for a high five. "How was your week?"

"Hey!" I slap his hand. "It had its challenges, but it's Sunday, and I'm ready to praise the Lord!"

The small room fills up quickly with seven-to-eleven-year-olds. I fell in love with this age group a couple of years ago when Nathan and I volunteered for a Christian summer camp for foster youth. Alexis, the child assigned to me, was eleven and new to the foster care system. She wanted nothing to do with God or the Bible, so I didn't push.

"I can't do it," Alexis said when she tried to build a birdhouse.

"Sure you can. I believe in you," I said. She held the hammer steady and gave it a good whack, but every time, the nail would bend.

"I think it's broken," she said. It turns out there was something wrong with the wood because even the instructor had a difficult time getting the nails to cooperate. Once we got it put together—it took three of us—she made it her own, painting a space theme on it. Her artistic talent impressed the other girls and coaches.

That experience with the birdhouse wasn't her only victory that week. Alexis stepped outside herself by teaching other girls how to feed animals. She experienced God's favor when, out of a selection of donated outfits, she discovered a plus-sized dress in her favorite color to wear for the tea party. And she overcame shyness by entering the talent show and teaching the entire camp how to draw cartoon mushrooms.

I prayed for her every night, and each day I saw a little more openness until finally, she was receptive to God's word. On the last day, she sang along with worship songs and read Scriptures to me. Alexis had broken through the wall that she had put up between her and God. I'd never witnessed a heart change of that magnitude in only four days.

Nathan and I continue to volunteer for camps each summer. Each one stretching and growing us as individuals and partners.

Marriage was difficult for the first couple of years. Like Alexis and her birdhouse, building a healthy home seemed impossible, like there was something wrong with the materials. Since experiencing forgiveness almost a year ago at the Sturgises' house, everything changed. And that took a third person as well: Jesus. No longer living in regret, I have the energy to invest in our relationship and pour out God's love into the community.

Now, I get to spend my Sunday mornings coaching children in God's word. I know how powerful the faith of a child can be, and I want them to know that God is with them now so that when they face challenges and temptation to lose faith amid a confusing world, they might remember how He carried them as children.

"Let's lift our hands up high as we sing to the God of heaven," Seth says, leading kids' worship.

"You are in control," we sing, as we raise our hands and follow the choreographed dance movements. It took me a while to get comfortable with that line. The Ministry taught we were in control of this world, not God. Once I left, their focus on power became clear to me, and I saw through Scripture that ultimately, the one who delegates authority is still the one with all the authority.

God may not control my decisions from day to day, and He may not control what other people do to me, but He provides the way out. He upholds the universe by the word of His power. He provides salvation and is in control of the eventual outcomes—things far greater than the scope of my mind. In His love, God set boundaries. And while there is still pain and suffering within those boundaries, there is far more capacity for joy and triumph.

"Coach Vic, Coach Vic!" a young boy says.

"Yes, what it is it?" I say.

"Look what I drew." He points to the black dry-erase board with neon drawings.

It might be a kangaroo or a giraffe. I'm not sure.

"It's a *wallabaloo!*" he says.

"Oh, is that right?"

"Yeah, you know, from the game . . ." He continues on about a video game. I know that it's not really about the game. It's about being seen and treated with kindness because Jesus cares for the children the same as all of us.

At the end of every kids service, we pray together. The children get to practice praying for each other without complex formulas. Their prayers are simple and honest from the heart. They reflect the personality of each soul and their attitude toward God in that moment.

After kids service, Nathan and I enter the main worship center and each take a small communion packet including a gluten-free wafer and grape juice to bring to our seats. They've thought of everything. On stage, the worship team plays with exuberance. Strong vocals supported by guitar, piano, and drums fill the space, and our hearts, with words of adoration. The beat and the Spirit move me to raise my hands high unto the one who holds it all. Nathan takes one of my raised hands in his and squeezes as the words hit home.

This time of praise and worship doesn't only help get our emotions aligned. It's a time of reflection on the truth being spoken, of repentance when needed, and of declaring God's position in our lives. He's our almighty defender, our loving father, a faithful friend, healer, refuge, strength, and our joy.

When the music fades, our pastor delivers a brief greeting and personal story for reflection, then leads us to take communion all before the syndicated teaching appears on screen. The message is always applicable to life today, welcoming seekers, new believers, and mature Christians alike. The weekly messages remind us of biblical ideas and Scripture references demonstrating both who God is and how we are to respond to Him. Every sermon provides actionable steps that help us apply what we've learned with the Holy Spirit's leading.

This body of believers called a church has become our family. Outside of seeing them on Sundays, we participate in growth groups where we share meals and pray for each other during the week. We celebrate successes and support each other through tough times.

Nobody is scrutinizing my theology or jumping down my throat for saying the wrong words. The elders don't expect us to involve them in our life decisions but are there if we need counsel. And through it all, God is guiding us to manifest more of Jesus in our life.

Lord, please show me how I can help the rest of the body of Christ experience this freedom from religious oppression.

I hear in my spirit, *Tell your story.*

My phone buzzes. It's just a reminder to drink water. I dismiss it without thinking and open the home screen where the photos widget displays a selfie I took with Rita on our hike one year ago today. I pause. *Of course, our author friend.*

I will reach out to her.

A child runs up to me in the lobby after the service concludes. "Coach Vic, Coach Vic."

"Yes, sweetie, what is it?"

"I forgot to tell you I memorized the fruit of the Spirit."

"You did? Let's hear it," I say.

"Okay, it's um . . . there's love, joy, peace . . . uh . . . patience, kindness, goodness . . . uh . . . faithfulness, gentleness, and . . . oh, I remember . . . self-control."

"Yes, that's right. High five!" I say as she gives me a strong hand slap and then giggles. I ask Seth to get her a prize and then say to her, "How do we get those fruits? Are they handed to us in a basket?"

"No," she says. "They're grown."

"That's right. And who grows them?"

"The Holy Spirit inside of us."

"Amen! Keep reading your Bible and ask God to grow that fruit inside of you every day. He's faithful."

"Okay!" she says and runs off to get her prize.

Nathan is gushing, "That was adorable!"

I turn to him and say, "I am truly more blessed than I've ever been, and yet I have more unanswered questions than ever before."

"You know God's got us," he says.

"I do. I trust God with the answers. It's not about me. It's about loving God and loving people. Just look around us. Our community is growing and our hearts are full because the Holy Spirit is moving in our lives. They may not be as active in spiritual gifts, but I see abundant fruit."

"That's how we know we are among God's people," Nathan says, "by their fruits."

But the Holy Spirit produces this kind of fruit in our lives: love, joy, peace, patience, kindness, goodness, faithfulness, gentleness, and self-control. There is no law against these things!

GALATIANS 5:22-23 (NLT)

ACKNOWLEDGMENTS

Above all, I thank my Heavenly Father God, Lord Jesus Christ, and Holy Spirit, who are with me always. When I started research for this book, I still had faith in the ministry I grew up in, but God knew what it would take to open my eyes and give me a heart of understanding. He set me free from bondage through forgiveness. He severed some relationships and restored others. I trust He will continue to replace false doctrines with a fuller understanding of grace and His word.

A heartfelt thank-you to the eighteen people I interviewed who trusted me to weave their stories into a work of fiction that would represent their collective experiences and unique viewpoints. I pray that reading this helps you on your journey of faith and healing.

Thank you to my husband for supporting my daily writing while unaware of the details. My mother, for cheering me on, praying for me, and proofreading several versions. My father for his support through prayer and encouraging me to follow God's lead.

Thank you to my editors, Carly and Alison from Catt Editing LLC, my co-laborers. This book would not be the same without them.

Thanks to my fellow authors with SelfPublishing.com, especially those who frequented the early-morning writing rooms. Your accountability, commiseration, and celebration helped keep me disciplined.

A special thanks to my beta readers who affirmed my belief in this book and saved me a round of editing costs: Jim M., Andy M., Rhi J., Bryn S., Cathy S., David B.

And of course, I can't forget my writing companion, foot warmer, and snuggle buddy when the tears were flowing—Skyler, our English labrador retriever.

LEAVE A REVIEW

If this book blessed you, please help spread the word.
Leaving a review full of stars could help others
find freedom and forgiveness.

Leave a review on your favorite platform:

Amazon
www.amazon.com/books

Good Reads
www.goodreads.com

BookBub
www.bookbub.com

ABOUT THE AUTHOR

Beth Sage is a truth-seeker who, like many born in the 1980s, unknowingly spent the first thirty-five years of her life in a high-control religious group.

She set out to write a memoir chronicling the miracles and revelatory teachings of her apostle, but as she researched, her work took a sharp turn. Allegations of abuse had divided her community, and seeking the truth meant confronting stories she could no longer ignore.

This quest for clarity would vindicate the accusers, but at what cost? After much prayer, she chose to rewrite the manuscript as a work of fiction to protect the privacy of the families involved.

A Messiah University communication graduate, Sage uses a journalistic approach to weave several personal journeys into a powerful narrative. She balances truth (as she and others remember it) with storytelling, inviting readers to connect with the universal themes of freedom, forgiveness, and spiritual healing.

Sage is passionate about biblical discourse and empowering others to grow in their faith. Her debut novel, *By Their Fruits*, emerges from her commitment to uncovering truth and honoring her relationship with God.

Along with her love of writing, she enjoys gardening, hiking, and dancing. She lives in Phoenix, Arizona, with her husband and their dog.

LET'S STAY CONNECTED!

Thank you for supporting this labor of love.

I would like to send you a free gift for joining me on this journey.

Scan this QR code to connect and claim your free gift: